CODE WORD: PATERNITY
A Presidential Thriller

Doug Norton

First published by Dog Ear Publishing
4010 W. 86th Street, Ste H
Indianapolis, IN 46268
www.dogearpublishing.net

ISBN: 978-1-4575-1555-2

This book is printed on acid-free paper.

Printed in the United States of America

For this is your duty, to act well the part that is given to you . . .
Epictetus, *The Enchiridion*

CHARACTERS

AMERICANS
Rick **Martin**, President of the United States
Graciela (Ella) Dominguez **Martin**, First Lady

<u>The National Security Council (NSC)</u>
       Statutory Members and Advisers (in addition to the President)
       Bruce **Griffith**, Vice President of the United States
       Eric **Easterly**, Secretary of Defense (SECDEF)
       Anne **Battista**, Secretary of State (SECSTATE)
       General Jay ("Mac") **MacAdoo**, U.S. Air Force, Chairman, Joint Chiefs of Staff (CJCS)
       Aaron **Hendricks**, Director of National Intelligence (DNI)

       Other Regular Attendees
       John **Dorn**, National Security Advisor
       Bart **Guarini**, White House Chief of Staff
       Scott **Hitzleberger**, CIA Director
       Ed **McDonnell**, Attorney General
       Sara **Zimmer**, Secretary of Homeland Security

Ray **Morales**, Congressman from Texas and General USMC, Retired. Former Chairman, Joint Chiefs of Staff (CJCS)

Oscar **Neumann**, Ambassador and United States Permanent Representative to the United Nations

Samantha (Sam) **Yu**, White House Press Secretary

INTERNATIONAL

Chen Shaoshi, Minister of National Defense, People's Republic of China (PRC)

Fahim, al-Qaeda's master bomb engineer

Gwon Chung-Hee, President of South Korea (Republic of Korea) (ROK)

Huang Bo, Ambassador and Chinese Permanent Representative to the United Nations

Jia Jinping, Minister of Foreign Affairs, People's Republic of China (PRC)

Akihiro **Kato**, Premier of Japan

Kim Jong-il, dictator of North Korea (The Democratic People's Republic of Korea (DPRK). Kim is addressed as "Dear Leader" by all North Koreans.

Ming Liu, President of the People's Republic of China (PRC)

Park Chang-su, Secretary-General of the United Nations, a South Korean

Young-san Ho, Field Marshal and leader of the North Korean military

A GLOSSARY MAY BE FOUND AT PAGE 274.

Chapter 1

THE PRESIDENT OF the United States was sitting in a puddle. The southeast wind gusted and President Rick Martin happily steered up into the puff, his tiny sailboat heeling and accelerating immediately as the wind hit its green-striped sail. He straightened his legs, hooked his feet under the leeward gunwale, and hung his dripping butt over the side, counterbalancing the sail's pull so the boat wouldn't capsize. Rick shifted the tiller extension and the sheet into his left hand and reached out his right, fingers trailing in the bay.

He lost himself in the rippling sound and the slick, smooth sensations of the warm water streaming past the small Sunfish he was sailing at the mouth of the Gunpowder River where it meets the Chesapeake Bay. The sky was an inverted blue bowl, just darker than robin's egg at its zenith and milky around its rim. To the west a fringe of low white clouds curled around the horizon like the remains of a balding man's hair.

A bit over six feet tall and wiry—the build of a swimmer or runner—Rick Martin looked streamlined. His salt-and-pepper hair was graying at the temples, but his face was quite unlined, except when he smiled. After six months in office Rick still projected the optimism, lively intelligence, and likeability that had fueled his rise from Maryland congressman to president. He appreciated Camp David but favored another retreat from the pressures of office: the Chesapeake Bay. The VIP guest house at the military's Aberdeen Proving Ground made a perfect base for the sailing he loved.

He guided the boat, reflecting that sailing was one of the few things in his life that had purity and integrity. *It's not that I expect politics to have either one,* he thought. *I take the hidden agendas and exaggerations and outright lies as they come and, let's be honest, do my share. But it's such a pleasure to enter a world, even a very limited world, where things are as they seem. The wind blows from where it blows—no man can control it or influence it. This little boat gives immediate and honest feedback.*

Honesty . . . I should be grateful to Glenna Rogers. Had I beaten her back then for the Democratic nomination, I probably would've made the same mistakes she did as president. Those mistakes left her vulnerable as few first-term presidents have been, as Jimmy Carter was, and for the same reason: Most Americans don't like feeling that the country has been humiliated, and when that happens they hold the president responsible.

* * *

As Las Vegas receded at a mile a minute, Fahim fretted, the I-15 ahead of his car as crisp and stark as fresh black paint on the yellowish, desolate soil. There was nothing he could do now, so he should put it out of his mind. But he could no more ignore it than his tongue could ignore a bit of food between his teeth. He knew he was taking a chance, but he had backup. The young man driving the truck would get his wish for martyrdom in any case, although he didn't know about the timer or the bomb's secret. Fahim, who didn't want to be a martyr, had directed the man who did to press his button at 10:35 a.m.

Interrupting his drive to California at 10:25, Fahim pulled to the shoulder and sat in the air conditioner's blast, sweating anyway. The sweat overflowed the barriers of his eyebrows and stung his eyes, which matched the black color of his hair. He compared his worries to the opening night jitters of an actor playing the West End the first time. Thinking of London theater brought to mind his father, a university professor of history who disapproved of his violent embrace of the cause but was nonetheless willing to admit he was cultured—for an engineer. He smiled at the memory of their fond arguments, his wiry body relaxing slightly.

Waiting for the event that would henceforth define him, he muted his humanity, burying it beneath hatred. He remembered the tens of thousands of Muslims America had killed. He remembered the suffering of his own Palestinian brothers at the hands of the Israelis, who owed their existence to Americans. He remembered the humiliation of Muslims at Abu Ghraib prison. He remembered Guantánamo.

Suppose he failed? Some stupid oversight? The Sheikh's memory would be mocked instead of glorified. Heart pounding, he gripped the wheel as if crushing it would ensure success.

At 10:30 a flash brighter than Fahim had imagined stabbed his rear-view mirror, which he had set for night to protect his eyes. He cried out, mouth a rictus that was part astonishment, part orgasm, then slumped in release as triumph embraced him. *I have just struck the mightiest blow ever against America! And I am going to do it again.*

* * *

The harsh sounds of jet skis and helicopter rotors were startling. Rick looked around and saw his secret service detail closing fast from their escort positions fifty yards away, followed by a small Coast Guard patrol boat. A familiar Marine helicopter was landing at the shoreline.

Agents surrounded his little sailboat. All but the one who spoke looked away, scanning for danger, hands on the waterproof bags he knew held weapons.

"Mr. President, there's a national security emergency and we need to get you to the helo! Get aboard behind me, please."

Feeling a stab in his stomach, but also a thrill, Martin clambered aboard, mind racing. *Another Russian incursion into the Ukraine? Something involving Israel? Maybe Korea?* Whatever it was, it might be his first crisis and he was secretly eager to tackle it, more than ready to be tested.

The crew chief jumped out of the helo—its rotors continuing to turn— trotted in a crouch to the president, and led him toward it. As if by magic the head of Martin's secret service detail, Wilson, appeared with a submachine gun and trailed him, followed by an officer carrying a briefcase. Rick moved to his familiar place, saw National Security Advisor John Dorn belted in nearby. The moment the president's soaking shorts squelched into his seat, the helo leaped skyward.

Martin, buckling his lap belt, looked at Dorn, saw his pale face, and said, "What!" in a sharp, flat voice that made it not a question, but a command.

"Sir, a nuclear bomb has exploded in Nevada, in or near Las Vegas! Because we haven't detected any missiles or unidentified military aircraft, we think it was a terrorist act. We have no communications—"

Dorn's lips kept forming words, but Martin's mind had stopped, like a sprinting soldier halted in mid-stride by a bullet. He sat back in his seat, folded his arms across his chest, and stared at the forward bulkhead. His gaze rested on the Great Seal of the President of the United States.

That's me.

He recalled, in a flash, his thoughts from many years past, thoughts that came immediately after he had once tumbled into a ravine, breaking an ankle while winter hiking alone in the wilderness during college: *Later this is really going to hurt, but right now you've got to put that away and figure out how to stay alive.*

Holding a satcom handset tightly to his ear against the chopper's noise, Martin asked General "Mac" MacAdoo, chairman of the JCS, "Do you have any doubt this was nuclear?"

MacAdoo responded from the Pentagon, "No sir! Two DSP satellites picked up a flash with the unique characteristics of a nuclear explosion. Besides, we have satellite imaging showing such destruction that it had to be a nuke, plus what they saw from Creech Air Force Base, about thirty-five miles away."

"Okay, Mac, but what's the chance that this was a ballistic missile attack and NORAD just missed it, somehow didn't detect a lone missile coming from an unexpected direction?"

"No chance, Mr. President. The old BMEWS radars might have missed one, the way you said, but now we have interlocking, multi-sensor coverage from six satellites. It's possible the warhead was put into Vegas using a short-range missile, or an artillery tube, but if so the firing point had to be within the U.S., probably within the state. It's also possible it was aboard a commercial aircraft."

"I understand . . . thanks."

Martin hung up and looked numbly out the window.

Well, now it begins. Nuclear terrorism was a nightmare and now it's real and mine to deal with. How vulnerable is my administration: did we fail to connect the dots?

How do you deal with tens of thousands of bodies on a radioactive rubble pile? Who did it?

Why Las Vegas?

What's next?

Rick's tongue explored his dry mouth. He wanted desperately to be anyone but who he was: the commander-in-chief. He felt drowsy, his lassitude driven by fear of acknowledging the terrifying expectations that now weighed on him. *I can't do this . . . I'm not ready . . . I can't handle what's coming.*

"Mr. President . . .

"Mr. President!"

Dorn, face grim and energetic, held out a sheet of paper. "Here's a draft agenda for the NSC meeting."

Martin came back from his despairing reverie, took it, and read. Soon he felt a lessening of the sharp pain in his stomach. *I don't have to do this all myself. There's an entire government, steered by smart, determined people who know what to do about some of this horror. I need to be worthy of leading them, but I don't have to have all the answers.*

"Thanks, John; let's go with that."

Dorn swallowed hard, eyes shifting around the cabin, shoulders slumped. "Sir, at this point we don't have enough information to get anywhere in this meeting. Maybe a few nuggets of useful output, but . . . mostly it will be . . . unhelpful." He squared his shoulders and looked at the president. "I think you should say a few words and leave the meeting to me while you go off to do what is, actually, the most important thing right now: figure out what to say to the country."

"You're right. There's going to be a lot of chest-pounding and butt-covering in that meeting, and right now I've got no need to listen. I'll take your suggestion. Thanks!"

Dorn, satcom to ear, said, "Sir, SECDEF has joined the call." Martin picked up again.

"Mr. President, we need military support for rescue and security in Las Vegas right from the get-go. I've alerted the Eighty-second Airborne, and if you approve, the ready brigade will be on their way in eight hours."

"Sounds right, Eric.

"John, unless someone in the NSC spots a problem, let's do that!"

Marine One banked and began a swift, jinking descent to Andrews Air Force Base, where three identical helicopters waited to begin his second journey.

But what if . . . ? With a sweeping motion, Martin grabbed the handset. "Mac, we've got to figure out whose bomb it was and we can't rule out one of ours. When you've completed a hands-on inventory, let me know right away!"

The chairman was startled because he hadn't thought of that, despite a head start on the president in absorbing the news. "Yes, sir!"

Well I'll be a son-of-a-bitch! This guy doesn't rattle. Right at the moment that thought made General MacAdoo feel pretty good. An instant later he didn't. *If one of ours is missing—not only missing but unreported—by the time those dominoes stop falling, the U.S. military will be shaken to its foundations!*

When the rotors had stopped, Rick Martin rose and strode from the helo, leaving wet footprints.

He felt on top of his game.

* * *

There! A hand! Steve Nguyen attacked the rubble like a machine.

The day the vulnerability of the United States was laid bare was a day off for Nguyen, a casino employee who lived in Las Vegas with his wife and two children. Now Steve dug frantically, with the maniacal strength of one who believes all he is or ever will be depends on it.

He found his younger daughter, her face angelic but her chest crushed. He began vomiting, not caring that he was bringing up blood. When he had extricated her small body and laid it to one side, he resumed digging. He knew her older sister would be nearby.

I have to get her out of there! I can't leave her!

He laid the body of his older child tenderly beside her sister. Squatting beside his daughters, Nguyen rocked on his heels, threw back his head, and howled. It was a cry of grief, rage, and helplessness. Had she heard it, First Lady Graciella Dominguez Martin would have known that cry well.

Chapter 2

SO, WHAT SHOULD I tell the country?

The president sat in a small room at the nuclear-hardened National Command Authority Relocation Site, tunneled into the solid granite of a Virginia mountain. He took in his sterile, musty surroundings: concrete walls, a desk, swivel chair, table, and two armchairs. *I'm the only president who's ever been in this room*, he thought, *and right now that feels better than the Oval Office, like a clean slate.*

Hands resting on the desk, Rick felt a stab of pain between his right shoulder and his spine. He relaxed his hunched posture, flexed his shoulders, and the ache vanished.

So far, nobody has claimed the bombing. Well, if Paternity works like they say, we'll find out. I doubt the bomb-maker was the bomber—too risky for another nation. Probably the bomber was al-Qaeda, but maybe not; we've had our own terrorists attack us with bombs and poisons.

Placing his palms flat on the desk, Martin stared at the legal pad silently demanding wisdom of him.

During the campaigns, every candidate promised to level with the American people. I made that pledge as a matter of course. Now I have to make a decision.

If I level, I'll say, "We don't know who did this and we may never know. We'll probably be able to make an educated guess before long, and then the question becomes what we do on the basis of that guess."

The president's mind continued saying words only he would ever hear himself speak: *"This is so terrible that we as a nation and certainly we political leaders refused to contemplate it, so we didn't take serious steps to prevent it or prepare for it. Now we're forced to take those steps. In order to protect you, your government is going to have to do things that so reduce the openness and free-dom of your lives that we will fundamentally change as a nation. I'm sorry, but it's come to that. And even after we do, your government won't be able to guarantee your safety.*

"I pledged to level with you and now I have."

Martin stood up, pushed his chair back with his thighs, moved to the table, and poured coffee. He intended to add cream and sweetener but forgot as his mind returned to creating his speech. He took a sip, grimaced, then added them. Cup in hand, he stood gazing at a landscape photo without seeing it.

But, of course, I can't and won't say those things.

Americans want to hear that I know who did it and we're going to get them and it will never happen again and nothing in their lives will change.

They don't really want their leaders to level with them when it's bad news. Jimmy Carter did that and it earned him derision. Mondale tried it in 1984 and got thumped by Reagan. And Glenna crushed her Republican opponent after he leveled about what would follow a heedless American withdrawal from Iraq.

No, I can't level with the American people unless I'm willing to be a one-term president, maybe even impeached.

Martin moved back to the desk, sat momentarily, then began to pace the few steps the room allowed.

So, I know what I'm not going to say. What am I going to say?

From somewhere, thoughts came. Rick stopped pacing, sat at the desk, and wrote. He paused, then added, "deal with them under international law."

But this is about more than recovery, accountability, and defense against another attack, he thought. *It's also an opportunity, a huge opportunity, to lead the world to a safer place! Nuclear terrorism is a game-changer.*

Martin paused again, then wrote furiously.

That's better; now it sets a new direction.

But I need some unifying theme. We're no more solidly united now than we were after Nine-eleven. Despite the United We Stand bumper stickers, solidarity dissolved within a year. I need something that will make people feel committed to each other, united by more than just shock and fear.

Then it came to him.

This'll be tricky! It's either going to work well or fall flat. Hitting the inter-com, he asked for his lead speechwriter and for Samantha Yu, his press secre-tary.

* * *

Everyone scrambled to get the technology and the president ready in the dank, sixties-era burrow. The broadcast crew snaked thick cables through the corridors and open blast doors, heavy on their hinges, to reach their satellite truck. Somebody realized about three hours before air time that the president didn't have a suit. His valet choppered in with it. Sam Yu and others hurriedly disguised the concrete bunker with a blue backdrop, skillful lighting, and the familiar flags left and right of the most substantial desk they could round up.

Air time rushed toward them. Rick's stomach was jumping, and he was sweating from TV lighting. He hurtled through space, flung by the explosion in Las Vegas, out of control, dreading the thought of another attack while he spoke. And still he had to get this right, must strike the perfect note, establish his leadership of the wounded nation, set the stage for seizing the great opportunity. He wiped his sweaty palms futilely.

At 10:12 p.m., the technicians having missed the announced air time, the networks, CNN, and Fox News cut to President Martin, seated at a desk. Viewers saw a man who looked slightly askew, slightly off-stride, but competent and determined despite that. Gripping his text, the president began speaking in a voice woven of outrage, sadness, and confidence.

"Good evening, fellow Americans of all ages, men and women, girls and boys. I come before you tonight in shock and sadness—and in anger and determination!

"We have suffered a terrible loss. We do not yet know the toll, but certainly tens of thousands of our fellow citizens and visitors from other countries were murdered today in Las Vegas, and many more were injured."

Martin put down the text and looked into the camera.

"I addressed you a moment ago as men and women, girls and boys. That's because this was an attack by enemies as intent on killing our children, our parents, and grandparents as they are on killing those of us leading active, adult lives. For these enemies, it was enough that their victims simply be at the place chosen for their attack.

"I don't know, *yet*"—stabbing the air with his finger—"who planned and carried out the nuclear destruction of Las Vegas. What those unidentified murderers did is something long and clearly urged by al-Qaeda and other extremist groups: the calculated murder of people who do not espouse their hate-filled views. But we will not rush to judgment; we are gathering evidence with open minds, recalling that terrorist attacks in our country have also been made by Americans."

Pausing, Martin willed beads of perspiration not to succumb to gravity and slide from temples to jaw.

Grasping his text again, he resumed: "This evening there isn't anything I want to say to you that goes beyond common sense and common decency. But although these words and the feelings that accompany them are just plain American common sense, it's important for Americans and for others—whether they wish us well or ill or are indifferent—to hear them from the president of the United States."

A camera tightened to a close-up, and Martin's voice strengthened, hammering each sentence.

"We will bury our dead with honor, succor our wounded, and be partners in rebuilding the hundreds of thousands of lives affected by this outrage.

"We will find the individuals who planned and carried out this attack. We will capture them for trial under international law. We will kill those we are unable to capture.

"We will find out how they got that bomb. We take it as a given that the terrorists did not make that nuclear weapon unassisted. One of the nations with whom we share this earth enabled them to get it, either as a deliberate decision or through failing to exercise the necessary safeguards.

"We will make it much, much harder for terrorists to attack us again with such weapons of mass destruction. As you have experienced since shortly after the attack, major sections of our transportation network have been shut down, and entry to many cities has been restricted. This will not continue long but is necessary to help us thwart any potential follow-on attacks.

"On the advice of the surgeon general, the governor of Nevada and I have isolated the Las Vegas disaster area. For their own protection, nobody will be allowed to enter the quarantined area. We are continuously monitoring radiation levels in all areas potentially at risk from nuclear fallout. At present that risk is not enough to require other evacuations.

"Although this is the worst attack upon the nation in history and has undeniably caused great suffering and loss, our nation—our citizens and our economy—have the resilience and determination to carry on and to recover from this blow! I will ask you for, and I am confident that you will make, the sacrifices necessary to protect our country and enable survivors to recover."

The president's voice changed in volume and pitch, dropping a notch from the driving force he had been using. The camera backed off and showed him turning a page, then putting his text aside. He folded his hands on the desk, leaned forward, and looked directly into the camera.

"Although this atrocity may have been committed by al-Qaeda, I acknowledge and I urge you to acknowledge that the murder visited upon Las Vegas was not by the hand of Islam itself. We will not hold one of the world's largest and greatest faiths responsible for the act of a splinter faction. As your president I will judge—and I ask you to judge—everyone by their words and actions, not just by the religion or philosophy they follow. I can assure all that every person in the United States will receive the full protection of our laws. I ask, and I expect, each of you to treat Muslims with respect and tolerance."

The president straightened, placing his palms flat on the desk.

"While we *will*"—Martin's right palm slapped the desk—"hold to account each individual and nation that struck us, or enabled that strike, we will not stop there! Those actions are a necessary, but not sufficient, response. We will not be content with them alone because this event shows so clearly that *all* nations are at risk from those filled with terrible hatred and in possession of terrible weapons.

"The United States will do more than it has in the past to lead the world in reducing the numbers of nuclear weapons and fissionable materials, and to obtain reliable safeguards on those that remain, wherever they may be. At the same time, we will join more vigorously in the search for equitable resolution of disputes that give rise to the hatreds of terrorists."

Rick decided this was as good a moment as he was going to get to blot his perspiring face, where a drop was preparing to dangle from the tip of his nose.

He gave a quick swipe with his pocket handkerchief and resumed: "I have just told you our situation, as I see it right now. You have heard my initial plan. With one hand the United States will pluck from hiding those who did this and those who enabled it—and deal with them. With the other we will reach out to all nations, seeking their ideas, cooperation, and actions to reduce the dangers to us all from hatred mixed with weapons of mass destruction."

To his surprise, Rick felt no trepidation about his risky closing. He could don sincerity as effortlessly as a favorite jacket, but this was genuine. He possessed a voice as supple and evocative as a violin, and now it seemed to become for his listeners that of every respected coach, every favorite teacher, every wise and loving grandparent.

"In the final moments of this broadcast I ask you to join me and the other leaders of your government—the government of, by, and for the people of the United States—as we each rededicate ourselves to the ideals of our country and to meeting the challenges ahead.

"I ask you to join us in the Pledge of Allegiance to our flag, but on this occasion honoring not only that flag, but each other. I'll pause a moment for you to gather and, if you are somewhere with windows, to open those windows."

Martin disappeared from the world's television and video screens as the camera cut to images of people purposefully striding along crowded city sidewalks, of children in classrooms, of family cook-outs, of a football team crowding together dedicating themselves to the challenge ahead, and, finally, of a huge, billowing American flag.

The president reappeared with the secretaries of state and defense, the speaker of the house, the chief justice, and General MacAdoo, hands linked.

"I ask you to join hands with those around you, as you see us doing.

"OK. Look at each other! This is for all those who died today and for all those we will, by our shared sacrifices, protect. I want all of us—and the entire world—to hear these words rising from the lips and hearts of three hundred million free and determined people. Shout them out those windows you opened!

"I pledge allegiance to the flag of the United States of America, and to the republic for which it stands, one nation under God, indivisible, with liberty and justice for all."

The camera closed in, offering the president's confident, determined features as a shield against the dangerous, uncertain universe.

"Tonight and for many nights ahead, we have far to go before we sleep, and promises to keep." Martin paused, gazing intensely into the camera, and said, with slower cadence and a harder tone, "And promises to keep."

Chapter 3

AS VIDEO FROM a Predator drone out of Creech air base streamed before them, Graciela Dominguez Martin, "Ella," squeezed Rick's hand as if in physical pain. The president's eyes, which had been drooping, opened wide. Ella saw him hunch, as if the sights were weights piling on his back. A few floors of some casinos were still standing, but mostly the view was of debris. Portions of the street grid cross-hatched endless views of rubble. As the aerial camera swept farther from ground zero, they saw the remains of automobiles.

People near ground zero had been vaporized or burned to wind-scattered ash. The bodies of others farther away looked like most other debris, mercifully disguised as scorched chunks of concrete or the charred beams of demolished buildings. But with distance from the explosion, shapes became human bodies. Rick and Ella turned toward each other. He opened his mouth, but before words came Ella nodded and he remained silent.

Farther out they saw survivors, figures that moved like people but didn't look like people, clothing, skin, and hair burned off. *They're like pulpy store manikins*, thought Rick, his gorge rising at the sight of their raw tissue. *How can they be alive?*

One manikin walked slowly toward the camera. In its arms were two small bodies, children's legs dangling and swinging as the adult tottered along.

"Oh my God!" he said, thinking about their own two kids. Then he thought, *get a grip! You can't personalize this; you'll do something dumb if you do. Anger is a distraction, a weakness.* Ella read her husband's mind, his character being as familiar to her as his appearance.

13

It was early in the morning, and they were on the couch in their cramped, underground quarters. Ella was near Rick but not touching him. As by unspoken agreement they gave each other space to process the video feed, but their hands crossed the gap, left holding right.

Ella's face was framed by shoulder-length black hair that appeared sable at times. She usually offered the world a friendly but earnest expression; an especially keen observer would sense that her earnestness was the tip of an iceberg of determination.

Rick punched off the parade of horrors and looked at his wife. "How're you doing, Ella?"

Her reply surprised him, the words darting at him like sparks from a fire: "It was murder! Murder! Those men, women, and children were killed for no reason other than that they happened to be in Las Vegas yesterday. They didn't die in a tsunami or a hurricane or an earthquake. They were murdered—by people who planned very carefully for a long time and who rejoiced when it was done. I want to kill the bastards who did this! I want to kill them personally and very painfully."

She means it, thought Rick, recalling her stories of childhood amidst the violence and vendettas of Mexico's drug wars. *Is that where we're headed now? Revenge? Will we ignore the rule of law and snarl off into the jungle, mauling every creature that crosses our path?*

After a moment he said, "What would you do if you were me?"

"I think I'd become a remorseless killing machine. Spend every waking hour pushing the FBI, the CIA, and the military to find the people who set off that bomb and the people who gave it to them."

"Would you hold both of them equally responsible?"

"Yes! After all, people hiding in caves in Afghanistan and Pakistan and Yemen couldn't have built that bomb from scratch. Some government gave it to them or failed to ensure it couldn't be stolen."

Rick looked sharply at her.

"Ella, we don't know that people hiding in caves did this. For all we know right now it could have been an American extremist group, using a stolen American nuke. It's too soon for me to become a remorseless killing machine! I don't know who to go after. Yesterday's NSC meeting was full of people pounding on the table without a clue what to do, except threaten. It was all heat and no light. There's no one to punch in the nose, yet, and nothing I can do to bring back Las Vegas or the people whose bodies we just saw!"

Ella looked thoughtfully at her husband of twenty-six years. He was optimistic by nature and believed compromise was always possible, although sometimes painful. Rick had both the instinct and the ability to defuse conflict, and she had seen him build consensus where none had seemed possible. Rick's world-view did not admit of undying hatred. He had never encountered a purely malevolent human being.

Ella shivered, because she had experienced both in the Mexican state of Sinaloa, in the person of drug lord "Chapo" Guzman. Guzman vowed to kill not only her father, Colonel Dominguez, but the entire family. Before his own death by assassination, Guzman did indeed kill her father, after torturing him for a long time.

She knew the world held some who were powerful, cruel, fearless, unmoved by reason or suffering, and utterly unwilling to compromise. Guzman and others like him were evil itself. Facing such demons, others either did as they were told or accepted a fight to the death.

Ella wondered if Rick would be able to find and harness the visceral force he needed now.

"Rick, what you said to the country a few hours ago was carefully reasoned and balanced. It was right for now. But within a few weeks Americans won't want a president who speaks in careful nuances. They'll want Winston Churchill, or maybe General Patton. You can't do what you have to do by your usual balanced, obscenely rational approach!"

She grabbed his forearm and challenged him, eyes vivid with outrage: "Rick, you've got to do whatever it takes to get the people who did this and keep it from happening again!"

"Ella, you can be certain that when the facts are in, I'll be Winston Patton."

Ella shuddered, recalling the awful scenes of Las Vegas and of her childhood. Churchill and Patton were fierce. Her father was fierce. Guzman was fierce. She didn't know if Rick was.

Chapter 4

SHOULDERS SAGGING DESPITE his sky-high caffeine level, Director of National Intelligence (DNI) Aaron Hendricks sat in an office near the ops room at the National Counterterrorism Center. He had appropriated it the day before and not left since, except to go to the bathroom or one of the conference rooms. Looking at his watch, he decided that the *New York Times* had posted the day's edition. He clicked his mouse and began to read the editorial:

> ## THERE ARE NO WORDS
>
> Just when we thought we had put 9/11 behind us, at a time when there are no U.S. troops engaged in questionable wars, just when we had eagerly embraced long-overdue social and economic reforms in the United States, comes the horror of Las Vegas. The irony and cosmic unfairness of it leave one breathless, as does the scope and scale of the suffering visited on the citizens of Las Vegas.
>
> There are no words. But words are what a newspaper has, so we'll try to make the best of them. We offer a half dozen.
>
> *Wisdom.* May we have the wisdom to reject preconceptions and instant answers from those who will uncritically blame the usual suspects and offer easy, comfortable answers and neat solutions.
>
> *Compassion.* For the victims and their families, but also for those who, by their appearance or dress, embody the stereotypical bogeyman that some will see on every street.
>
> *Focus.* Focus on aiding the stricken of a disaster that far exceeds Katrina, and on learning who attacked us and why.

Tolerance. For those who don't look or think as we do, who would otherwise be easy targets for the rage that will seek expression now.

Inquiring. Asking the hard questions. Rejecting the easy answers. Leaving no stone unturned, no assumption unexamined. We must know who and what failed to give warning of the plot.

Inclusive. Uniting the nation and the world to resist terrorism and to address and ultimately eliminate its causes.

President Martin's first words to the nation and the initial, even instinctive, reactions of his administration demonstrate that he knows these words and embraces them.

It's not going to take as long this time around, Hendricks thought. *One day after the explosion and the Times is already building the gallows.* Despite the pious call not to reach for easy answers, the DNI knew the intelligence community would be blamed.

Hendricks' eyes narrowed and his lips became a thin line as he thought about it. *Perfect, omniscient intelligence is the silver bullet that politicians invoke to avoid making hard choices. If the intelligence community is performing properly, they say, it will tell us who's going to attack, where they will strike, when, how, and also why. Each time the world demonstrates that intelligence is never perfect, politicians express shock and disappointment, restructure intelligence organizations, hand out some extra bucks for "technology enhancement," and announce that they have solved the problem, so long as the intelligence Neanderthals don't slouch back into their old ways.*

Director Hendricks gave it no more than a month before he would be seated before congressional committees, getting his ritual comeuppance, and making his ritual apologies. He knew *he* was safe; he was too far from the desks where raw intel was handled and judgments made. But this time, he figured, he'd have to throw some of the poor bastards who actually did that under the bus. Then Scott Hitzleberger, CIA Director, would probably fall on his sword to protect them and he'd have to go, too.

Glancing at a clock, Hendricks realized he just had time to pee before taking the chopper to the president's bunker. He logged off and headed for the bathroom, popping another antacid tablet.

Rick Martin, he thought, *smart, likeable, articulate, but I doubt he knows who he is, really. Like another president who faced an existential crisis right away,*

Jack Kennedy, he's never been tested big time. Kennedy at least had the PT-109 experience. Rick Martin's never done anything tougher than a presidential campaign, not that those are easy, but they're about the candidate, how much risk he'll take, what he can endure and put his family through, and what he's willing to do to win. Being president of the United States is about three hundred million people and the nation whose actions or inactions set the boundaries of what's possible in a lot of the world.

And Paternity! What's he gonna do with the evidence, compelling but not undeniable, not a smoking gun? He thought about their first discussion, on Martin's third day in office.

At his request, he and the president had had their first meeting not in the Oval Office, but in the White House SCIF, the Special Compartmented Intelligence Facility. Called "the skif," it was literally a room within a room, as secure as unlimited funds and technology could make it. The Oval Office was equally secure, but the DNI didn't control it, or the records of access to it, or the microphones that recorded conversations within it. The skif, however, was under his control. Also, he knew the value of theater when briefing a new president.

"Mr. President, I asked for this meeting with you alone, and here, to tell you about the most closely held intelligence asset this country possesses. The code word for it, which is itself top secret, is Paternity."

The president made a "go on" gesture with one hand and sat expressionless, signaling, Hendricks supposed, that *this* president's trust was not a given. Of course, that was *always* so with intelligence. Hendricks sighed inside and continued.

"Mr. President, Paternity refers to the scientific capability we have to determine the origin, the paternity one might say, of plutonium and highly enriched uranium, called HEU. By origin, I mean at least the country of its manufacture and in many cases the specific facility where the material was produced. We're able to do this by analysis of the HEU or the plutonium itself and by analysis of fallout particles in the atmosphere and the ground if it has exploded. This scientific capability has a number of potentially important applications, as I'm sure you will appreciate."

After pretending a bit too obviously to reflect, Martin said, "And one of those applications would be, if a nuclear weapon was detonated anonymously in this country, we could figure out who had made it."

Ignoring Martin's sarcasm but noting his vanity, Hendricks replied, "Indeed we could, Mr. President! And also if, as is to be hoped, we intercepted a bomb *before* it was detonated, for example by detecting it in a radiation portal scanner."

"Tell me something about it. How did we get this capability, how certain are you of the accuracy . . . and why keep it secret? It looks like a deterrent to me."

"It's a long story, Mr. President, which I will condense severely at this telling. But, as to the last of your questions, why is it that we don't we announce Paternity as a deterrent measure? Because it would reveal extremely sensitive intelligence sources and methods and because, if attention is directed to it, certain states will attempt, possibly successfully, to develop countermeasures. Better to keep this rabbit in our hat until we need it. That, sir, has been the conclusion of every president since Jimmy Carter began the program, which is called the Paternity Project."

"Mmmph! Well, *this* president may change that"

When Hendricks didn't react, Martin said, "Go on."

"When the Pakistanis tested six nukes in 1998, samples of the gasses that escaped from underground showed that most of the bombs used HEU from the Pakistani facility at Kahuta, but at least one of them used HEU from a Chinese enrichment facility. We know through investigation of A. Q. Khan's nuclear black market operation that the Pak bomb program had, indeed, obtained HEU from the Chinese.

"In 2006 and 2009, when the North Koreans tested plutonium weapons, also underground, analyses showed the plutonium was reprocessed at Yongbyon, something that the North Koreans publicly confirmed."

At this, he paused briefly before adding, with emphasis, "Paternity works, Mr. President!"

After a short silence, Martin said, "Who in the Rogers administration knew about Paternity?"

"Mr. President, since 1976 only a small group of intelligence people have known about Paternity in order to keep the program ready. Typically, presidents have directed that their national security advisor, secretary of defense, chairman of the JCS, and heads of the House and Senate select intelligence committees be kept in the loop.

"There've been variations: In 1998, President Clinton had Secretary of State Albright brought in so she could confront the Chinese ambassador about their assistance to Pakistan's nuclear bomb program. In Bush Two, no surprise, Vice President Cheney was in the program.

"In sum, it has been a tight circle—and with good reason. Since Nine-eleven, there have been occasional news articles suggesting that governments are trying to develop some capacity to determine the origin of nuclear materials. As a result of your predecessors' caution, there has never been even a hint about Paternity."

"You just said that Albright told the Chinese about Paternity—who knows who they've told?"

"That's so, Mr. President, but it hasn't been in their interest to reveal it. One doubts that this is an episode of which they are particularly proud. The Paks didn't ask permission before using the HEU in a test or even give the Chinese a heads-up. When Secretary Albright gave their ambassador a dressing-down, it caught the Chinese flat-footed. They don't like that sort of thing."

Martin thought for a moment. "Mac and the committee chairs already know—right?"

Hendricks nodded.

"Then for now brief only Eric and John. I'll bring Bruce in if he needs to get involved."

Hendricks knew the vice president, Bruce Griffith, would be upset if he learned of this decision because he'd see being in the program as a sign of prestige. It was revealing that Martin was cutting him out—an observation he filed away.

"Mr. President, a few minutes ago I mentioned A. Q. Khan, known as the father of the Muslim bomb."

Martin nodded.

"Dr. Khan didn't only enable *Pakistan* to go nuclear. We've followed his foot-prints through the clandestine nuclear weapon programs of North Korea, Libya, Iran, Iraq, and South Africa. We suspect al-Qaeda approached him. Kahn prob-ably rebuffed al-Qaeda, but he did sell uranium enrichment technology, equip-ment, and probably warhead plans—Chinese, we think—to those countries. He may also have sold weapons-grade uranium and plutonium to them or others. Truth be told, we just don't know all his customers, despite the fact that his activ-ities were revealed and—probably—halted in 2004.

Hendricks flicked a bit of lint from the left sleeve of his dark suit, some-how subtly linking that gesture to his words, "The Khan connection is just a footnote, but this seemed a good time to mention it."

Chapter 5

CRISP IN A navy suit, President Martin looked into the faces of the bedraggled White House press corps, crowded and hot in an underground concrete box, overflowing into a mildew-speckled corridor. Excitement, fear, anger, exhaustion, and a sour odor infused the humid air.

Sam thinks it's too soon for a press conference, Rick thought, *too risky because we know almost nothing, but dammit, I need to engage them. It's bad enough I'm in this hole in the ground. I can't hide!*

I might as well begin with one who'll probably be reasonable.

"Helen?"

"Mr. President, take us inside your head for a moment. What are you feeling, what are your priorities, how are you handling this shock yourself?"

"Helen, I'm saddened beyond words by this tragic event. Ella and I have seen the same pictures most Americans have on television and the Internet. It's heartbreaking—and also infuriating! As I told the nation last night, this country is going to support the victims, rebuild, deal with the killers, and take steps to keep this from happening again, not only to Americans, but to any people!"

The instant he stopped speaking shouts filled the air. He picked a question that served his purpose, pointing to a man in jeans and a wrinkled pink oxford, sleeves rolled up to forearms.

"Mr. President, if it was al-Qaeda do you believe they are capable of having made that bomb, or did some country sell it to them?"

Rick considered Paternity and the probability that it would soon provide an answer. "I'm not an expert in this, but while I wouldn't rule out the possibility that al-Qaeda has the expertise to build such a bomb, I think the odds

21

are they acquired it, most likely by theft, but perhaps with the knowledge of a nuclear-armed country."

As reporters scribbled, a booming, angry voice cut through the clamor that followed his answer. "Mr. President, your administration failed to protect the American people!"

Shifting his gaze to the rear where a damp stain marked the wall, the president saw a man whose name he didn't recall. *Well, it didn't take long to get to that*, he thought, and said, "Please repeat your question."

"Mr. President, the Martin administration failed to protect the American people from this attack, despite years of warning that terrorists could get a nuke. Why? What went wrong?"

Several journalists exchanged knowing glances.

He and Sam had crafted his answer, but Martin paused as if considering before saying, "Yes, the government did fail to protect the American people. Today the government is led by my administration, and having been president of the United States since January I accept responsibility."

Several shouted questions were follow-ups, but he didn't want to go there and instead answered a sharp-faced woman who said, "What about our nuclear forces—have you put them on high alert?"

"I don't think our nuclear-armed subs, bombers, and missiles are the most important part of our response right now. As a precaution we have put our military, including nuclear forces, on higher alert. But it's really others—the police, the FBI, Customs and Border Protection, the National Guard—that are the most important at this point."

"Mr. President, are you saying that nuclear deterrence has failed?" Rick knew the answer was yes, but he wasn't going there until he had answers for the follow-up questions, so he was glad to hear others shouting about Las Vegas. Pointing to one of them, Martin said "I think you asked me about Las Vegas, but I didn't hear your question clearly."

"Mr. President, Americans want to know how many people have been killed and injured and what's being done right now to help the victims and their families."

"I'm sure they do. Right now we don't know the numbers, although they are certainly in the hundreds of thousands. Greater Las Vegas has—had—a population of about a million. The scale of this attack, plus the danger to rescuers from radioactivity, is delaying our efforts to identify or even count the dead and assist the injured. FEMA, with the strong assistance of the Nevada National Guard and surviving Las Vegas first responders, has established an assistance perimeter around the city. Survivors who are able to reach this perimeter are decontaminated and given medical treatment and other assistance. Our military is helping, too; evacuation by C-17 cargo planes has begun.

"As we all are horribly aware, there are injured people in the high-radiation area, the no-go zone, who are unable to walk out. Rescue personnel can't reach them because radiation would be fatal to them, as it will soon be to those survivors. They will inevitably die, either from their burns and wounds, or from radiation poisoning. To their great credit, rescuers—particularly helicopter crews—have volunteered to enter the no-go zone anyway. But the hard truth is that wouldn't save a single victim and would not only cost their families the lives of those brave men and women, it would cost the country their desperately needed skills."

Rick thought of his debate with Sam Yu over whether to suppress the television helicopter video of mutilated bodies and dying survivors in the no-go zone. He had decided not to suppress it, partly because it simply couldn't be stopped—images filled the Internet—and partly because it was the new reality that the country needed to absorb.

Lights dimmed to a yellowish hue, then returned to normal. Martin flung a quip, reminding them that he had proposed legislation to modernize the nation's power grid. It fell flat. Without the amenities of the White House press room, or even chairs, the correspondents were becoming a scrum. As Rick watched, one who crouched to retrieve her pen nearly became road kill.

Rick considered the shouts, searching for just the right question. He heard it: "Mr. President, what's the impact of this on the lives of Americans?"

Glad that he recognized the questioner, Martin said, "James, I think it will take some time before we know the full impact on life in America. But I believe that as we deal with this, we must use methods within the bounds of what is best about our country. We will not become a closed and fearful society. We will not repeat mistaken policies, such as the internment of Japanese Americans after Pearl Harbor. We—"

Utter blackness.

The journalists, sweaty and claustrophobic, alerted and started like a herd of antelope scenting a predator. When someone yelled, "Smoke!" they were off, shoving and elbowing toward the only door, dimly lit by an emergency light.

Wilson and another agent grabbed Martin by his elbows, hustled him to a corner, then stood in front of him, weapons drawn. Things were happening so fast that Martin wasn't thinking, only reacting. That suited Wilson just fine, as he commanded over his shoulder, "Sit on the floor, Mr. President!"

Chapter 6

Pyongyang, North Korea (DPRK)—Twelve Months Previously.

The Dear Leader lit up and paced his office. *The Arabs—they were back again,* he thought. For years they had sought radioactive materials, any materials, from him. After he detonated a fission bomb inside a mountain, announcing his power to the world, they began asking for a complete weapon. For years he sent them away, but they kept coming back, each time honoring him more and offering more cash for the glorious future of Korea. And *this* time . . .

Kim knew he possessed wisdom far above others. He could solve any problem. He offered solutions freely to his countrymen, in farming, in fishing, in steel-making, in education, giving them on-the-spot guidance. He was so often disappointed that those to whom he gave his guidance were unable to carry it out. Despite that, he continued his patient teaching and kind leadership, as had his father, Kim il-Sung.

Kim crushed his cigarette and lit another.

Of all his talents, he was proudest of his skill as a media producer. Encouraged by his father, he had developed North Korea's filmmaking resources—the only thing of his the man hadn't denigrated. He spent thousands of hours studying the world's best films, even learning English and French the better to dissect the filmmaker's craft. He wrote, directed, and produced films and entered international competitions. When he needed skills lacking among his dear people, he ordered those possessing them kidnapped, then detained and exploited them at Choson Studios, which he bankrolled with gold from one of his mines.

Kim's pacing carried him near the closed door. "Come!" he said in a firm voice. Immediately a uniformed steward entered. The young man stood about eight inches taller than Kim, with an athletic build. Like all North Koreans, he wore a button displaying Kim's photo, as he had since early childhood.

"Yes, Dear Leader?"

"Tea!" The man vanished.

As the Dear Leader resumed pacing, his mind lingered on the robust young man. *What a lie—the story spread by Americans and South Koreans that my people are malnourished and stunted from decades of near starvation!* It was an attack on him. It was another way they mocked and underestimated him. He had shown them, when he tested his nuclear bombs and when he fired his missiles across Japan into the Pacific. Yet, still they refused to acknowledge his wisdom and power. Still they oppressed and threatened his people, who loved him and depended on him. Kim thought of that as his own failure and felt ashamed, then angry.

Through the haze of his anger, Kim sensed the return of the steward. He turned and pointed. After taking a sip, the young man put the cup on a nearby table. He stood next to it, eyes fixed on the wall, as Kim paced and smoked. After about a minute Kim looked intently at him, then dismissed him with a flick of his hand.

Kim continued pacing, now drinking tea. *The Americans were such fools in mistaking my patience and tenderness toward my people for weakness and irresolution. No, I am strong,* Kim thought, knowing it was given to him to see what others did not.

What he saw was that in a showdown the Americans would make noise but wouldn't hurt *him*. It was his skill as a dramatist and producer that revealed this to him, a skill acquired through his compulsive intake of America's films, talk shows, and political blogs. Americans couldn't face the images of themselves in battle that filled television, Internet, and films whenever it occurred. Images of the truck-bombed Marine barracks in Beirut soon forced their withdrawal from Lebanon. Images of soldiers' bodies being dragged through the streets drove them from Somalia, and those images had been burned into American memory by the fine film *Blackhawk Down*. Another excellent film, *Fahrenheit 9/11* had convinced them that their country's response to the attacks was cynically concocted to enrich the president, his family, and friends. Kim knew a thing or two about making propaganda, and he admired Michael Moore's craftsmanship in portraying an immoral government. Moore skillfully built his case that war is a means for the upper class to control the lower classes and then drew his conclusion, artfully framed as a question, that Americans should never trust their leaders again.

Over the last decade Americans had spent themselves as a force in the world, Kim thought. Having gone bankrupt during Bush's second term, they accelerated their decline under his successor. He would have expected nothing else from a woman! Glenna Rogers had withdrawn America's army from Iraq, which exploded into civil war. Then she threw both the army and marines—hurriedly pulled out of Afghanistan—back in again to quell it. Before the end—a Shia victory enabled by Iran—six thousand U.S. soldiers were wounded and two thousand killed. No one knew how many Iraqis were killed, but certainly tens of thousands.

Since their defeat in Iraq, Americans had no courage to use the power they still had. Images formed in Kim's mind: desperation in the faces of soldiers whose withdrawal to Iraq's airports had been under constant attack. Screaming women whose families had been pulverized by American airpower. *I'll make a film about this*, he thought. *It will be better than* Blackhawk Down, *or even* Apocalypse Now*!*

Bitterly, Kim recalled how he had tried and failed for years to get a meeting with an American president. He nearly had a visit from Bill Clinton, late in his second term. Clinton had sent his secretary of state, Albright, as a preliminary but then had turned his attention to the Jews and Arabs. Kim felt angry again as he thought of it. Clinton didn't even send a family member! He could have sent his wife, a powerful figure in her own right, but instead he sent a functionary outside his inner circle. That showed American arrogance and disregard for the dignity of Koreans. When Clinton finally came to Pyongyang in 2009, then an ex-president turned errand boy dispatched to collect two Americans Kim had ordered kidnapped, their meeting hadn't erased the earlier insult.

But that would have to wait. Tonight he was considering the latest offer: a billion Swiss francs for two nuclear bombs. In the past, his vision—his inner voice—had said the time was not yet right. This time he knew, as certainly as he knew his own destiny, that it *was* right. With that much hard currency he could purchase what his dear people needed to plant their feet firmly on the road toward his vision: the *Juche* society, entirely self-sufficient. And the destruction of two American cities would reveal to all what *he* already knew: the weakness, self-indulgence, and futility of the United States. After their protector was shown helpless to protect even itself, Koreans south of the DMZ would accept his unification offer, through which the principles of *Juche* would prove superior and would absorb their democracy. These events would restore the dignity and face he had lost over years of reaching out to the Americans and being rebuffed.

Still, his muse urged caution. He knew he couldn't be sure what the Arabs would do. They were crazy—they saw enemies everywhere! Suppose they decided to strike Russia or China or Pakistan, instead of America? He would have the money, but America would still appear powerful to South Koreans and others lacking his own sure vision. Or suppose they struck America with one bomb and used the other against the Russians, owing to some grievance on behalf of the Muslims in Chechnya? Unlike the Americans, the Russians had power they were not reluctant to use—in fact they were proud of it—and would undoubtedly retaliate against him in kind if one of his bombs was used against them. And the source of the bombs, wherever the Arabs used them, *would* become known. They might try to blackmail him with it, or perhaps just reveal it in one of their theological rants. So, he had to protect himself.

What he needed was a way to sell the Arabs nuclear bombs but retain control over how they were used. Tonight he didn't know how to do that, but he knew he would work it out it in good time, as he had the answers to all his dear people's problems.

* * *

Austin, Texas—Eight Months Previously.

General Ray Morales, now Congressman Ray Morales, looked across the breakfast table at his wife, Julie. "So forty years later, I'm a butter-bar again," he said, using the Corps' slang for a newly minted officer.

"Not exactly, Ray! You and I are new to politics, but we've got all the life we've lived, all the experiences. Neither of us is a rookie, even if they call you Austin's freshman congressman."

"Were you surprised we won?"

"Not really. First, because you were appointed to fill Lamar Smith's term last year and we spent a lot of time here building support. Plus, this has been a Republican seat for a long time. And finally, although it's a topic most people don't want to think about, you were right about Iraq when the president was wrong—and had the guts to resign over it."

"So I shouldn't feel too cocky about winning?"

"You mean *we* shouldn't feel too cocky about winning? Satisfied, yes, but not cocky." They grinned at each other.

"OK, coach, I got it!" Ray drained his coffee and ambled off to shave.

He had a blocky build, with powerful arms and thighs, overlooked by a broad face with a large, pug nose and a fleshy lower lip above a squarish jaw and broad chin. In repose his lips were usually a straight line, neither smiling nor frowning, both of which he did unmistakably when he wanted. His eyes were piercing, as if he were leading Marines on patrol, missing nothing and appraising everything.

As he shaved, Ray thought about the situation facing president-elect Rick Martin and Congress, of which he was a very junior member. Although the country's mood was hopeful, as its citizens anticipated the inauguration of a charismatic man who said that together they would make things a lot better, the economic facts were pretty bleak. And on the international side . . . it was as if Americans had decided to ignore the world and assume it would ignore them.

When things went to hell in Iraq, about halfway through the calendar-driven withdrawal he had refused to support, the weakened NATO effort in Afghanistan had faded. Special Operations units from several countries remained in the northeast searching for al-Qaeda leaders, but that was about it. And across the irrelevant border, Pakistan stewed and bubbled and lurched, caught in tribal and ethnic hatreds, menaced by both Islamist mujahedin and Hindu India—and possessing at least several dozen nuclear weapons.

Ray didn't think the world was going to leave them alone. It was going to settle old scores, real and imagined.

Morales had met Rick Martin a few times, the contact initiated by an old but intimate connection between their very different lives. That connection was Ella Martin.

Ray met Ella Dominguez on the Princeton campus after a Princeton vs. Navy track meet in their junior year. Theirs had been one of those episodic, passionate college romances that die after graduation. The sex had been incredible, for the same reason—total focus—that pulled them apart. Ella entered Columbia Law and Ray became a Marine officer. After he completed the grueling Basic Course at Quantico, they spent some weekends together and wrote a few times, and then it was just over.

Twenty-five years after parting, Ella and Ray found themselves in the same city. He was the new head of Marine Corps Plans, Policy, and Operations, a stepping-stone to becoming commandant, the top Marine. Senator and Mrs. Rick Martin were already in Washington. Both spouses knew the history and there were no sparks—well maybe one or two, he admitted—but mainly just a fondness and mutual surprise that the paths they had traveled now crossed. He and Rick got along well, if casually, each thinking the other was typical of his profession but somewhat better than the average practitioner of war or politics.

Now Ray had entered Rick's political world and wondered whether they would have a relationship. He doubted it.

* * *

Pyongyang, North Korea (DPRK)—Eight Months Previously.

The Dear Leader rose from the computer, bouncing to his feet with pleasure. He had discovered the solution, as he always did. He knew how to maintain control over his bombs after he sold them.

It had come to him an hour ago, around 1:00 a.m. as he sat in his private theater, drinking Hennessy Paradis cognac and smoking cigars, watching one of Marlon Brando's greatest performances, *On the Waterfront*. The screen framed men working in the hold of a freighter, unloading cases of Irish whisky. One of them, a cocky character named Dugan, pilfered a bottle, joking to his mates about it. That triggered Kim's insight. Suddenly, he *knew*.

A Web addict, Kim went to Google and entered "sea container tracking." It produced over a hundred thousand hits. Scanning the advertisements on the right of the screen, he read, "Track your assets around the world. RFID satellite tracking." Kim clicked it. He learned that a small device could report the location and operation of vehicles, worldwide. It had a one-year battery life and gave its owner the ability to track it anywhere in the world as long as it stayed within range of a satellite or a cell phone network.

Kim laughed as he read on. From any computer anxious parents could locate the family car and see how fast their teenager was driving, as well as obtain a history of locations and speeds. If the parents wished, they could send a signal locking or unlocking the car doors and even disabling the ignition.

One of those devices could be paired with each bomb, linked to the firing circuit in such a way that, if the device were tampered with, the bomb would be disabled and a small explosive would destroy the bomb and the tamperer. With the device in place and functioning, Kim would know where the bomb was and could, if he chose, disable it. Tomorrow he would tell the Arabs it was a deal, one he of course would dominate by selling old plutonium weapons that had never worked powerfully in tests.

Having solved the problem, Kim returned to his theater and *On the Waterfront*. Sadly for Dugan, the Mob killed him for taking their whiskey.

Later, riding through the deserted streets, Kim briefly considered the U.S. presidential election of the previous week. Since Kim's view of the world was Kim-centered, he viewed all others as either threats or opportunities. And since all his life he had his way in nearly everything, he tended toward opportunity when assessing people. None could match him anyway, he thought. He had long ago accepted his own genius and his destiny to create the perfect society for his dear people.

Martin would be another opportunity.

Chapter 7

PRESIDENT MARTIN ENTERED a small, drab room smelling of mildew. Cabinet officers and the few others rose, their faces mostly neutral. Some nodded and smiled slightly as his eyes met theirs. Others didn't hold eye contact.

Yesterday's press conference had ended in fiasco with the power failure and stampede. After Wilson's command Rick sat thinking, for just a moment, of people trapped in collapsed buildings in Las Vegas. As Martin was pushing away emotions, Wilson had tensed at a voice sounding in his earpiece. He then growled, "No fire, Mr. President, just some fuckin' idiot with an overactive imagination! We'll let the herd run away and then walk out of here. The generators will be back up in a few minutes."

Today the journalists, not wanting to admit they had panicked over a five-minute power outage, spun a narrative of the administration's failure to be prepared.

I'm not going to think about the people in Las Vegas, Rick vowed silently. *If I do, I'll become as paralyzed as Walter there*, he thought, contemplating the secretary of education. He slid the memory into the vault where he kept unwanted things.

"Good morning, ladies and gentlemen. Now we begin. The day before yesterday was, literally, the first day of the rest of our lives. The country expects us to aid the victims and prevent another attack. With God's help—and Congress's—we'll do that!

His face earnest, a look he could turn on and off at will but now was sincere, the president leaned forward, fingers interlaced in front of him on the table.

"I believe that each of you is up to the job. I'm not expecting perfection, but I am expecting best efforts, twenty-four seven. I need to hear what *you* believe, not just what I want to hear. We can't have leaks, not only for security reasons but for the other reason we all know. Fear of being hung out to dry causes people to hold back. I pledge to you this is a Woodward-free zone and you must each make the same pledge to me and to each other."

A brief ripple of smiles held Rick's attention, and he missed the frown that flitted across the vice president's features. Bruce Griffith's square face and ruddy complexion were topped by longish, white-blonde hair, carefully blow-dried and combed forward to conceal a receding hairline. But acne scars in his cheeks and chin kept him from looking like an aging movie star and seemed to connect him to ordinary folks, saying, "my life hasn't been all roses either."

"I also want to say that, as horrible as this is, it offers opportunities," continued Martin. "We need to keep them in mind, and I see that as one of my own key contributions going forward. Maybe, just maybe, other countries will be frightened enough for themselves to get behind a U.S. initiative to really, finally, end the spread of nuclear weapons."

The president gestured to National Security Advisor John Dorn, who nodded to Secretary of Homeland Security Sara Zimmer, whose face sagged with fatigue.

Zimmer's brownish hair, flecked with grey, hung barely to her shoulders and was tucked behind her ears, revealing high, flat cheekbones and chiseled jaw muscles beneath pale skin. She was just short of gaunt, no fat on a frame that, though normally wheelchair-bound, remained athletic from daily swims. Recalling her army service as pilot of an Apache helicopter gunship, cabinet colleagues readily imagined her swooping low over panicked infantry, cutting them down with efficient, well-aimed bursts of fire.

"Mr. President, medical personnel and other first responders are still trying to stabilize the situation. It's chaotic. There was an initial surge of thousands out of the no-go zone into the triage points at the edge of it. We decontaminate them, triage them, move them to temporary shelter, and as soon as possible evacuate those expected to survive. None of that is as orderly as it sounds, as we've all seen on TV and YouTube. But that's our process, and as we get more resources and more experience, it will get better.

"In addition to police and firefighters we have help from a lot of Eric's people—paratroopers, medics, engineers, military police, plus helos and transport planes. You want to speak to that, Eric?"

Secretary of Defense Eric Easterly was a compact man whose broad, flat nose dominated his creased and battered face. The dark pupils of his eyes contrasted sharply with their whites, which in turn contrasted with his mahogany skin. Something hard lurked beneath his polished manner, something that was almost visible every year when he ran in the Marine Corps marathon.

"Sure, Sara. As you know, Mr. President, we deployed the ready battalion of the Eighty-second Airborne about twelve hours after the attack. They were prepared to jump in, but the C-17s were able to land about thirty-five miles away at Creech Air Force Base. Most of the Seventeenth Airborne Corps is now on-scene, or on the way, to patrol the no-go perimeter and help out with decontamination, first aid, meals—anything they can do. The Transportation Command has already made a few relocation flights getting survivors out."

Rubbing her eyes, Zimmer resumed. "I'd like to bring in the surgeon general to give us the medical and public health picture."

The surgeon general, in a chair wedged against the wall, attempted to stand in the space between it and Zimmer's wheelchair. There wasn't room. With a shrug, he dropped back into his chair, peering around Zimmer until he made eye contact with Martin.

"Mr. President, it's a grim picture. We have tens of thousands of dead and even more injured. Needless to say, we need more medical people and more treatment facilities! Right now, most of the dead are in the no-go zone, but within a few days to a few weeks large numbers of those who were able to reach the perimeter will die, mostly from radiation sickness.

"That's a big issue we need to face. Thousands of survivors are going to die. There's no way to prevent that; all we can do is keep them comfortable." He sketched quotation marks in the air.

"While it might seem that the best for them would be to die in a hospital, any hospital, evacuating them will mean the majority will die among strangers. Most families won't be able to be with them. It'll also mean returning thousands of bodies to Nevada. And if we put the certain fatalities in hospitals, we won't have enough beds for people with a chance to survive. On the other hand, if we continue to set up field care units nearby, family members can be with them, and the handling of remains is not such a problem. It won't be pretty, but I think it's the kindest and most practical way to go; plus it saves hospitals for those who benefit most from them."

Rick glanced at his chief of staff. Bart Guarini's green eyes flashed out of deep, heavy-browed sockets, screened by partially lowered eyelids. The effect was a bit like a pair of snipers firing from formidable concealment: attract their ire and you die. Bart understood as if it were his own thought: Rick wants some pushback.

"Doctor, what do we say when survivors with radiation sickness and their families complain they're being warehoused to die, and warehoused in terrible conditions at that? The average high this time of year must be around a hundred degrees," said Guarini.

"We tell the truth: that they're going to die in any case and we need hospital beds for those who can live if they reach one. "

"That's a hell of a bedside manner you've got, doctor!"

"What would *you* tell them, Mr. Guarini?"

The chief of staff reddened as he formed a retort, but Eric Easterly was quicker.

"Doctor," said the secretary of defense, "Once we reach the period when most of the radiation deaths occur, how many can we expect a day?"

"I don't know how many received fatal doses . . . considering that about five hundred thousand were probably exposed . . . easily five to ten thousand deaths a day, beginning about a week after the explosion."

"Bart, I don't know about our national hospital capacity, but I *do* know about airlift," said Easterly. "Even with full mobilization of the civil reserve air fleet, I think moving that many bodies in addition to those with a chance to pull through, plus uninjured but homeless survivors, would overwhelm our capacity. And you're right about the temperature, which makes it even more critical to quickly evacuate those who *can* survive.

"We're in a war, and we have to adopt wartime measures. We bury people where they die, like in World War II, and later return the remains to relatives for burial."

No, thought Rick, unconsciously shaking his head, *we're not going there! I am* not *calling this war. Once that horse is out of the barn, diplomacy is dead.*

"Eric, I take your point, but not the way you've expressed it. I want everyone clear on this: we are *not* at war. We've been the victims of a terrorist attack. Until we know who's behind it, we have no country to go to war *with*."

The president's gaze swept the table like a death ray as he said, "We have terrorists to identify and apprehend, not a war to fight!"

Bruce Griffith kept his expression attentively neutral, but his mind shouted: *Victims! I hate that word! It implies powerlessness, helplessness. We've been attacked; we're going to find who did it and strip them of the power to attack us again. That's how I would put it, how most Americans want to hear it. And, "Apprehend." Apprehend? We should kill the bastards who did this!*

Chapter 8

MARTIN SHIFTED HIS gaze to Dorn, who said, "OK, let's turn to what Homeland Security is doing. Then we'll hear from Justice and National Intelligence."

Opening a folder, Zimmer began.

"We've made some assumptions; we'll adjust them as facts come in. First is that terrorists don't have man-portable weapons, suitcase nukes. So, we're concentrating on vehicles, rail, aircraft, and ships as possible means of delivery. The coast guard, with help from the other services, has the lead in searching all ships in our ports.

"We're assuming the next target is another large metro area. So, the FAA is diverting all flights to large cities or ordering them cancelled. We've banned freight trains from major metro areas but allowed passenger trains under heightened inspection. DOE deploys Nuclear Emergency Support Teams— NEST for short—to sweep for nukes whenever we find something suspicious.

"Cars and trucks are of course the biggest challenge. A few big metro areas, like Manhattan, have limited ingress and egress anyway, plus highway radiation portal monitors already in place, but everywhere else we have to use cops with handheld equipment. Frankly, it's a hell of a mess!"

She scanned their faces without apology.

"What's the plan if you find a nuke or something that appears to be one?" said the secretary of energy.

"It's one recommended by your NEST people: We check for booby traps and then move it to the nearest airfield, where it goes aboard a cargo aircraft with a military crew and a team of nuclear weapon engineers. The plane climbs to high altitude and heads out over the ocean, where the engineers go to work. They take photographs and record everything they observe, especially anything indicating origin. It's all immediately data-linked to your people at Sandia Labs and the Pantex plant. Then the engineers try to disarm it. If they are successful, the plane delivers it to Pantex. If not—assuming it doesn't blow—they dump it in deep ocean before coming home."

Rick squirmed to ease his aching back and cut his glance to the secretary of defense. Obediently, Dorn said, "Anything more, Eric?"

"Well, in addition to what Sara has already mentioned, we're sending field hospitals to Vegas and putting two hospital ships in port LA, a forty-five minute flight from there. And since every non-military aircraft is a potential nuclear bomb, we've reinstated the measures used after Nine-eleven: If a flight leaves its route and heads for a major city, fighters shoot it down if it won't turn away."

Easterly continued, but Rick's thoughts stayed with those words. *Some-body has to give that order. Should it be me? Whoever says shoot is ordering the immediate death of innocent passengers, maybe on a mistake. Could I do that? Is it the right thing to do? By what right do I take the lives of maybe a hundred peo-ple in order to prevent an attack that might or might not be happening? But by what right do I withhold permission to shoot and maybe sacrifice a city and many thousands of people who are just as innocent as those in the airplane?*

Martin held up a hand. "Eric, let's go back to those fighters. Who's going to make the decision to shoot?"

"Sir, that'll be the call of our general commanding the North American Air Defense Command or his deputy, a Canadian general. One or the other will always be in the command center."

"No!" The president made a stop gesture with his right hand. "I'm not gonna deal with the fallout of an American general ordering a Canadian air-liner shot down, or vice versa. Find another way!"

"OK, then I recommend each nation take responsibility for making that call within its own airspace. For us, it will be the flag officer on watch at the National Military Command Center."

"Agreed. What else?"

"Mr. President, we've sent army and air force units to support customs and border protection patrols."

"What results?"

"Well sir, they've located and stopped a number of four-wheel drive vehicles. They've all turned out to be what CBP calls the usual stuff: smugglers with Mexican illegals and lost hikers along the Canadian border. Unfortunately, a couple of vehicles coming from Mexico ignored halt orders and had to be stopped by fire. There've been three killed and about half a dozen wounded, all Mexicans."

Snapping his head leftward, Martin looked at Anne Battista, who shrugged. "Nothing yet from Mexico. I'm sure we'll hear from them soon."

Rick was surprised, then had a rare spike of anger. *Good God! We can't go lurching around smashing things like some wounded Godzilla. That's just what terrorists want us to do!* He glared at the secretary of defense.

"Eric, you and Sara have to find a better way! We can't go on shooting harmless illegals or start winging wandering hunters. It seems to me that if the vehicles are away from populated areas it should be OK to pursue and stop them eventually, without shooting them up."

Easterly's jaws worked as he absorbed the rebuke and then responded. "Yes, Mr. President. We'll put together new rules of engagement immediately and bring them to you for review." He glanced at MacAdoo, who nodded and left.

Chapter 9

"MOVING RIGHT ALONG!" said Dorn, attempting to lighten the mood. "Aaron, what are your trawls catching?"

Looking, as always, like his valet had just finished knotting his tie, Director of National Intelligence Hendricks cleared his throat and began speaking. He seemed to swell, reminding Rick of one of Maryland's red-winged blackbirds in mating season.

"I believe the most significant matter right now is that no organization has claimed responsibility. The chatter from low levels of al-Qaeda and Hezbollah is of course elation, but also puzzlement. Whoever did this is now the biggest dog on the block and must be bursting to strut. We're pretty sure it will come out, but it hasn't yet."

"What does Mossad think?" interjected Martin.

Hendricks scowled. "They have no leads either! Mordacai's hunch is that the longer there's no claim, the more it points to Hezbollah, because they have tight discipline. He doesn't think al-Qaeda or others could keep the secret very long."

"OK," replied Martin. "But as for Mossad's theory—remember, Israel would love to tie this can to Iran's tail."

Because he knew Hendricks would never go beyond generalities in this large group, Rick wanted to move on. "So Ed, what can you tell us? Any odds that American terrorists did this?"

Attorney General Ed McDonnell stiffened, struggling to appear cool. He was responsible for the FBI, whose job it was to find and thwart domestic terrorists. Although they had failed, the FBI director assured him they hadn't missed something as glaring as flight lessons. McDonnell prayed he was right.

He gulped and said, "Mr. President, the FBI, in close cooperation with the intelligence community, is reviewing the passenger list for every airline arrival in Las Vegas within the past thirty days, and the same with the backup copies of all hotel records. They are monitoring all Internet social media for chatter bearing on the bomber's identity, such as a martyr's farewell. They're examining the recent activities of every extremist organization in the country, whatever their credo, and locating all their known members.

"In addition—"

The president held up his hand to end the man's agony—it was clear he had no leads. "Ed, I have no doubt you and your team are doing absolutely everything to get a handle on the bomber! Keep at it and something will break our way."

Poor bastard! Ed doesn't know about Paternity, and I'm not ready tell him. At least I can cut him down from the gallows.

Dorn nodded to Secretary of State Anne Battista. In her official photo there is firmness in her expression that says "I've given up a lot to get here and now that I have, I'm going to make my mark." Her blonde hair, just brushing her shoulders, had been carefully tended to eliminate gray, but she made no effort to disguise the beginning of neck sag or deep grooves that appeared in her lower cheeks when her face was animated.

Speaking, Battista swept her eyes around the table. "There are widespread expressions of shock, sympathy, and support, with some pointed exceptions. We're not hearing much out of the Middle East, except of course from the Israelis. It's as if the Arabs and the Persians are waiting for another shoe to drop. NATO's sympathetic but frightened.

"As most of you know, President Volkov called President Martin on the Hotline, and they exchanged reassurances. The Russians and the Chinese have made statements condemning the attack. The Russian statement included the threat to retaliate—quote—with the full, repeat the full, resources of the state if terrorists should be so foolish as to attack Russia in this manner, unquote."

"If you nuke me, I'll nuke you," said the treasury secretary.

"Obviously," said Martin, glaring as if to say, you interrupted for *that?*

He looked back to the secretary of state. "Anne, please give us a thumbnail of Asia and what you're hearing from the UN."

"Well, the Chinese, as I said, condemned the attack, and I had a support-ive call from my Chinese counterpart, Jia . . . something I thought was odd: he said he assumed we'd know who did it soon enough. I said I agreed, but, frankly, I don't see how." She shrugged.

Paternity! Does Jia know about Paternity? The question speared Rick's stomach.

Chapter 10

MARTIN LOCKED EYES with Easterly, who understood the president's glance and remained silent.

Oblivious, Battista continued. "I'd say the Japanese government is very, very uneasy. Part of it is that some Japanese think this is karmic payback for Hiroshima and Nagasaki. But the heart of it is that they realize how we handle this determines whether our nuclear umbrella over Japan actually protects them. North Korea has nuclear weapons and missiles with plenty of range to reach Japan. If our pledge to protect Tokyo loses credibility in Pyongyang . . ."

She paused, sipping water, then resumed: "Seoul of course has a similar worry but is unwilling to say so. The Indians and the Pakistanis say they're shocked and horrified and will help us find the perpetrators. The Indians hint delicately that Pakistani extremists might have some connection. The Paks are clearly worried that they might be implicated, because of A. Q. Kahn and because al-Qaeda's leadership is somewhere in Waziristan. Australia wants to know how to help. The Indonesians have said nothing official so far."

Nodding toward the image of the UN ambassador on the teleconference screen, she continued: "Oscar tells me that during this morning's emergency meeting of the Security Council all members expressed sympathy and support. The council unanimously approved a resolution calling on all UN members to render what assistance they can."

"What would you add, Oscar?" said Martin.

All looked at the video screen as Ambassador Neumann responded. "Among the member nations at large—and UN officials, including the secretary-general—

I feel an atmosphere of watchful waiting. Will there be another bomb? What will the United States do? Is this the first domino in a rapid U.S. decline? What about countries allied with us—are they on the terrorists' target list? What about countries we've flagged as sponsors of terrorism—are they on *our* target list? What are we going to ask the UN to do? And last but not least, how much danger are all of *them* in at the UN complex here in New York?"

"Bottom line," said Battista, "we should appear injured but unafraid and angry but controlled. A lot of people, including many Americans, now believe Bush didn't really give diplomacy a chance after Nine-eleven, Mr. President. Your administration can do better."

Eric Easterly considered her words with invisible amusement. *Right, Anne,* he thought, *and you just happen to be in charge of the cabinet department that will have the lead in 'doing better.'* He saw her young aide scribbling furiously, making sure to record those words for her boss' memoir and for her own buddies' admiration.

Suddenly, Rick felt overwhelmed, drowning in information. He kicked hard for shore. "Thanks, Anne and Oscar," he said briskly. "The UN is going to be an important part of our response."

Catching the president's mood, Dorn said, "OK, Vijay, bring us up to date on the economic impacts and what you're doing."

Vijay Ramanna immediately began to speak. A former Federal Reserve governor, he had been a surprise choice, the first Indian-American to serve in a cabinet, and Martin had been pleased with the buzz.

Leaning forward, Ramanna spoke more loudly than necessary. "Mr. President, the Fed chairman agrees with me that the stock markets and commodity exchanges should stay closed for a few days in order to prevent panic selling. There's the Nine-eleven precedent, so we're not getting too much pushback. But, obviously, we can't keep the doors shut very long, because that would create an even bigger panic. We're watching liquidity closely, but for now we believe it's best to leave banks open."

Martin rubbed tired eyes, trying to relieve the gritty sensation signaling fatigue.

Ramanna continued: "Right after your address last night, I took action! Treasury is reaching out to our international counterparts and also requesting that all major banking centers report large transactions in which the amounts are unusual. If the bombers bought that weapon, there may be a money trail leading to the seller or the terrorists."

"Vijay, how far back are you looking?" said Vice President Griffith.

"First cut is six months, Mr. Vice President. That's just my guess. We'll adjust when we have more information. My hunch is that terrorists would use the bomb as soon as possible for their own security reasons."

"What does Justice think, Ed?" said Martin.

"That time window is as good a place to start as any. I agree with Vijay's hunch. We're working with CIA now to locate known bagmen for al-Qaeda or other terrorist groups. At some point renditions may make sense, so we can question them."

"Ed, that comes to the NSC before you grab anyone. I'm probably going to need a lot of convincing. This administration is *not* going to waterboard anybody, so I'm not sure that the gain from having them in custody would be worth the grief we'd get for snatching them."

Martin was watching the vice president's reaction, but Griffith's face remained neutral. *His presence on the ticket was crucial to me in Pennsylvania and several other states,* thought Rick, *but he's often wrong on civil liberties and national security. I'll bet he'll come to me on this before long.*

Three hours into the meeting, Rick was more than ready for a break. "Thanks, Vijay. He glanced at his watch.

"John, are we done?"

"Yes, Mr. President."

Martin rose, then paused. "No, don't get up. It's too crowded in here for that." The president examined their faces gravely before continuing: "This is going to take a long time. Pace yourselves and your people. It's a marathon, not a sprint. Once in awhile, go home in time to hug your kids and your spouses.

Chapter 11

AFTER A ONE-HOUR break, Rick eased into his chair and looked around the room, less crowded this time. Returning his gaze, or fiddling with papers and smart phones, were the members of the National Security Council (NSC), plus CIA Director Scott Hitzleberger and National Security Advisor John Dorn.

Martin spoke: "The purpose of this meeting is to discuss a CIA program, the Paternity Project, which only a few people know about." *Maybe that will fuzz it up enough to keep Bruce and Anne from knowing immediately that they've been kept out,* he thought. "This is a technical program—something called nuclear forensics—which could reveal the origin of the Las Vegas bomb. Over to you, Aaron and Scott."

Hendricks began to speak, and Rick let his mind wander while the DNI repeated what he'd heard from him in January. In a brief meeting just before this one, Hendricks had listened as Hitzleberger reported that initial analysis pointed to North Korea. Martin told them not to reveal it.

So we are close to having scientific information fingering the country that enabled terrorists to destroy Las Vegas, Rick thought. *Thank God it's not China or Russia!*

It's going to be awkward knowing what country it is but not knowing who the terrorists are. The existence of this information, right now, is itself a problem. How long before it leaks? If I can control it, do I want to keep it secret or tell the country and the world right away? When do I want the NSC to know? Pretty soon, because I can't get the full benefit of these good minds if I withhold information.

As he had aboard Marine One, Martin felt events running away from his control. Then his private smart phone vibrated. He saw it was Ella and, with a gesture to Bart, left the room.

"Rick, Dottie told me you'd gotten a call from Rog Phelps. My curiosity is killing me!"

"Yep! I think you can imagine what he had to say, most of it, anyway. I nearly passed him off on Bart, but figured in the circumstances I ought to at least *listen* to the Democratic party chairman, even if he did try to block our nomination last year."

"Let me guess. He was urging prudence, statesmanship, multilateralism— that sort of thing."

"That about sums it up. He cautioned me not to get the country into another preconceived war of choice, as he put it, which will infuriate the base and drag our party down for years."

"So after we've been attacked and tens of thousands of Americans murdered, Roger's main concern is the politics of it!"

"Well, Ella, he'd probably say that's because managing the politics is his job and that's best done unemotionally. I grant you he's not very credible to us—he was so wrong about our decision to run—but his message matters. We don't want to go off half-cocked, seeing everything through some familiar framework of us versus them that may not fit this situation."

"Look, Rick, we're not starting from a clean slate. America had several deadly enemies *before* Las Vegas was bombed. Not everybody is innocent until proven guilty—you can't disregard what was done and said before Las Vegas. We weren't attacked by men from Mars! I'm betting we'll find it was a group we already know. When that happens—"

"Ella, when that happens, we will decide what to do about it."

"Rick, has it already happened?"

"I'm sorry but I have to go. I ducked out of an NSC meeting. Love you."

"Love you, too."

Ella put her phone down and exhaled, her cheeks puffing as if blowing out a candle. *The murder of Las Vegas gets to me. Evil threatens my family and my people again. I've seen a society destroyed by the failure of good men to defeat evil men. It's not the same for Rick . . . He's put those scenes of Las Vegas away in a box.*

I want them on the table, in front of him like they're in front of me. I've got to get him out of his head!

Rick slid back into his seat knowing Ella realized he had ducked her question, but not ready for the conversation they would have if she knew what the spooks had told him. While he was away Scott Hitzleberger had taken over from Hendricks.

"At several points in the process of turning fissionable material into a bomb, the uranium or plutonium acquires characteristics, or tags if you will, that are unique to the particular manufacturing process. Uranium ore contains impurities—we call them trace elements—indicating where it was mined. Ore is crushed and mixed with acid, creating uranium oxide. To get the high concentration of U-235 required for a nuclear explosion, uranium oxide gas is spun through centrifuges. Then the U-235 is recovered as a solid that is compacted and machined into two or more pieces of uranium the right shape and size to produce a nuclear explosion if brought together."

Hitzleberger's hands mimicked squeezing an object.

"This manufacturing process causes the uranium in a bomb to have a distinctive mix of isotopes—U-238, -235, -232 if it's reprocessed fuel—plus traces of the impurities in the ore. When a nuke detonates, only about one percent of the bomb material is actually consumed. I know that's amazing, but we have data from sixty-plus bomb tests in the Pacific and in Nevada. We know exactly what happens when a nuclear weapon explodes, as do the other major nuclear powers: Britain, France, Russia and China."

The CIA director paused for a swallow of coffee from a paper cup bearing the presidential seal, then resumed.

"So, ninety-nine percent of the bomb is among the debris and fallout of the explosion and—again because of many tests—the techniques for collecting and analyzing the debris are well understood. Another amazing but well-documented fact is that the isotopic composition of the uranium debris is virtually identical to its pre-explosion state. In addition, trace elements of the uranium ore's impurities can be detected.

"Plutonium is created by nuclear reactors, using various methods. For now I'll just say this makes the tags on debris of a plutonium weapon more distinct and easier to match than those of a uranium bomb.

"Bottom line: every nuke has a signature.

"For both types of weapons the identification technique is conceptually like fingerprinting, or identification from iris patterns. It's not especially demanding scientifically, once the data have been collected . . . and the Paternity Project has been collecting that data for more than thirty years.

"Questions when you are ready, Mr. President." Hitzleberger sat down.

Griffith ignored his president and spoke, drawing several expressions of disbelief: "So tell us: who are the bastards that provided the bomb?"

Watching Martin, Hitzleberger followed instructions. "We're still running tests and collecting additional samples. One thing we learned right away: it was a plutonium weapon."

Rick said, "Bruce, once we have the report, naturally we'll all want to concentrate on what to do next. But right now, I need your help digging into the credibility of Paternity. With all due respect to Aaron and Scott, who weren't involved, I remember when the Agency said finding Saddam's WMD would be a slam dunk. We need to consider a huge issue: What reliance are we going to place on the results when we get them? And how will we convince others?"

Battista cleared her throat, something that Dorn always felt was contrived and annoying, then spoke. "Science is all about challenge. One lab produces a result and other labs rush to see whether they get the same result, independently. Scientists argue ferociously before they accept someone's hypothesis. Think global warming. If we present this as a purely scientific judgment, no matter how strong the evidence, we're going to get a lot of pushback! So, we should also be asking what other information would point to the bomb's origin."

She's right, Dorn thought; despite *her affectations she has a top-notch mind*. He said, "Well, we should certainly do what any good detective does: see who had motive and opportunity. Also, the old cui bono question—who benefits?"

Griffith said, "I'm betting this weapon changed hands for money, a lot of money. If we follow the money, it will lead to somebody. If money confirms science, we're looking better."

"So there may be some other indicators, beyond Paternity," said Martin. "But let's focus for a moment on the scientific case." He shifted his gaze to Hitzleberger as he spoke. "Scott, let's start with reproducibility."

"Sir, we're addressing that right now. We've got several teams working independently with the samples and the database."

"Yeah, that's good, but I meant non-government labs. How much sample material do you have? Enough to make some broadly available to the scientific community? If not that, then, say, to three or four other governments?"

"Sir, there's plenty of material within the fallout area. And airborne particles will circle the world up in the troposphere in quantities suitable for sampling for at least twenty days."

"So that means," said Battista, "we don't have to provide samples. Others can collect them independently."

"That's right, Anne," said Hendricks. "And that's exactly how it used to work. We'd do a test, or the Russians or the Chinese would, and the others would launch collection aircraft. American engineers became expert at deducing the power and even the designs of others' nukes. I'm sure the Russians, Brits, French, and probably the Chinese did, too. Since the end of atmospheric testing, in the sixties, most of those other sampling organizations have probably been disbanded, but the knowledge is there to reconstitute them quickly."

Griffith leaned forward. "OK, that raises a potential problem. Is this analysis demanding scientifically? I mean, suppose, say, the French scientists don't have good enough equipment, you know, not as sensitive maybe, so they get different results?"

After a glance at Hendricks, Hitzleberger responded. "The main scientific technique is spectroscopy, which is widely used in industry and science. I don't think that will be an issue." *I know what* will *be an issue,* Hitzleberger thought, *and I'm not goin' there!*

But Easterly did: "Analyzing a sample is only half the process. They've got to have something for comparison, and unless it's the same as our standard, there won't be a match. Scott, can we reproduce our standards, or let others use them?"

To Hitzleberger's enormous relief, Hendricks stepped in. "No, Eric, we can't! The samples came into our possession by extremely sensitive collection methods and through irreplaceable sources. They're items like copies of reactor operating records and tiny amounts of reactor fuel. To be used authoritatively, each must be identified as to time and place obtained. That information will compromise our sources.

"Let me make a point: Paternity isn't static. As current nuclear powers develop new weapons and others, like Iran, edge closer—Iran may have untested weapons now—we require new samples. For example, Pakistan's current warheads use uranium. If they go to plutonium, we need to update our sample library. We can't keep Paternity ready if we reveal our sources and methods."

The room was silent, all aware that Hendricks would not be moved on this, except by the president, who said nothing.

Understanding the president's silence, Dorn moved them to a different question. "There's more to the sources than their identity. There's the question of reliability. I remember some Iraqi scientist, who was the main source of information tying Saddam to an active biological weapons program, turned out to be bogus. How are we gonna handle the reliability issue?"

"We point to three instances when Paternity was validated," replied the DNI. "In 1998 the Paks tested six weapons underground. A plume of debris escaped, and we flew a U-2 collection aircraft through it. Analysis demonstrated, to President Clinton's satisfaction, that some of the HEU in those warheads was of Chinese origin and identified the specific facility that produced it. He had Madeline Albright call in the Chinese Ambassador and read the riot act, backing it up with specifics. We learned a couple of years later that the Chinese halted all nuclear cooperation with the Paks.

"When the North Koreans announced in 2006 they had tested a nuclear weapon underground we collected a sample the same way. Their bomb was plutonium and we got an exact match to the reactor fuel reprocessing facility at Yongbyon. Incidentally, we also determined that the weapon didn't work well; the yield was very low, probably because they didn't have a good understanding of beryllium tamping. We repeated that analysis when they tested again, in 2009."

"Well, that's just great!" said Easterly. "Two of our validators are presidents who are widely believed to be liars—Clinton about Monica and Bush about WMD."

"But," replied Hendricks, "we also have the Chinese government."

"That's what he meant!" said Anne Battista. "The Chinese foreign minister, when he said we'd know soon who did it."

Listening to Battista, Martin realized that her outburst would show Griffith that he was not the only one outside of Paternity until today, but Griffith's red cheeks and balled fists, resting on the table, told their story.

"Does *anyone* here think the Chinese would be willing to back us on Paternity?" asked the vice president, his right hand flicking imperiously to include everyone.

Battista looked at Griffith coolly and said, "A lot would depend on who Paternity points to."

The president stepped in. "You're right, Anne, and when we know that, the Chinese connection will be an aspect to pursue. But right now let me throw out a hypothetical: let's say I decide that we *must* have independent confirmation of Paternity. I then authorize sharing of portions of our database."

Martin turned to Hendricks, pausing for a beat, and everyone knew he was reminding him who was president.

He continued: "So how does that work? Who do we share with? How do we share credibly?"

"Well, I'd say for sure the IAEA," replied Battista, referring to the International Atomic Energy Agency. "And the permanent members of the UN Security Council. We're going to need their support to do anything at the UN, and probably each member still has expertise in analyzing fallout."

"Who are the strongest skeptics going to be?" asked Martin.

In unison, Griffith and Easterly said, "the press!"

"OK, and how can we handle their skepticism?"

"Well, we really should turn Sam Yu loose on that angle," Griffith replied, "but here's a top-of-the-head thought: How about if we bring Bob Woodward inside Paternity? He has a record of reporting from behind the scenes without either pulling punches or revealing the most sensitive information."

Well I'll be damned! thought Martin. *Bruce wants to be sure he comes out of this on the side of the angels. That's no surprise, but I expected he'd be more subtle. Well, if Woodward starts revealing inside information, I'll know where to look first.*

Easterly responded to the VP: "Hell, others are so jealous of him that they'll go out of their way to debunk whatever he writes! And he's a *Washington Post* guy. The *Times* would hate us if we did that. I bet Sam won't go for it."

"Just a thought," said Griffith. "Like I said, Sam's the expert."

"You know," said Battista, "somehow we've got to get away from Colin Powell briefing nonexistent WMD to the UN. We're going to see that footage played over and over."

"Mr. President," said Griffith, "the turn this discussion has taken shows the danger of trying too hard to be understood, to get everybody to agree with us. As it has here, the issue shifts from the terrorists to the credibility of the United States. I'm all for lining up support, but after we've considered the evidence here in this administration, we're going to have to do what we in Pennsylvania call takin' care of business. That's our responsibility to Americans!"

"Mr. Vice President," said Battista, "we have a responsibility to the world as well as to Americans. That goes with being the only superpower!"

Martin thought, *Yes, Bruce is going to be a problem! For many reasons I don't want to cut him out of this, but I need to find some way to insulate the process from his aggressiveness.*

The president closed his briefing book and slid his pen into his shirt pocket, those actions as dismissive as closing a door. "Bruce, when the time comes to take care of business, we will. And we've taken care of a lot of it here. We've had a discussion that points to some things we need to think through to make the most effective use of Paternity. John, I need your good staff work, soon."

Martin rose and left the room. As he walked, he made a decision: he and Ella would go to Las Vegas, soon.

Chapter 12

RICK AND ELLA made love that night, not passionately, but deeply, two people tenderly seeking to give and receive solace, knowing their lives had been changed forever, in a yet unfathomable way.

Rick had dropped quickly off to sleep, but now he was awake. It felt really good to be above ground again, at Camp David. He rolled and saw Ella, motionless in her bed a few feet away, heard her breathing slowly and deeply. Good—she wasn't awake. His mind was racing and he knew that sleep would not return.

The buck stops on my desk. Okay. Presidents get the issues that are basically insoluble. If they weren't, somebody else would have solved them. Most presidents muddle through, sustained by strong belief in something, *be it a political philosophy or a religion or both, and avoid the shame of a failed presidency because chance or fortune or a higher power—whatever you choose to call it—breaks about even over the course of a term. Bad decisions tend to be balanced by good. It's a fifty-fifty world.*

I've made tough calls, risky calls before, like running against Glenna Rogers. When you take on your party's sitting president, failure isn't an option if you want to stay in politics! I made that call and other tough ones during the campaign, and now I'm president. This is different, but . . . I can do it.

At five a.m. he quietly put on robe and slippers, stepping softly to the cabin's porch, feeling in a pocket for cigarettes and matches. As he moved, the Secret Service moved, too, murmuring into their microphones.

The president lit up and inhaled deeply. The cigarette's glow was the only light source on the shadowed porch, although the compound was lit. Birds were starting their morning chorus in the nearby trees, and the air felt pleasant.

Rick's mind returned to the cabinet meeting. His gut said they couldn't continue to govern from a bomb shelter. Yes, it would be chaos if a nuke in Washington got him, Bruce, the cabinet, and Congress. But the country couldn't shelter in a bunker and continue to exist as the United States of America. Americans had to get back to their workplaces and resume buying and selling and borrowing and lending.

If the people have to get back to their *cities their government should lead by getting back to its city, Washington. Bruce and I must stay apart so that one bomb can't get us both, but beyond that, this government has to go back to work in the capital. This morning I'll tell Bart to make the arrangements. We'll sleep tonight in the White House!*

Paternity! Sweet Jesus, what am I going to do with that *information? Aaron and Scott got the drift that I didn't want them to rush through the analysis, and that should delay the official determination another twenty-four, maybe forty-eight hours. But it's coming at me like a freight train, and it can't and shouldn't be kept secret.*

Suddenly it hit him: Suppose North Korea had not only made the bomb; suppose North Korea had also made the attack?

* * *

Low lights came up. Kim sat in his chair, alone in his theater.

He'd spent hours watching scenes of the devastation and President Martin's speech and news conference. He'd heard the president say, "we will find out how they got the bomb they used" and that America would deal with both those who carried out the attack and those who enabled it.

The devastation pleased him, and Martin's threat felt hollow.

As he had before taking the Arab's money, Kim assessed Martin's options. If the Americans attempted invasion—unlikely with the memory of Iraq so fresh—his fine army would bleed them far worse than al-Qaeda had. One frozen winter would be enough to send them crawling away, but it wouldn't even take that! If he simply threatened to use his missiles on Seoul and Tokyo, South Korea and Japan would force them to withdraw.

If they blockaded or imposed sanctions, he would get around them as Saddam had done. This was another way his creative genius would enable his triumph. He would flood the world with videos of his people's suffering, and America would have to back down.

Since Kim attached no value to lives other than his own, the issue for him was *him*. And the only way the Americans could actually harm *him* was with a nuclear strike.

In his mind's eye, Kim saw again the destruction his small bomb had created. He imagined how Pyongyang, *his* city, filled with statues and monuments to him and his father, would look after a much larger American nuke had done its work.

The Americans *would* find out the bomb was one of his. Kim felt an unfamiliar emotion: fear.

But then he saw, as if reading a screenplay, that he and his dear people would be protected from American reprisal by American doubters. American blogs showed that large numbers of them would always disbelieve their government. Kim thought for a minute of the film that Michael Moore would make and smiled; it would be even better than *Fahrenheit 9/11*!

Martin would order a nuclear attack only if he possessed undeniable proof of the bomb's origin—and only then if he could also stomach killing thousands of Kim's people, enraging the Chinese and South Koreans, and creating even more chaos among Americans. No. Everything in the man's life history shouted that he wouldn't. Kim knew there was no such thing as undeniable proof.

When the second bomb exploded, it would bring the Americans to their knees. It would also strip them of their allies. No nation would risk helping them for fear of drawing the Arabs' rage on themselves.

Kim decided to watch *One Flew over the Cuckoo's Nest*—he had always liked Jack Nicholson's work.

* * *

"A penny for your thoughts," said Ella softly from right behind him. She molded herself to Rick's back, reaching her arms around his waist and leaning her forehead into the nape of his neck, hugging him gently. With a guilty start he flicked away the cigarette then squeezed both her hands in his; he slowly unwrapped her arms and turned to face her.

"I was just thinking about getting us and the country back to work," he said. "The longer we hunker down, the worse it gets. Locking down our cities makes things go to hell for the economy much faster than anything we might gain against the bombers by doing it. What do you think it will take to get people back to their lives?"

"Setting an example and leveling with them," she said, and then: "Rick, what are the odds of more bombs?"

"I don't know, but if I ask myself, how many bombs these people—whoever they are—could have, logic says not many. Whether they bought them, stole them, or built them, there are so many constraints . . . limited bomb-making capacity, limited cash, and, I've got to believe, few sources, few nations that would be willing, or are so lax, that they would part with, or lose control of, more than a handful of nukes."

"So, worst case, we're looking at . . ."

"I don't know. Maybe two or three more bombs."

"Two or three more cities is what that means."

"Yeah."

"Can the country take that?"

"Depends a lot on which cities. If they were New York, Washington, and LA . . ."

"So, we don't try to defend everywhere. We defend the most critical cities."

"Try selling that to Congress and the press and the bloggers!"

Ella looked at him sharply. "Well, Rick, you may have to do just exactly that! Remember what you said about running an open, straight-talking administration?"

"Yeah. But I had in mind explaining the sacrifices necessary to make Social Security solvent, not trying to sell the idea that, depending on where you live, you may be expendable."

"Well, remember how England stood up under the blitz. They didn't try to defend every city as if it were London. Churchill sold that. Get the speech writers working on it!"

"Sir, it's six o'clock."

Rick and Ella knew that voice. It belonged to the president's valet, and with it their day began.

Chapter 13

Creech Air Force Base, near Las Vegas

STEVE NGUYEN WAS far gone toward death by radiation by the time Rick and Ella arrived at his stretcher. He had experienced several bouts of spontaneous bleeding, evidence of which was on his clothing, ears, nose, and the corners of his mouth. From somewhere in the morphine-induced haze that guarded him from most of the pain of his disintegrating body, Nguyen sensed a presence. He forced open his encrusted eyelids.

Rick was nearly overwhelmed by the smells: feces, infection, urine, vomit. As Rick and Ella paused beside Nguyen, he recognized them. "Mr. President!" Looking toward the hoarse, garbled, gurgling voice, they saw a man with red blotches and oozing patches on his skin and ulcerated, infected lip sores. He had pulled himself up on one elbow.

"They killed my family, my wife, my two little girls . . ." A rasping breath. "They killed me, too." Nguyen suddenly reached across his body and upwards, the motion tearing an IV needle out of his forearm, and grabbed the president's leg. As others reached for the man, Rick shook his head. He felt the strength in Nguyen's grip. "Find them. Punish them for what they did here. Promise me. Promise me!"

The president squatted beside the stretcher, his throat constricted, eyes prickling. *Why? Why? Nothing this country has done, no American policy, however misguided, justifies killing these people. I do not grant you the right to kill us! I will not accept this!*

For the first time since the bombing—in fact, the first in a very long time—Rick Martin felt emotion that he did not shunt to that separate place he'd constructed early in his life, when he resolved never to expose his feelings, never to risk allowing another to savage his unprotected emotional flesh.

"What's your name?" said the president, biting his lip.

"Steve . . . Nguyen."

"What are the names of your family?"

"Cindy my wife . . . Rachel who was three and . . . Carol . . . five."

"I promise you, Steve Nguyen. I promise!"

Nguyen winced, stiffened, and pulled himself upward, his muscles straining. Bleeding lips working, he shouted, "Don't let us down, Mr. President!" He let go of Rick's leg and slumped back down on the stretcher, hemorrhaging again in scarlet streams, his radiation-ravaged blood now without the platelets needed to clot.

Rick knelt, frozen, gazing at the dying man and smelling his suppurating sores.

Don't let us down . . . he holds me responsible for the outcome of all this. For bringing some sort of justice and closure and, yes, benefit out of this horror. He believes that's the president's job, my job. Well, I do, too, Steve!

Rick squeezed the dying man's hand, looked into Ella's eyes, and rose. They continued their journey through the dreadful landscape. When the first troops had arrived, Steve Nguyen and other survivors inhabited a scene like those recorded by American Civil War photographer Matthew Brady: the ground was carpeted with the wounded and dead. Survivors took precedence; the dead were left where they had dropped. Soldiers walked among them, giving water, rigging what shelter they could, injecting morphine from their battle dressing packs. These were paratroopers; they traveled light and slept rough and had few tents to offer. Very few survivors had shelter from the merciless sun.

By the day of the president's unannounced arrival, the soldiers and a steady stream of volunteers had filled every building and hangar at Creech with the injured. Their numbers, while overwhelming to those caring for them, were far, far fewer than the numbers of survivors remaining without shelter around the no-go perimeter. Even the fortunate ones at Creech were in grim circumstances. Most lay or sat on the tile or concrete floors in the squalor of festering wounds, overflowing waste, and head-to-toe crowding.

As word of the Martins' presence rippled through the base, a crowd gathered. Sam Yu, face like stone, moved alongside Rick as he paused at another stretcher. "Mr. President, you should speak to the survivors and the soldiers. I'll pull something together." Rick nodded and moved toward the next victim, his concentration broken only for a moment.

About forty-five minutes later, Rick and Ella climbed up onto the bed of a truck. Rick held a bullhorn and looked out over hundreds of people, the number growing as those able to walk streamed from all directions.

Wilson, leading the presidential protective detail, climbed up and took position about five steps—or one step and a dive—to the president's left. He was angry and jumpy; his eyes scanned ceaselessly for an expression or a movement revealing a shooter.

He felt like a plastic ball in a bingo caller's hopper. *One of these days, count on it, somebody's going to shoot at a president again.* When that happens, the agent whose ball had dropped from the hopper was either going to take the bullet or spend the rest of his life questioning his reaction in the instant that contained his entire reason for being. Wilson's stomach churned.

As he stood a few feet away, danger never entered the president's mind. *What should I tell them? What* can *I tell them?* To give himself a few more moments to consider Sam's hastily written words, he said, "Let's begin with a silent prayer for those who've been killed and those who are struggling to survive."

The president broke the silence: "The first thought I think we all have is what a monstrous tragedy this is. All the lives destroyed. All of us—federal, state, and local governments—will help. And I'm sure you join me now in thanking all the medics and soldiers and volunteers for their unceasing work to comfort and heal."

During the applause that followed, Martin looked around, seeing many people were without shelter. "We will improve conditions here as rapidly as humanly possible! I especially want you to know that hundreds of thousands of your fellow Americans are volunteering themselves, their tents and campers and vans, their homes, all of their individual talents, to help you.

"Ella and I are here because we want to be with you, to see and hear and try to understand and absorb the enormity of what you've suffered. What we have experienced today will be with us always and will drive us as we tackle all that's required to protect America, to rebuild, to bring the murderers to justice, and to reduce the dangers to mankind from nuclear weapons. The memory of your courage, your kindness, your skill, and above all your fierce urgency will drive us and sustain us when we tire.

"Right now we want to be with as many of you as possible in the few minutes before we must return to Washington."

Rick hopped down, took Ella's hand, and waded into the crowd. Wilson and other agents formed a scrum in a doomed attempt to keep space between the presidential couple and the surging crowd.

The Martins were engulfed in humanity. Voices from all directions. People reaching out to shake Rick's hand, to touch his shoulder, some sobbing, others grimly silent. *Every one of them needs something from me*, Rick thought, *but I have nothing left.*

"Mr. President!"

"Thank you for coming, Mr. President!"

"Mr. President, why . . . why?"

Suddenly he found himself pressed close to a thin woman whose face was framed by tangled shoulder-length grey hair. "President Martin!" she said in a voice that he heard with singular clarity amidst the hubbub. "My daughter was killed in Iraq. My husband and our grandchildren were killed here. Don't let this be an excuse for more killing! Don't give in to the ones who tell you to bomb, or invade. War isn't the answer to this. Find another way. *There's got to be another way!*"

The woman's eyes lanced Rick, impaling him with their intensity. "Yes," he said, "yes, I'll find another way!" Wilson shouldered between them, alarmed by the woman's passion and her position, pushing up against his president. She disappeared from Rick's view but not from his mind.

Chapter 14

AS THE AIR force Gulfstream V climbed, the president sat in the forward cabin, eyes closed, hands clasped in his lap. He was glad he'd insisted this be a quick, unannounced visit without journalists because he had no good answers for the questions they would be asking right now. *Well, the questions won't go away, so you'd better use this flight to get some answers.*

Rick opened his eyes and saw Ella watching him. His look asked her to speak.

"My God! That was something from hell. How are they ever going to get everybody under shelter? Conditions are so awful!"

"Yeah, I know. Let's see what Bart and Sam think." Unbuckling, Rick rose, opened the cabin door, and said, "Bart, Sam, come join us."

"OK, how do we manage this?" said the president after they were seated. "It's gonna stay on TV, twenty-four seven. It'll play as Katrina all over again.

"Sam?"

"We don't try to spin it. We don't try to soften it. We couldn't if we tried! We emphasize the scale and the suddenness. We blunt the comparison to Katrina with the facts of how much bigger this is. We come up with metrics that show progress. We give examples of the ingenuity and dedication and heroism of the victims and the responders. We highlight the volunteers. And as soon as we can, we get them to focus on your initiatives to make the country and the world safer."

Which I haven't figured out yet, Rick thought.

Guarini leaned toward him. "I agree, Mr. President. And I think that principle—get it all out there—*is* our communications strategy going forward. It's what you promised in the campaign *and* it's the best we have. You pledged to keep the American people in the loop. That's one of the places Bush and Rogers got it wrong. They let the reality perceived by ordinary Americans get way out of line with the reality *they* perceived."

"Yeah, but how can *openness* work, since the reality that *I* perceive right now, and that I'm betting you perceive, is uncertainty and fear of another attack!" Rick's voice rose. "We don't have any idea how they blew up Las Vegas, who *they* are, and whether they have another bomb, or two or three!"

Sam and Bart exchanged wide-eyed glances, acknowledging Martin's panic. Guarini was especially surprised because Rick Martin was not a let-your-hair-down guy. Even with Guarini, the man almost never let his emotions into the room. Early in their alliance and friendship, Bart believed Martin was simply ultra-cautious and that he, Bart, had not yet earned his full confidence. Later he realized that Rick was *always* in his head, weighing evidence, choosing his words, thinking things all the way through.

Guarini broke their strained silence. "Mr. President, we can be pretty sure that the *how* was loading the bomb in an SUV or truck and driving into Las Vegas. We also can be pretty sure that *they* are al-Qaeda or a group with similar motivations and roots. I'm betting that after DOE has analyzed the debris we'll know if the bomb was homemade or was assembled by experienced nuclear engineers. That'll give us a handle on who helped them do it."

Guiltily, Rick wondered if he should remain silent about Paternity.

"So, Mr. President, we're not clueless. I think that—actually—our biggest challenge is how to deal with what we're pretty sure of."

Even without knowing about Paternity, Bart, you've certainly got that right! thought Rick

"Yeah, you're right, Bart. And it's not only the *how*, but also *who*. A moment ago, Sam referred to my initiatives to make the country safer and to get better control of the world's nukes. Today those initiatives are just sound bites. We haven't had time to work on them. I'm thinking maybe I should pull back from recovery and internal security in order to develop and work those initiatives."

"Relief, recovery, and internal security are *huge* jobs and they have more daily impact on Americans than diplomacy!" said Yu. "Your administration can't appear to be leaving people to the bureaucrats. Remember Katrina!"

Rick's eyes widened, looking toward something beyond the cabin wall. Then he grinned. "How about putting Bruce Griffith in charge of all that?"

"Which takes him out of the main loop in our diplomatic and military responses. I like that!" said Guarini. "Of course, *he* probably *won't* like it, for the same reason."

"I can convince him it's in the country's best interest, because it is. Bruce *is* a patriot; he'll be able to see that this job *has* to be broken into two pieces and that the president is the one to be working with other governments. He'll also be able to see that, if he does it well, having this piece of the action will make him look presidential."

"We don't *want* him looking presidential during your *first* term," said Ella.

"I'll take that chance. What do you think, Bart?"

"I think it's a good idea. But it's tricky—it has the potential to give him more visibility, and favorable visibility at that, than you get. It's also tricky on resources. What resources does he control? Certainly, it'll have to be FEMA, but what about the rest of DHS, like the coast guard? What about the military units around Las Vegas? How do we link in the attorney general and the FBI?"

"Yeah, Bart, that's gonna be a mess to sort out." The president smiled at his chief of staff. "Looks like you'll have to earn those big bucks the government pays you.

"Sam, what do you have to say?"

Sam knew this arrangement would cause a ferocious turf war with the vice president's press secretary, but also saw both its logic and the fact that Martin and Guarini believed it was a good idea. She decided not to try to stop the train.

"Like Bart said, it's tricky. It's probably going to get ugly from time to time, but it sounds to me like it's what we need to do. I'm not so sure Griffith is going to want this; if there's another attack, or somebody gets caught scamming, like what happened after Katrina, he's going to be right in the line of fire."

"OK then, here's what we do next: Bart, set up a meeting, in the Oval Office, for the two of us and the VP. Let's see how that goes and what he wants to control." Martin smiled. "Let the games begin!" he said, in a self-mocking tone.

"Mr. President, Director Hendricks." As he spoke, the air force sergeant gestured toward the handset on the bulkhead.

Chapter 15

"HELLO, AARON. WHAT have you got?"

"Mr. President, the full Paternity analysis has been completed and double-checked. Our first indications have been confirmed."

Martin's stomach heaved. *It* was *North Korea!*

"I have Scott and his lead analyst with me now, but I'd prefer to have a face-to-face."

"OK, let's do that. We're due at Andrews at . . ." Martin looked inquiringly at the sergeant, who replied, "0030, sir."

"0030, I've just been told. Let's do it after the regular brief."

"Yes sir. Until tomorrow, then."

Martin replaced the handset. Rivulets of perspiration now ran from his armpits; he hoped they didn't show on his shirt.

"Aaron and Scott have information from analysis of bomb debris and fall-out. Let's circle back to what you said, Bart, about the possibility of getting a handle on the origin of the bomb. Let's assume we'll eventually accumulate considerable circumstantial evidence but that it won't be conclusive. What's our approach to that evidence? What do we do with it?"

"Well, first of all, we should put it out there," said Guarini. "I go back to my point about staying on the same page with the American public."

"Yeah, but suppose Aaron and Scott are goosey about revealing sources and methods—which they usually are!"

"You may just have to tell them sorry and go ahead. We don't have to hang *all* the laundry on the line, but for sure we have to say what this administration *believes* after considering the evidence."

Martin looked at Sam Yu.

"Mr. President, when Bush got it wrong about Saddam's WMD, and then so much of the world became persuaded that he had lied, it put the credibility of all future administrations in hock. To reclaim credibility, we would have to lay out *all* the evidence—air-tight. Short of a fully documented claim by al-Qaeda—assuming they're the bombers—there's *nothing* journalists would consider air-tight. Trust me, I am one!"

Yu made a wry expression and continued: "So my approach is to reveal as much as you and Aaron are comfortable with and then just deal with the disbelief as factually and unemotionally as I can. And, yes, state what the administration believes but only after it's your settled belief. Once it's out there, there's no credible way to change your mind without new evidence, evidence you're willing to put on display."

Martin nodded, then said, "now for the really *hard* question. What do we *do* about it if we believe the bomb was built by Nation 'X'?"

If Rick has one trait that bothers me, thought Guarini, *it's his preference for "we." All of us in politics use it reflexively because it serves our constant search for the cover of collective responsibility. Senators don't have "I" moments, unless they're talking about successes or failed policies they opposed. I'm that way for sure, so why should it bother me that he is?*

Because he's *the president.*

Having listened silently for a while, Ella suddenly spoke up, her voice cold and hard: "We hold them accountable. We do it in a way that tells anybody else thinking about providing a bomb that they'd better think again!"

Rick said, "Ella has no doubts! She wants an eye for an eye."

Ella's eyes flashed and narrowed at Rick's condescension, but she held her tongue.

"Well, Mr. President, that's surely gonna be on the table," said Guarini. "Another way of putting Ella's words is to say that deterrence has failed and unless it's restored, where's the barrier to more bombings?

"But doesn't what *you* do depend a lot on the identity of nation X? I'm not sure we learn much discussing it in the abstract. You're going to have to do *something* and most Americans have to feel it's right. Beyond that, what can anybody say right now?" Guarini shrugged, palms up.

"Dinner's ready in the rear cabin, sir."

"I'm not hungry; you all please go eat. I'm going to catch a nap."

Ella shot Rick a look that said, "Are you OK?" He nodded and smiled, hoping she'd go eat because he was angry but didn't want to have it out. She knew that, too, so she squeezed his shoulder and went aft with the others.

At first Rick's thoughts were a jumble. *What am I going to do? No, what are we going to do? I'm going to involve Congress and the public. I said I would be open and I will be open. But Bush got Congress and the public and the UN involved with Iraq and spent six months trying to find a course that had real support. No, he didn't exactly do that. He spent six months trying to develop support for what he had decided—invasion. I'll do it differently. I won't try to sell; I'll lead a genuine national and international dialogue.*

But what if there's another bombing? What then? And how much time do we have to sort this out? The economy is panicked. I laughed when Bush urged Americans to buy and sell, go to dinner, take that vacation, but he was addressing the problem I have right now: if Americans don't resume normal activity soon, we're going to have a meltdown. And that nightmare in the desert—I'm going to be blamed when it's not all tied up neatly in a month!

No! There are opportunities for me, particularly after I hand security and recovery off to Bruce. And after I hang the bomb on Kim, I can make a strong case that he has to go . . . hold summits to get the support of the Russians, Chinese, Japanese, and South Koreans . . . probably use this as the lever to unite Korea. And if I position the South to run the country, they'll support reunification. Maybe they'll even provide the troops if force is required to remove Kim. Then there's the opportunity to establish stronger accountability for nuclear weapons and materials, maybe give the IAEA real teeth.

I have the chance to put the world on a safer course!

* * *

The man being interviewed in front of a very large tent wore scrubs and exhaustion. "Yes," he said, "we've put the worst injured in these tents. There's nothing we can do except make them comfortable with drugs and give family members a chance to be with them."

The screen changed to a stand-up of a reporter looking almost as tired as the nurse.

"And so it has come to this," she said with a delivery that had once been brisk but now was slurred. "The American medical system is completely overwhelmed by Las Vegas. All of the technology, all of the drugs, all of the dedication of its people, and the best that can be done is to make thousands of terribly injured human beings *quote* comfortable *unquote* in a sweltering desert until their lives flicker out.

"Will the president's visit change anything? Now that he and the first lady have seen and felt the horror here, will the Martin administration do more? People here are praying it will.

"This is Ellen Shapiro reporting from Creech Air Force Base, near what used to be Las Vegas, Nevada—or maybe, from hell."

Chapter 16

The White House

THE PRESIDENT REREAD the *Wall Street Journal's* editorial:

> Where casinos like the Thunderbird and the Golden Phoenix once stood, another sort of bird rules. Las Vegas is now the home of a vast congregation of vultures, carrion crows, and even seagulls, in their thousands. The smell of death travels to the visitor and the survivor on desert winds.
>
> But this is more than the smell of death. It is the smell of Evil.
>
> We are well aware that any use of the term "evil" invites parody. Many in the president's party ridiculed the phrase "axis of evil" and still refuse to receive the idea of evil into "serious" political discourse, taking its use as evidence the speaker is simply another redneck clinging to guns and God.
>
> We would remind those who have banished this term of an observation by human rights activist Natan Sharansky, once a political prisoner in Russia's gulag, now an Israeli citizen and political figure. Writing about the differences between repressive social systems and free ones, he said, "Over the years, I have come to understand a critical difference between the world of fear and the world of freedom. In the former, the primary challenge is finding the inner strength to confront evil. In the latter, the primary challenge is finding the moral clarity to *see* evil."

We applaud the breadth and wisdom of the plan to which President Martin so eloquently rallied a shocked nation in the first hours after the murder of Las Vegas. As an intellectual construct, we could not improve upon it. Although it was more a wish list than a call to arms, it really is all that is possible right now because we don't know—as the president said, "yet"—whom to hold to account.

When we do know, we expect President Martin to have the moral clarity to reject the counsel of those who will say we brought this on ourselves, or who claim that retaliation is beneath a great nation, or any of the other echoes that persist of the puerile sixties refrain, "hey, can't we all just get along?"

The answer to that question is no, we can't, not after Las Vegas.

Martin gulped the rest of his coffee and walked down the South Portico to the Oval Office. If the *Journal's* editorial board knew what Aaron had told him last night, what would they call for him to do now? He was pretty sure he knew.

As usual, Bart Guarini and John Dorn attended the daily intelligence briefing. Afterwards, Hendricks looked at the president inquiringly. His look said, "now for Paternity. Do you want these guys in the room?"

Martin spoke: "Bart and John, we're going to hear from Aaron about a scientific analysis that may help identify the bomb. I've asked Bruce and Sam to join us."

When Griffith and Yu had poured coffee and taken seats, Martin looked around and said, "Aaron has additional information about the bomb. This information comes from something called the Paternity Project, which will be new to you, Bart and Sam. The NSC has had a presentation on Paternity and after this meeting I'd like you to go to the skif for that same briefing."

Well, that should make Bruce feel better, thought Rick. *He knows he was brought into Paternity before Bart.*

"Go ahead Aaron."

"Mr. President, let me begin by summarizing matters briefly for Bart and Sam. For more than forty years, we've been collecting, both clandestinely and openly, samples of nuclear material from around the world. This material is for the Paternity Project, one of our most tightly held secrets. The resulting library has given us the capability to determine the origin of the uranium or plutonium in a bomb, either before or after it has exploded. The Paternity analysis has already been used successfully on three occasions, one involving tests by Pakistan and two by North Korea. When the Paks tested, we revealed something about it to the Chinese. Las Vegas is the fourth time we've done this analysis.

"Our assessment has been conducted independently by two teams. Both reached the same result: Las Vegas was destroyed by a plutonium weapon, and the plutonium came from North Korea's Yongbyon fuel reprocessing facility. I have no doubt about that. Let me show you something."

An assistant handed Hendricks four charts. He gave one to Martin and passed the others to Guarini, who handed them around. Each chart had three patterns of vertical lines marching across it, one above the other, apparently identical. The top pattern was labeled "First DPRK Test." The middle pattern was labeled "Second DPRK Test" and he bottom one, "Las Vegas."

"These charts display the results of spectrographic analyses of the particles collected after North Korean tests in 2006 and 2009, and at Las Vegas. As you can see, they match.

"This is not the only evidence. Paternity has samples of the fuel rods used in Kim's research reactor and copies of its operating records indicating what the isotopic composition of plutonium reprocessed from those fuel rods would be. We ran another analysis, comparing the isotopic composition of the Las Vegas sample to the predicted isotopic composition of plutonium from Yongbyon. They matched.

"There is a third piece of evidence. It's not as solid, but it also points to North Korea.

"This explosion was weak, as nuclear explosions go. We estimate one to five kilotons. There's evidence that the uncontrolled chain reaction—the explosion—was poorly tamped. In other words, the force of the explosion blew the plutonium apart so rapidly that very little of it exploded. This matches what we found in samples of their test in 2006, which was also only about six kilotons, and in 2009.

"We believe the Las Vegas bomb was of North Korean origin, Mr. President."

Rick noted the qualifications in that careful statement, but of course Hendrickson *would* hedge.

He spoke: "Aaron told me last night, so I've had a little more time to absorb it. But I'd like to hear your initial reactions."

Dorn said, "OK, now we can start developing a specific strategy. How much confidence do we have in this information? That's question one. Two, with that figured out, what actions do we take? Three, do we put this out and if so, to whom?"

"I think we put it out there," said Yu. "It's going to leak. We can't have as many agencies and people as we need working on our response without a leak; it's a given."

"Before we do that, we probably should privately brief key ambassadors; and let the president make a few calls to heads of state, before we do that," said Battista.

"Don't forget briefing congressional leaders," Guarini added, to a chorus of agreement from all but the vice president.

"That's only window dressing!" said Griffith. "What really matters is what this administration is going to do about the fact that North Korea enabled terrorists to kill tens of thousands of Americans on June thirteenth. And it's not just about what they *did*. It's about blocking what they *may do next*. We must act!"

Martin's eyes narrowed. *There he goes again, half-cocked!* "Bruce, what about John's first point—what's our confidence in Paternity?"

"Mr. President, we've just seen the evidence and it's solid. Aaron says he has no doubts. That's good enough for me!"

"George Tenet believed Saddam had WMD and he was dead wrong."

The VP interlaced his fingers and leaned forward, forearms on the table. His voice rang with conviction: "This is not the same situation, not even close! One—Paternity is a proven technology. Two—we're not guessing Kim has nuclear weapons; he's shown the world by testing them. Three—Kim has a record: He sold missiles to Iran and Pakistan and helped Syria build a nuclear reactor to make plutonium. Four—the stakes are much higher now. If Kim continues to pass nukes to terrorists, more cities will be destroyed. America will come apart if that happens!"

The president, sitting with legs crossed in his back-tilted chair, thought about asking Griffith what he recommended but didn't want that discussion now. Scrambling like a quarterback, he lobbed a pass. "Bart, you haven't said much yet."

"That's right, sir. I really need the full briefing first. Sam and I should get up to speed."

Martin nodded. *Good ol' Bart! He always gets it.*

"Right! Let's wrap this up so you and Sam can do just that. Aaron, Bruce, and I need Bart for a meeting in an hour, so get to it now. Bruce, see you at ten thirty."

Right on schedule, Guarini and Griffith returned to the Oval Office. Martin motioned to the couches and sank into a wingback chair facing them.

"Bruce, last night I came to an important conclusion. The gravity and complexity of this situation requires unprecedented measures. No administration since Lincoln's has faced such a combination of destruction and danger within America's borders. On top of that, there are huge challenges abroad, beginning with the one we spoke about an hour ago. There is simply too much presidential-level decision making and leadership for me to do it all. I've decided to give you a very large, critically important set of responsibilities."

Martin paused, looking intently into Griffith's eyes, seeing curiosity, caution, and ambition. "Bruce, I'm putting you in charge of recovery, reconstruction, and internal security. Your authority and responsibility will be second only to mine in those areas."

The two gazed at each other, probing eyes, as Griffith did the risk-benefit calculations and took notice that he was not being invited to consider this role. It was being assigned. Realizing he had to accept, he decided to see what more he could get.

The vice president's voice grated, failing in its attempt to mask ambition with sincerity: "Mr. President, it means more than I can express that you have the confidence, in me, and in yourself, to create a co-presidency. That's in the country's best interest. Together, we'll bring America out of this stronger and better than she went into it!"

Martin straightened and set his shoulders. *Co-presidency! Right in my face. I can't let that pass!*

"Bruce, there's no authority in the Constitution for a co-presidency and neither of us can call it that. That is *not* what I'm saying to you! But you *will* have the second-largest executive role in this administration, a role without precedent for any vice president."

Griffith knew he had overreached but had no regrets, felt no embarrassment. He smiled. "Of course, Mr. President. I phrased that awkwardly, but I know you realize I meant what you just expressed much more accurately. You want Bart and me to work out the details and get back to you?"

"That's right." Martin looked at his wristwatch. "You might as well get started!"

As he left with the vice president, Bart wondered if they had just made a terrible mistake.

Chapter 17

"SIT. LET'S GET started—Aaron?"

The president spoke as he crossed the threshold of the main conference room of the Situation Room, removing his coat and loosening his tie as he moved to his chair for the NSC meeting. Martin had considered including Sam Yu but decided against it; the discussion might cover plans she would need to deny.

Tuning Hendricks out, Rick thought, *how did we let it get this far? We've had evidence for over twenty years that the Kims were selling weapons and we've known for nearly that long the current Kim had nukes. Those aren't dots; they're flashing lights, at least now. But nobody wanted to open that can of worms.*

Hendricks wound up: "So that's what we've got, and we believe it's conclusive."

He looked at the president, who said, "I'm going to leave you to discuss this. I want you to challenge Paternity, because for sure others will.

"Something more . . ." Martin's eyes found theirs, each in turn. "I have decided to put the vice president in charge of all relief, recovery and internal security operations. His authority in those areas is now second only to mine. It's a huge job and without someone of Bruce's abilities and patriotism to handle it, I'd be so consumed I wouldn't be able to effectively pursue critical international initiatives.

"Bruce, thank you for stepping up to the plate on this."

Preening, Griffith said, "Mr. President each of us in this room would do anything to help the nation through this crisis. I will dedicate myself to being worthy of this trust."

"I know you will, Bruce. There are some details to be worked out, so we'll keep it under wraps until we're ready to announce the full scope of your role."

As he left, the president frowned: *could Guarini and Dorn keep Griffith from grabbing control of the meeting?* And the hurt in Sara Zimmer's face when he'd announced Griffith's new role—he'd have to take her aside and reassure her.

After a moment, Easterly said, "Mr. Vice President, you've been handed an incredibly tough job. You'll have my full support." The others voiced a hub-bub of similar sentiments.

"Thank you all. Now let's get to work on a plan for North Korea."

Dorn spoke quickly: "Yes, well let's take it step by step, based on our earlier discussion."

"What's to discuss?" said Griffith. "North Korea must be made to pay an appropriate price."

Battista said, "Yes, but what's appropriate, and when and how is the price to be paid? How will our actions be perceived by our allies? By our enemies? We have a lot to consider."

"Let's not make this harder than it is," said the vice president. "Look, we got a break here. Kim Jong-il is one of the most isolated and disliked leaders on the planet. In fact, he probably is *the* most isolated and disliked. He's a brutal dictator who's allowed his own people to starve. Nobody's going to feel sorry for him when we nail him. We give him an ultimatum: step down or we take you out!"

"Does anybody else think that sounds like what the Bushies told Saddam Hussein?" said Easterly, brow furrowed. "Saddam was all of those things, but when we 'took him out' as you say, look what happened! We don't want to repeat that."

"Eric, this isn't Iraq! We have the smoking gun—Las Vegas. In fact, it's the *opposite* of Iraq! We invaded Iraq to keep Saddam from passing nuclear or chemical or bioweapons to terrorists when he thought the time was right. We didn't wait to be hit: we prevented a hit. Or some would say, since we didn't find WMD, we were fooled and fought an unnecessary war. On the other hand, we've done nothing but negotiate with North Korea. We waited, and they hit us. What I'm speaking of is hitting back, not a preemptive strike."

"Bruce, what do you have in mind when you say hitting back?" Griffith preferred to be called Mr. Vice President, as Anne Battista well knew. Using his first name felt good—petty maybe, but good.

"Order him to leave the country! I don't even care if he goes someplace we can't get him. Just so he goes, and takes his henchmen with him."

Easterly waded back in. "Well, putting aside for now the loose ends that would leave, what do you have in mind if, like Saddam, he denies everything and refuses to go?"

Griffith glared at the secretary of defense. "We remove him forcibly!"

"And how would we do that?"

"General MacAdoo, what are the prospects if we invade North Korea to remove Kim?"

"Mr. Secretary, my estimate is that it would be worse than the first time we fought in Korea, and that was a long, bloody slog. And this time around Pyongyang has missiles that could reach Japan and maybe Hawaii, plus, apparently, nuclear warheads to put on them. And there's South Korea—Kim could pulverize Seoul in a few days using conventional artillery if he didn't want to use a nuke. Plus, of course, there's China. The last time they sent over a million soldiers to help North Korea."

Griffith leaned forward, face set. "So, instead we send special forces and grab him or kill him."

"That's an option, Mr. Vice President, but I don't think the odds would be in our favor. North Korea is the world's most closed, tightly policed society. Kim's location and movements are extremely hard to know. I'm sure Secretary Easterly will present you with options if asked, but that's my top-of-the-head thinking on it."

MacAdoo looked at Easterly as if gazing at an oracle. Guarini thought again that Mac was a kiss-up, more bureaucrat than general.

"Mr. Vice President, I've thought some about that—not studied it, just kicked it around. On the one hand, it's a classic special ops mission. But the challenges to a team inserting and lingering undetected until Kim did something that made him vulnerable, like traveling out of Pyongyang to one of his palaces, are huge. I'll look at it in more detail, but I think Mac just gave a good summation of the risk and odds in general."

The vice president glanced down at the table, fiddled with his coffee cup, sighed, then spoke. This time there was none of the hectoring, challenging tone he had just displayed.

"In that case, we must consider responding in kind. We could take out Kim by destroying Pyongyang with a nuclear missile. That would change the regime and even the score in one move, without a single U.S. casualty."

His words washed over them like ice water. No one else spoke or moved.

Without even acknowledging it, thought Guarini, *he's proposing to forever change America's relationship with the rest of the world and with itself, with its own soul. But the hell of it is, he's right, if you consider only meeting the threat and preserving American, South Korean, and Japanese lives. His thinking is so different from Rick's; he doesn't see the big picture! That option is going nowhere while Rick is president—but it's going to appeal to a lot of Americans. We've got to keep this guy contained!*

Feeling certain that he spoke for the president and everyone knew it, Guarini said, "Well, it might come to that, but there are still options we haven't discussed."

Griffith nodded, tight-lipped.

"Here's one," said Easterly. "We blockade North Korea as a means of preventing any other nuclear weapons leaving the country."

"Blockade is generally considered an act of war," said Battista.

"So is everything else we've been talking about!" said Easterly.

"I just wanted to be clear about that," she responded. "I'll get the department's lawyers on it immediately. What they tell us might matter a great deal. But that's about what we *call* it, not what we *do*. I think some form of action along those lines may be a good option."

Dorn perked up. "OK, let's examine the blockade option," he said, drawing a grid on his notepaper. "Mr. Secretary, how does blockading North Korea strike you as to the level of effort and the chances of success?"

"I'll have to get the details, but it appears doable and I see no reason it wouldn't be successful. Aaron, am I correct in believing that not much moves in or out of North Korea anyway, by sea or air, I mean?"

"That's right."

"OK," said Easterly, "a nuclear weapon in a confined space is hard to hide from an alerted and well-equipped search party with plenty of time to work. The ships would be pretty easy. Dealing with aircraft could be tough. Once one is airborne from Pyongyang we've either got to shoot it down or force it to land for inspection or take possession of it as soon as it reaches its destination. That could be tricky. Suppose it lands in China, or Iran?"

Battista leaped in: "North Korea has two land borders. Probably to the south we could induce the South Koreans to cooperate with the blockade and even assist us—although that's not a given. But China in the north? I don't think so. I think our blockade would have a big hole in it unless we persuaded the Chinese to participate."

"So," said Dorn, "blockade is feasible but not effective unless the Chinese and the South Koreans do their parts. Not so good as it appears at first." A spoiler's sly smile flitted across his face, but Easterly ignored the jibe.

Dorn said, "I think the group has developed several options: forcing Kim out by political pressure backed up by the threat of force; capturing or killing him with a special forces operation; blockading North Korea to prevent Kim from sending more nukes out to terrorists; using a nuclear weapon to kill Kim and thousands of residents of Pyongyang, thereby creating regime change." Dorn looked around the room expecting conclusion, but Guarini stuck a foot in the door he wanted to close.

"Hey, Aaron and Scott," said the chief of staff. "We haven't talked about CIA playing an operational role in this. Have you got capabilities for snatching Kim, or for anything else that would help us here?"

Hitzleberger responded immediately, and everyone saw his pleasure in taking up a topic about which he had more expertise than his boss, Hendricks. They all knew he hated the fact that CIA now worked for someone other than the president. "We have nobody inside North Korea. We do have formal intelligence-sharing agreements with South Korea. We also have assets inside the South Korean government who pass us additional snippets of what their agents—who are very good—learn about the North."

"How about using those Predator drones of yours, like you used to take out al-Qaeda leaders?" Guarini made a pistol of his right hand and leveled it at Griffith. Battista stifled her smile.

"Sure, Bart. They could be part of the mix, but the North Koreans have an air force and plenty of SAMs. The drones couldn't loiter over the DPRK the way they do above northeast Afghanistan. They'd be shot down. We could keep 'em on alert in South Korea and send them north to support an op there—assuming the South Koreans allowed it—but they might be detected and alert Kim that something's up. Conditions are just not good for drones."

"OK, thanks, Scott." Guarini looked around the table, the others' silence acknowledging his authority. *That peacock!* thought Griffith. *Never been elected dogcatcher, never heard a shot fired in anger; my three senate terms and Purple Heart . . .*

Guarini ignored Griffith's obvious feelings. "This has been a very useful first discussion. The president will study John's report of the options carefully and will want to discuss them with you soon. I don't need to tell you that any option involving a nuclear strike will be last on his list, at least for the present.

"There's something else I think he wants discussed: what should be our strategy with the information that Aaron's just given us, that the bomb was North Korean?"

Dorn winced at his oversight as chairman but said, "Right you are, Bart!" He glanced at his notes as he spoke. "I believe we concluded that going public quickly was the right approach. Another point of interest is that we should share Paternity data with the IAEA. Because they've done so in the past, we can assume that Britain, France, Russia, and China will collect samples and do analyses of their own. And we're going to face doubt because of the debacle over Saddam's WMD."

He's such a technician, thought Guarini. *I wonder if he's the right guy for these times.* He spoke: "I think the first thing we need to recommend is the approach the president should take. Is he just going to announce this, or is he going to follow the announcement with his plan of action?"

Griffith said, "Bart, he's got to say what he's going to do! He can't just say he's going to think it over. He doesn't have to position it as the full response or go into detail, but there's gotta be payback for what the North Koreans did to us."

Happy to tweak the vice president, Battista said, "Bruce, the North Koreans didn't necessarily *do* this—they probably provided the bomb to others."

Christ! thought Griffith, *she's so legalistic.* "Anne, we don't know who actually detonated that bomb and might never know. It would be disastrous to focus only on the perpetrators. The world would conclude that there's no penalty for enabling terrorists to nuke us! We have to treat the North Koreans just as if they planted the bomb and pushed the button. We can't afford to make a distinction between nations who provide WMDs and the individuals or groups who use them."

He smiled bleakly. "We should announce that Las Vegas was destroyed by North Korea. That would *really* wrong-foot them! Force them to make a case, if they can, that it was al-Qaeda or Hezbollah, or whoever!"

Battista's lip curled. "But that's completely contrary to the principles of our laws! We don't hold the manufacturer of a pistol responsible when someone uses it to kill a convenience store clerk."

Griffith rolled his eyes. "Anne, that law is based on the premise—which I agree with—that society must and can stand letting some otherwise preventable murders happen because some of the steps necessary to stop them all are worse than the crimes. But now we're talking about events that our society *cannot* withstand. If we can't prevent nuclear attacks, America is done! And if we have to prevent them solely by defensive measures, that also will destroy us—we've seen what happens. We have to *deter* nuclear attacks, and only one side of the unholy partnership between nuclear powers and terrorists can be deterred!"

The VP's fist slammed the table.

This has gone far enough! thought Guarini. "OK, I take your points. This is going to be one hell of a tough call for the president. I guess that's why they play that fanfare when he enters the room," he said, referring to "Hail to the Chief" in an attempt to cut the tension. It wasn't successful, but he no longer feared Griffith might reach across the table and start shaking the secretary of state by her Hermès scarf.

John Dorn made haste to end the confrontation. "I'll write this point up as a key pending issue requiring further consideration. I think that will be all for now." Fingers moving with the dexterity of a bank teller, Dorn neatly stacked his papers, clipped them, and retreated through the door, followed by Hendricks and Hitzleberger.

Hendricks paused at the threshold and turned to Battista. "By the way, Anne, be sure your lawyers take into account that the Korean War never ended. There's a cease-fire, nothing more." He flashed a "gotcha" smile.

The man is insufferable! thought Battista. Then the vice president stepped toward her. "I'm sorry that I got a little loud. But this really is critical—we can't let North Korean off the hook!"

"And we can't beat them by being like them!" said Battista, eyes boring into his. Griffith appeared ready to let fly, but pulled himself up. "We'll discuss this again, Madame Secretary."

Guarini and Battista were alone in the room.

"That man is dangerous, Bart!"

"Maybe, but he might just be right. I hate to sound like Dick Cheney, but Bruce reminded us that this really *is* an existential threat we're facing."

"You've changed, Bart."

"Probably. Working for the commander-in-chief is a whole lot different than working for the chairman of the Foreign Relations Committee."

No way is Bart going to lecture me. I've been with Rick as long as he has, hung in there when it seemed hopeless and self-destructive to keep fighting Glenna Rogers.

"No shit, Sherlock, but that doesn't mean shelving your principles!"

"I'm not shelving them, but I have to consider the cost of sticking to them!"

"Remember Lord Acton, Bart?"

"Yeah—'power corrupts and absolute power corrupts absolutely.'

"Anne, he had a good ear for a phrase, but, except for one lackluster term as MP, the guy never accepted responsibility for anything other than his own well-being. I don't deny the aptness and even the wisdom of his observation. But I can't forget that it was made by someone living in a bubble protected by the immense power of his class and the British Empire. He didn't find power corrupting when it was his! He *may* have been a reformer; for *sure* he was a hypocrite. You should keep that in mind, Anne."

Battista's mouth flew open, a volcano's maw, then clamped shut as her eyes went from fiery to uncertain. She shut her briefcase and stalked out.

What brought that on? she thought. *Is the pressure too much for Bart?*

Chapter 18

An Army Compound in Pakistan.

"OF COURSE, THE Americans are frantic to get their hands on everyone who could possibly be implicated in the bombing or help them find out who is."

President Bahadar Sharif was speaking, his eyes probing the group. "Two days ago I received a call from Martin. The Americans want access to A. Q. He was polite but clear: if we do not grant them access the consequences for Pakistan will be as bad as he can make them. Martin gave me his version of Bush's declaration that those not with the U.S. are against it."

The men sat around a table in a room as full of tension as it was of cigarette smoke. They rarely gathered, this group: the current and former political and military leaders of Pakistan. Some had imprisoned or exiled others; some, or their fathers, had hung or blown up close relatives. One had become president after others assassinated his wife, whose father had been hung by his presidential successor. On this occasion, the threat they felt was enough to make them put aside animosity, even hatred, and accept the invitation of Pakistan's president to meet secretly.

One of Sharif's predecessors, General Pervez Musharraf, smiled bitterly. "At least *he* told you that. *I* got that speech from a deputy secretary of state."

The general who headed Inter-Service Intelligence, the ISI, said, "The Americans are naive, but they are powerful. They are confused, but they are dangerous. Even a blind tiger can kill you, eventually, if you if are locked in his cage. Since American nuclear missiles can reach anywhere on earth, we are locked in the tiger's cage."

Looking around, Sharif said, "What do we know and what is the worst we might not know?"

Musharraf said, "What we *know* is that al-Qaeda did this to avenge bin Laden, or even if they didn't, will happily bask in rumors that they did. That some al-Qaeda leaders are still in Pakistan, where they have been sheltered by certain of us for years. That our own, esteemed father of the Muslim bomb, Dr. A. Q. Khan, ran a nuclear black market for over twenty years and we don't know the full extent of his customer list. That in response to far less deadly attacks in 2001, the Americans decimated the leadership of al-Qaeda and every group thought to be involved in the attack or potentially able to launch new attacks. That in the process the Americans invaded and conquered two countries, hanging the leaders of one of them."

Musharraf felt their complete attention now and gave a tight little smile.

"The worst we might *not* know is that A. Q. is directly linked to making the Las Vegas bomb. He denies it, but of course he would, now. However, I can tell you that in 1999 I heard that he was airlifting some irregular cargo to North Korea. I tried hard to find out what it was but could not."

The chief of staff of Pakistan's army said, "This is not 2001! The Americans have learned the costs and limits of the power they are willing to use, their non-nuclear power. Even after losing tens of thousands in the attack, President Martin has made statements less threatening than Volkov's—and the Russians didn't even get bombed! What do we have to worry about, even if A. Q. *did* enable the Koreans to have nuclear weapons and they sold one to al-Qaeda?"

Musharraf said, "You can *say* that, even after they easily penetrated the heart of Pakistan to assassinate bin Laden?"

"We knew the bird was there; he was in our cage. We could pluck him out and hand him over to the Americans at the time of our choosing. Who could have known bin Laden would be so careless, so incompetent, as to allow couriers to lead the Americans to him?"

Musharraf looked at the group, shaking his head, a teacher saddened by obtuse pupils: "What you have to understand about the Americans is that they themselves do not know how bloody-minded they are; or, at least, they're unable to acknowledge it. Because those idiots, whoever they are, used a nuclear weapon, the world is in a new situation. Now, the only resolution Americans will accept is the total destruction of the individuals and countries they hold responsible. In the case of Korea–or Pakistan–that can be done in about one hour, with less than a tenth of America's nuclear missiles.

"President Martin is giving speeches about responding to this tragedy by building a safer world for all, but behind him American anger is building. Before long, Martin will find himself scrambling to catch up to the cowboys who want to find everybody who had a hand in this and nuke them until they glow, as I believe their expression goes."

"So," said Bahadar Sharif, "where does that leave us?"

"In great danger," said Musharraf.

The group was quiet.

"So let's preempt the cowboys!" said a former head of the ISI, General Daud. "Let's feed the blind tiger, so that it won't eat us. Let's round up some Arabs and hand them to the Americans. And A. Q., too! That bastard lied to us, Pervez, and never shared the millions he got from being a nuclear peddler. I'm sure that money is in Switzerland. Let's give him, too, to President Martin!"

Musharraf started to respond, but the chief justice of Pakistan's supreme court said, "What about the reaction among the people if we do that? There will be terrible unrest! A. Q. is a hero to our entire nation."

"I for one don't want to explain to Pakistan's people why their government turned A. Q. over to the Americans!" said the leader of Pakistan's second-largest political party. "A. Q. is old, sick, and rightly admired for giving us the bomb. Without him, we'd have to cower every time those Indian bastards fart. The Americans haven't asked to take him, only to speak to him. If they do ask, then we decide. No, let's give them some Arabs, but not A. Q., at least not yet."

Sharif looked at the others, saw agreement. He said, "We in this room are the heart and soul of Pakistan. If we are agreed in taking this step and each of us controls our followers, unrest will be manageable."

"How will you do it?" asked Daud.

"That's for my government to determine," responded Sharif. "But, I don't mind telling all of you what I'm thinking. We'll give that greedy bastard A. Q. one chance to save his miserable skin: We will require that the American interrogation be conducted in A. Q.'s home, under our supervision. If he is clever enough to avoid implicating himself, he stays in Pakistan. If he does not, we will let the Americans have him.

"Martin will be so grateful that, even if it does turn out that A. Q. helped build that bomb, he'll be willing to shield Pakistan."

Bahadar Sharif went around the table, and each man agreed. It was done. The group dispersed rapidly, glad to be free of each other.

Chapter 19

"ELLA, I'VE BEEN thinking about what I said on the plane, about you wanting an eye for an eye. That was mean of me. I apologize."

Her look told him she was glad for his apology but wasn't going to let him off the hook.

They were together in the White House family quarters but alone, each cocooned by festering anger. Rick knew Ella wanted to talk about his dismissive words on the plane. He also knew she wouldn't bring it up. After a day of nonstop decision making, he felt as if he couldn't form even one more coherent sentence. But he knew continued silence wasn't an option.

"Rick, it's not our disagreement: it's the way you handled it. You acted like I'm some hockey mom who doesn't have a brain! I have a law degree from Columbia, for God's sake, and my GPA was better than yours. I'm as smart as anyone on that plane!"

He grimaced, hands up in appeal. "I said I was sorry!"

She slammed her book shut. "I don't think you get my point, dammit! If you include me in meetings I'm going to express opinions. I'm not going to sit there like a piece of arm candy. And if you dis me again, I'm not just going to take it quietly! You know, Rick, you're admired for listening to all points of view. All, that is, except mine. It's time you started *hearing* me."

"OK, OK—Uncle!" he said, flashing his never-fail disarming grin.

"And you are going to begin now!"

Rick groaned inside. This conversation was a chasm between him and bed. "OK, what's on your mind?"

"As if you didn't know!"

"What?"

"An eye for an eye."

"What do you mean?"

"I mean you can't dismiss it. There're lots of Americans who think that's the way to go when we find out who did this. Maybe they're not the people who voted for us, although I'll bet some did, but you're going to have to engage their point of view. You can't just look down your nose at it and them. And you are going to have to do it *soon*."

Rick's eyes dropped. "I know."

"And you are going to have to consider it *seriously*. That call from Aaron during the flight tells me we've figured out where the bomb came from—at least as solidly as we can. You haven't said anything and you don't need to. It's got to be either North Korea or Iran, or, just maybe, Pakistan. None of the other nuclear governments is so out of touch with reality as to run the risk or, like Pakistan, so lacking control over their country."

She looked into his eyes. "What are you going to do, Rick?"

He held her gaze. "What's best for this country and the world."

"Suppose what's best for this country isn't what's best for the world?"

"I'll deal with that if it plays that way."

"Which comes first?"

"This country, of course—why do you ask?" he snapped.

"Just wanted to hear you say it! Rick, do you realize that you haven't once said 'my country,' or 'our country'? That seems disconnected to me, as if you're some impartial judge. *Is* this about *your* country and *my* country?"

Rick shot to his feet as if her words were electricity. "Ella, you're being silly, like those people who think it matters whether or not I wear a flag pin!"

"No, Rick, I'm not! Answer my question."

Her eyes felt like searchlights probing for his soul. "All right. *Of course* this is about my country and your country!"

"Rick, you're famous for your cool. You've accomplished some amazing things because you stayed detached, didn't get caught up in emotions. I understand why you're that way—you saw your parents destroy each other with their anger. But remaining emotionally unattached also means you can only draw strength from yourself, from that cool, quick, bright intellect of yours, and from God."

She glared. "You with me?"

He nodded.

"Rick, could you order a nuclear attack on North Korea or Iran? I don't mean do you have the authority, I mean could you *do* it?"

"Ella, it's not going to come to that."

Her eyes flashed. "Don't duck the question, Rick!"

The searchlights had found their target. He looked away, then back. "Tell me why I would do such a thing, something that would make me as bloody as whoever set off that bomb, as bloody as Saddam, as bloody as that butcher in Serbia!"

She flung her right hand toward him. "How about your duty as president of the United States, how about the oath you took to preserve, protect, and defend?"

Rick's eyes narrowed. "I didn't agree to become a mass murderer when I took that oath!"

"What *did* you swear to do?"

He took a breath, exhaled slowly. "I swore to preserve, protect, and defend the *Constitution*. The Constitution is about life, about living freely—not about murder. There *will* be a way to do this without becoming a murderer like the ones who destroyed Las Vegas!"

Ella sat up straighter, glanced at the book in her lap, then said, "Rick, I pray you're right. But this may reach a point where there's no way to protect the people of our country, except by destroying the country—and its people—whose government is giving or selling nukes to terrorists. And if that happens, you'll need more than your intellect and detachment. You'll need at least some fraction of the feeling of belonging to the tribe, the tribe of Americans, which led other Americans to endure torture in Hanoi, to attack the men with box cutters knowing it meant crashing their airliner, to endure the sickness and the terror of Guadalcanal, and to stand sentry barefooted in the winter of 1778."

Then her words stabbed: "I don't think you have that feeling right now, Rick—you'd better begin working on it!"

Wonderful! Rick thought, scowling. *You've just asked me to become part of mankind's greatest problem, tribalism. The tribe is* mankind, *not Arab or Jew, Korean or American!*

He felt like countering with a zinger, but Ella had begun her diatribe by ordering him to *hear* her. He knew he would lose her respect and earn her anger if he tried to brush by this moment, so instead he did something unusual: He spoke without calculation or circumlocution.

"Ella, I'm not sure if I can do that." His face was troubled.

She stood, facing him and taking his hands. "Tell me what you felt when Steve Nguyen appealed to you."

"That my soul is accountable to his soul and the souls of his wife and kids, for making this come out OK." He felt her hands squeeze his.

"That's a start. What else did you feel?"

His eyes narrowed. "Rage. Nobody has the right to do that to the people of this country, no matter what our differences may be!"

"The people of this country. Would those be *Americans?*" She smiled at him. Smiling back he said, "Yes—*Americans.*"

"OK. Keep thinking about them. Keep thinking about those doomed, suffering *Americans* we watched wandering the no-go zone until they collapsed."

All right, she thought. *He is strong enough to do this! I just have to keep helping him break through his detachment, his damned neutrality.* Suddenly she was bursting with tenderness for this good man who was facing a decision so horrible that he could not yet acknowledge it.

Pulling him to her she said, "OK, bedtime. You come wit' me, sojer. I show you good time."

Rick couldn't stay awake for the good time.

As she watched him sleep, Ella thought, not for the first time since arriving in the United States, what an odd sense of self many prominent Americans exhibited.

It's as if they think of themselves as people who happen to live in America, rather than as Americans. Do they consider that because they "happen" to live here their lives are longer, richer, safer than if they "happened" to live in the Congo or Yemen or Sudan or . . . Mexico?

No, they show no sign of realizing that their safety and freedom are not givens.

Are they aware that if America "happens" to become less secure, less wealthy, less free, their lives will change for the worse? They don't act like it. It's as if they believe they have only to click some "opt out" button. Observing their detachment, I think of dinosaurs munching placidly, while their changing environment prepares to kill them.

Chapter 20

A BURLY FIGURE pounded the treadmill in the gym provided for members of the House of Representatives. It was 5:45 a.m., or 0545 to Ray Morales, who still thought in military time. There was a scattering of others but Morales was alone, engrossed in thought.

I've heard a lot about helping the victims but not much about how we're going to prevent more attacks. We haven't got anything yet on who planted the bomb or how, so preventing another attack is that much harder. Al-Qaeda probably did it, but other than motive there's zip connecting them so far. This thing could have been done with far fewer people in the know than Nine-eleven, and some or all of them were vaporized in Las Vegas.

The president laid out an ambitious plan in his speech, but since then I haven't observed, or heard from my Marine buddies, anything more than dealing with Las Vegas. Rick and Ella were smart to make that quick trip to the scene. Video hit millions of bloggers and crackberry addicts, plus saturating cable and network news programs and social networking sites. Slick!

So our president has shown us his compassion. I hope he's about to demonstrate leadership and fidelity to his duty as commander-in-chief. I figure the bomb must have come from North Korea or Iran. When the scientists in DOE figure out who made it, what then, Mr. President?

Morales accelerated. Sweat streaked his face and his pace drove his thoughts.

And what, Mr. President, if the dragnets sweeping the country snare someone who probably knows who did the deed, or who probably knows about another attack in the works? What will you do, Rick Martin? If you stick by your statement that the country doesn't need to compromise its ideals in order to defend itself, you'll never find those answers.

Morales shifted to high gear. He felt the regular rhythm of his stride seeming to give order and discipline to his thoughts. A quick smile as he admitted that, secretly, he'd always liked marching, its precision and certainty.

Ideals are important, but if you stick to them while someone with a different set is using yours to kill you, you're gonna die. I know that from experience. If you play nice, Rick, if you salve your conscience, how many more Americans will be killed in an attack that you might have prevented or disrupted?

And then there's Ella, her life in Mexico, her father—how he died and why. She believes that beyond a point, negotiation and compromise won't hack it; that it's sometimes foolish to wait until struck to strike yourself. She knows what it is to be stalked by an implacable killer. One got her father and would have murdered her if he hadn't sent his family to Los Angeles. I wonder what she's thinking and saying to Rick?

At the end of his workout, Morales grabbed his towel and blotted his forehead, breathing heavily.

"Ray, glad I ran into you!" Fred Stanton called out to him from across the way. Ray knew him slightly from the Armed Services Committee, knew at least that he represented a district in Massachusetts. Fred came striding toward him with an expectant look.

"Hello, Fred. What's up?"

"I was wondering . . . you know . . . since you're a military man, what do you think of this situation?

Ray thought, *what the hell does that mean? I think it sucks—who wouldn't?*

"What I think of it is I'd rather we weren't in it! But we are, and now the issues are how we protect ourselves and how we recover."

"There are those who say that we brought this on ourselves."

Morales sucked from his water bottle, swirled the liquid noisily before swallowing. *Well, Fred, if that's what 'those' say, what do you say? Let's cut to the chase—I want my shower.*

Morales said, "Does that matter much now? Isn't the point that it happened and we have to deal with it? Isn't the point that some group killed at least sixty thousand Americans living their daily lives in one of our cities and that we can presume from what's been said by al-Qaeda and the president of Iran that there's more to come, unless we prevent it?"

Squaring his shoulders, Stanton looked eager as a terrier waiting for his ball to be thrown. "It matters because if we know why they did it, we can reconsider our policies; amend them in some way to address their grievances. We can prevent more attacks by eliminating the anger, hopelessness, and alienation that caused this one."

Eyebrows raised, Morales said, "OK, but wouldn't you agree that while we're doing all that we need to protect ourselves?"

"Of course, but not by nuking some country, or bombing people with cruise missiles!" Stanton's prominent Adam's apple worked vigorously. "We protect ourselves by demonstrating we are ready to engage fully to find a negotiated solution, and by finding better leadership for the intelligence community that failed again. I'm not against using force in self-defense, but I do insist that it be used discriminately, against the right targets."

Flicking his towel as he spoke, Morales said, "Well, Fred, let's leave aside that I think that some of their grievances, like the existence of Israel, aren't things we should yield on. How about this: if a nuclear attack leads us to change course to suit the perpetrators, *and* they suffer no harm, how do we deter other groups from doing the same thing?"

"By getting out ahead of the curve for once! By adopting a forward-looking foreign policy. By engaging in a dialogue with all who have legitimate grievances.

"Getting a nuclear weapon isn't easy. At the least it's expensive. I think, given the choice, the others will prefer constructive dialogue over bombing again."

Morales draped the towel around his muscular neck, grasping the ends in his hands, making fists. Anyone who didn't notice the towel would think he was about to punch Stanton.

"Fred, do you know anyone who lost someone close to them in Las Vegas?"

"No."

"How about in Nine-eleven?"

"No, but—"

"Would you risk the lives of the people who live in your district?"

"Of course not!" Stanton's face puckered with displeasure.

"Then isn't our difference really about perception of risk? You don't perceive high risk to people you know or feel responsible for. I do. I hope the president does. Where you sit on risk and responsibility probably determines where you stand on these issues."

Forcing a smile, Ray clapped Stanton on the shoulder. "Please excuse me, but I've got to get showered and out to a breakfast meeting. Have a good workout!"

"OK, Ray, good to talk with you."

* * *

As NSA Director Pete Hsu continued to describe his Argus eavesdropping system, three stars glinting from his shoulders as he gestured, Attorney General Ed McDonnell looked at others around the table and wondered who else felt uncomfortable with the relentless slide toward Big Brother that chilled him.

Wearing her usual, no-nonsense pantsuit—this one in charcoal—Homeland Defense Secretary Sara Zimmer was intense, McDonnell thought. *She still has the mission focus the army taught her and her mission is prevention. She's all for prosecuting the perps, but not at the cost of letting them do their deed. If Sara is concerned about the destruction of civil liberties occurring in this room, it doesn't show.*

Head throbbing, McDonnell shifted his eyes to red-eyed FBI Director Brian Leek, wondering whether his lips were compressed in concentration on Hsu or in holding back exhaustion. *He's been through the first World Trade Center bombing, Nine-eleven and its investigations; Brian knows nothing remains secret and everything will eventually be sliced and diced with the sharp knife of hindsight. He's a dedicated law enforcement officer, but also a proud man, proud of himself and especially proud of his FBI. He'll maneuver to protect both of those interests.*

It's up to me.

"Thanks, Pete," said McDonnell. "That's an amazing system. I don't mind telling you that what this government has the *capability* to do frightens me a little." No one reacted. Disappointed but not surprised, he said, "Now lets get to our recommendations because it's not long until we conference up with Bart."

McDonnell looked at his notes. "These are the working group's recommendations that I believe we've decided to send to the president: We focus our defenses at our borders, where they'll be less disruptive to essential economic and social activities. Using our strength in technologies, including Argus, we vet every person and every cargo on arrival. This will cause backups, but better there than all across America."

Now comes the part that really worries me, he thought. "Some problematic individuals and cargoes will inevitably slip through this screening, so our second line of defense will be nationwide random operations that stop people and transporters—road, rail, airliners, river barges, subways—identifying the individuals and screening the transporters and cargo for nuclear indications.

"These stop and search operations will require new legislative authorities. We will propose legislation as necessary. The first proposals are a national, biometric identity card and a modification to *posse comitatus* to permit the routine use of regular military units in domestic law enforcement."

The attorney general looked up from his papers, seeing agreement on their faces. With a sigh he pushed his reading glasses up and looked at Zimmer. "Sara, are you *sure* it's necessary to use the army? It's for good reason that for over two hundred years the government has severely limited the use of our military in law enforcement."

"Ed, I have no doubt," she said bluntly, "especially right now. There's no mechanism to control and coordinate the use of local police forces to do what's necessary. The state police are more centrally organized, but there aren't enough of them, and anyway both local and state cops still have their regular functions to perform." She waved toward Leek. "You know the Bureau can't stretch any further! And even if there were enough law enforcement to do this job alone, we couldn't yank them away from their normal duties without creating chaos.

"Mobility's another issue. We've decided that, to maximize effectiveness while minimizing disruption, these operations must be unpredictable, quick hits. For example, suddenly seal off a section of highway, inspect intensely for an hour or two, and then on to another, unpredictable location. That means lots of helos and people, and only the military has enough right now."

Under Zimmer's flat gaze McDonnell felt like she was centering crosshairs on his head.

"I share your concerns and so does the army. They do *not* want to do this." Zimmer rapped her fingers on the table. "We can sunset the authority after two years, during which we build out the law enforcement capacity."

As he looked without result for objections, McDonnell thought, *I should go to the mat against this, but . . . right now, prevention is the name of the game. And it was my guys, the FBI, who failed to prevent "Six-thirteen," as it's being called. And we still haven't found evidence of the actual bomber. These days, I have about as much wallop as a snowball in July.*

Shoulders slumped, McDonnell said, "OK, we're agreed on the recommendations."

Chapter 21

"OK, LET'S GET started."

"Mr. President," said Dorn, glancing at the other NSC members, "Secretary Ramanna has information about a suspicious transaction that Treasury uncovered."

The president beamed. "That's great—what do you have for us, Vijay?"

"Mr. President, I persuaded the director general of SWIFT to resume cooperation with us. You recall that group, the Society for Worldwide Interbank Financial Telecommunication that handles trillions a day in transfers. It's in Brussels.

"They were pretty reluctant, because when the *New York Times* outed them, describing their cooperation with Bush, they got a lot of heat. Eventually, though, I broke through their resistance."

Ramanna paused, preened, and took a sip of water.

"Using their data I was able to uncover a suspicious transaction that happened last January. I confronted my Swiss counterpart—also very reluctant—and got him to run it down for me.

"I uncovered the transfer of a billion Swiss francs from Iran's central bank to an account in a private client bank in Zurich. At my insistence, the bank revealed the account holder: a member of Kim's family!"

Ramanna's triumph filled his face.

"Great work, Vijay!" said the vice president, smiling. "Mr. President, now that money corroborates the other evidence, we've got an even stronger case!"

"If I may play devil's advocate for a moment, tell me what this establishes, besides the fact that the Kim family is stashing money in a Swiss account," said the attorney general.

Spots of color appeared on Griffith's cheeks. "Ed, it shows that Kim did something last January that earned him a billion francs. He sure didn't get that from the lousy movies he makes! It must have been from selling the bomb—or bombs!"

"It certainly could have been, Mr. Vice President, but not necessarily, said McDonnell. "We know the DPRK sells missile technology and maybe missiles themselves to Iran, Myanmar, and, probably, Syria. It also hauls in money from counterfeiting and sells uranium ore. They may also be selling enriched uranium or plutonium from Yongbyon. A billion is a big number, but it could have come from those other sources, plus speculation in gold, which we're pretty sure Kim has been squirreling away for years. With gold at a thousand an ounce and still climbing . . . you see what I mean?"

Griffith's face showed he did, and didn't like it.

Martin's tone said he didn't want to listen to their sparring: "Vijay, this is really an important piece of the puzzle! Keep on working those channels you pried open. That's all we need for now, thanks."

Looking crestfallen, Ramanna left.

"I've reviewed your options from our first meeting," said Martin. "I've asked John to walk us through them, except for nuclear." He scanned the room, broadcasting his determination, then continued: "I'll tell you now I'm not even going to consider nuclear unless and until every other option has failed!"

That was pretty much in Bruce's face, he thought. *That should keep him off the topic!*

Griffith flushed, although his expression remained politely expectant.

"John, please take us through the other options."

"All options are based on our belief that absent a forceful U.S. response to the Las Vegas bombing, Kim—and perhaps others—will continue to supply nuclear weapons and other hardware, perhaps ballistic missiles, to organizations or governments that will use them against us."

"Wait a minute!" said Martin, hand raised. "Why would Kim *do* that? What's his motivation to run such a risk?" He looked challengingly around the room. "Anne, you and Scott have both served in major positions focusing on the Koreas—do *you* agree with John?"

Hitzleberger, a former ambassador to South Korea, wanted to let Battista, who was once State's senior regional official for East Asia, test the waters.

At his deferential gesture she began speaking. "Mr. President, we believe Kim's motivation is to remain absolute ruler of a viable North Korean state. I feel pretty confident of that, but I feel very little confidence in predicting how that motivation will translate into action."

Battista's face became animated. "He and his father did some amazingly provocative and dangerous things, which would seem to fly in the face of his motivation. To begin with, in 1950 the first Kim invaded the south, the Republic of Korea. In 1968 the North Koreans attacked and captured USS *Pueblo*, an intelligence-gathering ship, in international waters, and they have kept it to this day. They gave back the crew, living and dead, after about a year. In 1969 they shot down an unarmed U.S. Air Force surveillance plane, in international airspace, killing everyone. The Kims have made several blatant attacks on ROK leaders. One killed the wife of South Korea's President Park. Another killed several of the South Korean cabinet during a state visit to Burma and barely missed their president. Some say this was when the younger Kim made his bones."

Relishing their attention, she continued. "The Kims kidnapped citizens of the ROK and Japan to satisfy what most would say were minor, if not frivolous, needs. And they permitted famine that could have destroyed the country and their own positions in order to hold fast to their ideology of self-sufficiency, called *Juche*. We're pretty sure they've sold missile technology to Pakistan and Iran. In the midst of negotiations about their nuclear program, the current Kim, Kim Jong-il, ignored both carrots and sticks and tested a nuclear weapon. Two years later he did it again. He once ordered the test firing of a ballistic missile right across Japan! There's a pretty good case that he contracted with Syria to help them build a facility to produce nuclear weapons material. And of course during the Rogers administration, the current Kim's regime torpedoed an ROK patrol boat and shelled South Korea itself.

"It's really a long record of acts that, frankly, I wouldn't have predicted from the Kims' motivations."

A gleam in his eyes, Martin pounced: "So, Anne, if his actions don't track with his presumed motive, maybe you really don't understand what they've been after! Did you ever think about that?"

Battista's temper flashed through her eyes. "Not often, Mr. President. Over the years I've spent more time thinking about how to *deal with* the Kims' actions."

Martin gave her a professorial smile and turned to the CIA director.

"Mr. President, I agree with Secretary Battista, and I, too, have sometimes been surprised by what they've done. I'll add that, in seventy-five or seventy-six, North Korean troops killed two U.S. soldiers at the DMZ. But I don't think we should focus on North Korea alone. Perhaps, as a former ambassador to the ROK, I can make a few useful points.

"The Kims have about seventy million enablers: the people who inhabit the two Koreas. The people of the north suffer terrible conditions, but the great majority genuinely revere Kim Jong-il, just as they revered his father, Kim il-Sung. We tend to dismiss their reverence as forced and comical. Some is forced, but most is not, and *none of it* is comical, believe me! This tiny country has a larger army than we do, plus ballistic missiles and nuclear weapons."

Hitzleberger twirled his pen between fingers, as if unrolling a scroll.

"The North Koreans aren't a restive people. There isn't, and hasn't been for about fifty years, any serious popular opposition to the regime. In a twisted way the Kims' power has come from the people they rule, because they go obediently to work in factories, farms, and in the army; concentrate on keeping themselves and their families alive; and don't look for opportunities to rebel."

The pen became a baton, flicking upward.

"And here's something else that's twisted: While ambassador to South Korea I saw and heard every week that people there think they have an *American* problem rather than a *North Korean* problem: America periodically upsets the north, and American troops are present in the south. Most South Koreans aren't worried about Kim. They just want to be left alone to make the economy grow and enjoy its fruits—and believe if we leave, they will be."

Martin nodded.

"So, naturally, politics in the ROK is about riding the voters' beliefs. Keep the north placated, usually by providing food and fuel, and push back at U.S. policies that upset Kim."

He downed the pen with a distinct smack.

"Oh, and one more thing: unification." Hitzleberger pointed to a map. "Both governments say they want unification, but nobody who matters in either country means it. They all know it would be too hard and too disruptive to their personal interests. Everyone pays lip service, but it's the last thing they want."

Martin's eyes sparkled with interest. "So Scott, how do we change the playing field, in the north and south, to something we can work with? What we've inherited isn't good enough!"

"Right now, I can't say, sir. We've got a lousy hand, but it looks to me like we're going to have to play it."

"Anybody else? Does anyone have ideas?" The president looked slowly around the silent room. "This simply isn't good enough! I need—the country needs—fresh thinking. We can't just keep on doing the same old things and hope that somehow they start working. The families of about eighty thousand dead expect—and deserve—more from their government!"

He rapped the table.

"OK, John, let's hear those options, and hope I get some original thinking as we discuss them."

Dorn glanced nervously at his papers. "Mr. President, Option A is to force Kim out, using economic, political, and military pressure. We wouldn't insist on his prosecution for any crimes, either against the U.S. or against the people of North Korea. Behind the scenes we assist in finding a country that will take Kim and his cronies. This is the 'Regime Change without War' option."

Dorn looked up to safe, noncommittal expressions.

What the hell, thought Griffith. *I'm not going to be intimidated. Somebody has to take the lead; why shouldn't it be me?*

Looking at Martin, the vice president said, "This option probably won't work, but it does some things for us. First, it shows we want to avoid using force. Second, it gives us an opening gambit with the Chinese, who are certainly going to play in any deal that involves regime change."

Rick grimaced. He wanted to sideline Griffith, but here the man was emerging as first among equals, or at least making a play for it.

Guarini sensed this and, if he could have reached Battista's shin, he would have nudged her. Since he couldn't, he said, "Anne, how do you think the Chinese would react—would they help?"

"Well, I don't think this will work, because surely Kim anticipated discovery and made up his mind to tough it out. But that's no reason not to try, particularly since it helps us avoid a rush-to-war charge. As for the Chinese . . . I'm sure Ming Liu's position will be driven by the succession question: who will rule if not Kim?"

"And what do you say to him, Anne? What's the successor government we have in mind for North Korea?"

"Huge issue, Mr. President, and I'll admit I haven't reached a conclusion yet. Some options that have occurred to me are rule of some sort under a UN mandate leading to self-government, unification with the south, or a Chinese protectorate."

Throwing a warning glance at Griffith, Martin said, "Anne, at first glance the most attractive is unification. How do you think that would play with President Ming?"

"He wouldn't like it, Mr. President, although I can perhaps see him eventually deciding it's his least bad choice. But our problem in working with the Chinese is that they don't want any change. Kim is just fine with them; he gives them a client state on their border, a communist buffer that reduces the visibility and influence of the capitalist economy booming in the ROK. Not that Ming is completely happy with Kim—he doesn't like it at all that Kim has nuclear weapons. But pragmatically, Kim's DPRK is better for Ming than anything else available."

"Well, a new world began on June thirteenth, and surely Ming will come to see that the old solutions won't work anymore!"

"Mr. President, if I may?" Martin made a go-ahead gesture to Aaron Hendricks.

"I wonder whether we're putting the cart before the horse. We haven't asked the key question: is the United States going to hold North Korea as responsible for the bombing as we do those who carried it out?"

Guarini winced and thought, here it comes!

Griffith leaned forward, his forearms resting on the table. "That's exactly the key, Aaron, and I think we can deal with it quickly!

"We have no choice but to treat North Korea as if this entire murderous attack was their doing. In fact, we don't have any evidence that it wasn't! We don't think Kim would dare, but that's just an assumption. The only *evidence* we have is that a North Korean nuke destroyed Las Vegas. That's what you should tell the world, Mr. President! Let Kim try to save his skin by implicating others—if he can."

He's wrong, but I'll tell him privately, thought Martin. "Bruce, you've put forward a bold, intriguing approach there. Put the squeeze on Kim and see if he throws someone under the bus."

Martin looked to Easterly, thinking he'd save Battista for the closing argument that would make his case. "Eric, let me hear your thoughts on that."

"Mr. President, we have to be pragmatic. During our recent Principals meeting, the vice president urged that same approach, but he also spoke to a larger issue: deterrence. Among ourselves we should acknowledge that nuclear deterrence has failed. If it's not restored, governments with nuclear weapons may conclude there's little risk in providing nukes to terrorists. If we don't restore deterrence, Las Vegas could represent not only a disaster in its own right, but the first step in the destruction of our country!"

"And how should we do that?" said the president, eyebrows raised.

"By hitting back hard at North Korea, Mr. President. And there's where we have to be practical. We have to act within our means. I don't believe that invading North Korea and defeating the regime in a conventional war is within our means. It would take longer and kill more people than the public would tolerate."

Well, Eric, neither do I, thought Martin, *and besides that's not what I want to do. Still, I'm surprised and pleased that you've gone on record about that right now. That should slow Bruce down!*

"Eric, is it left to us alone, using force, to restore deterrence?"

Easterly looked dubious. "I don't see any other country doing it on our behalf!"

"How about the rest of you—any ideas?" Martin's outstretched arms invited comment.

After their silence, his voice lashed them, his face hard.

"Aren't any of you capable of moving beyond the old ways of thinking? Can't you see that this is about more than defending the United States?

"Look, every government on the planet is put at risk by this failure of deterrence! Every government is thinking of enemies who might do this to *them*! The Russians have the Chechens, and probably the Georgians and the Ukrainians, too. Ming Liu has to worry about the Uighurs and maybe the Tibetans, plus the Indians and the Paks. The Paks and the Indians have each other to fret over, plus their own extremist groups who might do a bombing that implicates their government. The Brits, French, and Germans are concerned about their unassimilated and disaffected Islamic populations. The Israelis have Hezbollah, Fatah, and others to fear.

"Las Vegas is a horror and a disaster, but also an opportunity! Now is the time, if there is ever going to be such a time, to strengthen the Nonproliferation Treaty, to reduce the number of nuclear weapons, to use an IAEA with more staff and teeth to lock down nuclear materials all over the world!"

Martin's fervent eyes swept their faces like a searchlight. "I ask you: if not *now*, when? If not *us*, who?"

Face still shining, Martin looked around, seeing careful neutrality in most expressions, surprise in a few, and anger in one. *Now I've set the tone. All right, Anne; let's see you hit one out of the park!*

"Sorry to run on. Anne, how about you?"

Battista's shrewdness warred briefly with her spirit. Her spirit won.

"Mr. President, thank you for directing our attention toward a higher goal than we—at least I—had considered. I think we could do a lot diplomatically. But there is still, as Eric said, the matter of practicality. The program you laid out is probably the work of years. Right now we have a pressing need to protect ourselves, guided by Paternity."

Martin was surprised at his anger. *Dammit! I pulled the car out of the ditch and she drove it right back in there! Once again this group has shown itself to be unimaginative and unproductive. I've had enough of them for one day!*

The president's face was set in hard, flat lines that warned against resistance. "Anne, I understand that by the usual diplomatic practice what I outlined could take years. But now's not the time for business as usual! I have in mind a series of summits, beginning soon, without the normal lengthy dance of agenda-making and precooked outcomes.

"As for Paternity . . . I want this group to get on with that. I'll leave you to it, but with this charge: as you work the details, keep the larger goal I've described very much in mind!"

He headed upstairs to the Oval Office.

Guarini's gaze took in the unsettled, uncertain group at the table. *Now what? Where's Rick going with this?*

Nodding to Dorn, Guarini left them.

Chapter 22

THE CH-47 CHINOOK hung from its twin rotors above I-95, twenty miles north of Philadelphia. Secretary of Homeland Security Sara Zimmer squinted in the sun's glare and dropped the visor of her flight helmet. Now she saw something she would never have believed could become commonplace in America: the sudden envelopment of a mile of highway by army and FBI to screen every vehicle and person, like fish in a net. Most would be released, but some would be kept. It was called Operation Sudden Touch, and she owned it.

State police cruisers blocked all lanes. Twisting in her chair to gain a view out the side door around the load master's green-clad bulk, Zimmer saw, flanking the highway, soldiers training machine guns at the bottled-up cars and trucks.

Zimmer keyed her helmet mike. "Captain, how many of these ops have you done?"

"Couple of dozen, ma'am," said the pilot.

"Ever see anybody try to boogie?"

"Nope. Would you? Lookit all those Eleven Bravos and Hummers."

Zimmer clicked her mike twice in acknowledgement and sighed. *Would* the gunners take down someone who bolted? Probably not, if that was all they did, scamper. She would "suggest" to General Harper they drop the flanking machine guns—a deterrent that wasn't necessary and an accident waiting to happen.

Continuing her scan, she saw soldiers expertly sifting the vehicles and their occupants, working from both ends toward the middle of the jam.

Sprinkled among them were FBI, identified by black windbreakers with big yellow letters.

While their comrades worked the cars, pickups, and SUVs, other soldiers directed drivers to clear paths into the median strip or onto the shoulder for the large trucks. Troops and agents inspected the big rigs with dogs and tools ranging from long-handled mirrors to radiation detectors and forklifts.

After about half an hour, Sara noticed civilians under guard inside an area marked by parked Humvees. They were, she thought, people who didn't have their identity cards, or were wanted by police. The FBI would take them into custody. Illegals or those with warrants outstanding would enter the criminal justice system; the others would be released after establishing their identities as citizens or properly documented aliens.

Cleared vehicles and occupants were released at each end of the locked-down highway. Those cars fortunate enough to be among the first inspected were on their way in less than forty-five minutes, but those toward the middle were stuck for hours. As for the truckers, smaller trucks with all in order were on their way in about an hour, but Zimmer knew the eighteen-wheelers were typically motionless for three to four hours.

I've seen enough.

"OK, Captain, I've used up my daily ration of fresh air. Gotta go back to the bottomless inbox. Drop me at hotel sierra one, please."

"Yes ma'am."

The Chinook's nose dipped and the pilot accelerated toward her personal Blackhawk chopper, waiting on a softball field five miles away. From her wheelchair just aft of the flight deck, Sara Zimmer gazed over the pilot's shoulder and cycled her eyes across the instruments. She drank in nostalgic odors: jet fuel, oil, hot metal. There wasn't much challenge flying the "trash hauler," as the attack pilots called the lumbering Chinook, and Zimmer was pretty sure these pilots wanted attack birds, as she had. She'd felt prouder the day she qualified as an Apache pilot than the day she'd pinned on her wings. Then one night the tail rotor failed on the Apache that Zimmer was flinging through valleys and over treetops. The crash left her a paraplegic. She sealed off her devastation at that sudden end to the focal point of her life. Shit happens. You go on—in her case to law school and the DOJ.

Her wheelchair clamped in place at the special desk in her Blackhawk, Zimmer opened her briefcase, but paused rather than diving into papers as she intended. *No wonder so many people are scared and angry about this,* she thought. *It really is spooky police-state, Nazi-occupation stuff. I just saw about a thousand lives ominously disrupted, dozens of kids frightened, and a whole bunch of freight delivery schedules screwed up. About the best you can say is that it's the least bad option. It really sucks. The soldiers hate it. The ACLU is running ads quoting George Orwell.*

She knew that Sudden Touch operations happened around a hundred times a day, nationwide. The president had proposed authorizing legislation at the same time he ended the nationwide transportation lockdown. The National Security Emergency Powers Act required everyone sixteen and older to carry state or federal government-issued biometric ID and authorized the Sudden Touch program, including the military's role in it. This legislation was to sunset in twelve months, but even with that provision, Congress was debating fiercely. President Martin launched Sudden Touch under his authority as commander-in-chief, pledging to stop the program if Congress failed to pass authorizing legislation within a month.

She remembered the first lawsuit had gotten to the Supreme Court in five days and been adjudicated in three. The justices, as frightened as other citizens and mindful of presidential responsibility for national security, ruled for the government while making clear that the door was open for other challenges. Several were on the way.

Zimmer recalled the attorney general's worried, almost shocked face when they debated using the army and her own poker-faced insistence hiding her private concerns. She was glad the ACLU was crying foul, even though she believed that "N-SEPA," as it was called, was necessary right now. *It was 'we can't beat them by becoming like them' versus 'we can't beat them if they destroy our society,'* she thought. *I agree with the first statement but right now am more persuaded by the second. After we're safer, we can roll back things like Sudden Touch. If we can't achieve that—if I can't achieve that—and we continue to lose cities, we'll become a mob, with the survivalists in charge. If that happens, Sudden Touch will seem like the good old days!*

* * *

The president looked up to see John Dorn about to rap on the doorjamb. "That's OK, John, come in."

Rick was in his small private office, connected to the Oval Office by a short corridor, not ten feet long, and done in Ella's selection of bright southwestern hues that kept it from feeling claustrophobic. He saw Dorn's agitation and felt what Ella called "rabbit energy," an aura of urgency and uncertainty tinged with readiness for flight.

"What's on your mind?"

Dorn's words tumbled out: "Mr. President, you've got to go to the country very soon with a response to North Korea's role in the attack! If you don't, it will leak. There are tens of thousands of Americans dead, thousands more dying from radiation—and one of our cities is rubble. You've got to tell the country what you know and what you're going to do before Paternity leaks and this gets out there ahead of us!"

Dorn's lips made a thin, angry line while his eyes flitted between Martin's and a point over his shoulder.

Well, if he feels so strongly, thought Rick, *I'd better take this seriously, even though he's wrong.*

"John, I know that. But I have to get it right. This is probably the most critical decision any president has ever faced. North Korea isn't going anywhere. It's not as if we have to act before they escape. I need to be sure I make the right decision."

Dorn gulped his anger, choked it down, and said, "Mr. President, you *do* have to act before opinion gets away! You have to announce this and you have to say what you are going to do about it. We have to get out in front of—"

Martin stood, his action cutting Dorn off and conveying the ancient message of defending territory. The room rang with their collision: Martin by nature utterly self-confident, Dorn a man of historical trends and political analyses and facts on the ground.

"John, you're speaking as if this is just another issue to be managed politically. It isn't! This isn't a decision to be made solely by me, within the next few hours or days. Millions of lives will be affected, and I will not take sole responsibility for deciding what to do going forward. Congress and the people of this country have to have a say in it. I *will* decide on a plan, but I will *not* decide in a vacuum!"

"Please, have a seat." Martin waved to the chair, sitting himself.

"Eight months ago I won a presidential election. In that campaign I pledged my administration would lay out the facts, level with the American people in a crisis, and not rush to decisions. We beat Glenna Rogers for reelection because she didn't face facts on the ground in Iraq and because she made decisions hurriedly, without preparing the public.

"I'm not going to operate that way!" Martin's face radiated enthusiasm.

"We could have prevented this, you know! If we nuclear powers and the UN had been serious about preventing the spread of nuclear weapons, this wouldn't have happened . . . but we refused to see the threat. Well, now that threat is plain and it's huge! This could happen again, to any country. I believe the world is frightened enough to join us if we lead in finally locking down all the loose nukes and making deep cuts."

Bracing his shoulders, Dorn tried to speak, but Martin surged up and over his attempt like a wrestler going for the pin. Dorn's left hand squeezed his notebook hard enough to whiten his fingernails.

"Despite what Anne and Scott think, there's opportunity around Korea! This could be the opening for regime change, not by blowing up North Korea, but by forcing Kim and his cronies into exile or even arresting them and putting them on trial at The Hague. Unification is a big carrot for the ordinary people of Korea. Yes, the elites are wary of it, but with the right preparation, the south may be able to open the border and reunify peacefully. The United States and others could provide financial and trade support to enable the south to absorb the north into a single, democratic country, the way Germany went.

"John, as we study this and get input, the wisest course of action will become clear. Perhaps, in the end, we must nuke them. But as long as I am president, that is our last option, not our first!"

His own anger and astonishment jolted Dorn like electricity. *This isn't a panel discussion, or a campaign speech!* he thought. *Don't you get it? Television and Internet show soldiers burying our dead in mass graves. We have to use the army for internal security. The stock market had a meltdown. Factories are limping because one hundred percent of arriving cargo has to be inspected. Layoffs are rolling through America. There's panicked buying and hoarding.*

But Dorn deployed none of those facts in rebuttal; his anger obliterated caution. Instead, in a voice choked with frustration and fear, he uttered a single sentence: "Mr. President, that is either the wisest decision—or the most foolish—any president ever made!"

The words hung heavily in the air, kept aloft by both men's desire to preserve their relationship and by mutual shock that their disagreement was so profound. The room felt hot, stuffy, thick with unreleased anger.

Martin's eyes popped, then narrowed to slits. Rick acknowledged his outrage—*how dare he!*—then sent it away. He leaned back.

"John, I know you feel strongly about this, and I appreciate that you've come to me. Candid discussions will continue in the NSC; that's what it was created for. I want to hear all views in those meetings, especially yours. I promise you I'll think hard about what you've said today."

Martin rose and, impelled by his instinct to smooth disagreement, held out his hand, as if they were fellow senators after a contentious committee meeting. Dorn, feeling his head whirling at Martin's sweeping, unmoored vision, took it, without meeting his eyes.

"Thank you, Mr. President."

Alone, Rick sat down and exhaled heavily. His national security advisor had come very close to calling him a fool. Bart had warned against giving the post to an outsider. Was Dorn, like Griffith, a loose cannon? Disloyal?

Or could he be right?

Chapter 23

RICK FELT THEIR tension as he entered. *I bruised a lot of egos when I left the last meeting, to shake them out of their ruts. I hope I won't need to repeat that performance today, but if they still haven't come around, I may just have to dispense with these meetings and drive everything myself!*

The NSC waited around a rosewood table in a conference room dominated by five large video screens. Staff and experts were along the walls. shelved in their chairs like reference books Several odd-looking semicircular glass enclosures, of the type that usually contained revolving doors, bulged from the walls, each sheltering a pair of encrypted telephones, one with video and one without. Intended to permit a participant to step away for a private conversation, they existed because of some techie with a big budget and a desire to make the world's coolest conference room. No one used them. Anne Battista spoke for all when she said, "Standing in one of those bubbles makes me feel like I'm stripping in Macy's window."

Plastic water bottles and paper cups were positioned within reach of the participants. Several laptops gaped open near their owners. Encrypted smart phones sat on every blotter, and people hurriedly fingered them to silence their bleeps, wondering what mood would sweep into the room with the president.

Dorn looked apprehensively toward the president, wondering whether Martin, or maybe Guarini, would make those little moves that show he'd lost the president's confidence.

Martin made a go-ahead gesture.

"Mr. President, I'll start by summarizing the courses of action we've developed. We believe that taken together they constitute an initial response to Paternity's implication of North Korea, plus a way forward. We also believe that we should have your decision on these measures today or in the very near future."

Martin's face revealed nothing as he waited, fingers steepled on the table. *Maybe you will, maybe you won't,* he thought. *It depends on what you offer.*

Dorn read from notes: "The United States will declare that Las Vegas was destroyed by a North Korean nuclear weapon and that we hold the North Korean government responsible; that any further such attack will cause a full nuclear retaliatory response on North Korea; that we will lead the UN to condemn North Korea for a breach of international peace and security, a finding that obligates the UN to address the matter; that we go to the UN for sanction and cooperation for a blockade; and that we convene two summit conferences—NATO, and the Northeast Asia regional powers: China, Japan, Russia and South Korea.

"Subsequently, we propose demanding that Kim step down, going to Congress for authorization to use force if necessary to remove him, and making a comprehensive proposal for a UN-led scheme to prevent nuclear terrorism by denying terrorists access to nuclear weapons or materials."

His list complete, Dorn looked uncertainly at Martin.

Not bad, thought the president. *I see Bruce got the nuclear option back in, and I'm not having it, but their thinking is coming along.*

The president looked around the table, his gaze a sunlamp warming Dorn as he spoke. "Overall, this is a good package. I do want to tweak it, and I'm not going along with the threat to nuke North Korea.

"You don't mention any terrorist group. I suspected al-Qaeda and told the country that the day it happened. I still suspect them. So, why not say that?"

The attorney general spoke from Martin's right: "Because, so far, we have no evidence at all linking any person or entity other than Kim and the DPRK to Las Vegas."

"Besides which," the vice president barged in, "by laying it all at Kim's door we have the possibility he will not only deny it but finger the terrorists, *and,* if we make no mention of al-Qaeda, they might not be able to stand being ignored and make their claim."

They're right, thought Martin, *let's put some pressure on North Korea and see what happens.*

"OK, Bruce.

"Anybody else. . . . No? Fine, that's the way we'll go."

Dorn relaxed a little; the president wasn't going to retaliate, at least right now, for his blunt words in the private office. But he felt the emotional barrier between them and he knew that Guarini, and maybe Battista, would sense it the way sharks sense an injured fish.

"The second item was threatening a nuclear response. I remember my grandfather—he was a Chesapeake waterman—saying that if you have to *tell* people you're tough, then you're not. Real toughness doesn't need to be announced. It's obvious that we could obliterate North Korea. I don't need to say that, and if I do, some people who would otherwise support us would call it saber rattling and back away. I want Kim to be the one sounding warlike, which he surely will when we point to him. Who disagrees?"

Surprise and irritation flared in Guarini. *Who disagrees? That's not inviting debate; it's trying to bulldoze the NSC! Who's he after? What happened to the guy who wanted a full exchange of views?*

Seeing Griffith gather himself, his shoulders tensing, Guarini spoke: "Mr. President, the number of dead and missing is nearing eighty thousand. A lot of Americans—not all of them right-wingers, by any means—want payback. Right now that's focused on al-Qaeda, but when we announce that North Korea's responsible, a lot of folks, including some big-name bloggers and newspaper editors, are going to call for retaliation. Plus, the scholars of nuclear deterrence will point out that it needs to be restored, which is an indirect way of urging retaliation.

"We all agree with you a nuclear strike should be our last option, not our first. The part about retaliation isn't really a threat. It is, as you just said, a statement of the obvious. Making it gives you some pushback against the nuke 'em now crowd and also against the think tanks' hand-wringing over the failure of deterrence."

We aren't goin' there! thought Rick. *Once we suggest nuclear retaliation, it'll suck all the air out of the room. Nothing else will get any attention from the press.* "Well, Bart, I just don't want to make a chest-pounding threat like that. How else could we do what you recommend?"

"How about by low-keyed actions and leaks?" said the secretary of defense, as intent as Guarini at heading off a clash between Martin and Griffith.

"Like what, Eric?"

"Like . . . we make some unannounced but discoverable moves with the nuclear force. Say . . . we surge missile sub deployments to get an extra boat or two to sea. We deploy strategic nuclear bombers to Guam . . . I'm sure Mac and the chiefs can come up with more ideas. Maybe we leak that we're updating nuclear strike plans. Things like that. And we need to go to higher alert in the region in anyway, to be prepared for what Kim might do after we finger him."

Bart's probably right, thought Martin. *This is a bit of chest-pounding for those who want it, but it's not me on camera. OK.*

"Bart and Eric, I take your points. We'll do it that way."

OK, we're two for two! Cheerfully, Martin shifted his gaze to Anne Battista and UN Ambassador Oscar Neumann sitting across the table from her. "Anne, how about you and Oscar tell me how the UN will play in this package of ours? I believe the UN is an important resource."

"Well, Mr. President, I have some ideas, but Oscar's our expert. Oscar, why don't you walk us through this?"

Neumann began eagerly. "With respect to obtaining a Security Council resolution condemning North Korea, there's good news and bad news. The good is, it's not unprecedented. In fact the council has done that before where North Korea was concerned, in 1950. The council also found, in 1991, that when Iraq invaded Kuwait it committed a breach of international peace and security. The bad is this time we don't have tens of thousands of troops crossing a border. There are no North Korean attackers to show on CNN. So, getting the resolution depends on presenting credible evidence that North Korea bombed Las Vegas. I don't have to tell you that since the 2003 WMD fiasco U.S. credibility isn't high at the UN. It will be a struggle to get what we want from the Security Council."

Martin's face became a thundercloud.

What the hell—in for a penny, in for a pound, thought Battista, who said, "Oscar, what about UN approval for a blockade to prevent North Korea from passing more nukes to terrorists?"

Neumann pursed his fleshy lips, aware that his boss was pushing him onto thin ice. "More of the same, I'm afraid. There are precedents; after Iraq's invasion of Kuwait the council approved a resolution that, although it never used the word, sanctioned a blockade of Iraq. After the DPRK's first nuclear test in

2006 the Security Council passed a resolution, 1718, that could be used to legitimize international inspections of all shipments moving in or out of the DPRK. But neither China nor South Korea wants to impede North Korea's trade because they fear a complete collapse of the country if they do that. Neither wants the chaos and risk from North Korea falling apart right next door. With its veto in the Security Council, China can stop us cold."

I can't believe, thought Martin, *how frozen and unimaginative professional diplomats are. They make the generals seem forward-thinking!*

"Ambassador Neumann, I'm going to give you the same reality check I gave your colleagues! The game changed on June thirteenth! Terrorists with nukes aren't just a problem; they're annihilation itself! The old equations for calculating self-interest no longer apply. If you have as much diplomatic skill as I have been told you have, you'll be able to make them understand that. If you cannot, I'll replace you with someone who can!"

The president's threat left everyone unsettled. In Griffith's case, it was more than unsettled. He was boiling. *This is outrageous! If this man doesn't hear what he wants to hear, he shoots the messenger. We can't have this!*

Guarini felt Griffith's anger rising but kept silent. It was the secretary of defense who maneuvered them around the wreckage, speaking calmly, as if Martin's outburst never happened.

"Mr. President, it seems to me we've reached a workable plan—challenging, but workable. May I suggest we direct the staff to follow up, then meet again tomorrow afternoon?"

OK, I'd give them about a B-minus this time, and if I slap down someone else, they'll sulk. Martin agreed and left to prepare for calls to the leaders of China, South Korea, and Japan.

Griffith, too, had some calls to make, but his were local.

Chapter 24

AS HE OFTEN did when receiving sudden and momentous news China's president, Ming Liu, let his mind go blank, then thought of earth, trees, and sky and waited for ideas to grow. Soon they began to appear, like shoots poking through soil into spring sunshine. Except in this case there was no sunshine.

Ming leaned back in a wicker armchair and gazed out the window at his beloved vegetable garden. He braced his elbows against his chest, steepled his fingers, and rested his chin on them. *I must call Jia and Chen, but first, I will think a few minutes.*

Parts of President Martin's call began to replay themselves. Martin's tone of voice was hard to read because his own English was poor. Still, his impression mirrored that of his interpreter: It was the voice of someone under great strain and carried much sadness.

Next to appear in his mind's eye was the dissolute face of Kim Jong-il. *Damn that man!* Whether or not he had done it, his behavior over many years had made him the Americans' prime target, and an inviting one at that. Kim was outrageous, capricious—no, crazy—and that prepared the world to believe he was fool enough to have done what Martin was soon to announce: detonate a nuclear bomb in an American city. He had to admit that soon after hearing about the explosion he, Ming, had wondered if Kim was involved. He had pushed the thought away, and now here it was again, not a thought, not a suspicion, but an assertion by the leader of a country easily capable of erasing all life in North Korea. Which direction would the radioactive fallout drift? He needed to find out, since only the Yalu River separated North Korea from China.

Martin said he wanted to avoid nuclear retaliation if there was any other way to make his country safe again and give a just response to Kim's attack. I believe him. That's the only thing about this that is not a disaster for China. The rest—it's all terrible news for us.

Well, perhaps not entirely terrible. The likely outcome, loss of North Korean sovereignty, is certainly bad. Our buffer will be gone. But . . . Martin knows he needs China's support to accomplish anything other than nuclear retaliation. He told me that I'm the first foreign leader he's called and that he will call only Gwon and Kato before making his announcement two days from now. He's acknowledging that China is much more important in this crisis than Russia. I'm certainly not going to hear any more prattle from him about human rights, or about our currency! So, it's not all bad.

A few minutes later Ming had Foreign Minister Jia Jinping and National Defense Minister Chen Shaoshi on the line.

"Martin wants to convene a five-party conference immediately to agree upon measures to screen or block all North Korean exports so that no more of Kim's bombs get to terrorists. Us, Russia, South Korea, Japan and them. He wants us to host it. What do you think, Jia?"

Jia marshaled his thoughts. After perhaps five seconds, he said, "It's not unprecedented. This is actually a revival of the Six-Party Talks of the Bush administration, but without North Korea."

Ming knew his foreign minister had no initiative, so he was not surprised by Jia's non-answer. He was, however, surprised by what Jia said next.

"Have you spoken with Comrade Kim yet?"

Ming had in fact thought of it while contemplating his garden, but let it go. *What was to be gained?* It would be an unsatisfying conversation and would, as always, leave him feeling soiled. Kim was a liar, a lecher, and a bombastic idiot. *But . . .*

Ming said, "To what purpose, Jia? He'll deny it, and then probably make some outrageous public statement that will preempt President Martin's speech to Congress. I've just told you how China can gain from working with Martin in his time of desperate need; why risk that opportunity? Martin would surely know where Kim's information came from!"

"I know, but isn't it possible the Americans are wrong or are lying, that the bomb was not North Korean? I'm sure, Comrade President, you would want to be prepared for that possibility."

Ming sighed. "Jia, surely you have no doubt that Kim is erratic enough to do something like this and that the analysis of nuclear explosions has been a well-established fact ever since China and others did it in the fifties and sixties? And, yes, the Americans could be lying, but I doubt it. Martin said he was going to make the evidence available for independent verification."

Chen Shaoshi's voice sounded from the speakerphone. As he listened, Ming lit a cigarette. "Comrades, there's nothing for us in telling Kim what's up. In fact there's a risk: if Kim responds by doing something that frightens the South Koreans and makes him look guilty—the man is crazy enough to admit it and dare the Americans to do something about it—that will make Martin's task easier. We want him to need China badly in order to assemble his coalition. That way he will be forced to give us something substantial in return, as you said Comrade President—Taiwan Province, perhaps, or a reduction in military sales to Japan. We have Martin by the balls and I want to keep it that way."

"Jia, I think Chen just summed up the situation. No, I'm not going to call Comrade Kim."

"Comrade President." It was Chen again. "Did Martin say whether he was taking any immediate military measures?"

"Yes, Chen. He is sending several cruisers to the waters between Korea and Japan. They have rockets that can shoot down ballistic missiles that Kim might launch toward Japan. When he speaks to Gwon, Martin will offer to send Patriot antimissile batteries to protect South Korea. And today he has ordered the American aircraft carrier that is based in Japan to put to sea and move within attack range of North Korea. He assured me that when the danger is resolved, his ships will leave."

"That's what I would do, in his place," said the defense minister. "I think I will send a submarine or two and perhaps some destroyers to help the Americans remember that we have a true navy now."

After emphasizing that Kim was not to be alerted and directing Jia to be skeptical but helpful when his American counterpart arrived in about fifteen hours, Ming hung up.

China's president exhaled, crushed out the cigarette, and went into his garden. He was a husky six-footer who walked with a slight limp. His hands were large enough to palm a basketball.

Do I truly have Martin by the balls? Maybe, but we may actually have each other by the balls. China will suffer if Martin turns North Korea into a radioactive wasteland and the fallout and the survivors come here. There's also a problem—perhaps more of a problem—if he unseats Kim and unifies Korea under southern rule. Still, the united Korea will be weak for many years; repairing the social and economic devastation the Kims created will be a huge drain. On balance, I'd rather deal with unification.

Ming's mind returned to Jia's skepticism. *Yes, they could be lying, but why should they? That would be very risky. And they* do *have the technology. Albright told our ambassador some of the uranium that produced the Pakistani explosions had come from our enrichment plant in Heping. She was dead right.*

That's it! It is I who have Martin. Ming smiled at the tomato plant he was spraying. *He'll be desperate for China's confirmation of his technology! He needs us so badly that I may be able to get him to withdraw American support for Taiwan Province. I could bring them back into the nation, just as Jiang Zemin brought Hong Kong back. Now that would be something!*

Chapter 25

"MR. SPEAKER, THE President of the United States." As the ceremonial announcement ended, Martin began moving down the center aisle.

He felt the applause as much as he heard it. From the countless times he had proceeded to a podium amidst applause, Rick judged its promise. Some welcoming applause was ebullient, warm, and eager, sweeping under him like a surfer's dream wave and lifting him for a long, exhilarating swoop down its face. Not tonight, he realized. This applause was fearfully expectant. It was brittle, capable of being shattered into splinters of silence or jagged shards of rage by what he was about to say.

Rick knew this was the speech of his life. There could be others of even greater moment as he brought the nation and the world to a safer place, but those speeches wouldn't happen unless he got this one right.

Working down the aisle, through the ritual handshakes, Rick and Wilson shouldered through tension as thick as the crowd of legislators. Keeping his expression solemn and confident, Rick chanted "Hi, Hello, Thanks" and heard the bland greetings of uncertain politicians fearful of uttering anything that might power an attack ad come next election: "We're with you, Mr. President; God be with you; lead us through this; the nation needs wisdom and prudence, Mr. President."

Congressman Ray Morales observed the scrum, thinking that many of those elbowing to get into the TV coverage with Martin would never support him; they just wanted a free ride on his video coattails.

Reaching the well, the president shook hands with congressional leaders and his cabinet, the joint chiefs, and supreme court justices. He caught Ella's eye, easily spotting her standing dead center in the balcony, and then climbed to the rostrum. The brittle applause continued; Rick accepted it for only a moment before motioning for silence. Above and behind him he heard the Speaker's gavel and his call to order.

Solemnly and proudly, Martin recounted destruction and heroics at Las Vegas, the resilience of the American spirit, and the support of other nations. He acknowledged and praised the efforts of America's defenders, who were screening cargo, scouring the globe for information, and had so far prevented follow-up attacks.

Rick paused, scanning the packed chamber. *OK, that was the easy part. They're a jaded bunch, but right now they're scared enough to be hanging on my words. Now for what I want them to do.*

He took up the theme of balance between civil liberties and measures to uncover and block the next attack. He told them actions like Operation Sudden Touch were bearing fruit and thanked Americans for their cooperation.

Before leaving the topic, Martin threw down the gauntlet. "I will say to you and to the American people that the measures in N-SEPA are vital to the protection of the country. But no president rules by fiat; no president is above the laws of this land. So even though I believe we place ourselves at greater risk if I order an end to measures like Sudden Touch, I will do so unless Congress approves the N-SEPA legislation within the thirty days to which I have voluntarily limited my authority to act alone. The president is the commander-in-chief but does not have sole authority or sole responsibility. In their wisdom, the framers of our Constitution also gave authority and responsibility to the legislative and judicial branches. I ask both branches to consider that and act to help your president protect the American people."

Morales joined the applause, but it was scattered and most of Martin's own party were silent. Not one of the justices applauded. Ray thought Martin was doing the presidency no favors by saying the president's authority and responsibility as commander-in-chief were shared.

Well, most of them didn't like that at all, Rick thought. *I wouldn't have liked it either, as a senator. I just told them that they would be required to share responsibility and couldn't avoid it by legislative deadlock. Whether they act, or whether they do not, they share this responsibility for balancing civil liberties and public safety.*

The president turned next to the link between terrorists and nuclear weapons. After walking through the collective failure of vision that had allowed the link to be forged, he announced his intention to initiate, through the UN, a program to break it. That got solid applause.

Of course, he thought, *who would be against* that *and, besides, I'm not asking them to take responsibility.*

Martin let the applause die, then gazed around the crowded chamber. For a moment his eyes became opaque as he looked inward, gathering himself. He felt the wetness in his armpits as his body anticipated what he was about to reveal. Hands grasping either side of the lectern, gripping hard, shoulders back, he saw his listeners reacting, feeling the imminence of a moment of climax.

Ella kept her face impassive but felt doubts surround her again. *He's still not strong enough on this; he's going to look weak, out of touch.*

"I close with serious, but fundamentally hopeful, news. Through a technical program whose evidence we will make available to all, a program begun over forty years ago by a far-sighted American president and several times validated by events . . . I can tell you tonight who is responsible for the attack that destroyed Las Vegas."

His words seemed to absorb every other sound in the chamber. Martin swept his gaze across the crowd, eyes hard. He gathered them all, held them all, then spoke.

"Las Vegas was destroyed by a North Korean nuclear weapon and we hold the North Korean government responsible. The bomb derived its nuclear explosive power from plutonium reprocessed in the facility at Yongbyon. I have seen the evidence and I believe it."

Morales wasn't surprised and didn't join the uproar that filled the chamber.

Rick paused, letting the moment drain like a lanced boil.

He spoke into the hubbub: "I promise you . . ." He stopped, waiting for silence.

"I promise you that accountability for this attack will be stern and certain and appropriate."

Rick heard a few shouts of "nuke them." Concealing his satisfaction, he spread his arms wide and raised them above his head. "No," he said, "at least not now.

"To hear this for the first time is to experience rage and the urge to strike back. I know, for I felt that too. I am conscious of the fact that, as commander-in-chief, I could give the order and North Korea would be entirely destroyed within a few hours. But I am aware, as you will become aware when thought replaces rage, as it will, that North Korea is ruled by an absolute dictator."

Bruce Griffith fought to keep a poker face. *And what will you do, Mr. President, when what you call* thought—*I call it temporizing*—*fails to prevent another attack?*

Martin continued: "Responsibility rests with that dictator, Kim Jong-il, not the people of North Korea. He and those who help him enslave the North Korean people are the ones we will hold accountable. That accountability, and ensuring Kim is unable ever again to attack any nation with nuclear weapons, is my first goal. I believe it will become a goal shared by most Americans and indeed by most nations."

The president paused and sipped water, creating a moment for his listeners to reflect.

"We have, therefore, within the last few days begun the process of consultation with North Korea's neighbors, countries that would be deeply affected by a worst-case resolution of Kim's threat to the United States. I am pleased to report that their initial responses have been positive. At this moment Secretary of State Battista is in Beijing, where the Chinese government has agreed to host a meeting of the United States, China, Japan, Russia, and South Korea. I expect that this will prepare the ground for a summit meeting of this same group in the near future."

Morales, as a junior congressman jammed in far to the rear, watched live video on his smart phone. Seeing a close-up of Ella, he knew they had the same thought: negotiation won't make Americans safer from nuclear-armed terrorists any time soon.

"I have also asked the nations of NATO to meet at heads-of-state level immediately and urged UN Security Council action to condemn North Korea for this attack and to develop a work program to address the threat that nuclear terrorism poses to all countries.

"I recognize that, despite our hopes and efforts, my plan for the peaceful resolution of this deadly threat might not succeed. In that case, let there be no mistake: the United States *will* . . . act *forcefully* . . . to protect itself." Martin emphasized each pause with a slash of his hand. Applause thundered.

Has he no shame? thought Griffith. *He touts what he is least likely to do in order to get at least one sound bite of solid applause.* Griffith tasted bile.

"This appalling situation and the threat it highlights for *all* nations saddens me but also gives me hope. The community of nations has far too long ignored the growing and inescapable danger of nuclear terrorism, a danger as universal as climate change. It is my expectation—and my prayer—that out of the pain of Las Vegas will come broad and effective international action to break forever the connection that now exists between terrorists and nuclear weapons."

New, sustained applause told Rick he was over the hump. *They've gotten over their first shock. Now for a tip of the hat to Bruce, a nod to the sensibility of the Congress, and out. This is working!*

"These diplomatic initiatives at the highest level will, obviously, require a large share of my attention. The country is fortunate to have a vice president of such ability that he can be my strong right arm in the crucial work of recovery and homeland security."

Martin turned to look at the man seated behind him and to his right. "Vice President Griffith, I salute your energy, skill, and patriotism!"

The vice president preened, disdain swept away by vanity.

When the applause for Griffith, who had been a popular senator, had died, Martin spoke again.

"Being sons of the Congress, the vice president and I understand, respect, and value the crucial role that each of you plays in the life of our country. And while we cannot claim personal experience with the role of the judicial branch"—he gestured to the black-robed justices—"we are equally aware of its importance, particularly in keeping America true to herself. I pray that God will give all of us the wisdom and strength to do our duties in this time of unparalleled crisis and unparalleled opportunity.

"May God bless the United States of America!

"Good night."

Sweaty and elated, President Martin plunged into the departure ritual, working his way up the aisle toward the massive doors.

On the dais, Griffith leaned close to Speaker Ron Nielsen. "What do you really think, Ron?

"I think he just handed you the hardest, riskiest part of his job, while refusing your recommendation to attack North Korea. You got screwed without getting kissed, Bruce!"

Chapter 26

FAHIM WAS ALWAYS alert, but especially while driving. Heading north on Interstate 5 from San Diego to Los Angeles, intently scanning the shoulders, Fahim noticed a pair of police cruisers parked perhaps a quarter mile ahead on his right and, across the median, another pair on the shoulder of the southbound lanes. Reacting immediately, he slowed and pulled out of the traffic stream, halting on the shoulder before reaching the cruisers.

While miming the actions of a conscientious driver pulled over to respond to the bleat of his smart phone, Fahim scanned the highway behind, then ahead, watching the torrent of cars flooding the concrete riverbed.

Suddenly cops left the cruisers on each side of the median and ignited highway flares. About fifteen seconds later, the cruisers nosed into the traffic streams, matching speeds, and then braking rapidly. Behind them, beside the flares, other police made emphatic "slow down *now*" gestures. Within a minute Fahim's car was no longer being buffeted by the slipstreams of vehicles passing at seventy miles per hour. The freeway had become a parking lot.

Fahim heard the distinctive sound of Blackhawk helicopters. He knew it well from his days in Iraq, and that history was why he was so cautious. Fahim imagined other drivers cursing and muttering about "the idiots" who thought these precautions were necessary, but he was relieved. He had, as the Americans say, dodged a bullet. As he steeled himself for a long delay, he thought things over.

A Palestinian born and educated in England, Fahim had felt compelled, as if drawn by a magnetic force, to go to the land of his fathers and help his people fight for their land and rights. An electrical engineer with a minor in computer

125

science, Fahim had been, once he convinced the hard men of Hamas of his loyalty, a welcome addition to their relatively small corps of bomb-makers. Eventually he was drawn to al-Qaeda in Iraq.

Fahim considered President Martin's speech. *The movement's strategy of not claiming the attack was shrewd. It deprived the Americans of an indisputable enemy. Martin had pointed to some scientific program for evidence that North Korea was that enemy, but science could and would be challenged.* Shaking his head, Fahim was amazed at Martin's willingness to spare the country he had identified as the deadliest enemy in American history while he negotiated. His lips twisted, as if he had bitten something foul. It was ludicrous that Martin would not strike back for fear of harming "the people of North Korea."

He felt contempt for Martin and America wash over him, carrying away his own fear and loneliness. And he recalled his orders: "Detonate each bomb in a major city. Try for one in the east and one in the west. Do it this year."

I destroyed Las Vegas because it was the easiest western target. The fact that it had symbolism as the very epicenter of unrighteous behavior, and that neighboring Creech Air Force Base was the site from which Predator attacks were controlled, was fortuitous, but no more than that. And no one, not even I, knows yet where or when the second bomb will be detonated. This too will be determined by circumstances after it arrives in about three weeks.

Fahim squirmed into a new position and drank from his water bottle. His reverie broken, he noticed a highway patrolman speaking to the driver of a car ahead of him.

What's going on? Why's he talking with that driver? We're both outside the inspection area!

What's that in his hand?

Fahim feared several electronic devices the Americans used. One took digital fingerprints and quickly compared them to several databases. Another did a facial scan and compared the biometric indices with its own internal file of the ten thousand "most wanted," a file updated daily. He knew he had been identified and physically catalogued in Iraq and would be in those files.

His stomach twisted as the cop walked toward him.

* * *

The Dear Leader paced and smoked. Martin's speech continued the American way of ignoring Korea's *kibun*, feelings. Martin was as arrogant as all the others, speaking without regard for *anshim,* the obligation to act in a way that is harmonious. Kim felt his anger rising.

He and his brave people had been brazenly accused of attacking America and then threatened with retaliation—no, annihilation—before the entire world, as if they had no choice but to accept this disrespect. *Well,* thought Kim, *Martin would soon learn that the Democratic People's Republic of Korea is not helpless!*

Unlike the Rogers administration that had ignored him, the Martin administration would be forced into engaging him, and engaging him as an equal. And, in the way of Bush and Clinton, Martin would find out that Korea, like the spiny sea urchin, drew the blood of those who tried to grasp it.

While one aspect of Martin's speech had been surprising, it was a mere tactical detail. The surprise was Martin acting as if the Arabs played no part. This was an interesting gambit, but no more than that. Kim paused at the window in the east corner of this office and gazed out at Pyongyang, but what he saw in his imagination was President Martin.

Martin's feeble trick did not change the situation because he knew the weak American president was afraid of using the only weapon that could hurt him. UN sanctions? Kim would flood the Internet with video of starving Korean children. He would declare sanctions equivalent to war and mobilize the brave people who loved him so. He would order the relief agencies to leave; then they would exert pressure on the UN to desist from sanctions so that they could return. Attack by American bombs and missiles? He would unleash another flood of video, this time of mutilated children. Kim knew his skill as a dramatist would triumph over sanctions and bombs. He smiled.

An attack by the American army? His soldiers would outnumber the Americans and would be defending their beloved homeland's rugged terrain. That alone would be enough to defeat them, but he had even more. He would attack Japan with missiles, and Tokyo would demand that Washington withdraw. His agents would spark rioting in every South Korean city. And undergirding all that was China, which could not, would not allow American soldiers to win, even if they somehow bled their way northward.

Kim felt a confident glow; his father would have been proud of him now. Like the Great Leader, he would defeat the Americans and shame them. He knew, though, that his father would expect him to take revenge for Martin's arrogance. And that was the most satisfying of all the opportunities Martin had presented. By his gambit, Martin had ensured that when the second bomb was detonated, it would be seen not as the Arabs', but as Kim's, his defiant, crushing retaliation.

* * *

Flee or brazen it out? Fahim's mind stuttered, then froze, marooning him behind the wheel.

As the cop strolled toward him, Fahim strained to identify the object he held. He gripped the wheel with both hands, tightened his arm muscles, and leaned forward, as if he could literally pull it into clear view. All he could determine was that it was book-sized.

Suddenly the officer was there, a couple of yards ahead and off to the left of the car. Holding the object in both hands, he made some keystrokes with his thumbs.

Sweat beaded along Fahim's hairline and spread over his forehead. His eyes darted left and right.

Now the officer was at his door, looking down at him. Fahim observed the man register his Arabic appearance. Fahim stiffened in reaction but forced himself to calm. The officer bent over slightly and spoke. "Good afternoon, sir. Sorry that you're being delayed, but you know how it is these days."

Fahim looked up at the cop and put on his most patient, resigned smile.

"That's quite alright, officer. It can't be helped." Fahim observed his British accent blunt the cop's suspicion.

"I see you're on the shoulder. Do you have car problems?"

Should I say yes? Can't tell where that will lead. Better use the phone explanation.

"No, officer. Just before you shut down the highway my mobile sounded and I pulled over to see the message." Fahim had deliberately said "mobile" instead of "cell phone," careful to use his native British pronunciation of the word.

The officer smiled. "Wish more people would do that. I've cleaned up after more texting wrecks than you can imagine!

"Look, we're going to reverse the flow back to the exit; it's about a mile." He pointed. "So just sit tight until the car behind you U-turns, then you do the same and you can get out of this parking lot."

With a wave, the cop headed for the next car.

For a moment Fahim sat motionless, hardly believing he was out of danger. Then, in a torrent of softly spoken Arabic, he praised Allah for deliverance. Although wary of attracting attention, Fahim opened his door and stood on the pavement, stretching, restoring flexibility to muscles knotted by fear.

The Las Vegas bomb was easy; the second bomb will be harder. Before Las Vegas there was virtually no chance of the bomb being discovered as I drove it into position. Now, with radiation detectors many more places, there's a chance, still low, but it's there. And the danger is more than the discovery of the bomb. There's also the chance, maybe the biggest chance, I will be discovered before I can complete my mission.

I will reconsider my plans to drive to the East Coast. Although an airport is very dangerous, my exposure will be short if I fly. But if I drive . . . these cursed round-ups are everywhere. I must think on it.

Chapter 27

DRAWN TOGETHER BY the crisis like many other families, the four Martins gathered in Washington. Now, for the first time in ten years, the question of what next for Rick's career didn't surround them, wasn't a companion at every family gathering and a factor in every decision. After Six-thirteen the danger everyone faced and the impact of the tens of thousands of deaths had become a shield between the family and their clamoring ambitions. In an unexpected closeness forged by the bombing, Rick and Ella were getting acquainted with the young adults who had replaced their children.

The family was finishing dinner when Mark, a senior hanging on by his fingernails at Yale, said tentatively that some of his friends thought the country had brought on the attack as a result of bad policies and brutal instruments for carrying them out.

Stifling her irritation that Mark was so typically unwilling to commit himself, Ella said, "Mark, let's say your friends are right. Where do they go next with that train of thought? How do we stop the attacks? Or do we just accept them as well-deserved punishment?"

"Well, they don't go there. They talk about how criminally wrong Bush and Rogers were and say that we must address the grievances we've created and only then will we be respected and able to live in peace."

Rick said, "I agree with some of that, Mark. But what do we do in the meantime, while we're addressing those grievances? That's what I'm wrestling with, the here and now of tens of thousands killed and at least a quarter million homeless, and maybe more of Kim's bombs headed our way."

Their daughter Gabriella, a sophomore at Columbia, entered the conversation while Ella sipped her coffee in silence. "Dad, isn't *protecting ourselves* what we have to do? And don't we have the power to destroy Kim and his country, just blow it off the map?"

"Gabby, we do have that power. I control it. What would you think of me if I ordered the Pentagon to blow North Korea off the map? It's not only Kim; there're about twenty million people who'd die with him. It may well be that their only connection to Las Vegas is that their ruler made a terrible mistake; he sold bombs to terrorists. Should *they* all die for that? What would you think of me if I ordered their deaths and General MacAdoo killed them in a single afternoon? He could, you know!"

Gabriella didn't respond and Ella broke the silence. "Gabby, what would you think of your father if he declined to use that power and Kim destroyed San Francisco? Or Chicago? Or Washington? Or all three of them? Is it OK for tens of thousands more Americans to die because Kim is allowed to use his people as a shield?"

Mark looked at his father. "God, Dad, you're really between a rock and a hard place, aren't you!"

Overcome, Rick nodded mutely, throat tight and mind churning.

And how would I feel if, like Steve Nguyen, I found my kids' bloody bodies and Ella was gone forever, not even her corpse left on this earth?

He recalled Ella's words the day it began. 'I think I'd become a relentless killing machine.' *Is that what I would do if Kim killed my family? Am I bound to become that because he has killed others' families? Or am I bound to find a way that doesn't take more lives, as that woman at Las Vegas said?*

Mark's voice brought him back. "Dad, don't we have ways to get Kim without using nuclear weapons, without killing so many people?"

"Yes, we do have other ways. I could order an invasion of North Korea to push Kim from power—maybe even capture him for trial—and take away the country's nukes and the means to build more."

"That sounds better to me," said Gabriella.

"Well, but the last war in Korea killed millions and didn't change the North Korean leader," said Rick. "Chinese and North Korean soldiers battled South Korean and UN soldiers. Most of Korea's cities were destroyed. The result of all that blood and violence was stalemate, ending up right back where the war began. Kim Jong-il's father, Kim Il-sung, became even stronger, and here we are facing his son and grandson. About thirty-six thousand American soldiers were killed in Korea."

"And on Six-thirteen the same regime killed many more American civilians, right in their homes," Ella said coldly. "What's the count now? Sixty, eighty thousand?"

"Did we have nukes back then?" asked Gabriella, with the historic cluelessness of the young, even those well educated.

"We did," said Rick.

"Did the president think of using them?"

Rick drank some coffee and replied: "Yes, he did. But he chose not to and actually fired his top general partly because the man, Douglas MacArthur, kept pushing it.

"That president was Harry Truman. In World War Two he allowed the military to A-bomb Hiroshima and Nagasaki. In Korea he made the opposite call. In his memoirs he wrote that he feared a full-scale war with China had he agreed to nukes. But I have to wonder if he was so sickened by the earlier bombings that he couldn't do it again. He said not, but we'll never know."

"So is that how you feel, Dad, that you just couldn't do it?"

Rick stole a glance at Ella. Her expression cut him like a knife.

"Before I answer that, there's more to consider. Kim has between three and ten nukes, as best we know. He has missiles that could explode over South Korean and Japanese cities—maybe even reach Hawaii. If we were to invade, Kim might launch those nuclear missiles. Japan, Korea, and America have defensive missiles that could probably shoot down some of those North Korean missiles. But we don't have many of them and we haven't tested them much—so, who knows?

"So, could I do it, could I order a big nuclear attack on North Korea? I could, but only if I was sure it was the only option to protect us. I'm not sure yet."

Ella thought that 'only' option might not be the same as 'best' option, but didn't say so. Instead she said, "*When* will you decide, Rick? *When* will you know enough?"

"I can't say, Ella. But I *will* know!" Rick's face flushed, and Mark and Gabby traded knowing glances.

Ella held Rick's stare and wondered when he would accept that the only way to deal with Kim was kill him or imprison him. Like the drug lord who murdered her father, Kim was a law unto himself, more a force of nature than a man.

"Dad," said Gabby, "would a big nuclear attack on North Korea keep Kim from shooting those missiles at us and the Koreans and the Japanese?"

"General MacAdoo says so and I think he's right."

"Then tell Kim that's what you're going to do unless he gives it up."

"If I confront him, give him a deadline—that may provoke him to launch his missiles. And he certainly will make threats that cause riots in South Korea and scare the Japanese half to death, not to mention Americans, who are already spooked!"

"OK, but isn't that better than killing twenty million people without a clear warning?" said Mark.

"Do you have any reason to think Kim would heed your father's warning, Mark? I don't know how much you know about North Korea under Kim and his father, but that man allowed tens of thousands of his people to starve to death by insisting upon his own harebrained schemes for farming and then diverting international food supplies to his huge army. You can't sway Kim by threatening harm to his so-called dear people!"

"Yeah, Mom, but even Kim needs a country to rule. If his country is blown up, he's out of a job!"

"Do you think that hasn't occurred to him, Mark?" Ella shot back. "Does Kim seem stupid to you?"

"Well, no, but I just think we should go the extra mile for peace and spell out exactly what's going to happen to him if he doesn't step down."

"Go the extra mile? Mark, don't you think your father has already *done* that? Kim destroyed an American city and killed tens of thousands. Since Six-thirteen your father has given everything he has to negotiate a solution to this threat to our very existence and hasn't ordered a single shot fired. I'd say he's already gone the extra mile!"

"So, Dad, *do* you think Kim can be pressured into giving up his nukes or going into exile?"

"I can't say for sure, Mark, and I'm still trying that, but I'm certain the problems I'd create by making an or-else demand and starting my stopwatch would be huge."

"Rick, you've done all anyone could possibly do to solve this crisis in a humane manner! You're giving everything, you can't sleep, you exist on caffeine and cigarettes—yes, I know you're sneaking a pack a day—and you're getting an ulcer. . . ." She ran out of words, but her angry eyes continued to speak: 'diplomacy won't work.'

Ignoring her message, Rick smiled at Ella and took her hand. "As usual, your mom has summed up something complicated in a few well-chosen words.

"Come on, get ready—we'll be leaving for Aberdeen in five minutes. The wind forecast is perfect, and I don't want to miss a minute of sailing!"

As he watched his family bustle off, Rick thought that Kim wanted to kill them or, for a price, enable terrorists do it. This time he didn't scold himself for getting personal.

Chapter 28

VICE PRESIDENT GRIFFITH exploded into the conference room at Creech Air Force Base, his energy and impatience flung outward like shrapnel as he entered.

"OK, let's get started! Harry, what the *hell* is the problem with shelter for the survivors? People are still jammed together in tents like sardines—those lucky enough to be *in* tents, which most are not! Where are the trailers?"

Harry Fisher, the FEMA onsite leader, reminded himself that the VP was willing to hear the truth, however unpalatable it might be. If you pushed back at Griffith, he listened. He would rip your head off if you didn't have your facts straight, but if you did, he faced them. So, he leaned into it. "Sir, we learned all over again after Katrina: when you want it bad you get it bad. Thousands of trailers turned out to be unfit for habitation. We ain't goin' there this time! We're not sole-sourcing or short-cutting. We've got a competitive bid process with all the oversight needed to prevent another fiasco. Until that's done, tents are the best we can do. And, by the way, sir, we have every damn tent in North America out here now!"

"So why settle for that? They've got tents all over the world! Go get 'em!" Fisher and his colleagues understood that Griffith's tone and eyes added, 'Thanks for busting your butt. I've got your back.'

Now humorless, the VP said, "OK, Harry, let's take that apart. Where are you guys in the trailer process?"

"We have valid bids from five firms. There's one six hundred pound gorilla in the business, Horizons, and all the rest fight over the crumbs. So, it's kinda like Paul Bunyan competing with four of the Seven Dwarfs."

"How long 'til the trailers arrive if you play out the bid process?"

"Well, I'd say it will take another ninety days to award the contract, then after award—if there's no protest from any of the losers—another forty-five until trailers begin arriving, and six months until the full production run is delivered."

"Harry, do you trust the Horizons guys? I know they have stockholders and a profit imperative and all that b.s., but do you *trust them* not to screw us?"

Fisher's mind cranked: *OK, what's going on here? Is he setting me up? He's getting ready to tell me to go sole-source if I say I trust 'em. Then he can say I assured him and duck the shit if it goes south. Would he do that? You know, I don't think so, and besides, he's right: it's just unacceptable that these people, after all they've suffered, don't have decent shelter yet!*

"Yes sir, I do. They'll take their profit, but they're not assholes. They want to help. They can't do it for free, but at the end of the day, they want to help the country. Yeah, I trust them."

"Then sole-source it. You get any flak from Les Moore or anyone else, you tell 'em that's *my* decision and call me if they want to argue the point."

Griffith looked to his right.

"OK, Arnie, now tell me how you Feebies are earning your keep! I know, The Book says FBI will be in charge on-scene after any terrorist-related event, but damned if I can figure what evidence is left. It all vaporized, didn't it?"

FBI Assistant Deputy Director Arnold Cantwell grinned at Griffith. "Well, the physical evidence did, but that's not all we're working on. We interviewed around fifteen thousand survivors, the most seriously injured and irradiated first. About ten thousand died from radiation in the first two weeks, and we got statements from nearly all of them."

"And?"

"And, nothing *yet*. But that doesn't mean nothing ever! This has to be done, if for no other reason than to cover our asses, sir. But I'm here to tell you we could come up with some gold dust; it wouldn't be the first time I've seen the bureau crack a case by just plain ball-busting, mind-numbing persistence. It's what we do, boss."

"So I've been told. Keep at it!"

Griffith turned to Major General Stanley Karnow, the Pentagon's on-scene commander.

"So, Stan, how are your troops handling burial duty? I know they'd rather be jumping out of perfectly fine airplanes, like good little paratroopers."

"Yes sir, you got that right. This really sucks! But despite their bitching, my soldiers realize that with this many dead, only the military has the people to handle it the right way."

Karnow's blue eyes went cold. "I'll tell you what: if my troopers ever come up against the guys who did this, we won't need Guantánamo to hold the prisoners."

The vice president grunted, then snapped, "What about security? Any looters?"

"A few, but the radiation scare has done more than my airborne division to keep 'em away. Radiation poisoning is such a shitty way to go, and because so many of the dying have been on TV and the Internet, the scumbags have stayed away, by and large."

"Yeah, that's certainly safer. What about your soldiers—any radiation problems?"

"No sir, because they stay clear of the no-go zone and wear protective gear near it."

Griffith stood. "OK, flight time! Let's go have our look around."

The vice president strode from the Creech Air Force Base commander's conference room with gusto, glad to be handling his recovery duties far from Washington. *First, it gets me out of Martin's shadow,* he thought. *Second, it gives me my own press pool: I'm not covered by those prima donna White House correspondents; I've got younger, hungrier reporters, still trying to make it. And I can sit in the same room with the players; when my ass is on the line, I don't want to be deciding from some big-screen shot of a guy expounding from two thousand miles away. I want to be close enough to see the lines around his eyes, to smell sweat—or bullshit.*

After forty-five minutes above the ruined city, during which Griffith kept up a steady fire of questions and instructions, the group parted and Griffith headed for another "town hall" with survivors.

As each of the agency leaders knew full well, there Griffith would "do a Rudy," copying the outspoken, decisive style of New York Mayor Rudy Giuliani after Nine-eleven. But though contrived, it wasn't bad, because it got results and generated great press, for their agencies as well as for him.

Back in his office at Creech, Arnie Cantwell smiled at a memory. After being hit with survivors' anger at spoiled food, the VP had ordered the FBI to fetch the CEO of that company. He'd enjoyed his phone call launching agents toward corporate offices in New Jersey, whence the surprised executive was escorted to an FBI Gulfstream. In flight to the undisclosed destination the agents had deli sandwiches; the CEO was served one of his company's meals. Forty-five minutes after touchdown at Creech, the CEO had received a memorable chewing-out and was back aboard the Gulfstream with Griffith's list and his forty-eight hour deadline. Cantwell smiled. *What a righteous use of power!*

But Griffith's blunt criticism of the president's diplomatic activities felt off, a taste of milk going sour. *His assumption that they shared his opinion and were his guys was flattering but . . . it's almost as if he's holding auditions for a Griffith administration,* thought Cantwell, rubbing gritty eyes, then cursing when their sting told him he had gotten sun block in them again.

Chapter 29

"HELLO, EVERYBODY." DORN spoke, trying to sound brisk but not succeeding; he was tired. They all were.

"The president wants an update on international support for his initiatives. I know it's been a busy forty-eight hours for everyone." Dorn glanced at the video screen and said, "Ambassador Neumann, first to you."

Air Force One was out of Zaventem for the fourteen-hour flight from Brussels to Tokyo. Martin, Easterly, and Dorn sat in the large cabin, which served as dining room and conference room, squarely over the Boeing 747's huge wings.

"Good evening, Mr. President. We've circulated a draft security council resolution charging North Korea with a breach of international peace and security. As anticipated, we're running into considerable skepticism, not that a breach occurred, but as to the identity of the offender. As expected, the pushback is about the authenticity of the samples. While we have a chain of custody for the Las Vegas sample, we don't have one for the Yongbyon sample. We are being told that in such a grave matter the Security Council can act only on the basis of incontrovertible evidence."

"Aaron," said the president, "can't you give Oscar more to work with?" His tone and gestures milked the cliché 'What? You can't do better than that?'

Hendricks' video image took that with lips clamped tightly, then spoke: "No, sir. I'm confident the material was obtained from Yongbyon and that it is unadulterated, but our chain of custody began after my agents got out of North Korea."

"Mr. President," interjected Griffith, head bobbing on the screen, "with all due respect to Oscar and the good work he does at the UN, I just don't think this is worth a lot of your time. Given what happened in 2003, there's no way we'll be able to move the focus from U.S. credibility to North Korean culpability. Oscar has to keep trying, but there are much better uses for *your* time and prestige than trying to get the UN to tackle this."

Martin glared at Griffith's image. "Well, you may be right, Bruce, but getting UN support is almost a necessity, as far as I'm concerned."

Addressing Neumann, whose bald head reflected light as he sat before a blue background across which the words "U.S. Mission to the UN" filed, the president said, "Oscar, keep at it. Are you reminding your colleagues that the world changed on Six-thirteen and that ducking this issue will put their own countries at greater risk? What do they say to that?"

"That slides off like water from a duck's back, sir. Among the Perm Five, only the UK supports our draft fully. The French, Chinese, and Russians all sing the same song: Each nation must deal with this changed world in its own way; each of them is quite confident it can do so without the UN, and so should we be. In other words, dealing with North Korea is *our* problem! Unsurprisingly, there is in conversations with the Chinese and Russian a common undercurrent: While this is an *American* problem, North Korea is *their* neighbor, and they expect to have a say in their neighborhood. As for the rest of the Security Council," Neumann's hands appeared, framing his face, "I don't think any of them feels threatened by North Korea or by Islamists with nukes, not so long as there are higher profile targets, like us."

Rick, listening with his right hand cupping his chin, thought *Damn! That's what I got from NATO. Don't they get it? I guess I owe Oscar an apology for the other day.*

"Well, Oscar, I know you're the best we have for a very tough job. I've just experienced something like that, and it gave me a new perspective on your challenges. Let's both pledge to keep butting our heads against those walls, because unless we knock them down, the world will miss its last chance to put the Armageddon genie, state sponsored nuclear terrorism, back in the bottle."

Smiling, Neumann said, "That's a deal, sir."

In a corner of his mind, Rick congratulated himself: *Armageddon genie. That's a great sound bite; I'll use it at my press conference in Tokyo.*

"So, I might as well go ahead with my update." Martin paused, looked down and rubbed the back of his neck.

Looking up, he said, "In brief, my counterparts were sympathetic but just barely willing to invoke Article Five. I really had to do some arm-twisting. That's pretty shocking, considering the North Atlantic Council invoked Article Five soon after Nine-eleven, without much fuss. But today they were reluctant to go on record that a North Korean attack on the United States is an attack on every NATO nation, even though that's precisely what the treaty requires."

"What's your take on that, Mr. President?" said Bart Guarini from the White House.

"Bart, I'd say it's the usual suspects, self-interest and fear. Our more willing supporters in Brussels see themselves as high enough on somebody's target list to want NATO backup as a deterrent. The others don't feel threatened now but fear becoming targets by supporting us."

"So, we've gotten all the help we're going to get from NATO!" said Griffith, who was with Guarini in the Situation Room.

"That's what it looks like to me, Bruce," said Martin.

The president's smart phone chirped. He glanced at it, then dismissed the alert. He motioned to Dorn, who said, "NATO foreign ministers told me that if we decide to use force, we're on our own. The French foreign minister, by the way, seemed to take it for granted that we intend to retaliate by taking out at least one North Korean city. He certainly made it clear that's what France would do!

"I got some skeptical questions about our analysis of the bomb debris. The Belgians and the Germans think we're repeating our WMD mistake. The Turkish foreign minister was pleased that we aren't pointing to al-Qaeda, or another Islamist group, because that would push Turkey into a corner."

Martin glowered, shaking his head. *When are they going to get* over it? *I'm not George Bush. The world has changed!*

"So, let's hear from you, Anne," he said. "How do things look for the summit?"

Battista sat up straighter in her chair in Beijing, will overcoming fatigue. "Not great, but not impossible either, Mr. President. As you know, since your speech there's been violent unrest in South Korea. Thanks to your call to President Gwon, his internal security forces were ready and quickly forced back the protesters storming our embassy."

At the bottom of the screen Battista's right wrist could be seen rocking up and down. Eric Easterly registered the familiar mannerism: She was tapping a pen on the desk.

"Bottom line on the South Koreans: they are *very* conflicted. Both the elites and ordinary citizens believe that Kim is difficult but someone they can live with. They believe that he will die soon and his son will be easier. Slowly, they'll move toward closer ties between north and south. Now, suddenly, they are presented with an alternative universe where Kim has attacked the United States, their own key ally, leaving North Korea open to nuclear retaliation. The consequence of a U.S. nuclear attack on the north is disaster for the south. For most South Koreans this must be like an out-of-the-blue diagnosis of a fatal cancer, 'Hello, you have only a few weeks to live.' Not surprisingly, they're in denial. At the least, they want a second opinion. And, until they accept that second opinion, they're furious at the U.S. for, as they see it, putting them in danger."

Martin rocked his chair back and interlaced his hands behind his aching neck. That felt better. "Do you think President Gwon shares my view that there's a silver lining here, that it offers an opportunity for unification?"

"No, sir. Quite the opposite. He doesn't want to unite the north and the south in a single, chaotic event, liking marching across the DMZ as Kim leaves Pyongyang. He fears that would impose huge costs, both financially and socially, as it did when Germany unified almost overnight. He wants a unification timetable of years."

"So Gwon is someone else who doesn't realize the world has changed, that he's out of his comfort zone whether he wants to be or not?" The president scowled.

"I'd have to agree with that, Mr. President."

"Well, I guess I have work to do, then! What about the Japanese?"

Battista's expression said 'that's a different story.' "They've been working at acknowledging Kim is a threat for much longer than the South Koreans. They're worried about what Kim may do to them to force us to leave him alone. Their defense minister told me that, if a decision is made to remove Kim by force, it must be done quickly; otherwise Kim will surely hit them with a nuke. Their price for supporting us is your commitment to take Kim's government down fast and hard if that's what you decide to do. Gradualism will cost the Japanese a city; that's the way Minister Sato put it to me."

"Well, I may not give that commitment, if 'taking Kim's government down fast and hard' requires killing a lot of North Korean civilians!"

Dorn's eyebrows shot up and he said, "Mr. President, we should think hard about the consequences of failing to prevent Japan from being hit with a nuke. Our larger goal—*your initiative*—is to put the brakes on nuclear proliferation. If Japan and others see that the result of forgoing their own bombs and trusting us to protect them is not protection, but great pain, there goes nonproliferation!"

Slapping the table, Martin said, "Well, I'm not going to murder a bunch of people who bear no responsibility for Kim's actions!"

In Washington, Griffith looked at Guarini and shook his head. He scribbled quickly and shoved the note to him.

Chapter 30

"MR. PRESIDENT, WE need Japan's support, and we won't get it unless you make that commitment!" said Battista, her eyes muted by the video screen but compelling nonetheless.

Silence.

Guarini stepped into his role as defuser-in-chief. "Anne, what, specifically, do we need from Japan?"

"A lot! Cutting off funds to Kim's regime from the significant Korean population in Japan; supporting the blockade; continuing use of our navy and air force bases in Japan, which Kim will undoubtedly threaten to attack. Next there's supporting us at this summit and in the UN, and then supporting nonproliferation itself.

"The Japanese could have a nuclear capability in two-three years, wouldn't you agree, Aaron?"

The director of national intelligence nodded. "That's a fair estimate. A nuclear Japan would be a huge shock to China, one that would surely drive them into increasing *their* nuclear forces."

Silence reigned again. Guarini, reading his boss, said, "OK, food for thought. What about Russia and China, Anne?"

"The Russians, ah, the Russians!" Battista threw up her hands. "They're the wild card. They're less affected than the other three; the Russians live in the neighborhood, but not on the same block. Volkov is still angry about America's part in the dissolution of the Soviet Union. So, I think he's looking for an opportunity to make you squirm, Mr. President. He probably also sees a chance to get something big in return for Russia's support. With each of the other four we have sticks to work with; with the Russians, only carrots."

"Well, Anne, you and John better work on finding us some sticks!" said Martin, pointing at each. "And China? Anne, what do you and Ambassador Caulfield think?"

"China will push for the status quo, but President Ming knows we have to do *something*. Foreign Minister Jia told Barton and me that he fears catastrophic consequences if we attack North Korea. He said under some circumstances, like invasion, China would be compelled to assist Kim. And he said that a nuclear attack on North Korea would be *quote* unacceptable *unquote*. But, he implied that a conventional bombing campaign would not necessarily trigger their military intervention. One way to read those comments is that they describe the sticks we have to work with."

Battista brushed her hair back and tucked it behind her ears. "As for carrots, I'm sure President Ming will have a list. One could be the withdrawal of our support for independent Taiwan so that they can take control of it as they did Hong Kong. Another might be establishing a preferred status for Chinese investments in U.S. Treasuries."

"Do you think Ming will threaten to dump their holdings, or to refuse to buy more?" said Griffith.

"Well, Mr. Vice President," said Barton Caulfield, "that's certainly a possibility, but the GOC didn't buy Treasuries to do us a favor. They did it because it was a sound investment. They've got a lot riding on our recovery— our success in preventing other attacks and our economic health. They stand to lose not only those billions in Treasuries but also a crucial export market."

He paused then said, "Mr. President, as the secretary and I have been discussing, we have another carrot, one I believe is very high on Ming's wish list! He wants to emerge from this conference as the leader of America's super-power partner. Since the demise of the USSR, we've stood alone. If we now acknowledge China as our equal partner, clearly more important than Russia, it will be a huge feather in Ming's cap. With that, plus something significant on Taiwan, Ming's place in modern Chinese history would seem assured, not to mention his ability to stay in power."

Martin perked up. Observing, Guarini relaxed. "What do we need from Ming Liu?" said Martin.

Battista responded: "Mr. President, we need a *lot*. We need China's cooperation in the blockade of North Korea, just as we need South Korea's. Without either one, no blockade. We also need their cooperation at the Security Council—at the very least, not using their veto."

Caulfield added, "Also, Ming is in a unique position to help us attain peaceful regime change. China is not only the DPRK's most important source of support; culturally China is their elder cousin. If anyone can talk Kim into giving up his nukes or going into exile, it's Ming."

Across the table from Guarini, the DCI spoke: "There's one more thing, something Ming is uniquely able to do." Hendricks paused for dramatic effect, then continued: "He can validate Paternity. He can recount Albright's assertion about China providing HEU to the Paks and tell everyone it was true."

Martin rocked forward in his chair and planted his elbows on the table. "That would be huge!" he said. "If they did that, and supported us in the Security Council, we could probably get the UN to act.

"So, everyone, how should I approach Ming?"

Dorn, who usually waited to sum up, surprised Guarini by speaking immediately. "You need to two-step this, sir. At this meeting you need to get Ming's cooperation, but you can't give him that equal partnership. If you do, the Russians will surely block us at the UN. Once it's clear we are granting China the status that the USSR had, Russia's main objective will be to block the two of us in everything. They will be obsessed with showing the world they still count. So, we need to get the blockade going and get the necessary UN actions before you anoint China."

Battista leaped in. "I agree, Mr. President. This is going to be very delicate, very subtle. In other words, right up your alley!" She cringed at her blurted words, but Martin loved them.

"Right you are, Anne! This is a challenge, but we're up to it. Well, I've got a busy thirty-six hours ahead: Premier Kato, President Gwon, and then on to Beijing. I'd better grab some sleep, unless there's something else right now? . . . Fine. Thanks everyone!"

The screens went dark.

Rick tossed, sleepless, in his cabin in the nose of Air Force One. The aircraft rode smooth as silk, but he couldn't drop off.

This is a huge opportunity! It's what I've been preparing for all my life. It's one of those rare moments when world politics shakes free from the web of uncertainties and self-deceptions and short-term imperatives. It's an opportunity to hit the reset button. Many leaders haven't realized that yet, and my challenge and opportunity is to show them.

I can do that! It's what I've always done. And when I've done it, the world will be safer and saner than it was before Six-thirteen.

The secretary of defense sat alone in the senior staff compartment, a nightcap in his hand. Disdaining the spiffy Air Force One leather flight jackets available, he wore an old, olive-drab nylon jacket with a worn leather patch on the left breast displaying the Navy SEAL insignia and "LT Eric Easterly, USNR" in faded gold. His gaze inventoried the cabin: leather upholstery, indirect lighting, polished wood, thick carpet, eagle glaring fiercely from the Great Seal of the United States on the bulkhead.

Here, we're surrounded by all the trappings, he thought. *It's easy to believe that if you conceive a plan, the power this airplane evokes will make it happen. But power is situational and IQ won't stop a bullet. I wish the president had the experience, like me, of being pinned down by an illiterate peasant with an ancient rifle and every intention of canceling my ticket.*

The race doesn't necessarily go to the swiftest. He smiled at his play on words, then dozed.

Chapter 31

Beijing

RICK'S TEMPLES SCREAMED as if being squeezed by the tongs he used as a teenager working summers in the ice-making plant at Easton. His proposal that the five nations impose a quarantine on North Korea had been received coolly—by closed minds—with South Korean and Russian doubts that Paternity's evidence was sufficient. Japan's Premier Kato supported him strongly, and cleverly, too. Rick was grateful—as Kato had intended, the president wryly acknowledged.

Martin let his gaze rove the room as Ming Liu, their host and honorary chairman, spoke. Ming, whose face was dominated by a broad nose and topped by a thick head of perfectly controlled hair, fidgeted with his earphone, a bit uncomfortable but essential for a meeting conducted in five languages.

A plastic flower arrangement sat at the center of the large, circular table. It contained five tulips, each a different color, and at the moment four were lit. Each lighted tulip signaled that a translation was in progress. Observing them, a speaker could tell when the translation of his words was complete. It was an odd but useful device that had been a fixture in the talks with and about North Korea for years.

President Ming smiled like a beneficent teacher as he completed his opening statement, his teeth showing nicotine stains.

"Even from our brief discussion so far it is clear that this is a complex situation requiring careful study. We must not rush into something heedlessly. President Martin, we all offer our sympathetic support to the people of the

United States in this difficult and distressing situation. We have a range of views on the table. China is not at odds with any of them. No nation knows better than China how, um, troublesome Comrade Kim can be at times. Still, we feel a great deal of fraternal unity with the Democratic People's Republic of Korea. This is a unity born of our common belief in communism as the best organizing principle of society and of the personal bonds between our two peoples, who together gave much of their blood to ensure the independent existence of the DPRK."

OK, I know where this is going, thought Rick. *This group is deadlocked, two to two, and Ming's going to cast the swing vote. But not until he's demonstrated that I can't succeed without his support.*

As he spoke, Ming's mind probed for Martin's. *So, Rick Martin, do you feel my hand squeezing your balls? Of course you do. You know I've got you, that you cannot emerge from this meeting with what you need unless I grant it.*

"It is a profound thing, President Martin, that you come here asking us to do, to join the United States in removing the leader of a sovereign nation. If that were not weighty enough, the leader you would have us remove has nuclear weapons. And your proposed quarantine is actually a blockade and as such is an act of war.

"You assert that the DPRK attacked the United States, destroying Las Vegas with a nuclear bomb. As proof of your assertion you offer a scientific analysis of bomb debris compared to nuclear material you tell us came from Yongbyon. China does not dispute the possibility that such an analysis could be accurate. Like America and the Soviet Union, China has made considerable use of such analyses in the past, and we understand that a great deal can be determined by analysis of fallout. But you are asking us—and indeed the world—to accept the United States' assurance that the comparison sample is indeed from Yongbyon. All hinges on that. You will, I'm sure, not take offense when I say we must consider this most carefully."

With an expression that perfectly suited a cat playing with a mouse, Ming continued: "Well, this has been a most useful opening session. I thank you all for your candid and helpful statements, each illuminating the situation faced by the United States from a different perspective, perspectives that I'm sure President Martin appreciates and will consider most carefully.

"The morning has flown; unless there are objections, I propose we adjourn for lunch."

Ming looked at Martin challengingly and, hearing nothing, nodded and pushed back from the table.

In a large, airy room well provisioned with drinks and finger foods, the delegations swirled like schools of fish, now intermingling, now separating. The conversations in five languages were an interpreter's nightmare, with those harassed individuals constantly scanning to see where they were needed and hustling to position themselves. President Ming, ever the genial host, worked the room. Approaching the Americans, who were in conversation with the Russians, Ming caught Martin's eye and pointed aside with his chin. Martin took his leave and joined him, trailed by his Chinese interpreter and his Secret Service agent, Wilson.

"May we talk for a moment in private, Mr. President?"

"Of course, President Ming, and please call me Rick."

Ming ushered Martin to a door and opened it. Following Ming into the room, Martin saw two men whose backs were turned. One wore khaki trousers and jacket; the other, a dark suit. At the sound of their entrance the two men turned.

Martin felt shock so profound he nearly stumbled—the man in khaki was Kim Jong-il.

Kim smiled and strode confidently toward Martin, who stood as if rooted. Ming spoke through his interpreter: "I thought it would be helpful if you two met." Ming gave Martin an avuncular pat on the shoulder; then he and his interpreter left the room.

Rick's brain exploded: *Jesus! Here I am with this guy, and there's no Korean interpreter except his. It's now on record that we've met and talked, and there are no bilingual witnesses but his guy. Kim or Ming can later announce whatever they want about our discussion, and there's only my word to contradict them. Maybe I should just leave the room . . . no, then Kim would figure I'm unwilling to listen; it might prevent a dialogue that could lead him to step down.*

Ming, you bastard!

Suddenly Kim was in front of him, holding out his hand, smiling face masked by those trademark sunglasses. Reflexively, Martin took Kim's hand and then almost jerked free as he wondered whether he should take the hand of someone who had recently killed about eighty thousand people. Martin was rattled, speechless. His interpreter was not and took out a notepad. Seeing that matter-of-fact action helped Rick get a grip.

Kim acted as if this were a normal first meeting between heads of state. He spoke and paused for his interpreter.

"Good afternoon, President Martin. I'm very pleased to meet you. I'm quite delighted to meet a serving American president, at last. This has been my wish for twenty years."

Martin's ability to begin speaking before he had decided what to say— sometimes a blessing, sometimes a curse—kicked in.

"Mr. Kim, this is a surprise . . . I'm not sure how you wish to be addressed."

"Oh, Kim will do."

Finding his feet, Martin bored in.

"Kim, why did you do it? Why did you bomb Las Vegas?"

"I did not, Mr. President. You have made a very great mistake by accusing my dear people and me of attacking you."

"Kim, we have proof that the bomb was North Korean."

"No, you have only brazen lies! You concocted a so-called Yongbyon sample, making it match your sample from Las Vegas."

Martin's jaw dropped, then snapped closed, seeming to catapult his words. "Kim, I believe you and your regime are responsible and I am going to act on that belief! The United States and the other nations meeting here today will not allow you to continue to rule North Korea, nor will we allow North Korea to keep its nuclear weapons."

Like the governor that keeps an engine from over-speeding, a voice spoke in Martin's head: *Watch it! You're getting angry. Don't let him turn this into a chest-thumping contest. You mustn't let yourself care whether or not you face him down or what he thinks of you. The goal is a nuclear-free Korea ruled by someone less dangerous than Kim. Focus on that.*

Kim adopted a pained expression. "Mr. President, my dear people depend on me. They would be lost without me. It would be very difficult to leave them.

"We need not quarrel, Mr. President. The Democratic People's Republic of Korea wants only to be the friend and ally of the United States. For many years I have tried to reach an agreement of mutual respect and nonaggression. Each of your predecessors ignored my offers.

"I am a patient man, and despite your false accusations I bear you no ill will. Eventually you will discover that a regrettable error was made by your scientists. I'm sure our countries can then reach an agreement."

Holding a hand out, palm up, Martin said, "Kim, I share your concerns for your dear people. It is possible that they would, regrettably, be harmed if you refuse to step aside. Thinking of them, I ask you to consider this: Many Americans want me to order a nuclear strike on your country. Of those who oppose such a drastic measure, most believe you *must* give up power, if not by agreement then by economic and military force. We bear your dear people no ill will and will help them with trade and support for economic development after you leave and the country is nuclear free. But they will suffer if we are forced to compel you to go."

Casually, Kim removed his sunglasses and held them out. His interpreter took them.

Kim erupted in agitated, impassioned speech. "Mr. President Rick Martin, you are disrespectful to the people of Korea and to me! My patience has limits. You speak to me without sincerity, without honesty, and without respect! We will not accept this!"

His guttural words continued, incomprehensible to Martin, lava from Kim's depths. Kim's interpreter paddled valiantly in the torrent of Korean, trying not to get swamped by the fiercely swirling words.

He sounds like President Gwon, exploding because he feels disrespected! But what else could I say to him? Rick stepped back, stomach stabbing, sweat popping at his hairline.

Taking a step forward, Kim said, "We demand you respect us! You do not have the power to bend us to your will. If you attack us in any way, we will turn Seoul into a lake of fire! We will make Japan a radioactive wasteland! We will kill your invading soldiers in such number that their bodies will pile as high as Mount Baekdu!"

Kim's face distorted. His eyes narrowed and their obsidian pupils glared at Martin, who was unable to banish the thought that this was like watching Jack Nicholson play one of his manic characters.

Wilson, who usually tuned out the president's conversations, felt Kim's hostility and went on the alert, planning what he would do if the man laid hands on Martin.

Gathering himself, Martin started to speak, but Kim hurtled on, fists clenched at his sides: "And do not think those you are with today will help you, Rick Martin! I have been listening. Gwon and Kato will not help you; they do not dare face my people's weapons. Ming and Volkov will not either! China needs my leadership of Korea and the Russians hate you and want you to fail."

Rick was hypnotized by the utter chaos and pure hate in Kim's eyes, which seemed to attack his soul.

"No, I do not fear either your diplomatic efforts or your nuclear missiles!" Spittle sprayed. "Your people recently tasted nuclear destruction. The Japanese people remember their suffering. Neither will risk another bath in atomic fire, a bath that I promise them if you threaten—"

Ming reentered the room and Kim stopped in mid-sentence. An eerie calm settled across his face. He held out his hand to Martin, who ignored it. Pausing for a beat with hand outstretched, Kim said, in passable English, "A pleasure, Mr. President," and stepped toward Ming.

"Thank you for arranging this meeting, President Ming. It was most productive."

Ming nodded, grasped Martin's elbow, and guided him out of the room.

Ming halted apart from the others in the reception room and spoke quietly through Martin's interpreter. "Rick, I know you are angry with me, but I have done you a favor. I have given you an opportunity to take the measure of Kim in private so that you will know who you are dealing with. When your anger fades, you will appreciate that, I'm sure."

Martin, tight-lipped, nodded.

"I leave it to you whether to mention this to the others." Ming shook Martin's hand with a smile and ambled off toward the South Koreans.

Chapter 32

RICK'S THOUGHTS SWIRLED as delegations resumed their places. *Should I say something now? Yes. That'll put me back in the driver's seat; besides, if I don't take the initiative, Ming will spring it whenever it suits him.*

Ming, thinking to stir the pot by calling on Volkov, caught Martin's motion and recognized him instead.

"President Ming, I now have even more to thank you for. Ladies and gentlemen, through our host's good offices I have just had a brief meeting with Kim Jong-il."

The many English speakers in the room went on alert like pointers, unsettling those awaiting translation.

"I can tell you I felt our meeting was useful but not productive. Kim denied his attack. After I rejected his denial and called on him to step aside for the good of Koreans, he became angry and started shouting. He threatened to destroy Seoul and Tokyo, as well as defeat any invasion and bathe the U.S. in atomic fire, as he put it. He also said that diplomatic efforts to remove him would fail. I'm summarizing now from memory, but my Chinese-language interpreter took notes of what I said and of the English translation as Kim spoke. I will make those notes available."

Martin watched his counterparts as the tulips winked out one by one. Gwon looked alarmed, Kato concerned, Volkov eager to speak, and Ming wore a slight, wry smile.

Rick gave Volkov no opportunity. "Some of you—certainly President Ming—have experience working with Kim. We will all benefit from your observations and comments. For myself, I have the sense that Kim is off balance and fears that this group of nations can, indeed, force him to give up power. I find that encouraging and I suggest we redouble our efforts around this table so that we do just that."

Watching the tulips flicker, Martin scribbled a note to Battista: When I write my memoirs, I'm going to call this chapter 'waiting on the tulips.'

Battista smiled, nodded, and passed the note to the other Americans.

Dimitri Volkov watched them and wondered if a trap was being laid. Were Ming and Martin setting him up? Was that "surprise" meeting part of their plan to marginalize Russia?

Deciding to preempt any such move, Volkov seized the floor, barely waiting for Ming's recognition. He asserted that Kim threatened South Korea and Japan because they had allowed themselves to become U.S. client states. This triggered a long, angry response from Gwon that amused Martin, who allowed himself a smirk. There, Dimitri—now you see for yourself how difficult it is to deal with Koreans!

While the heads of state were engaged, a group of officials nearby were struggling to agree on a communiqué. Anne Battista, part of her mind following the leaders' discussions, reviewed the latest draft. This would never do! She could see the headlines: Leaders Fail to Reach Agreement. The document was a dollop of pabulum that deplored the attack but spoke only of "agreeing to consider appropriate measures" when the attacker had been "conclusively identified." She murmured to Eric Easterly, then slipped out the door.

Martin was less than half-listening to Volkov about the critical uncertainties and grave dangers of taking action against a sovereign state on the basis of unverified information. *I think I detect movement in our direction. When I put it all together, with allowance for Chinese subtlety, I believe Ming's hinting that he could be convinced. Of course, he's already convinced—he knows damn well it was Kim's bomb and that we know it the same way we knew about China's HEU in Pakistan's bomb tests. I think he's preparing the record for a shift in position and signaling me to come horse-trade.*

Volkov rolled on, conveying in diplomatic terms that it would be a cold day in hell before the Russians supported the sanctimonious bastards who had lectured them about dealing with the Chechens.

Slipping into her seat, Battista passed a note to the president. Martin examined her under arched eyebrows. She nodded.

"Mr. Chairman, I wonder if we could have a short recess."

Ming looked around and, seeing no objection, agreed.

After moving into a corner of the room—which, they assumed, was bugged—Martin turned to Battista.

"Anne, that's good timing. I was thinking Ming is shifting and signaling it's time for the two of us to talk. So what's the problem with the communiqué?"

"We're at an impasse. Let me show you" Warily, Battista wrote on a steno pad:

If you bring Ming, can force Gwon into line, leave only Russians out of quarantine. Without Ming, only Kato with us. Ming's price probably Taiwan.

I've got to get a quarantine agreement, thought Rick. *Lots of people are demanding a military response and I can't ignore them, even though they're wrong. Without quarantine, my softest military option is gone and I'm looking at invasion, bombing, or nukes. By protecting them from Chinese attack, we've given the Taiwan government over fifty years to work out an agreement with China. I don't think history will judge us too harshly if I call a halt to that when the stakes are this high.*

Martin scribbled "OK," then scanned for Ming and saw that, although appearing to be in conversation with his foreign minister, Ming was watching him. Martin nodded and walked in Ming's direction.

Ming met him and motioned toward the same door through which Martin had passed to meet Kim. *Remember who you've got to deal with—you need my help.*

Trailed by their interpreters, foreign ministers, and bodyguards, the two entered the room. Ming looked at Martin with a neutral expression, silent. Rick felt his heart accelerate.

"President Ming, history will not deal kindly with us if we fail to find a way short of nuclear retaliation to deal with despots like Kim."

"President Martin, history's verdict reflects the writer. China will write a lot of the history of the twenty-first century."

Martin said, "You and I could talk for hours. There would be many things we agree on. I think they would outweigh the matters where we don't agree. I wouldn't say that to Dimitri Volkov."

Ming looked at him, expressionless.

Rick's anger surged and he didn't banish it immediately. *You sonofabitch! You're not going to help me at all, are you? All right—let's get this over!*

Straining to keep his voice even, catching himself before hands clenched into fists, Martin said, "I will impose a quarantine on North Korea. If China does not support it, I fear military confrontations between our forces. I'm sure neither of us wants that, but it could happen, without either of us intending it."

Pulling a battered cigarette case from his pocket, Ming said, "Military confrontation is possible, Mr. President, but my concern is greatest in another area, the Taiwan Straits."

Martin waited, searching Ming's round, bland face, hoping Ming would continue, but he did not. He was making Martin propose the betrayal. In the long silence, an aide lit Ming's cigarette.

"So, let's resolve both our concerns now," said Martin. "It would resolve America's concern if China undertook, at this meeting and at the UN, to support a quarantine of North Korea by sea, land, and air. If China did not challenge U.S. actions at sea and did not allow North Korea to use Chinese airspace or export through China, that would resolve U.S. concern. How might the United States resolve China's concern?"

Eyes hooded, Ming exhaled, then replied, "If certain U.S. military undertakings with the rebel government of Taiwan Province were set aside, I would no longer fear confrontation in either area."

Rick nearly choked on his words: "I see a clear alignment of our interests in this matter. I suggest we instruct our foreign ministers to work out the specifics."

Burying the sound of victory beneath a glacial tone, Ming replied: "Yes. They should be able to do that in the next few minutes, do you not agree?"

Rick's stomach flopped. *Is there no way to build trust here?* Then he nodded.

Ming dropped his cigarette, crushing it heavily as he spun away from Martin, then strode to the door. Martin followed him back to the conference room.

Ming made a short, graceful statement that China had concluded, reluctantly, that quarantine was necessary. At Kato's suggestion he called it an outbound quarantine. Ming even managed to avoid saying China accepted American evidence of Kim's culpability, terming the quarantine "a necessary interim step while evidence is gathered and evaluated."

As Ming's words were translated, Martin observed their impact. Gwon looked angry but also stricken. Kato remained unruffled. Volkov smirked, knowing he had forced Martin to crawl and pay a high price. To his left, he saw Battista huddled with her South Korean counterpart. He knew what she was saying: join us, or no ship or aircraft that has touched South Korea will be allowed to enter the U.S. Nor will South Korean companies be allowed to do business in America. They all knew the South Korean economy couldn't withstand that.

Notes were passed and Gwon gave in. South Korea joined the quarantine.

President Gwon Chung-hee stalked from the meeting in a black rage. The Americans had ruined his presidency by accusing the north and today they had humiliated him. He felt a nudge; his foreign minister leaned close and whispered that President Volkov would like a few minutes. Gwon smiled and followed him.

Chapter 33

SHORTLY AFTER SEEING his other guests off, President Ming sat down in his study with Kim. Ming wanted to savor his success over a favorite meal, followed by puttering in his garden, but knew he could not relax in the long summer twilight until he had spoken to Kim.

"Comrade Kim, I trust you feel this has been helpful."

Kim, who knew Ming didn't like him, hid his own dislike, as he always did with the Chinese leaders. He replied in Ming's language, "Indeed, Comrade Ming. I thank you for arranging my meeting with Martin."

"What did you think of him?"

"Unsure of himself when confronted. He doesn't know how to deal with a leader who doesn't fear U.S. power."

"Comrade Kim, I have been advised that the American scientists made a mistake; this bomb was not yours. But, the Americans are skilled at this analysis, as are we Chinese. It is unlikely they would be wrong twice. It would be very uncertain and very challenging if they were to point to you a second time."

Ming stared at Kim, who returned his look unfazed, silent. "Comrade Kim!" he said, more sharply than he intended. "An elder cousin cannot protect a younger cousin, no matter how he may wish to, if the younger is foolish!"

"Elder cousin, I am not foolish."

Ming stood and extended his hand. "I'm sure you are anxious to return to your dear people."

Kim smiled, shook hands, and took his leave. He took pleasure in remaining silent about the second bomb, the one Fahim was waiting for, the one that would show the world that he, Kim Jong-il, had brought the Americans to their knees.

* * *

"We got handed our heads!" said Easterly, making a chopping motion with his right hand that made ice cubes in his glass tinkle. He polished it off with a grimace, as if the tea were castor oil.

He was sitting with Secretary of State Anne Battista and National Security Advisor John Dorn in an area of Air Force One designated for senior staff. The richly furnished cabin contained a small table and four chairs and was next to the main galley. The aircraft rushed homeward through black subzero sky, making just over six hundred miles per hour at flight level four zero—forty thousand feet above the earth. Dinner had been served and cleared. The president was in his suite about seventy-five feet forward, maybe sleeping, maybe not.

The hard man continued, shaking his head. "Can you *believe* that Kim Jong-il? He's decided we can't get to him and is telling the United States to go fuck itself! And that's what the South Koreans, Chinese, and Russians told us, too, just a hair less directly. We had to pay in blood to get Ming's cooperation, and I'm sure when I talk with his defense minister about quarantine ops the haggling will start all over again. The ROKs will be even worse! Only the Japanese are really with us!"

"Come on, Eric—it wasn't *that* bad!" Battista glared at the defense secretary, thinking that the man had absolutely no subtlety. "We did better than you think.

"The president reinforced his personal relationship with each of his opposites—excepting Kim, of course—and that will come in handy later on. You and I had some useful nuts-and-bolts conversations with our counterparts about ways to put military and diplomatic pressure on Pyongyang. Rome wasn't built in a day. You didn't *actually* think each of them would just salute"—she made a vague wave toward her temple—"and ask where to sign up to our plan, did you?"

"No, but I figured we'd at least get willing support for the quarantine."

"*At least*? Eric, supporting quarantine is a *huge* undertaking for Gwon and Ming! They've had very little time to consider it. I'd have been stunned if they'd agreed easily, figured Scott's boys and girls must have slipped something into their green tea!"

"How do you think the Kim meeting went down with the president?" said Dorn.

"I think he was surprised at how Looney Tunes the guy is!" said Easterly.

"Yeah, he was surprised, but he realized that he could outmaneuver Kim, that Kim's world was unreal, that he could be manipulated," said Battista.

"What about Kim's threats?" said Dorn.

"That was the best news of the trip!" said Easterly. "When somebody who's just murdered eighty thousand of your people tells you to your face he'll do it again if you piss him off, it has to get your attention. I think the president needed to hear that."

"What do you mean, Eric?" Battista said, her arms folded across her chest and her face wearing a skeptical look.

Easterly sighed and grimaced. "Anne, what I mean is that the president has, from day one, refused to discuss using nuclear weapons against North Korea. But those weapons are our best military option, in fact our only realistic military option. I mean, we sure as hell aren't going to invade and chase Kim out with our infantry—he's got as many soldiers as we do, plus several million local defense forces, and they've spent fifty years digging in on some of the most rugged terrain you can imagine."

"Can we make the quarantine work with the support we've got?" said Dorn.

"Yes and no," said Easterly. He planted both feet on deck and gave a shove, tilting his chair and extending a footrest. Feet up, he went on: "We can seal them off pretty well by sea, especially if the president gives us a free hand. But stopping aircraft—that's a big problem. To be honest, we probably can't, at least not without shooting at civilian planes."

"But can we *look* like we're sealing them off?" said Battista.

"For a little while. But the press will dig hard to catch us out, to show we're exaggerating. It's what they *do*," said Easterly with a shrug.

Dorn looked at him. "Eric, let's go back to options. I'm wondering if there's another one—short of bombing, invading, or using nuclear weapons."

"You mean a special ops option? "

"Yeah, or CIA."

Easterly grinned. "My question to you is, 'to do what?'"

Dorn and Battista looked at him mutely.

"Yeah, you see the problem. The United States doesn't assassinate leaders of other countries. When you eliminate that, what's left for a special op or the CIA, kidnapping? No way that's doable! We could kill him, maybe, if all the stars aligned. But grab him and hustle him out of his own country, a country he controls absolutely and where our guys are as obvious as Martians? Impossible!"

"What about using spec ops to destroy their nuclear capability?" said Battista.

"How?" Easterly's hands flew wide, palms up. "The facility at Yongbyon is large. Spec Ops troops could never lug enough conventional explosive to seriously damage it. Plus, there're probably other facilities that we don't know about and couldn't penetrate if we did. No, if we want to take out their nuclear weapons, it's a job for missiles and planes, not spec ops. And, short of using nukes, it's no sure thing."

Rick lay on his bed, mind churning.

The short-term, tactical thinking at that table today was shocking—crazy! Well, no, Ming's thinking, and Kato's, is strategic. But Gwon and Volkov were so focused on the pre–Six-thirteen universe I can scarcely believe it!

Kato—now there's a clever guy! By explicitly expressing confidence in U.S. protection from Kim's missiles when he supported me in that meeting, he obligated me to do just that. After I refused in private, he got what he needed by going public and daring me to refuse again.

Ming forced me to do something many will call feckless and disgraceful. Well, there was no choice. Now I have to figure out how to deliver the news to the Taiwanese government and how to announce it. That's going to be a bitch!

No doubt—I put the needs of our tribe above the needs of outsiders. He smiled; *Ella would approve. And, it was my decision. There wasn't any "we" about this. I feel vulnerable but also good, and I'm sure it was the right call.*

And Kim! I've certainly seen delusional thinking before—it's not that rare in politics—but never someone who expressed his delusions with a nuclear weapon. With a jolt he remembered Kim yelling that he would bathe his opponents in nuclear fire.

But wait a minute. This isn't just me and Kim, like two gunslingers. Messy and disappointing as it was, the summit produced agreement between four nations to a quarantine that will keep Kim from getting another nuke out of North Korea.

I've put Kim in a box. Still . . .

Rick shoved doubts into the lockbox where he kept unwanted realities, commanded his mind to go blank, and concentrated on deep breathing until sleep took him.

Chapter 34

BRUCE GRIFFITH BOUNDED onto the platform as if he were campaigning, smiling and waving to the reporters gathered at Creech Air Force Base, followed by Fisher, Karnow, and Cantwell. *The timing is great,* he thought—*this'll get lots of coverage. Not only are the president and the White House press corps in flight, off the radar for sixteen hours, the president isn't bringing home anything to celebrate. Sorry, Mr. President—I tried to tell you, but you didn't listen.*

"First question!" Griffith made a show of scanning the room, then chose the one he'd preselected for his pugnacity. "OK, Larry," said Griffith, pointing to a reporter in the second row.

"Mr. Vice President, the administration's response to Six-thirteen has had an ad hoc, make-it-up-as-you-go quality that has disturbed and angered many people. Many victims suffered because shelter and food were slow to arrive and distributed carelessly. Why were you so unprepared?"

Griffith stopped just short of licking his chops before saying, "Larry, of *course* our response was ad hoc! In the blink of an eye, about five hundred thousand innocent people were smashed into a mix of dead, wounded, and homeless persons, and in the desert at that! No government prepares at scale to deal with an attack of this size. We certainly had plans, well-practiced plans, but never rehearsed on this scale.

"I'm not *apologetic* that our response had an ad hoc quality, I'm *proud* that it did! Because, if it didn't, we'd still be standing around with our thumbs you-know-where, waiting for someone to hand us a plan. The people led by these men with me have done a heroic and, I'd even say, inspired job of improvising. They continue to do that every day. I'm damn proud to be associated with their efforts!"

The vice president's eyes sparkled. He waved his arm as if painting a heroic mural on the wall behind the press, who were scribbling furiously.

"But what about the slow arrival of food, shelter, clothing, and other relief supplies?"

Griffith devoured the question like a hungry man eating breakfast.

"Slow? What's slow when you're working on this scale? Remember, folks, when you include victims and survivors' family members, whom we're also supporting out here, we're dealing with a group about as large as the whole U.S. Army. Even the entire supply chain of Wal-Mart doesn't hold enough food and bedding at one time to take care of that many! And even if it did, it would take every eighteen-wheeler in North America a month to move it here."

Griffith didn't know whether that was true or not, but he knew the press didn't know, either. His stance challenged them, Wyatt Earp ready to clear leather.

"So you're saying that everything that *could* have been done to prepare for this *was* done, and everything that's been done since Six-thirteen was right—there are no lessons to be learned, nothing to do differently?"

"No, not at all! There *are* lessons in this. First, we must never again let ourselves get in such a position that a rogue state like North Korea would have so little concern for our retaliation that they attack us. And, if I may put on my other hat for a moment, my Homeland Security hat"—Griffith placed an imaginary hat on his head—"we need to realize that we can no longer permit our borders to be porous, and we are probably going to have to readjust the balance between civil liberties and national security.

"I know that's not a popular thing to say in some quarters. But I think most people, whatever their feelings prior to Six-thirteen, if they dealt up close and personal—day after day—with the destruction, pain, suffering, and broken lives caused by this murderous attack, would agree: when you balance the possibility of abuse against the flesh-and-blood reality of Las Vegas, you give primacy to defeating new attacks over theoretical concerns that American officials might abuse temporary emergency powers."

"Mr. Vice President, there are rumors that you had a very persuasive conversation with the CEO of a food service company that should best remain unidentified. Can you confirm that and tell us what happened?"

Griffith fought off the grin about to burst forth, holding it to a modest smile. "Well, yes, I did. I won't accept business-as-usual responses in this crisis! Again, I suppose that comes from spending a lot of time with the victims of this despicable attack. I felt that particular company wasn't giving its all-out support, which we sorely needed, and felt the CEO probably didn't understand our situation here. He needed to see for himself. I made that possible and also gave him an overview of the situation as I saw it. Armed with that new information, the CEO returned to his company and led them in much-improved performance, for which I am most grateful."

When the appreciative laughter subsided, Griffith continued: "And that reminds me of a thought I had earlier, regarding the speed of our response. I guess I got off onto some other aspect. Anyway, someone commented about lack of speed in our response. I want to make another point about that.

"I'm well aware of the saying 'when you want it bad, you get it bad.' When it came to, say, temporary housing, we certainly wanted it bad. I had a choice. I could insist on rigorous contracting and quality control measures in order to avoid or at least reduce fraud, waste, and abuse. But that would take more time, too much time in my judgment. I decided to minimize processes in order to get tents and trailers here as quickly as humanly possible. As a result, we've had to discard some because of shoddy or unsafe workmanship, and, as sure as I'm standing here, there is someone listening on TV or radio that is cheating the people of Las Vegas and the nation. I say to that person and others like him, shame on you! If I catch you, you'll bitterly regret your scamming at the expense of these sufferers. But I won't let fear of the few like you delay us in getting aid to those who so desperately need it!"

The vice president performed for about forty-five minutes. His delighted press pool preened and lobbed targets into the kill zone of his rhetorical missiles. It was a win-win, with the media getting video that spread virally across blogs and cable and talk shows, and Griffith getting the opportunity to sound on top of things—decisive and inspiring.

Later it would be clear that on this day the tide of American opinion turned against the president's strategy.

* * *

Siebersdorf, Austria

Erika van Bruntland sighed and shifted in her chair. She was balancing the good of her organization, and her career, with an unwelcome truth in the report before her.

Erika was short, florid, loved Dutch beer, was addicted to *Gauloises* cigarettes, and fought a losing battle to follow the instructions of her keen mind
to take better care of herself. That keen mind was now wrestling with a problem for the International Atomic Energy Agency (IAEA) Safeguards Analyti-
cal Laboratories, which she headed.

Entitled with perfect bureaucratic opacity, "Forensic Analysis of Certain
Plutonium Isotopes," the report contained a sensational and potentially deadly
conclusion: the isotopic signature of a sample of the Las Vegas fallout,
obtained independently by the IAEA, matched that of a plutonium sample
taken by the IAEA from piping at Yongbyon. That sample had been taken in
1990 by inspectors observing a strict protocol and chain of custody, with the
permission of the North Koreans. The IAEA's Yongbyon sample was genuine
and unadulterated—unchallengeable, unless one alleged the IAEA was knowingly part of a U.S. deception. The lab had also compared the IAEA's Yongbyon sample to that alleged by the United States to be a sample from
Yongbyon. They matched. The U.S. accusation of North Korea had a credible
scientific basis.

The problem, she knew, was that the IAEA director-general didn't want to
point to North Korea, because that might set the stage for the country's
nuclear destruction by the United States. The fact that the UN secretary-general was South Korean made his predicament even worse.

Unfortunately for the director-general, the U.S. government had asked
the IAEA to gather and analyze a sample of the Las Vegas fallout, and he felt
unable to refuse. Also unfortunately for him, the manager responsible for the
analysis was van Bruntland.

It wasn't that she cared much for the United States or its policies; it was
that she cared for science and truth and fairness and had courage. Somewhere
in her DNA was the readiness to risk all to do the right thing that had moti-
vated some of her countrymen to protect Dutch Jews from the Nazis. Van
Bruntland had slow-rolled the lab work and report, but she had not yielded to
pressure to "overlook" the agency's own Yongbyon sample.

I'm going to play this absolutely straight, she thought. *Even so, I'm going to
make some of the bigs furious.* She felt her stomach jump. *I've got my pension, but
I'm scared.*

Van Bruntland closed the cover with a snap, heaved herself to her feet, and
left her office, telling her secretary she was going to confer with her boss.

Chapter 35

RICK PUT DOWN the report he had been reading and Ella said, "So what about Kim? What's your gut saying about the prospects of getting him to give up his nukes or step aside?"

They were sitting in the one room of the White House that was truly theirs. Officially it was "The Washington Sitting Room," but at Ella's insistence it had been redecorated: every stick of furniture, everything on the walls, every piece of décor had come from their home. "When we leave," she had said, "Washington can have his room back."

He massaged his temples, then stood and began to pace. "I wasn't at my best when we met—it was such a total surprise! Still, I pushed him—*hard*—on his responsibility for Las Vegas. I told him clearly he had to step aside or there would be severe consequences."

Scowling, Rick continued: "But the way it ended, he may have gotten the impression he can run over me, because we got interrupted. Like I said, he was raving like a Jack Nicholson character about destroying Japan and South Korea, and piling up a mountain of dead U.S. soldiers. Then, Ming comes in and Kim stops in mid-sentence, thanks me—in English, no less—turns and thanks Ming, and then Ming ushers me out. I didn't have a chance to respond to his anger and threats. He might think I had no response, that he bullied me into silence. That concerns me."

"What Kim may think won't matter if we kill him, like bin Laden."

Rick's eyes widened. "Ella, how can you say that? Kim's not some terrorist; he's the head of state of a nation with twenty million people and a seat in the UN!"

"Rick, Kim is the absolute ruler of a country we call a state sponsor of terrorism! Why doesn't that make him a terrorist, more dangerous than bin Laden was? Kim kills over twenty times more Americans than bin Laden, but we won't touch him? Explain that!"

"Dammit, Ella! I will *not* become a killer in order to deal with one. . . . Besides, it's too personal. Everybody would see it that way."

"Rick, with the radiation deaths, Kim has now killed about eighty thousand Americans. *Shouldn't* it be personal?"

"But he's a head of state. If we open that can of worms, where does it stop? Do we take out the leader of every country that we fear, that we disagree with? Do other nations start doing that? Once that genie is out of the bottle, the world's nations are essentially at endless war with each other—there's nothing to stop those who say, "She disagrees? Kill her!""

His face working, Rick turned away and stared out the window. A thunderstorm had engulfed Washington, announcing a respite from the day's heat.

Rising, Ella said to his back, "Do you worry that Kim might bomb us again because he thinks he cowed you?"

"No, he knows our identification technology works and would point to him. He'd have to expect a nuclear attack in response."

"Would he be *right* to expect that, Rick?"

The president was silent. Ella waited. He said in a low voice, "I'd have to consider it seriously. It would be about all we could do . . . and I'd be impeached otherwise."

Ella gripped his shoulder and her voice was hard and sharp, a blade: "Could you give the order, Rick?

He turned but didn't answer. His eyes met hers, then cut away. Staring over Ella's shoulder, Rick said, "Well, I still have time to think about that. It may not come to it. I'm determined that it *won't* come to it! Look, we've got a lot of balls in the air now. We're sealing off North Korea so no more bombs get out. We're pushing hard at the Security Council, and my speech to the General Assembly could put us over the top."

His speech accelerating, as if velocity gave certainty, Rick said, "And then there's Ming Liu. I think the reason he sprang that meeting with Kim was to show that Kim is erratic and defiant, but he has leverage over him. He wanted to demonstrate how much the United States needs China's support. I know Ming wants more than we can afford to give, but I don't see why we can't meet in the middle. After all, Ming can't want to see me forced into using nukes right next door to China!"

Rick's like a fox, thought Ella, *surrounded by hunters and dogs, darting to familiar escapes only to find them blocked. He's being driven toward the corner he fears most, toward a decision only two other presidents ever faced. He's still twisting and turning, trying to squirm through openings, thinking he can outrun the jaws of his duty, but they're getting closer.*

Ella's eyes filled and her throat ached. *He believes he can escape, but he can't. The president can't. Oh, God! What will those jaws do to Rick's soul!*

I've never faced anything like this. How can I help him?

Chapter 36

THE WORLD'S CORRESPONDENTS, editors, anchors, pundits, and "experts" of all sorts shouted with the frenzy of songbirds' dawn chorus in mating season. The most titillating aspect of the UN special session on combating nuclear terrorism was that Kim Jong-il would attend "to correct and rebut the vicious lies and fabrications of the arrogant and foolish President Martin." Some journalists saw Kim's decision as a sign that he respected Martin and wanted to engage diplomatically to work things out. Others said Kim had bullied him in Beijing and was coming to the UN to do it again. That week a video portraying Kim as a trash-talking criminal threatening a bumbling Martin made YouTube's Most Popular list.

As the hour for his speech approached, the president sat with Oscar Neumann, Bart Guarini, and Anne Battista in Neumann's UN office. As they talked, Sam Yu worked the phones, breaking off when Martin beckoned.

"Sam, what does it look like to you right now? What's the story line?"

"Well, Mr. President, there's no doubt Kim's going to drive a lot of the coverage. Many are going to lead it as a sort of OK Corral showdown, with words instead of six-shooters. Some will approve, maybe recalling Churchill's comment, 'to jaw, jaw is better than to war, war.' Others will play it as a predictable consequence of your decision to work through the UN, one that grants a world audience and de facto equality to Kim and puts the United States in the dock."

Martin grimaced. "So what can you do to mute the negatives?"

Yu glanced at her bleeping smart phone, silenced it, and said, "Well, a lot depends on Kim." She ticked off points as she spoke. "If he disagrees in a sober, diplomatic way, we say that you wisely brought him to the table to give peace a chance. If he foams at the mouth, we say you lured him into a public display that demonstrates his erratic and volatile nature. If that happens, we'll imply that his behavior is consistent with the irrationality it would take to attack the United States with a nuclear weapon. On background we'll say: you guys saw him—was that the behavior of a rational man? How could any administration do more than we are to protect the country without resort to our own nuclear weapons?"

We've got the bases covered, she thought, head tilted back to look Martin in the eyes.

Jamming his hands in his pockets, Martin said, "Yeah, either of those spins will help with the Left, but what about the Right, the nuke-'em-til-they-glow bunch?"

Shaking her head, Yu said, "Mr. President, nothing short of removing Kim will placate those groups! They want you impeached because Kim's still there and you haven't pushed the red button. They'll continue to shout about that no matter what you do today."

Rick shrugged. "So how're we doing with the rest?"

"Well, as usual, polling shows people are not thinking about this in a consistent or disciplined way. For example, a large majority is against any measure that would seriously harm large numbers of North Koreans. But when asked more specific questions, turns out they would support actions that caused a lot of Korean casualties if they believed they were necessary to stop further nuclear attacks on the U.S."

The president sighed. "In other words, the majority want me to make the North Korean problem go away but not make *them* feel bad about it!"

Guarini spoke: "So how do we look regionally, Sam?"

Stealing a glance at her vibrating phone, Yu said, "Generally speaking, the closer someone is, geographically or personally, to Las Vegas, the more negatives about how we're handling things. A clear majority in the Northeast think your diplomacy is the right approach. There's an exception to that—right here in New York City. For obvious reasons, the people here feel connected to Las Vegas. Out on the West Coast, opinion splits evenly, but the trend is negative. About two-thirds of those in the South and the Mountain states are negative. The Midwest and upper Midwest are split, with support for you increasing as you move north."

Turning to Martin, Guarini said, "Mr. President, we need to get something out there showing we have a tough Plan B."

"And what is *that*, Bart?" said Battista, eyes flashing.

"Come on, Anne! You know that if what we're doing now—quarantine, the UN, the IAEA, the Northeast Asia Group—doesn't soon show signs of getting Kim out, we've got to try something else. We can't stick with this approach if it's a loser!"

Seeing Battista's hands snap to her hips as she yanked her shoulders back, inhaling to propel her riposte, Rick thought, *great—my two oldest advisors are like eighteen-wheelers about to collide!*

Not far away, President Ming sat with the Chinese permanent representative to the UN. In his office, Ambassador Huang Bo advised Ming from a comfortable chair across a low table.

"Martin is in a very difficult position," said Huang. "None of his initiatives has budged Kim, who proclaims innocence and threatens to destroy South Korea and Japan if attacked. The quarantine is working but only because we have sealed our Korean border, refused over-flight to any aircraft bound to or from the DPRK, and held our navy back. The Americans' polls show a trend away from Martin's policy. He is being undermined not only by Kim's defiance and clever manipulation of opinion but also by his own vice president. Vice President Griffith has become quite popular—something rare in their politics for a vice president—and he is advocating a harder line. Sources tell us that Griffith is quietly contacting legislators, testing their stomach for Martin's removal, which they have the power to do through a process called impeachment. If Martin is impeached, Griffith immediately becomes president. Martin may believe you hold the key to his survival."

Ming peered at him over steepled fingers, then said, "What might he be prepared to offer?" Prior to being appointed to the UN, Huang Bo had several postings to Washington, ultimately as ambassador. Ming thought Huang understood Americans and their government better than anyone else in China's leadership.

"Martin is a man of great self-confidence. Perhaps he does not yet believe his position is as precarious as it is. We Chinese are not being forced by events to take any position. We are not in danger from Kim, or from al-Qaeda. America is facing the dragons: we are not."

Ming was mulling that over when the Americans arrived. During a few minutes of small talk he decided Martin did, indeed, seem supremely confident. But although his senses were dulled by the intervention of interpreters, Ming discerned, the way he might sense an object hidden by the sun's glare, that Martin knew he was running out of time. And Battista: squinting, body taut. He saw her brittleness, the gambler facing long odds but forced to play.

The two leaders and their foreign ministers moved into Huang Bo's official office while he and Neumann went to his private office. Martin said, "President Ming, this is a historic occasion! History will mark it as the point at which mankind turned from the seductive but terribly dangerous path of nuclear proliferation. I'm grateful that you are here."

Ming nodded, holding his face blank.

"Let us talk of history for a moment, the history of your country and mine. Am I correct that you have been briefed, as I have, about the discussion between our governments after the Pakistani nuclear tests in 1998?"

"I certainly recall the tests, but what about them?"

"The U.S. government analyzed gasses that vented from the underground test chambers and determined that some of the nuclear material was of Chinese origin. Our secretary of state called in your ambassador and, I am told, not only protested strongly but identified the Chinese facility that had produced this material."

"Perhaps this occurred as you say. I could make inquiries."

Feeling a weight on his shoulders, Martin thought, *he's not going to deal now. Ming's going to make me come to him, ask for what I want, and then put me off. I'll still need his support next week, next month, and next year; he can take his time, wait for me to put more and more carrots in front of him, knowing I have no sticks. There are things China wants at play in this situation, but not things China needs.*

No, that's not right—China needs North Korea as a buffer! Rick bridled his excitement.

"President Ming, I hope we have the same understanding of the situation between the United States and North Korea. Kim attacked us, and as long as *he* remains in power, we are at risk of other attacks. That is intolerable. But if a coalition removes Kim and his successor agrees to verifiably end their nuclear weapon programs . . . we have no need to further change the character of the

DPRK. China could earn the gratitude of the United States and the entire world if you led such a coalition."

Martin's eyes held Ming's in silence.

Anne Battista gulped. *Rick's so often cited the reunification of Korea as an example of how good might come from the tragedy. He just abandoned that, without even being asked. I know we're in a weak position, but this means Rick's desperate.* She felt slickness on her palms.

That's interesting, thought Ming. *He just told me that North Korea could remain a sovereign, communist nation. Let's see what else he'll give me.*

"Mr. President, what you suggest would be difficult for China, maybe impossible. Perhaps a situation could arise in which such a change would benefit the people of the Democratic Republic. That would be worthy of consideration and further discussion. However, in the few minutes we have left, I would like to hear your plans for nuclear weapons."

Rick winced, stomach acid burning in his throat. *Ming just pocketed my concession and told me the price is higher still. He's got the power and he's going to use it—bastard! Why doesn't he see this is in China's interest?*

Martin resumed: "As important as those plans are, Mr. President, I believe that at this moment there is a more urgent matter. I'm speaking of the U.S. proposal that the Security Council declares the DPRK has committed a breach of international peace and security. Will China support it?"

I don't want Bruce Griffith to replace Martin, thought Ming. *Griffith is far more likely to do the one thing that would cause serious difficulty for us: attack the DPRK. I need to give Martin enough to keep him limping along on the negotiation path, a step or two ahead of impeachment.*

"Mr. President, most assuredly *someone* committed such a breach. But you are asking a great deal of China, to condemn a neighboring, friendly people and accuse them of a very grave act, without conclusive evidence. You are also asking China to take a position that would create disharmony in our relations with the DPRK, which would in turn leave us less able to assist Kim privately in understanding the benefits of restraint and cooperation.

"Yet, *I* know what it is for a nation to lose ninety thousand in a day and see another half million made homeless. That was what we faced after the Sichuan earthquakes in 2008. I understand the forces that arise in such a circumstance, forces demanding government action. Perhaps China could abstain when the Security Council votes. I will discuss this with Huang Bo."

Studying Ming, Rick couldn't read anything in his expression or body language, and Ming's voice itself, rising and falling in the five tones of the Chinese language, was no help. *It's like I'm blind and deaf,* he thought, *trying to wring truth from Braille.* He took a slow, deep breath, fighting panic.

The continuing silence delivered Ming's message. Doggedly, Martin turned to his proposal to counter nuclear terrorism.

"President Ming, the United States will, one way or another, deal with the threat of the Kim regime. But I don't believe that's enough. The destruction of Las Vegas showed the danger, to all nations, of nuclear attack from foolish or nihilistic groups. That attack demonstrates the world has, truly, entered a new era. As I said the very day of that attack, the United States will do more than just deal with North Korea. We will work with others, through the UN and IAEA, to establish effective global safeguards against nuclear terrorism."

This Rick Martin is certainly bold and confident, thought Ming. *A strong proposal, if agreed and enforced, would prevent nuclear terrorism. But that is not a serious threat to China, and, if we were attacked, China could absorb one bomb and then take such vengeance that we would never be attacked again. The bombing of Las Vegas did create a new day for China, but not as Martin believes. What's new is America's desperate need for China's support. I can get a lot in return!*

After reading nothing in Ming's appearance and glancing at his watch, Martin broke the silence. "Will China support this program?"

"We look forward to learning full details. Might this approach resolve your concerns about Kim?"

Always, Ming puts me over a barrel! thought Rick, jaw muscles working. *Now, he wants me to defer dealing with a grave danger, one that threatens China, too, if only he could see that!*

"It certainly could, Mr. President, if the U.S. proposals are adopted quickly."

"China is always interested in exploring proposals to make the world safer."

Martin rose. "It's time for us to go to the General Assembly, Mr. President. I'm glad we've had this conversation and am encouraged by your words."

Trailing her president into the corridor, Battista felt her heart hammer. Martin's reversal on the DPRK had been as fluid and effortless as an Olympic swimmer's flip turn. *Does he have no scruples?* she thought. *And Ming—does he have no appreciation for the dangers?*

Chapter 37

KIM JONG-IL preened at the center of the UN delegation of the Democratic People's Republic of Korea. The great auditorium curved away to his left and right, rows of nations before him descending toward the dais and ascending behind him. Seeing how often other leaders and delegations glanced his way, Kim thought, *once again I have seen and done what others could not.*

I took an old TV spot from Lyndon Johnson's campaign and adapted it using an American media company that thinks its client is Las Vegas Families for Peace. My video creation went viral, as I knew it would. It's so easy to control others when you understand how simply they perceive the world! Primitive though it was in comparison to my work, that "Daisy" spot was a huge success in its day; by juxtaposing childhood innocence and nuclear holocaust, Johnson defined himself as the man of peace and his opponent, Barry Goldwater, as the man of nuclear war. It was the most effective piece of political priming ever produced—until mine.

And my purpose is much more subtle and complex than Johnson's! I'm not just trying to influence beliefs about me or Martin. I'm using emotion to create an alternate reality, in which Americans can be angered by the destruction of Las Vegas while being inoculated against the urge to retaliate with their own nukes. The emotions I've created act as a filter through which Americans interpret information from their government.

And of course it's working perfectly, allowing many Americans to feel anger and patriotism, while triggering their opposition to an attack, particularly a nuclear attack. Their so-called free press writes what I want: "Kim is despicable and dangerous and must go, but we have no quarrel with Korean children, who are already suffering under a U.S.-led quarantine that may well prove to have been unnecessary."

Kim smiled. *I'm looking forward to the next few minutes.*

Anne Battista waited in the chair of the U.S. representative. *For God's sake! Back there Rick offered Ming the chance to put his own man in as Kim's successor! Why didn't he show some interest? I don't know which is worse: the fact that Rick made the offer or that Ming seemed not to even notice.*

Secretary-General Park Chang-su concluded his introduction, and Battista gave her full attention to the scene before her. Applause for Martin was brief and far from universal. Besides Kim's delegation and the Russians, most Middle Eastern delegations sat silent and impassive, as did the South Koreans, several African nations, and a few South Americans.

As she thought about it later, Battista couldn't believe how quickly things unraveled.

Martin framed the destruction of Las Vegas in both American and universal terms, then built the case against North Korea. When he stated unequivocally that Kim was responsible, Kim stood and interrupted, angry but controlled. Like everyone else, Battista got the translation of Kim in one ear and the president in the other. Later, she would watch the video go to split-screen at this point, displaying both men in close-up. With two statements pouring into her ears simultaneously, Battista had difficulty understanding, but clearly Kim was calling Martin a liar and Martin was soldiering on with his speech.

Kim took off his headphones, managing to appear both angry and dignified, and marched out, followed by the DPRK delegation. Martin deviated skillfully from his text to decry Kim's departure and then returned to his themes.

Minutes later, unbeknownst to Martin or Battista, Kim began a press conference that was covered by virtually every cable and network and was shown in split-screen alongside Martin's address to the assembly. While Martin spoke to the remaining diplomats there, Kim spoke to the world about his unceasing efforts for peace despite years of American rejection and arrogance. Periodically an aide handed Kim notes of some point in Martin's speech, and Kim did his best to ridicule and refute it.

As Rick began describing his plan for countering nuclear terrorism, his eye caught a sudden movement to his left. Iran's ambassador was on his feet. *So he's going to stage a walkout. That's not too surprising, and it helps make my point.*

Another flicker of motion. *He threw something! A shoe!* Rick tensed to duck, but saw it fall short.

The Iranian's action was repeated by the representatives of Iraq, Syria, Saudi Arabia, Afghanistan, Yemen, Sudan, Lebanon, Somalia, Congo, Nigeria, Uganda and Zimbabwe. Finally Hugo Chavez, acting as if this had never occurred to him before, heaved a shoe and left. None of the shoes reached Martin, who completed his speech, his shock becoming anger and finally, rage.

As Battista left the auditorium, her British colleague pulled her aside. "Isn't it about time you tell the emperor he's naked? My god, Anne, Martin has been turned aside with fuzzy words by the UN, by NATO, by every country he's asked, including mine. As we stand here, he's being mocked by Kim Jong-il. He's leading a parade, but no one's marching behind him, except a few Left-wing loonies! His diplomacy has gained nothing, and it becomes ever more apparent that the United States has no adequate response to terrorists with nuclear weapons. Martin's dithering endangers us all! Anne, you've got to do something!"

Stunned, Battista nodded, shuffled out with the crowd and fled to Neumann's office.

When she got there, Martin, red-faced and shaking, was berating his ambassador. He glanced her way as she entered but didn't interrupt his dressing-down. White-faced, Neumann said, "Mr. President, I didn't predict this, didn't warn you, because it was not predictable! Nobody in this room, nobody in the U.S. government, suspected this would happen! Who can know the mind of someone like Kim?"

Neumann's taken enough, thought Bart Guarini. *He should have gotten wind of the shoe-throwing plan, but he's right about Kim. The man was not only unpredictable, he was clever. We all underestimated Kim. At least there's a silver lining: this fiasco will help me sell Plan B.*

The chief of staff spoke: "Mr. President, I, too, fault the ambassador for failing to warn of the shoe throwing, but what if he had? It wouldn't have stopped you from speaking or changed what you had to say. And we all—we *all*—underestimated Kim. That's what we need to take away from this and incorporate into our planning going forward."

Bart's right, Rick thought. *I knew Kim was dangerous because he has nuclear weapons but dismissed him as a political force. That was a mistake. He understands the media all too well!*

Martin took a deep, shuddering breath. His determination never to let anger cripple him reasserted itself. "Yeah, Bart, you're right on both counts. Ambassador Neumann, you should have done better about the shoe throwing, but you're right about Kim. I apologize. I guess I should be thankful that nobody in that bunch but Chavez comes from a nation that plays baseball. All the others had lousy arms. Chavez had a pretty good peg, but he was farthest away. Come on, let's go."

As she headed for the helo pad, Battista knew Guarini would have a receptive audience when he pushed Plan B, whatever it was.

Congressman Ray Morales muted the three televisions, leaving a total of ten sets of jaws flapping soundlessly at him from the screens. It was just before seven, so the world had had about nine hours to react to the spectacle at the UN. That was plenty of time for story lines to be shaped and floated; now talking heads and bloggers were hard at work whipping up the mix of support and disagreement they needed to fire up their followers.

Ray had scribbled a few notes as he watched in the morning, then decided he needed some brain time, as he called it. So he sent his chief of staff to the two cocktail parties he was slated to attend. When the last staffer was out the door, Ray locked it, went to the refrigerator, pulled out a beer, and dropped into the one truly comfortable chair.

He took a pull on the beer. *We certainly took a beating today. Kim really sucker-punched Rick Martin!*

Objectively, Kim's performance wasn't all that good. But at the time, the live images—Kim unafraid to go toe to toe with Martin—surely resonated powerfully in parts of the world. So did the shoe throwing. And I know, because I've humped a pack on patrol in some tough neighborhoods: there will be extra attacks on the grunts in the next few weeks because of those images.

His cell phone rang. Caller ID was blocked. He considered ignoring it but then mashed the green button with a blunt finger. In his present mood, if it was a telemarketer, he would enjoy tearing the guy's head off.

"Morales!"

"Ray, this is Bruce Griffith. Thanks for taking my call."

Morales' eyes widened.

"Mr. Vice President, how are you?"

"You mean, other than the play, Mrs. Lincoln, how was your day?"

Ray couldn't help smiling. "Yes sir, I guess that's all I *could* mean."

"Look, Ray, I'll get right to the point. I know you don't like to beat around the bush. I'm sure today's spectacle sickened you, as it did me. I believe—and I'm going a bit off the reservation here—that you and a few others like you need to be in the loop, for the good of the country. So, I'm putting together what you military guys call a Red team. You know, some trustworthy, experienced folks who will tell me the unvarnished truth and, frankly, do some preliminary planning for other options that this administration isn't willing to consider, even after this morning. What do you say?"

Planning for other options? What other options? Assassinating Kim? A strike on North Korea? Could the man be talking about a coup? At the very least he's trying to get me on the impeachment bandwagon!

Carefully, Morales said, "Mr. Vice President, I know what Red teams can do. You've got a good idea there, but I guess I'm a traditionalist. I believe in the unity of command. I'd be honored to serve on a Red team that reported to the president, but this one sounds a little different. So thanks, sir, for thinking of me, but no thanks."

Griffith's voice changed. Its tone said, 'I've done nothing untoward here, and if you ever suggest that, I'll tie you in knots.' "Ray, the team reports to me for now but eventually will report to the president. You'd be a real asset and I'll ask again as the situation develops. Listen, it's nearly eight and you should get home to that lovely wife of yours, Julie—have a good evening and please remember me to her."

"I'll do that, Mr. Vice President."

"Goodbye, Ray"

"'bye sir."

Griffith is smooth and he's got balls . . . I'll say that for him. "Eventually will report to the president"—yeah, when he is president! Well, it seems there's no end to today's surprises. The question is what, if anything, I do about this call. I gotta say I agree we need to come up with some better plans for dealing with Kim. How can I get involved with that? Should I get involved?

I need to talk to Julie!

Morales deposited the bottle in the trash and headed home, oblivious to his surroundings as his mind wrestled with this problem.

Listening to their call a few hours later from an Argus intercept, General Hsu frowned. *Morales' refusal was predictable; Griffith shouldn't have risked asking.* Hsu thought nostalgically about the old days, when NSA only eavesdropped on the Soviets and their helpers. He was walking a fine line now and it scared him.

Chapter 38

HEAD UP, SMILING, Rick strolled along the South Portico. *Things are breaking my way. That IAEA confirmation of Paternity was huge! We're getting some momentum, and I'll bet my numbers are up.*

After Bart and Sam were seated in the Oval Office, Martin said, "I think the IAEA announcement is a game-changer, Sam, don't you?"

Yu thought, *that announcement is a big plus. A game-changer? Uh-uh—but I don't want to burst his bubble.*

"It's a great development, Mr. President—sure silenced the WMD-all-over-again crowd!"

"It's also taken away the Security Council's escape hatch," said Guarini with a grin. "They've had to call Kim's actions a breach of international peace and security. Oscar's done a nice job!"

"Yeah, he believes that before the week is over the council will support our quarantine," replied Martin.

"So how're we doin', Sam?" said Guarini.

"Well, it's a little soon–only forty-eight hours—but even so, there's a five point increase in people who feel the country's on the right track. The newspapers that doubted you are at least no longer expressing those doubts, and some have explicitly changed their positions. With bloggers, less so; they tend to hold their opinions tenaciously."

"What about that war-is-not-the-answer video? You know, the one they call Daisy Two? Have we learned anything about Las Vegas Families for Peace?"

"Only that the organization doesn't exist; it's a cover. That hasn't reduced interest in that video or several others they've posted. The mystery and the power of their messages keep interest up and they spread like wildfire."

"I'm not surprised. I've seen them and they're good! It's pretty effective to use a clip from one of my campaign speeches, where I was pointing out that we don't need to compromise our values to remain secure, and couple that with an assertion that nuclear retaliation would do just that. And, frankly, I agree with them."

"And that's a point we should explore, Mr. President," said Bart. "You might have to go beyond negotiation. Plan B. Remember Glenna Rogers cooked her goose by making a big course change in Iraq without preparing the public; might be we should start, just as a contingency."

"I remember, Bart!" Martin said with a glare. "But this is not the Rogers administration. Our favorables are *much* higher than theirs were, despite the blip caused by adjusting our Taiwan policy."

Adjusting? thought Bart, frowning. *We threw them to the wolves. And the reaction wasn't a blip; it was an eruption.*

"Look, we've put Kim in a box!" continued the president, wagging a finger at Guarini. "He's sealed off. He can bluster and lie all he wants, but that's an irritation, not a danger. Now that there's IAEA confirmation that Kim did it, the Chinese will seriously consider our ideas for removing Kim peacefully, especially since Ming knows I won't push reunification. He can help us dump Kim and still have his communist buffer."

Yu read tension and frustration in Guarini's face as he said, "But suppose Kim got several bombs out of the country *before* the quarantine? Suppose there's a team here now, getting one into position, or waiting for it to arrive on some container ship or an eighteen-wheeler slipping in from Mexico or Canada? If we base our policy entirely on the assumption that we've rendered Kim harmless and then lose another city—"

Interrupting, Martin wore a superior smile. "Bart, suppose you're right? Suppose there *is* a team with a bomb already on the loose? Moving more aggressively against Kim wouldn't change that; they'd still be out there. Where we need to be aggressive is homeland security, to break up any terrorist attack, and Bruce Griffith is certainly doing that!"

Guarini recognized that Rick hadn't accepted or even considered his point; he had just used the debater's trick of redirection to slide by it. That worried him; he had fought to control his friend's reflexive optimism as long as they'd been together.

Seeing he wasn't going to move Martin, Guarini said, "Speaking of the vice president, what are we gonna do about him?"

"What do you mean, Bart?" said Martin, head tilting.

"Sam, what are Griffith's favorables?"

"Pretty darn good, almost as good as the president's and trending up."

Martin shrugged. "I knew that would happen if he was successful, and it doesn't surprise me now. It's a price I'm willing to pay for what Bruce is accomplishing for the country. He's doing well—I say he's earned his favorable numbers."

"Has he earned the right to start greasing the skids for your impeachment?"

Martin's eyes narrowed and he beckoned for more. Yu's jaw dropped.

"I heard from Ray Morales yesterday. He got a call from the vice president that he believes was to sound him out on impeachment. He says Griffith is building a coalition on the Hill to impeach you if there's another attack."

"That doesn't make sense. If there's another attack, *he's* the guy who failed to protect the country; *he's* the guy in charge of stopping attacks!"

"It makes sense if he's built a case against you for preventing him from doing more out of civil liberty considerations, or out of squeamishness about aggressive interrogation. And if you study his press conferences, you can see that thread."

"Sam?"

"If you're asking whether I've heard any impeachment talk, my answer is yes. But I've considered it just background noise from the far Right. This is the first I've heard linking the VP. Oh, I've had some shouting matches with his press secretary about some of his remarks, but like you, I was expecting trouble, so I didn't think his motive was anything more than the usual VP ambition."

Dottie Branson's voice from the intercom: "Mr. President, Ambassador Chernowski is here for his appointment, to present his credentials."

"OK, Dottie, we're wrapping up."

Martin leaned back, crossed his legs, and gazed out a window. *Could Morales be right? Is Bruce beyond the usual ambitions of a vice president? I'd better start paying more attention! I remember Ella worried that Bruce's star would rise too fast.*

He stood. "OK, that'll have to be it for right now. Let's all keep our ears to the ground, but let's also remember that every VP wants to be president and not read too much into this."

"Bart, what's your read? Is Morales angling for something; maybe floating the idea that he'd be a Trojan horse . . . What do you think?"

"I think he's pretty straightforward. Remember when he resigned as Rogers' JCS chairman? He just took off his uniform and went home to Texas—didn't run off to do the talk shows, or write a book, or be a talking head on Fox. He's still pretty much a Marine and I think he's offended by the disloyalty of what Bruce is doing or, I mean, what he *thinks* Bruce is doing."

"OK, thanks. Sam, on your way out, ask Dottie to send in the ambassador.

"Bart, where are the Speaker and the Majority Leader on this?

"They support you, but they haven't clamped down on the discussions."

Which means, thought Rick, *they think Bruce is on to something.*

Chapter 39

IT WAS A typical, sweaty Baltimore summer day and Larry Cosgrove was puzzled. The scarred, grimy sea container on the battered eighteen-wheeler chassis passing slowly through what looked like a giant croquet wicket was sending an unexpected signal. Larry, clad in jeans and a tank top, sat in a hot, windowless room near the Consolidated Data and Inspection Portal (CDIP) at the Seagirt container terminal's exit, monitoring data emitted by each container. These data, transmitted to receivers within the CDIP, identified the container and sometimes also identified specific shipments within it. The portal also contained other sensors that looked for other things, but that wasn't his concern.

Larry worked for a freight consolidator serving shippers without enough cargo to fill an entire "box," forty feet long by eight square. The systems he monitored confirmed that not only had the container arrived, the separate shipments within it were there, as they should be. Nobody had screwed up the container manifest or taken contents out at the last minute to place in another container for some made-sense-at-the-time reason or stolen them.

The extra signal really wasn't his concern, but because he was bored, Cosgrove clicked his mouse. Seconds later a truck driver swore. A yellow LED blinked on his dashboard, signaling him to pull into the further-inspection lane. Moments later, a harsh voice came from the cheap speakers in Cosgrove's computer. "Hey, Larry, what's with APL sixteen four fifty-eight?"

"It's gotta extra emitter," he said through a mouthful of candy bar. "My gear's getting a signal that doesn't correlate to any RFID tag in my system."

"Dammit! This is the fourth load diverted for inspection on my shift. I'm gettin' real fuckin' tired of this shit!"

Cosgrove, who didn't like this particular federal agent at all, flipped him off invisibly and munched the rest of the candy bar.

A stumpy man wearing sweat-marked blue-black fatigues with a badge denoting Customs and Border Protection (CBP) stalked across grease-spotted concrete. Pulling himself up onto the cab steps, he told the driver, "Awright, run us through the Vassis." He was referring to the Vehicle and Cargo Inspection System, or VACIS, another portal, one much more sophisticated than the CDIP.

As the trucker pulled the container through the portal, a light blinked red and a horn sounded. The driver and the CBP officer both swore.

"Bananas! Fuckin' bananas, five'l get you ten." The CBP officer was referring to the tendency of the VACIS to alarm on naturally occurring radiation, such as emitted by bananas, or several kinds of granite, or cat litter, some types of porcelain, and a long list of other harmless items.

"OK. Pull it over to dump and thump." That was the area where CBP opened containers and inspected the contents, sometime removing them—"dump"—and sometimes tapping on them—"thump"—in search of hidden cavities.

During the journey, Gus the CBP officer thumbed his mike and said, "Larry, what's the manifest say for this bitch?"

"It's a grab bag. Consumer electronics, plus some portable generators, and yeah, some toilet fixtures, probably porcelain."

When the truck reached dump and thump, the K9 team—the explosive sniffer—was waiting. As the box was unloaded the handler looked bored; the German shepherd looked happy. When the dog reached the portable generators, he went to alert. The shepherd became elated; the men became engaged.

The handler called out, "K9 has a positive!"

Gus' anger became alertness. The dogs got fooled sometimes, but they were a lot more accurate than the VACIS. Gus keyed his radio. "Blue Diamond. We have a Blue Diamond at site Charlie Three." He and the driver and the K9 backed off about one hundred feet. Other CBP officers set up a security perimeter around the tractor-trailer, which sat patiently in dump and thump with its doors open.

* * *

After working about an hour, army EOD Specialist Breanne Murphy disarmed an explosive device, a relatively small—meaning it wouldn't have killed anyone but her—amount of Semtex rigged to be triggered by a commercial asset tracking and control apparatus.

EOD—Explosive Ordnance Disposal—is a craft that demands an audit trail. If the device blows, it's crucial to know everything the dead technician did, especially the fatal move. Thus, the soldier "in the hole" describes and discusses every finding and every planned action with others at a safe distance.

Murphy paused for a moment, wiping sweat from her face. So, was that it—or was it sucker bait to lull her into tripping a booby trap or failing to search thoroughly enough to find the main charge?

God, it stinks in here! They musta used this box to pack recyclables headed to Asia. But I do love this shit. It's a head game for sure, to make the bet you've got it figured out, then snip the wires and see if you're still alive the next second.

She swigged from her canteen, then carefully, with step-by-step commentary, opened the generator's weather shield and saw something that literally terrified her.

With a mouth so dry she could hardly speak, Breanne said, "Jesus! I see a probable implosion device."

"I ain't Jesus. I'm even better—I'm a first sergeant," said the team leader, observing the edge-liver's code of keeping it light.

"Are you sure?"

"Damn right I am! It's about the size of a basketball."

"Any timing or triggering device?"

"Shit, I can't tell. Not an obvious one but there're a hell of a lot of wires!"

"What's your PRD read?"

Breanne, on her belly peering under the "generator," scooched around so she could see her belt-mounted radiation detector.

"Fuck me! It's at the upper end of the yellow, about 25!"

"OK, video everything, take a couple of IRs, and back out."

* * *

"Mr. President, the NEST team has confirmed it's a nuke."

Sara Zimmer's voice came from the speakerphone in the tiny White House bomb shelter. "They do not, repeat do not, see any timing device. That doesn't mean it's not armed, though. There could be an electronic detonating device, say a cell phone. They believe the bomb is stable enough to move. Our plan is to helo it to the air base at Dover, Delaware. That's a rural area; plus an aircraft out of Dover is over the Atlantic almost immediately. I've given instructions to handle it according to the protocol we developed—get it out over the ocean, analyze it, disarm it, and deliver it to the Pantex plant near Amarillo for detailed study."

"OK, Sara, I remember you briefed us about that procedure at an NSC. That seems like the right thing to do."

"I'll keep you advised, Mr. President."

Martin broke the connection. Hearing someone enter, he half-turned in his chair and saw Ella. He reached up; she grasped his hand. They sat in apprehensive silence.

That silence was broken by Bart Guarini's arrival. "Mr. President, Ella. You'll need to go on TV tonight! I've got the speechwriters working on two— one if we lose another city and one if we don't."

Rick tried to think of a quip about how one speech would differ from the other, but he couldn't.

Discouragement washed over him. *This changes so much, just when we were making progress! There's going to be panic, anger, another stock market collapse, more congressional hearings, and most of all, demands for action. But what action? Against whom? Is this Kim or someone else?*

Ella said, "Kim?"

"We haven't analyzed the bomb yet, but surely it's Kim's. How could there be another leader who'd run that risk? God help the world if there's another like him out there!"

Guarini spoke, with an edge of fear: "Mr. President, if it's Kim—and I agree it surely is Kim—we have to go to Plan B immediately! We can't wait any longer. We've got to remove him from control of North Korea and its nukes!"

Another voice said, "I agree." Guarini and the Martins saw John Dorn, who reached the doorway as Bart spoke.

So here we are, Rick thought: *Four people in a bomb shelter trying to figure out how to save civilization by destroying a portion of it. It's come to that!*

No, stop being dramatic. This is not about saving civilization; it's about saving the United States and the Martin administration. Or maybe the other way around, if I'm honest.

"Sir, we've got to take the gloves off!" said Dorn.

"What does that mean, John?" said Martin.

"That means taking Kim out any way we can—assassination, kidnapping, hitting Pyongyang with a nuke. Whatever it takes!" Dorn's face shone with sweat.

The president held up a hand and spoke sharply: "So, the end justifies the means? It's really *not* possible to defend ourselves without compromising our ideals?"

Dorn fired back: "Sir, the people who agreed when you made that statement didn't feel threatened! If we lose another city, *everyone* will feel threatened! Every city and town will become a fortress. The economy will collapse. No security measure will be too intrusive or too destructive of civil liberties. You could be impeached.

"If that bomb goes off, and probably even if it doesn't, the people of this country are going to be scared to death and mad as hell. We can either ride that wave or be drowned by it!"

"What do you think, Bart?"

"I agree with John!"

"Rick." The three looked at Ella.

"The end does not justify the means, not now, not ever. But that's not all there is to it. Sometimes things have to be done that cannot be fully justified. They have to be done by those who have accepted responsibility for others. A family. A tribe. A nation. Those who have responsibility sometimes have to accept the cost of doing the unthinkable, of paying an awful price personally because it's their duty to others who trusted them."

Rick was about to speak when Dottie Branson's voice came from the speakerphone. *I wonder where she is . . . still at her desk while I'm safely in this shelter? Who else is in the usual place, risking incineration? I hate the idea that I have to be preserved, above all others, as if I'm some totem or god whose very existence will save the nation. I know I'm not and, right now, I have no damned idea how to save the nation.*

"Mr. President, Sam's on for you."

"Sir, there's breaking news. The networks and cables are running live feeds of police activity on the Baltimore waterfront and speculating about it. The press room is filling with reporters expecting our statement."

Looking into Martin's eyes for understanding and seeing it, Guarini spoke, leaving Martin deniability. "Sam, tell them inspectors found a powerful bomb in a container at the port." Still looking intently at the president for some sign and intuiting agreement, Guarini continued: "Experts have safed the bomb, and it's being removed now to a military base that for security reasons will not be identified. People in Baltimore are not in danger from this bomb. Oh, and Sam, characterize this as a preliminary report."

"OK, Bart." Sam knew the president had not been rushed to the bomb shelter because of a truckload of TNT in Baltimore. She also knew not to ask. Still, she refused to fly completely blind. "Bart—should I be prepared for substantial revision to this preliminary report?"

"Yes."

Dorn said, "I'd better get the NSC together."

"Right," said Martin, "and we can't do it from down here—no teleconference equipment in this hidey-hole."

He turned to Wilson. "Look, the bomb's being managed. It's time for me to get back upstairs, at least to the Sit Room. The hunkering down is over."

The four of them watched the head of the presidential protective detail consider briefly, then heard him agree. They trooped upstairs, the president, Dorn, and Guarini striding away from Ella at the corridor leading to the Sit Room. After a few steps, Rick spun around and went to Ella, putting an arm around her shoulders and leaning in close to her ear. After a brief, whispered conversation, they hugged and parted.

As they approached the Sit Room complex the agent in front of Martin cupped his hand to his earpiece, then turned to the president. "Sir, Secretary Zimmer reports the helo has arrived at Dover OK." Martin gave a thumbs-up and followed Dorn and Guarini into the large conference room, where five screens displayed the networks plus CNN and Fox News.

Suddenly, all the screens cut to a worried man at a podium, glancing down at notes. Rick felt a stab in that familiar spot in his stomach because it was the mayor of Baltimore.

Chapter 40

HUMAN BEINGS USUALLY oversimplify and then misapply lessons of a notorious disaster. Katrina-driven lesson number one in Mayor Funk's head was 'evacuate at the first sign of serious trouble.' The second was 'if you don't know the risk, overstating is better than understating.'

He put both lessons to use, announcing that a nuclear bomb had been discovered in the port of Baltimore and people in the area should immediately evacuate to a distance of at least ten miles. He promised further updates when available and introduced the director of public safety, who read evacuation routes and other instructions in a frightened voice.

Rick watched in helpless fury.

Soon every building and parking area in Baltimore's Inner Harbor district was gushing people and cars, but quickly the gush became a trickle as vehicles and humans filled all available streets and sidewalks, congealing in a heaving, shouting mass that pulsed angrily but went nowhere.

Guarini's phone rang. Samantha Yu exploded in his ear: "Bart, I need a statement to release or somebody at policy level to speak to the press, and I need it *now!*"

Guarini agreed and was about to tell her he was on the way. Click! *How about the vice president?* said a voice in his head. He asked Yu.

"Bart, that's crazy! He's in Nevada today."

"So what? We can patch him to the press room and he can answer questions. He's the guy the president put in charge of homeland security; let him face that wolf pack!"

"Bart, don't you *get* it? He's out there with his own coterie of reporters. Guess which group will get the lion's share of his attention! He'll marginalize the White House press and play to his pack of wannabes. The White House reporters will never, ever forgive the Martin administration. It's a non-starter!"

Shit, I should have thought of that!

"Sam, you're right. OK, I'm heading your way."

"Thanks, Bart."

"Sam needs help and you're going, right?" said the president.

"Yes."

"Right decision, wrong guy. You stay here and help John pull together the NSC and work up some options. I'll help Sam."

The chief of staff's disagreement was so sharp he forgot protocol: "Rick, you *can't* do that! You don't know any more than John and I do, which is not jack shit! They'll skin you alive and then fight over your bones!"

"I don't know more than you do about this bomb, but I do know this: I'm the president. I'm the one with the red button. I'm the one who will make the decisions about how we respond, so I'm the best one to go live now and calm things down. We just defeated a major attack without the loss of a single life—unless someone gets trampled in Baltimore. People need to hear me say that."

Guarini nodded and hit speed dial to Sam.

"Ladies and gentlemen, the president!" Sam barely had time to utter the words before Rick was at her side. The room's uproar dropped to a low hum.

Martin stood at the podium, the White House logo visible behind him. He had about him the calm of absolute certainty.

"Ladies and gentlemen . . . Ladies and gentlemen! I want to give you and the American people a brief report on what just happened in Baltimore and what it means for America."

The immediate, total concentration of dozens of journalists seemed to suck all extraneous sound from the room.

"A few hours ago, alert and courageous homeland security forces in the port of Baltimore detected a nuclear bomb being smuggled into the country inside a sea container. The various security systems worked correctly, people responded alertly and bravely, and we now have the bomb under examination aboard a military aircraft out over the Atlantic. I am sure you join me in prayers for the safety of that air crew and the bomb experts, who as I speak are doing their duty at the risk of their lives."

Rick leaned over the podium, projecting himself into the room, eyes hard and certain.

"Although some will try to tell you otherwise, this is a great victory for the United States of America! We have defeated an attack that was intended to push us into panic and despair, without—so far—the loss of a single life. We have taken from those who tried this attack an irreplaceable asset: the nuclear weapon they intended to use. From that weapon we will determine its origin, its paternity if I may say so, and take appropriate action. We will take that action deliberately and calmly, bearing in mind both the safety of Americans and our country's ideals. Our defenses are strong, as demonstrated today, and our resolution is even stronger. We will not only prevail over nuclear terrorism—this nation will work successfully with other nations to put measures in place that will end this twenty-first-century scourge!

"I must go now. May God bless and protect those in that airplane and this country!"

Martin left swiftly, ignoring questions, buoyed by a belief that in this moment the country had turned the corner.

It had, but not the corner he believed. Panic surged from Baltimore faster than any flash flood ever roared down a valley. Via Twitter and instant messaging, MySpace and Facebook, blogs, texts, and e-mail, the raw emotions of several hundred thousand frightened people were connected directly to the nervous systems of friends, acquaintances, business associates, and total strangers. Those they touched passed that fear along to their own contacts, often adding their own concerns.

Panic spread at Internet speed.

A few officials reacted as best they could, uploading video of the president's press room appearance to YouTube and the president's Facebook page. The keeper of the president's Twitter account sent reassuring tweets as fast as she could think of them.

Their efforts were sandbags against a tidal wave.

*   *   *

Fahim turned off the motel television. The whore he'd brought for cover, so no one would wonder why he was checking in at 2 p.m., was snoring gently on the bed, unused of course.

195

He knew he'd just been touched by the hand of Allah.

How had they found it? Perhaps some new technology, perhaps just luck. Except it wasn't luck; whatever happened to the bomb was the will of Allah. It was not Allah's will that the United States be bathed in his fire again. In the instant of Allah's touch he *knew* that.

I will continue to fight. I will go to the mountains, perhaps to Idaho, or Montana. No one will notice me among the panicked Americans fleeing their cities. They accept loners in those mountains; I will not be unusual or suspicious if I live by myself in an isolated area. The Base knows I will do that and they will find me and send me bombers to wear my vests and drive my trucks.

Fahim methodically wiped the room of their fingerprints. The woman stirred and mumbled. *She's an infidel whore and she can identify me. Tonight I'll kill her and dump her somewhere; it'll be easy in the confusion.*

Allah made me his instrument for cleansing Las Vegas and humbling the Far Enemy. Now he's chosen me to serve in another way. I'm a skilled maker of bombs, not nuclear ones but all sizes and types of explosive bombs. With the knowledge in my head, the skill of my hands, and materials easy to buy or steal, I am a weapon! Not a suicide bomber but the creator of suicide bombers.

Many of them!

Chapter 41

THE PRESIDENT SAUNTERED toward the Sit Room after his triumphant statement. He was in no hurry, enjoying his thoughts in this snippet of time between meetings and public appearances.

It's all in how you choose to look at things. Yes, it's shocking and infuriating that Kim would try another bombing. Kim? Well, not yet proven, but who else? Anyway, you could either be furious and frightened that Kim was still trying, or else be calmed and steeled by today's success. I know there'll be plenty of people who'll be furious and frightened, but I'm not going to give in to them or their way of think-ing—we won big today!

Rick began whistling, then stopped because he didn't want to appear over-confident. Hands in pockets, he nodded to the Marine holding the door, passed through, and glided athletically into his seat. Chairs scraped, people rose. He waved them down and looked at Dorn.

"Mr. President, you were magnificent in there!"

Martin offered his lopsided grin. "Thanks, but I don't mind telling you I know those defenses won't succeed indefinitely. Time is *not* on our side. We've got to move quickly, not only because we need to put an end to this danger, but because the momentum of this great success gives us leverage.

"What have you got for me so far?"

"Mr. President." Sara Zimmer's voice interrupted over a bad connection. "The engineers believe they've safed the bomb! I'd like your permission to send them to Pantex."

"What's the risk, Sara?"

"They'll be routed direct to Amarillo at forty thousand. If the bomb should detonate at that altitude, ground effects would be minimal."

"What's minimal?"

"Well, there would be little fallout and that bit would stay airborne. If someone below should be looking right at the aircraft when it explodes, there might be some vision damage. Electromagnetic pulse effect—EMP—would scramble some computers for a while. Radiation is a non-issue; the ground is way too far below for gamma or neutrons to be a problem, much less alpha."

Martin pursed his lips then said, "What if it blows at Pantex?"

"If that happens, we're in a whole new ballgame, but the engineers wouldn't be recommending delivery there if they believed it could. These guys *live* near Pantex, with their families."

Fist striking palm with a smack, Rick said, "That sure *would* be a new ball game! That would turn the tables on us; it would be like they had successfully targeted our key nuclear facility. No to that plan!"

He looked around. "Any ideas?"

Easterly and McAdoo had their heads together. Then Zimmer's voice: "Well, the bomb's aboard a C-130 with aerial refueling. We can send it anywhere you want, Mr. President."

Easterly said, "Kwajalein."

"Surrrre," replied Zimmer. Martin looked puzzled at the understanding in her tone.

"Kwajalein Atoll, sir, in the Marshall Islands," said Easterly. "It's the most isolated military base we have with enough infrastructure for scientists to examine the bomb. It's perfect!"

"OK, send it there! And have the FAA keep other planes far enough away that they won't get zapped if it blows, despite the confidence of those engineers. Keep the bomb under two-person control and continuous video monitoring. I'm going to invite the IAEA to send a rep to participate in the analysis. No further digging into it until IAEA gets there.

"Got that, Sara?"

"Yes, sir."

"Anne, get with the IAEA to arrange it."

"Yes sir . . . Mr. President, I think you should invite a Chinese scientist to participate."

"Why?"

"I don't have a reason. It's just a hunch that having them in this from the beginning could turn out to be important."

"Yeah, like if the bomb turns out to be one of the Chinese designs that Khan was peddling," said DNI Hendricks.

"Good!" said Martin. "Let's do that."

"Mr. President, I think it would be a good thing if you called Ming and made the offer directly," said the vice president. "It may get you inside his head a little and also let him know that *we* are aware of the design possibility and don't intend to call them on it. We can be pretty confident that if the warhead design *is* theirs, they didn't give it to Kim, knowing him as they do."

"OK, Bruce. I'll do that."

Martin's phone bleeped. "Sir, this is the Sit Room watch officer. Television is showing huge numbers of people leaving East Coast cities. We've seen reports from New York, Boston, Philadelphia, here in DC, plus Baltimore of course."

Instantly, Martin's stomach flamed. *Shit! It didn't take long for the fear mongers to regroup. Should I go back to the press room? No, I don't want to overdo that. How about if Ella and the kids and I visit big cities around the country, spend a day in each, show there's no imminent danger?*

He led a brief discussion of this new development and his idea, then called Sam and told her to make an announcement. He looked at Guarini. "Bart, get the show on the road for this! The Secret Service will hate it, but they'll just have to suck it up."

After calling Ella, Martin returned his attention to the NSC. "OK, John, you have me again. What should we do to leverage this success and move our agenda forward?"

Dorn was once again astounded, and angered, by Martin's relentless optimism. It was hard for him to work for someone who saw opportunity in every development, when he himself more often saw problems.

"Sir, we're all just starting to get our arms around this thing. We don't even know yet where the bomb came from, much less who was trying to smuggle it in or what they intended. We're going to need some time."

Wrong answer! thought Guarini. *John still doesn't understand that you have to work with Rick as he is: a confident opportunist who wants to run when he's feeling good. To bond with Rick, you always have to have something to give him when he wants to go full throttle.*

And I do: Plan B.

"Mr. President," said Guarini, "I agree with John that there's a lot we don't know right now. But I think we can make some assumptions without being irresponsible. For the present, let's assume the bomb is Kim's. Let's take the same approach: unless there's a case made otherwise, North Korea is once again the perp, acting alone. So the question is, how are we going to respond to Kim's second attack?"

Battista saw Martin nod attentively. *Bart's wrong, but, damn, he's good with Rick,* she thought. *Eric and Mac look prepared—Bart must have put them to work on Plan B already. He kept me out of the loop. Well, if he figures he can roll me, he's going to be surprised! She cut her eyes to Bruce Griffith's image on the monitor. Is he also out of the loop? Can't tell.*

"Bart!" He glared at her. "Let's not forget that we have the option to call this bomb an attack, or something else; emphasize increased threat or improved defense. So, we are *not* considering our response to Kim's second attack *unless* we decide to handle it that way. Obviously, if we've been attacked again, we must respond strongly. But it's not a given that this was an attack; we may have caught them before they could set up the attack."

"Good point, Anne," said the president.

Guarini grimaced, then smiled. "Point taken, Anne. But I think the president has already characterized this as an attack, in the press room fifteen minutes ago. We could, I suppose, walk that back. But for now, let's consider that we just defeated a second attack."

Guarini's glance at the president drew a nod.

Dammit! thought Battista, *they're not taking me seriously!* Her face flushed as she felt her betrayal.

Guarini said, "We have these options, it seems to me, to force Kim from control of the DPRK: we can continue our present line of activity, diplomacy and quarantine, or an augmented version of it—or we can start really using military force.

"Since we just found a nuclear bomb in Baltimore, I submit that our current activities aren't handling the threat we face."

"They may actually have increased the threat," said the vice president. "By not striking the DPRK we may have led Kim to believe we're unwilling to do that, so he feels free to take nuclear potshots at us."

"Perhaps," replied Guarini, shocked at Griffith's open criticism of the president's chosen course.

"I know the risks of diplomacy!" said Martin, slapping his palm on the table. "Proceed, Bart; tell me something I *don't* already know!"

"Well, sir, I doubt if any of this will be new to you, but I'd like Eric and Mac to review some military options."

Easterly said, "Mac, why don't you walk us through this?"

Nodding, General MacAdoo took a sip of water and began to speak.

"Mr. President, we're contending with a nuclear power ruled absolutely by someone who is, as you have experienced, given to fits of rage. Our use of *any* military force might cause Kim to go nuclear. The DPRK appears to have the capability, using Taepodong-two or Nodong nuclear missiles, to hit South Korea, Japan, Okinawa, and perhaps Guam, Hawaii, or Alaska. We don't know this for a fact, but we do know that three of Kim's nuclear weapons have been detonated successfully and the DPRK has tested the Taepodong to ranges well beyond Korea and Japan. Plus, DPRK aircraft could nuke South Korea or Japan. We also know that the north has tons of chemical weapons stocks. We must assume they have the capacity for large-scale chemical attacks on anyone within aircraft or missile range. This is the backdrop to anything we may consider."

Looking at Hendricks, the president said, "Aaron, how many nukes does Kim have now?"

"We certainly don't know, sir, but we think somewhere between three and ten."

"Mac, haven't we got some defensive weapons against Kim's missiles?"

"Yes, sir. Our navy and the Japanese and ROK navies have cruisers with Aegis missiles that can probably knock down Nodongs. We're less confident about Taepodongs. And our Patriot missiles, which both the Japanese and the South Koreans have too, have some chance of getting them. We also have one aircraft with a laser able to destroy a missile early in flight, but the weather must be clear for it to work."

"I'm not hearing a lot of confidence, General!" said the president.

"No sir, you're not. Although Bush Two withdrew from the ABM treaty that banned our testing, following administrations decided to observe it, so we haven't tested against live targets in years. The Nodong is based on the SCUD, and we downed some SCUDS during the Iraq campaigns. The ABL—that's the airborne laser—has a lower probability of success than Aegis or Patriot. It's had one successful shot, but in comparison to the others, we haven't tested it much."

"Aaron, how many Nodongs and Taepodongs?"

"We don't know exactly. Except those they've tested over the past ten years, the missiles have been hidden from our satellites. We get an occasional sniff from communication intercepts, but since the DPRK has almost no cell phones and few telephones, there's not much. We estimate they have a couple of hundred Nodongs operational. As for Taepodongs, it's more likely a couple of dozen than a couple of hundred."

"Aaron, I have to say, your intel on the DPRK is awful!"

"Yes, sir, it is. The DPRK is the toughest intelligence target on the planet."

"How about Gwon's people . . . do *they* have anything better?"

"Probably, sir, but Gwon's mad as hell at the United States; plus cooperation began drying up early in the Rogers administration after she outed those detention centers they were operating for us."

Cords stood out in the president's neck as he said, "What I'm hearing so far boils down to saying *we have no military option!*"

Chapter 42

SECRETARY OF DEFENSE Easterly, face and tone carefully neutral, said, "No, sir, we have options, several of them. None of them are clean or sure, but we've got 'em.

"You can change our policy and we can try to kill Kim. Or we could take out Yongbyon and all his other known nuclear sites with cruise missiles and hope that the ROK, Japan, and our bases could survive any of Kim's missiles we didn't get. Or, we could destroy any part of the DPRK, or all of it, with nuclear weapons delivered by cruise missiles, ballistic missiles, or stealth bombers."

Flinging his briefing paper toward a wastebasket, Martin said, "None of those are options!"

The vice president cleared his throat, turning all eyes toward his image. "Sir, I submit that those are indeed options. Horrible? Yes. Unprecedented? No—but worse than any president since Kennedy has faced."

As if trumping, Martin said, "Eric, if we nuke Pyongyang, how many people die?"

"Sir, the population is between three and four million. Depending on the size of the warhead, burst height, and other technical decisions, I'd say from one million to all of them, however many that is."

"And *what* would we accomplish?"

"Maybe kill Kim and his gang. Maybe convince him to go into exile. Maybe the shock of a nuke would get Ming to cooperate with us in pushing him out. Maybe create such fear among the elite that a coup would come out of nowhere and take him out."

Rick felt the blood rising in his neck. His face flushed. Leaning forward, eyes sweeping the room like shotgun barrels, he fired into the crowd: "Look, I want some *graduated* options! I refuse to believe we've got nothing short of violating our principles by assassinating Kim or using a nuclear weapon! Bomb his palaces. Destroy Pyongyang's airport. Shoot down their air force. Level a small city with conventional bombs. Engineer a coup—he must have *some* rivals. Don't give me only choices between surrender and Armageddon!"

Everyone looked at Guarini.

Bart knew Rick was trying to bulldoze his advisors, as if that would change the facts. *Why? I'm as political as he is, but I can see we can't tolerate Kim much longer. Why doesn't he see that?*

Immediately he knew the answer: *Because he's the one who would have to sign Kim's death warrant or push the nuclear button!*

Knowing that he might be the only one able to move Martin, the chief of staff said, "Sir, we could do any of those things—except the coup—but they each lead to the same terrible outcome. For example, let's say we bomb Pyongyang's airport and Kim responds by lobbing nuclear missiles at Japan and one gets through the Aegis and the Patriots. Can we make the case that we took a reasonable risk, or do we look foolish and callous, ready to fight to the last Japanese city? And Tokyo wouldn't be Kim's only option. He could put one into Seoul, too—and hit Okinawa. A Taepodong-two might even have the range for Anderson Air Force Base on Guam."

Cautiously but firmly, hoping to gentle the president around, Guarini said what he hoped his friend could accept as bedrock truth: "All options to break Kim's control short of eliminating him or flattening the DPRK in one blow run a high risk that he will devastate South Korea and Japan and maybe hit us again."

Eyes narrowed, voice stinging, Martin said, "Look, Bart—all of you! We started this meeting to figure out how to leverage our extraordinary success in Baltimore to move ahead in the UN and the Northeast Asia Group. Now you're talking as if Baltimore had been blown up. It wasn't. *We* won this round! I refuse to talk about doomsday scenarios! Now get busy and get me something better!"

Martin stood and said in a tight, quiet voice. "John, you were right—this group *doesn't* have its arms around things yet!"

Anne Battista recalled the British foreign minister at the UN but said nothing, telling herself this wasn't the time. The room's silence was broken only by the sounds of Martin leaving.

Feeling like he had been punched in the stomach, Guarini looked around the table, glanced at the faces on the screens, and drew a shaky breath. "He'll come around. It's just that this is so terribly, terribly hard. He's facing choices he never thought he'd face—that none of us thought we'd face after the cold war. This is the conclusion of a slow-motion train wreck that began when we—the world—gave Kim time to make nuclear bombs and build missiles. We laughed at him; we made him a joke—the crazy uncle locked in the attic—instead of preventing him from becoming a deadly threat to millions. Now we have to deal with that—*the president* does—and there are nothing but awful choices and not much time."

Vice President Griffith's voice, as clear as if he were seated next to each of them, froze his distant colleagues: "Bart, is he up to it? *Can* he do it and do it in time, before we lose another city?"

If he's bold enough to ask that question in this meeting, thought Guarini, *he must think he's got the votes for impeachment!* His gut heaved.

"Yes, he can! Since you have doubts, Mr. Vice President, you should return to Washington immediately and speak with the president!"

Griffith's voice was calm: "I agree, Bart.

"Look, you all probably think what I just said is the worst of all political crimes: disloyalty. But, I ask you—do you think the man who just ranted about the Baltimore debacle being a *victory*, then stormed out when others differed—do you think that man should be leading this country right now when it's coming apart at the seams? As for me, I have my doubts!"

His face carefully composed and voice more sorrowful than angry, the VP continued: "I want Rick Martin to succeed. But the oath I took—and the ones you each took, too—were not to him. Our oaths are to uphold the Constitution, which right now means protecting Americans from attacks by Kim. If the government doesn't do that—quickly and convincingly—well, then you see the face of the new America right now on CNN: hundreds of thousands of frightened people fleeing! The president told us time isn't on our side, but in the end, all he did was put off decisions.

"I'll fly back right away!"

* * *

Behind his closed door, Guarini yanked his tie down and unbuttoned his collar. *Griffith's smooth confidence scares me. He's moved from secretly encouraging impeachment talk to openly questioning the president's fitness to remain in office. Rick's going to have to do one of the things he hates: go toe to toe. This is so Rick! The man can't bring himself to recognize flaws in people on his team. I think—*

It hit him like a sledgehammer: *the army, the military. They're already in position to control the country; we put them there with N-SEPA! The internal security troops report to Griffith. And what about the FBI? A big part of its field force is under Griffith's control. Is that why he's so bold?*

Guarini nearly stopped breathing. *Would they follow Griffith in a showdown, if he claimed it was the only way to protect the country and stop society from unraveling?* Hairs bristling on his neck, he glanced at the door.

Chapter 43

"PRESIDENT MARTIN CALLING, sir. Your interpreter is on."

Ming was watching a Xinhua News Agency feed showing jammed American highways. *With such a crisis, why would Martin take the time to call me? Could* Kim *be his reason?*

Surely Kim wouldn't have . . . A few minutes ago, I considered calling Kim. He never, ever takes phone calls. He will call back but is never available when called. And, at this point, Kim could lie to me with ease—better to see if the weapon is identified.

But what if the Americans have already identified the bomb's "parent," as they called it? What if it is Kim?

Ming picked up, feeling sweat in his palm as he grasped the handset. "Good evening, President Martin. I'm watching the flight from America's cities. You have a hard task to get matters back under control!"

Stifling irritation and hoping his antacid tablet would kick in, Martin said, "Good morning, President Ming. Yes, you're right, but I believe that once our people realize today's events show the strength of our protective measures, they will return. As you may know, my family and I will be spending the next week in our major cities, demonstrating that they are safe.

"But I'm calling about something else. The bomb we seized will be delivered to our military base at Kwajalein, in the Marshal Islands. Scientists and engineers will examine it carefully and will determine its origin. I'm calling to invite you to send a personal representative. I will also invite the IAEA"

He didn't mention Kim! Ming exhaled but said nothing.

Martin went on. "As you can imagine, consequences will flow from the identification. I want no question to arise about the accuracy of this analysis. I also want everyone to know that China and the United States operate on a basis of mutual trust and mutual respect. We are not and never will be adversaries when it comes to combating nuclear terrorism. Rather, we are the two nations who should lead in putting an end to it through our coordinated diplomacy. As the two most influential nations in the world, we have a special obligation to do this."

As Martin intended, his final sentence brought a slight smile to Ming's face. *Martin is coming the rest of the way to us! He accepts China as America's equal! So, let's see whether he will say it publicly.*

"Mr. President, that is both bold and wise of you. China accepts your offer. Perhaps we should issue a joint statement along the lines of your words."

That's why I said them, thought Martin. *I have to have your support.*

"Certainly, President Ming. I'll instruct our ambassador to work with your government on that. And, Mr. President, there is another reason we will welcome your representative's presence. It's possible the warhead is a design we know was sold by that bastard A. Q. Khan. That design is said to be Chinese; of course, only Khan could tell us where and how he got it. As you know, we are questioning him. If the design is Chinese, Kim and others might attempt to use that to divide us. I want to tell you now that I am certain China did not provide a warhead design to Kim Jong-il. If the design proves to be Chinese, I am sure it was stolen."

Ming's smile returned. *This is getting better and better! Martin has just eliminated one of China's vulnerabilities in this affair. But why? What does he need from me?*

"Mr. President—Rick—Americans are a resilient people and I am sure that only a relative few are now in panicky flight. Others are reacting differently, are they not?"

"Ming, public opinion is overwhelming that we must eliminate Kim's power to attack us. There are still those who favor diplomacy, but that number is dwindling, and I expect what happened today will drown them out, even though I am one of them. I'm sure you have an understanding of our impeachment process. I believe opinion will soon reach the point that, unless I take military action, I will be replaced by someone who has no doubts about using our military, Vice President Griffith."

Pausing, Rick thought: *OK, now you know both the carrot and the stick. Let's see if you're willing to do what I need.* His chest tightened.

Ming said nothing. Earnestly, Martin resumed: "I believe that China and America, working together, can prevent war in Northeast Asia, but we don't have much time. So I ask you: if America determines, with the concurrence of China and the IAEA, that this bomb is also Kim's, will you use your powers in concert with ours to force him into exile and replace him with someone who will dismantle the DPRK's nuclear capacities?"

Ming thought, *so, Rick Martin, now I know what you ask and what you offer. I don't want Griffith, but I cannot control Kim. I don't have the means to force him from power, other than having him killed or taking over the DPRK, and I am not willing to do either, at least not now. No matter—I'll have the joint statement and you'll have to settle for what I give you. As for Griffith? Huang Bo said impeachment is a deliberate, public process. I'll have time to adjust.*

He said, "Rick, as Korea's elder cousin, China will urge that accommodations be made. But we are a family and family members do not attack each other. Between 1950 and 1953, a few years before you were born, China sacrificed over eight hundred thousand soldiers to superior American firepower in order save the DPRK. One of them was my own father. The cigarette case I use is all of him that returned to us. Perhaps I can persuade Kim to do what you suggest without loss of face. Face is important to Kim and to all of us in what you call Northeast Asia. Think on that, I urge you."

Martin's mind said what his lips did not: *You should think, too, Ming! Think what it would mean for China if the U.S. went to war with your younger cousin. Think about the face in that!*

Instead, he said: "Thank you for that, Ming. I pray your efforts with Kim will be successful, because the effects of war between America and China's younger cousin—and neighbor—are unpredictable. I think we truly are balanced now between a bright future for our two countries and a disaster for both of us. Let us choose wisely, despite Kim's efforts to divide and confuse us."

Scowling, Ming said, "We have an understanding that will prevent difficulties. We will issue the joint statement immediately and send our representative to Kwajalein. I will be my most persuasive with Kim if our joint inspection of the bomb proves it to be his."

"This has been an excellent discussion, and we have reached important agreements. Good day, Ming."

"Good evening, Rick."

Martin looked anxiously at Battista, Dorn, and Guarini. "Any reactions?"

"Well, he agreed to the deal we wanted, Mr. President," said Battista.

"That's not quite what I heard," said Dorn. "He agreed to give it a try, then reminded you what a big stake China has in the DPRK. I think he was signaling that he'd ask but wouldn't hold a gun to Kim's head."

"It's important that he agreed to send a representative to Kwajalein!" said Battista. "I think we have some leverage if it turns out to be a Chinese bomb design."

"That was certainly better than if he'd refused our offer," said Guarini. "Now, Anne and John, if you'll excuse us, it's time for the president's meeting with the vice president."

Rick felt his stomach, which had just subsided, flame again.

Chapter 44

THEY HAD DECIDED on a show of power, so the president was seated behind his desk, with Guarini to his right and Attorney General McDonnell to his left, when Dottie Branson ushered in the vice president.

Griffith gestured at the three, saying, "Looks like the firing squad for me! Do I get a last cigarette and a blindfold?"

The jab stung Martin. *So here I am, the guy who's never needed more than wits and words to face anyone, now presenting myself in the panoply of commander-in-chief. But, dammit, I am commander-in-chief and this man is challenging me head-on!*

Rick tried to lighten it up: "Sorry, smoking isn't permitted in federal buildings. How about a Nicorette?"

"May I sit?" said Griffith, his disregard for Martin's attempt at humor shouting his message: 'Fuck you.'

"Of course, Bruce," said the president, ignoring it. "We're here for a discussion, not a sentencing.

"Bart, you called this meeting. Get us started, please."

The chief of staff felt sweat bead at his hairline, not only from the situation, but from the fear he didn't dare reveal. He spoke as he'd rehearsed: "Sir, after you left the NSC meeting yesterday, the vice president questioned your fitness to serve as president, indicated he had doubts you were up to the task. To be fair, he did so reluctantly and in the context of what he believes is mortal danger to our country. But he did it nonetheless, in front of the entire group. In view of that, I asked him to return to Washington immediately and meet with you."

Griffith waved a big, blunt-fingered hand.

"Bart, there's no need recounting what I'm sure the three of you have reviewed on video several times! Look, I know I was way out of line as vice president yesterday. Because you left suddenly, Mr. President, I had no opportunity to express those views to you. But, had you stayed, I would have. I wasn't speaking because you had left; I was speaking because America is fast running out of time to take measures that may, *may,* preserve it in some semblance of what it was when this administration took office."

Don't let him bait you, said the same voice that had spoken during his encounter with Kim.

The VP charged on: "We've got to get Kim's hand off the nuclear trigger. Every minute he remains in control of the DPRK is a minute in which hundreds of thousands more Americans could die!"

Rick's mind acknowledged that Griffith had just said what many Americans believed, something he couldn't dismiss out of hand. But his answer boiled up from someplace else, someplace he rarely visited.

"Bruce, surely you don't believe there's a button on Kim's desk connected to bombs in the U.S.! Save the sensationalism for your next press conference!"

Griffith hurled his response like a rock: "Mr. President, surely *you* don't believe any longer we have the time or leverage to negotiate our safety with Kim!"

The two glared at each other. The attorney general took notes, scribbling furiously. Guarini started to speak, but Martin beat him to it.

"Look, Bruce," he said in a calmer voice, "I *don't* believe we can negotiate Kim into giving up his nukes. He has to go and he *will* go. I just had an important conversation with Ming Liu. He agreed to pressure Kim into stepping down, going into exile, and working with us to replace him with someone who'll give up the country's nukes."

I wonder what you gave away to get that? thought the VP.

But he said only, "I'm glad to hear that, sir. *When* do you expect Kim to leave?"

"Soon. Within a couple of weeks."

Yeah, right, thought Griffith, who leaned forward in his chair, elbows on knees, fists clenched, eyes mocking. "How many things has Kim promised to do and then not done, in the last twenty years? What's your backup? What will you do if Kim is still running the country fifteen days from now?"

This time Rick contained his anger and thought of the long conversation he and Ella had had the night before: *Then, I'll have to protect our tribe. I might as well tell you, because I won't have any choice if it happens.*

"I'm not setting a deadline of exactly fifteen days. But if we can't pressure him into stepping down, I'll use force to remove him."

Griffith looked surprised, seemed to relax a bit. But inside, he was on high alert. *I don't believe him, but I'm not going to say that here, with the tapes running.*

"Well, I worry about letting him stay even for two weeks, but I guess we're on the same page. I'm very glad to hear that, sir."

Then Martin said, "And now *I'll* be glad to hear your pledge to stop bad-mouthing your president!"

The VP's eyes bulged in his suddenly red face. "If what you mean by bad-mouthing is disagreement, I won't give that pledge!"

The president stood up behind the big desk crowded with symbols of his power, placed his hands on either side of the blotter, leaned forward with blazing eyes. "Dammit, Bruce, you *know* what I mean!"

Griffith visibly considered his reply, then rose and said, "I will not question your ability to do the job unless you fail to take adequate action, should Kim remain in power past the deadline you just gave."

"Deadline is your word, Bruce, not mine! I haven't set a deadline, but I think two weeks will tell whether Ming can talk him out."

They stood glaring at each other as McDonnell continued to scribble.

Guarini gazed in horror at the spectacle of a vice president going toe to toe with his president, arguing as an equal. *Has this ever happened before?* he wondered. *Probably between Nixon and Ford, maybe between the Clintons and Gore, and in each case impeachment was on the wind. These two are very nearly out of control.* He swallowed hard, eyes roaming the room vacantly. *I've got to end this! But how?*

McDonnell, the silent scribe, kept his head down.

Dottie Branson's voice startled them: "Mr. President, it's time for your meeting with the Wisconsin Cheese Queen, accompanied by Senators Presley and Robbins and Representative Bays, in the Roosevelt Room."

Martin looked as if she had just pulled him back into his body, and he was surprised to find himself standing.

Griffith's face turned even redder, then his shoulders shook. Unable to suppress it, he began to guffaw. Suddenly they were laughing until tears came.

Griffith regained control. "If it's not one damn thing, it's another, isn't it, Mr. President?"

"That's right, Bruce. Sorry to end this discussion, but now I have to do something *really* important!"

As Rick walked toward the Roosevelt Room, Dottie moved to his side. She whispered, "I made that up, Mr. President. It sounded to me like you gladiators needed to break." She turned and walked rapidly toward her desk.

Martin had just settled in his private office when Guarini's head and shoulders leaned in. He saw that his friend's once starched collar had wilted and knew his own had, too.

"So, Bart, she fooled you, too!"

"Yeah, and thank heaven I didn't open my big mouth when I realized that *wasn't* on your schedule!

"Something else I held my tongue about was that timeline for Kim. When did you decide that?"

"Last night."

Guarini was silent, waiting for more. When nothing came, he said, "Have you told Eric and John?"

"No. I guess I'd better do that!" Rick flashed his disarming grin.

"Yeah, you should.

"So now what's your take on the vice president?"

"Bart, I believe he's a patriot like you and me but sees things through a different lens. We've stopped him encouraging impeachment talk, but he'll start again if Kim doesn't give it up and step down soon.

"And I think—and that's why I gave the timeline—it will stiffen Ming's resolve knowing there *is* one and that military planning to remove Kim is underway."

"How's Ming going to know that?"

"Because you, Bart, will orchestrate the necessary leaks."

"Am I leaking nuclear?"

"No, you are *not.*"

The chief of staff bit his tongue. Rick was threatening military action when the only effective military action was something *he* refused even to discuss. Eric was going to love that, not to mention Premier Kato when he got wind of it! And what about the fear he didn't dare name, even to himself?

About to unburden himself, he realized his friend's brittleness, knew he couldn't imagine the pressure Rick felt, and said instead, "OK, boss," with as much spirit as he could muster.

* * *

"It saddens me that the Arabs are incompetent," said Kim, belching gently after swallowing a last bite of sashimi prepared by his excellent Japanese chef. "Too bad for them! As for us, we are accomplishing our objectives. I met President Martin and frightened him with the strength and determination of our beloved Korean people. Then I made him lose face at the UN. He has made threats, but they have only strengthened the ardor of our people to defend our homeland. And those same threats have thrown the fools in the south into confusion and terrified the Japanese. Our elder cousins to the north are a disappointment because they have supported the illegal blockade, but I know they cannot afford to let the American pirates prevail."

Supping with Kim were his youngest son, designated to succeed him in the indefinite future, and Field Marshal Young-san Ho, head of Kim's military. Gazing at Young-san with the menacing inscrutability of a python, Kim said, "Tell me, Comrade Field Marshal, what is the state of your preparations?"

Young-san, who had attained his rank by always having the right answer for Kim, said, "Dear Leader, our soldiers have sworn to become human bombs and bullets, to hurl themselves against the enemy. Our pilots have pledged to shoot down ten for every loss to them. Our brave sailors are ready to put to sea in swarms of fast attack boats and submarines. We are ready!"

"And our missile strike forces?"

"Also ready, Dear Leader! At your command they will destroy Seoul, Pusan, Osaka, Sasebo, Yokohama, and Tokyo."

Kim's eyes grew opaque as he looked inward at firestorms and shock waves and ruined cities blazing. *I have the powers of a god. Even my father could not have done what I can!* He felt a rush of achievement.

"Thank you, Comrade Field Marshal. Remain alert! The call may come at any time."

Chapter 45

MING LIU PATROLLED his garden, hoe ready. *I enjoy caring for this plot so much!* he thought, savoring the smell of earth wet from a summer shower. *I wish I could pluck China's problems as easily as weeds! Kim is pushing Martin closer to the worst for us, a nuclear attack. He's a fool, and like most fools he leaves it to others to deal with the consequences of his follies. My duty to protect China won't even leave me in peace to tend my vegetables for an hour!*

He threw down the hoe, startling the aide who hovered at the edge of the plot. His mind recycled conversations with Kim—telephone conversations because he refused to come to Beijing. Kim had turned aside both compliments and threats. He would not leave the DPRK for a retirement of honor and luxury in China.

Ming stooped and cupped a ripening tomato in both hands, then picked up the hoe and resumed patrolling.

Throughout their conversations Kim was cheerfully confident. He knew he occupied Martin's every waking moment, which gave him face after so many years of being ignored by American presidents. He feared nothing from American power but a nuclear attack, and he was absolutely certain—in fact he was gleeful about it—that he had shaped American public opinion so as to prevent it.

Kim boasted about the videos he was using to control Americans' perceptions. He was especially pleased with his latest. It featured two Korean children playing a haunting duet of "You Were Born to be Loved" on violin and piano, standing near the altar of a Christian church. The genius of this one, Kim bragged, was that the video would also appeal to South Koreans because the song was popular there and was in fact written by a South Korean.

There! Ming slashed so hard the handle vibrated. *Kim deceived me about the second bomb! He was willing to let his elder cousin, who protected him, lose face. Kim gambles with the very existence of life on the Korean peninsula, betting the Americans won't retaliate a hundred-fold, as they could in a single, cataclysmic instant. Only a crazy man would risk that!*

Of course, we do have agents high up in the DPRK. But they are Korean after all, taught by a lifetime of conditioning to venerate Kim. So there are limits to what they will do for China. And they lack commitment; mostly they are working for us to ensure themselves a safe haven, should Kim turn on them for some imagined transgression.

There are too many questions: Can I have Kim assassinated? Could I control what happened if I did? Could China seize the DPRK's nuclear bombs and end its capacity to build others? Would China have to deploy half its army to keep millions of starving, brutish North Koreans from crossing our border?

Those are huge unknowns carrying big risks—big for me if I order certain measures taken and big for China. I don't want to gamble at those stakes!

The worst of it was Martin's demeanor when I gave him the bad news! He was defeated, resigned to the failure of his diplomacy and ready to use force to remove Kim. He even asked whether I had the means to "surgically remove"—meaning assassinate—Kim. Of course I gave a rambling non-reply, but Martin's response was alarming: "Then I am now left only with terrible means to protect my country and must use them soon."

China is caught between a desperate man and a crazy one! Ming stood stock-still, gazing across his plot with unseeing eyes.

Still, I doubt Martin would order an invasion to remove Kim, much less a nuclear strike. So much of his life, and his entire presidency before Six-thirteen, has been about how dialogue and the glue of common humanity could defuse even deep hatreds. I don't believe that, but I think Rick Martin probably does.

And Huang Bo told me that a significant minority of Americans, including an influential part of Martin's political base, angrily reject attacking North Korea: War is not the answer. Find another way. We don't have to kill Korean children to protect American children.

Ming snorted. *Fine sentiments, artfully planted and nurtured by Kim, but having no place in the real world—except America, where Huang is certain they are deeply felt by groups that Martin can't ignore.*

The English have a saying: the leopard cannot change its spots. I hope they are right!

Chapter 46

DOTTIE BRANSON KNEW her boss was deeply tired, bone tired, working until his brain was mush, sleeping fitfully if at all. She fought off the urge to check on him in his hideaway, rising and then returning to her desk. Rick had absorbed so many blows on Six-thirteen and since. But worst of all must be his knowing that every arriving minute could carry news of another bomb.

Rick tilted his chair back and put his feet on the small desk. He wanted a cigarette but not enough to walk outside. He fiddled with his notepad, doodling, then wrote "Kim" and underlined it twice.

Kim is the key. He's the one who controls these weapons. But let's say I could make him vanish by snapping my fingers; wouldn't someone else just grab power and continue to kill Americans and threaten America? Plus Japan and South Korea? Not if I could convince that person that giving up those nuclear bombs was in his personal interest. But I haven't been able to convince Kim, so how could I convince someone like Kim, his son or his top general? Probably only if he knew I would make him vanish, too. But there's no magic wand. The ways I have to make people vanish are all violent—seize them or kill them. All my life I've rejected the politics of violence. Now . . .

Anyway, how could I negotiate directly with Kim after Baltimore? I'd be impeached! And besides, after I placated Kim, if I placated him, who'd be next? What if Iran's Supreme Leader calculates the same odds—or has a vision—and gives Hezbollah a nuke with our address?

His left arm and hand wrapped over his skull, fingers rubbing his aching right temple, a pretzel of anguish.

About the only thing Americans agree on is that I'm wrong. The Left shrieks that we're veering toward genocide in North Korea; the Right thunders that my indecision and squeamishness will be the end of America. And in less than two weeks Griffith will be back on the impeachment warpath, if he ever stopped!

Rick rubbed eyes dry and itchy with fatigue. Despair stalked him, a jackal just beyond the campfire's light.

I'm going in circles. I don't have the time, with two clocks ticking, one marking the days until another city is bombed, another counting the days until the House votes to impeach me!

He felt pounding in his temples.

Needing space, Rick left his cubbyhole and slouched into the Oval Office. *Last night, after Ming's awful call, I sent for Bart and the NSC. We gathered here and paced and drank too much coffee and re-plowed the same ground.*

Again, we considered the military options; again most quickly proved doubtful or impossible. Not only is assassination against our principles, we haven't got a quick, sure means to kill just Kim. Conventional air and missile attacks are more likely to lead Kim to nuke South Korea and Japan than to scuttle into exile—and he'd try even harder to nuke us again.

Invasion is a non-starter: Gwon won't help, and fighting without his army, we'd be outnumbered and take heavy casualties; invasion would lead to DPRK attacks, probably nuclear, against South Korea, Japan, and any U.S. base or city Kim could reach, and it might bring in China. Then I'd have a bloody shambles, like Truman's war that killed or wounded over four million, devastated the entire peninsula, and ended back where it began, without regime change.

That leaves nuclear.

With a grimace, Rick moved behind his desk and chair and stood, hands in pockets and shoulders slumped, looking glumly out the thick window to the small patio and nearby trees.

Eric and Mac say that if we hit key targets simultaneously Kim won't be able to launch nukes. Afterward, the DPRK would no longer be a functioning society; half to three-quarters of its population would be dead or dying. All urban areas would be radioactive no-go zones like Las Vegas. Hundreds of thousands, maybe millions, of survivors, including some fatally irradiated, would surge across the borders into China, Russia, and South Korea.

That vision had sickened Rick and his advisors. And no one knew what the simultaneous detonation of nearly two dozen nuclear warheads would do to the planet. By unspoken agreement they rejected that option.

Over desperate hours, what emerged was a plan to use a weapon that no longer existed. If European war had broken out in the late sixties, America had a nuclear answer to waves of Soviet tanks racing across Germany: a warhead that produced a huge, momentary pulse of radiation, killing tank crews. Enhanced Radiation Warheads produced relatively little fallout and less blast and heat than other nuclear weapons. After the cold war, the first President Bush had them dismantled, but the components were stored at the Pantex facility. Several could be assembled within weeks, and Martin had ordered it.

Such a weapon—called the neutron bomb—could be used to ravage a North Korean army or city without creating cross-border fallout or global ecological damage.

Rick rose on his toes, flexing tense muscles.

Nuke one target. Would that cause Kim to flee? Motivate a coup by some hastily formed opposition group? Convince Ming to remove Kim by force? Induce Gwon to cooperate?

Or would it cause Kim to launch his nuclear missiles?

Turning, Rick gazed across the Oval Office, thinking about the annihilating weapons he had ordered to be prepared. *Morally how, if at all, does this differ from the Nazis' Final Solution? How am I different from Himmler if I sign a bombing order that kills tens of thousands of civilians?*

Rick felt a giant vise squeezing his chest, a finger of pain tracing his neck and jaw. He pushed a thought away. *Not now, God . . . no time.*

Is there no other way? Rick asked the bust of George Washington. *The only feasible military option is so awful; why not continue working diplomacy and internal security, with faith that they will succeed? After all, we stopped the bombers cold at Baltimore. We defeated them there. If we did it once, we can do it again! And diplomacy is working. The UN has condemned North Korea and demanded that it dismantle its nuclear weapons.*

Rick glanced at the presidential flag flanking his desk, the eagle's fierce gaze.

But . . . with that second bomb this became about more than defending. Right now the country's on its back. We're seeing the dissolution of our social contract. No longer believing their government—their president—will protect them,

Americans are withdrawing into enclaves and arming themselves. All but the most disadvantaged have fled our cities, leaving them to looters. Our economy is collapsing. Anyone who looks Korean is attacked on the street, or at the least gets cursed.

At this point there's no gradual path to recovery. We can't reverse the disintegration without an act as dramatic and game changing as the bombs that drove us there.

And now I'm back to the neutron bomb.

Rick sat down heavily at the presidential desk, drummed his fingers on it.

But I don't have to do what others say is necessary and right if I think it's wrong. I can stick to what I believe is right. Let them impeach me!

His lips twisted. *Yeah, but then the country would get Bruce Griffith. He'd probably go for the full nuclear strike package. So, because I'm morally offended at the options facing me, I open the way for Bruce to choose the most morally offensive of all? Where's the morality in that? Besides, I don't want to be a failed president! And what about Ella's belief that duty must sometimes override morality? Is she right, or is that thinking like a guard at Auschwitz?*

How many times did I say it during the campaign? Must have been hundreds. With stern face and firm tone: "I will do whatever is necessary to protect the American people!"

Now I'm face to face with myself. I know what I said, but I don't know what I believed. When you scrape off the campaign gloss, what did I mean by "whatever is necessary"? Anything? No matter how repugnant? What did I mean then? What did others believe I meant? Am I now bound by those words?

He picked up a letter opener and, unconsciously, held it like a dagger.

I didn't think about what those words meant; what they might require. They were just a check-off, like my pledge to always level with the American people. The price of entry. Pay to play. Saying certain things was as necessary as having campaign funds. Lacking either one, I'm out. Any presidential candidate would be out.

So there are huge mitigating circumstances. Like someone who is pressured into signing a contract without understanding it. Like a home buyer taken in by a predatory lender. When I said those words, I didn't really mean "whatever." My listeners, if questioned, would have said they didn't expect it to be literally anything. Circumstances have changed since I said that. A foolish consistency is the hobgoblin of little minds. No, I don't feel bound by those words to nuke North Korea!

Rick poured coffee and scuffed back to his private office. Placing the mug on a coaster with the presidential seal, he dropped into his chair.

But the price of not doing whatever it takes is so huge, and it's paid in deaths and mutilations and cancers and orphans and fear—deep, deep fear that's destroying us right now!

It's not that I'm running out of options. It's time I'm running out of!

What am I going to do before one of those clocks ticks zero? His stomach cramped.

All the supports of his life, everything that held him, protected him, stood as a bulwark between him and chaos, had been swept away. He was dizzy, in a fog, disoriented, unable to concentrate, wandering through mental loops that always ended in disaster.

Like other politicians, Rick Martin had acknowledged his faith, taking care not to give offense to anyone. He regarded religion as no more than one of several sources of inspiration, guidance, and optimism.

Until this moment.

The words of a familiar scripture, one he had intellectually acknowledged as expressing profound distress but never thought about, much less felt, now pierced his soul.

Desperately, he knelt and said, "Lord, let this cup pass from me!"

Alone in his hideaway, Rick felt those words erupt from his soul. Though he knew the words, he didn't have the courage to finish the passage.

He stood up. *Somehow, I feel better, no longer alone and beyond any help or comfort. I'm probably tricking myself, but I feel buoyed by something.*

Chapter 47

IN THE PRESIDENTIAL Briefing Room, Rick prepared with fatalistic intensity to learn the recommended target for annihilation. Unsuccessfully, he tried to block images and voices of Las Vegas. "Find them, Mr. President. Punish them for what they did here!" *No,* he thought. *This is about protecting, not avenging. But I don't know if this will protect; all I know is it will kill a lot of people who had nothing to do with Las Vegas. Maybe I'm just tired of the strain of trying to find a way without more killing. Maybe if I keep looking, I'll find it.*

Secretary of Defense Easterly spoke, the volume of his first words and the pause after them signaling that he was pulling Martin back from wherever he had gone.

"... We recommend the city of Sinpo for our demonstration attack. It's on the east coast of the DPRK, near the widest part of the Sea of Japan, and about equidistant from the Chinese and ROK borders—roughly a hundred miles from each, and about one fifty from Russia. Our best estimate—guess, really—is a population of about one hundred fifty-eight thousand."

Martin, usually chatty with his briefers, was silent. Easterly glanced from his notes to the president. *Poor bastard! I don't think he wants to know much about Sinpo.*

Bart Guarini, ever conscious of how his boss and friend would appear to history, tried unsuccessfully to will Martin into engaging, probing, questioning the choice.

Silence.

At last Guarini said, "Eric, tell us why you chose Sinpo, rather than a military target."

"It really came down to geography. We want to have as little effect on the DPRK's neighbors as possible. Most of the North Korean army has moved into positions close to the ROK border, the DMZ, and the ROKs have a large force facing them. They're pretty close together, too close to be confident the ROK troops wouldn't be affected if we put neutron bombs on the North Koreans. Plus, northern soldiers who weren't killed outright would probably come storming south, into the ROKs, starting the land war we're trying to avoid.

"There are two other army concentrations. One is in and around Pyongyang and the other is along the Chinese border, probably to keep Kim's dear people from fleeing. Since we don't want any impact on China and don't want to hit Pyongyang on this first strike, we can't hit those troops.

"Bottom line? There are no military targets right now for the neutron weapons."

"OK, go on," said Martin flatly, a forefinger repeatedly tracing the rim of his coffee mug.

"Sir, since the neutron bombs have never been tested in the atmosphere, we have only an approximate idea of their kill radius. In order to be certain of inflicting heavy casualties, three weapons are assigned. They'll be delivered by cruise missiles. Time on target will be mid-morning in Sinpo."

Rick tasted bile. *I'm sitting here planning to kill thousands of people, just blot them out in the midst of an ordinary morning.* How can I do this? Horror fought exhaustion for dominance of his mind. Then he heard a gargling voice and knew it spoke from a mass grave in Nevada. "Don't let us down, Mr. President!"

"And how many people am I going to kill at mid-morning in Sinpo?" he said dully.

Guarini was appalled that Rick Martin, once the master of "we" and the passive voice, was now taking all this upon himself. Hurriedly, he said, "It's *we*, Mr. President. We *all* believe we must do this to protect Americans and enable our society to recover."

Martin nodded, stone-faced, awaiting Easterly's answer.

"It's impossible to say for certain—there are too many unknowns—but surely tens of thousands. Say, fifty to seventy-five thousand." Easterly shrugged, frowning.

"And after I sign that order, it happens? How fast?"

"We can have the cruise missiles on target within an hour, or you can specify a time. As I said, we recommend mid-morning Sinpo time."

Jesus! Like having pizza delivered! Martin's finger, the one tracing the rim of the coffee mug, began to twitch. He didn't notice as he sat in silent contemplation of piles of Korean bodies covering up piles of American bodies. Desperately, he told himself that he was still pursuing other options, that until he actually signed the order—maybe even for a few minutes after he signed—one of them might work. Ming, or even Kim, might see reason and he, Rick Martin, would not become a mass murderer.

He realized the three were staring. "OK," he said in a hollow voice, rising from his chair like a zombie, knowing he had moved another step toward becoming the evil he was fighting.

MacAdoo and Easterly watched as he left, followed protectively by Guarini. "My God!" said Easterly. "Did you see that?"

Chapter 48

RAY MORALES WALKED toward the White House through the tunnel from Treasury, met by a silent, impassive Secret Service agent whose one moment of human contact was to look him in the eye and say, "Semper Fi, sir!"

Morales responded automatically but proudly, "Semper Fi, Marine."

Semper Fidelis . . . Always Faithful. After The Corps, many Marines gravitate to positions where, at some point, they'll be required to stand firm. Perhaps that's why there are so few of us in politics. The Art of the Possible isn't a high calling after Always Faithful. When the fact that something looks impossible justifies inaction, what have you got? The best of my congressional colleagues accept responsibility, but none of them even understands duty, much less embraces it.

Trudging behind the agent, Morales shook his head. *And now I'm on my way to meet the president of the United States. I have no idea what he wants. Ella wouldn't tell me, just said she can't help him and she's praying I can.*

He entered the private office, and Martin rose from a small desk, hand outstretched.

"Thanks for coming right away, Ray."

"Mr. President, when the bell rings, old fire horses feel the same adrenaline as young ones. Pavlov was right."

The president smiled, although it was clearly strained, and gestured to the chair.

"Ray, you haven't been in the White House loop, but I'll bet you know what I'm dealing with these days."

"Yessir. As my Marine buddies would say, you're deciding how big a can of whup-ass to open up on North Korea or, as my congressional colleagues would put it, you're searching for the most appropriate combination of carrots and sticks."

"You got it, Ray.

"Can we agree that this meeting is in strictest confidence, entirely between the two of us?"

"Certainly, sir."

"Ray, could you stop calling me sir? I need your frankness much more than your deference!"

"You'll have my frankness, sir, but you're The Man. When I was a brand new second lieutenant, my Marines always called me sir. They also let me know when I was being a dumb-ass. I'll be frank, I promise you . . . sir."

Yessir, nosir, three bags full. I wonder if this meeting Ella insisted on will be a waste of time. But after all, this man is the only JCS chairman ever to resign on a matter of conscience—and he was right. No, Ray Morales isn't just a Clint Eastwood poster.

"Ray, what's it like to kill someone? What's it like to give orders that kill a lot of people?"

Jesus! thought Morales. *Are we going into psychoanalysis?*

"That's quite a question, sir! Under what circumstances?"

"In the military, in doing your duty."

"Well, sir, depends a lot on who's getting killed. I never had second thoughts about plinking some bastard trying to kill me or my Marines. I've had many second thoughts about orders I gave that got Marines or civilians killed."

"But every time you ordered an attack, usually Marines, or civilians, or both were killed. How can you carry a burden like *that*?"

"Because what I meant was, killed unnecessarily, killed because I made a mistake, because I missed something or because I just fucked up."

"So killing is OK with you when it's not the result of a mistake?"

"Depends on what you mean by OK, sir. It's never OK in a cosmic sense. God doesn't like it. I'll have to answer for the killing I've done. But it's also part of being human. We've got a lot of good in us, but we're also weak, confused, greedy, jealous, cruel, the whole nine yards."

Morales' voice rasped from deep inside: "So I've killed because it seems to me that in this world as it is, a group that doesn't protect itself will be killed—or enslaved. God help me, I'm willing to kill to prevent that happening to me, my family, my friends, my country!"

My country, thought Rick, leaning forward. *That's how Ella puts it; if only it were that simple! If we can't see beyond country, the world will never have peace.*

He forced himself to back off. "I'm sorry, Ray, I just started firing questions at you. Would you like some refreshment? I don't mind saying I could use a taste. It's been a long day."

"Sounds good, sir. Can the White House come up with a Miller?"

After the steward had delivered their drinks and withdrawn, Morales said, "Sir, why'd you ask me to come over tonight? I'm flattered, but I know I'm an ex-general who'll probably serve only one term in Congress. I'm the most junior member of the House Armed Services Committee. And I'm a Republican, to boot."

Well, here goes, thought Rick.

His words tumbled out: "Ray, I've never knowingly harmed anybody in my life and now I'm being urged to sign an order that will kill at least fifty thousand people!"

"And?"

"I don't know if it's the right thing and I don't know if I can live with myself if I do it, even if it *is* right!"

"So how do I fit into that situation?"

"I don't know exactly, but Ella insisted I speak with you about it."

"You know that Ella and I . . ."

"Are way over it. But she respects you. Frankly, I don't know whether she respects me any longer."

"I'm not a marriage counselor."

With a scowl and a dismissive wave, Rick said, "That's not why you're here!

"Look, the only other president who ever used a nuke did it after six years of bloody world war had conditioned him and this country to killing and death just like they were conditioned to the weather! It was part of life. It couldn't be predicted exactly, but it happened each day and you lived with it."

"Sir, the bulldozers are still scraping trenches in the desert to bury our dead. We're damn lucky they're not also at work in Maryland! And somewhere out there those bastards are pulling together another attack. Look, if eighty thousand dead—and civilians at that—isn't bloody warfare, what is?"

"Ray, nobody but Himmler has ever—*ever*—signed an order to kill fifty thousand human beings in cold blood, and even he couldn't do it in a single moment, like Zeus throwing a thunderbolt. That's what they tell me I should do, but how *could* I?"

Morales saw agony, indecision, and fear as Martin sat bolt upright in his chair.

"Tell me what happens if you don't do it."

"I don't know of course; that's one part of the hell of it! But the NSC believes Kim will continue bombing, or furnishing bombs; my domestic advisors believe the country will unravel beyond repair; and I'm certain to be impeached in favor of Bruce Griffith, who *will* sign that nuclear attack order."

"What else?"

"What do you mean?"

"How are you going to feel if they're right about those consequences?"

"Terrible, but not like a murderer!"

Morales nodded. "OK. Look, sir, you're having to learn in a few weeks what people like me learn to live with over years. That's hard, really hard, but you're going to have to. Or, if not, you're going to have to accept what happens as the price—to others as well as yourself—of protecting your own soul."

"But, Ray, what's right? How can killing fifty thousand human beings be right?"

"Let me tell you a story. I was about five years too young for Vietnam. But I got my first Marine officer training—we call it The Basic School, TBS— from men who'd led Marines there.

"In wartime, people get killed. There's nothing a second lieutenant, or a general, or a president can do about that, until both sides decide to end it. You have an ability to influence how many get killed and who they are, but there's no course of action in combat that's free of killing. Marines are taught this from their first day; I imagine most presidents have to learn it.

"One of my TBS instructors called this situation prepping the tree line. It's a Vietnam story, but it applies to most wars and I think it describes your dilemma.

"Imagine you're leading your platoon through open ground toward a village in a group of trees on a slight hill. Your job is to occupy this village, today. You know from experience the enemy will be waiting, hiding among the trees and huts, keeping the villagers under guard until you get real close. They may even have a few out in the open doing normal things. As you reach the village, the enemy will open up from cover and kill a lot of your Marines before they can overrun them.

"Unless . . . unless you prep the tree line. That means calling for artillery and air strikes to kill some of the enemy dug in there and shake up the rest, before your guys get within range. Doing that will also kill villagers. And of course, there's always the chance that there are no enemy in this village today, that it's just as it appears.

"What do you do? You prep the tree line."

"How can you live with that, with knowingly killing people who have done you no harm and in fact couldn't harm you?" Martin asked.

"Duty. Because it's your duty to occupy that village today. Because you have a duty to your Marines, who trusted you to value their lives and use them wisely and carefully."

"You sound like Ella. She calls it protecting the tribe." Morales saw skepticism in his eyes.

"OK—that's another way to put it, I guess.

"My own combat was Gulf One, and I was a battalion commander. That's not as personal as leading a platoon or a company, but still I made several of those decisions. Each time, I lost a little piece of my soul."

"But you were prepared."

"As prepared as you can get by listening to others. It tore me up inside anyway."

Rick gazed off, seeing Las Vegas. He thought about Steve Nguyen, who wanted punishment, and the grieving woman, who wanted no more killing. But he was left with Nguyen's final words, words that had drained the last energy of this life from his soul: "Don't let us down!"

Seeing Rick's sight turned inward, Morales waited. After a while, he said, "Sir, is there any better way to do your duty than signing that order, anything your advisors might have overlooked or withheld from you?"

"No, I don't think so."

"Then what's stopping you?"

Martin picked up an index card and tapped it on the desk, gathering his thoughts.

"Maybe because it's so personal. I've selected a North Korean city for death and I'm going to kill it. I'm going to kill the same kind of people who were killed in Las Vegas—grandparents, infants, kids playing."

"Yes, you are. But the words you just said make no connection between those people and the bombing of Las Vegas. I'd say there is a connection. Those eighty thousand Americans were killed by North Koreans. And you're killing the North Koreans to protect Americans from more of the same—right?"

"Yes, but the North Koreans I will kill have no control over what Kim does. They are as much his victims as the Americans in Las Vegas!"

"I don't agree with that entirely, sir, but if you're correct, doesn't that mean responsibility for what happens to them is Kim's? You're going to destroy this city because Kim continues to threaten the people you took an oath to protect, after already killing eighty thousand of them. You're doing it for no other reason than to force Kim from power before he can bomb again—right?"

"You're talking as if North Korean lives have less value than American lives!"

"No, sir. You're not listening carefully or thinking clearly. I believe that, to God, all lives are equally valuable. But you aren't God. You're the president of the United States. Didn't you swear an oath to carry out the duties of president? Don't those duties include defense of our people and the preservation of the Constitution? Aren't they both being attacked by North Korea? You're not some mediator. You're our leader—and God help us if you refuse to act like it!"

Martin's eyes flashed. "I don't have to kill thousands with a nuclear weapon to be your leader!"

"Then what *do* you have to do, Mr. President?"

"I have to find another way out of this."

"What else, sir?"

"What do you mean, Ray?"

"What's the rest of that sentence, the one that begins I have to find another way"

Rick looked away. *I know what he means. Can I say it? If I do, I'm back up against it again. I can deflect his question, and if he were a reporter, I would. But he's not. He's someone who's trying to help me. After I asked him to.*

Rick turned back to Morales. "Yeah. The rest is before Kim bombs us again."

"Yessir. And how much time do you have?"

"I don't know."

"And will destroying that city stop it?"

"It might, by getting Kim out of power."

"Is there anything else that might?"

"Finding out what he wants and giving it to him."

"Can you do that before he bombs us again?"

"I don't know."

"So, you're weighing something specific you can do now that might stop Kim's nuclear bombing of Americans against something as yet unknown that also might stop it, unless Kim sets off another while you're searching for that something. And what's in the balance is tens of thousands of American lives, the lives of people who believe you will protect them because you said you would during the campaign and swore you would on inauguration day!"

"You didn't mention Korean lives in the balance, Ray."

"You didn't swear an oath to protect Koreans, Mr. President. You have a great duty to Americans. I'd say you have a much lesser duty to protect Koreans."

"Because they're not in our tribe, is that it, Ray?"

"Yes, if you want to put it that way. But they still count; you're going to have their lives on your soul forever, sir, just like me and every other leader who's ever decided to prep the tree line."

So my duty demands my soul. That's what Ella said.

No! I won't make that trade!

Then what trade will *you make?* said a mocking voice from somewhere beyond.

To prevent more attacks I have to close the North Korean nuke store—now. *I've tried everything else. This is the only way left!*

He heard another voice: *Don't let this be an excuse for more killing. Find another way. There's got to be another way!*

"I'm sorry," mumbled Rick, feeling something die inside, "so sorry! I can't find another way."

Morales waited. Finally, the president said, "Ray, what does the country want me to do? What's your read on public opinion?"

"Sir you've got experts who can answer that. I pay close attention to my district but not nationally."

"I'll ask my experts, but right now I'm asking you."

"Most people are very frightened. They're afraid of more nukes, but also just afraid in general. YouTube is full of Islamist videos screaming, in English, that now the infidels will pay. People want protection.

"You were right—grabbing the Baltimore bomb handed the terrorists a huge defeat, but frightened people tend to see the glass half empty. The people in my district are on edge. Their lives are on hold, waiting, hoping for something telling them the danger is over so they can go back to their homes and jobs in Austin.

"But there's more to it. With the second bomb, people passed a tipping point. Before that, it was like Nine-eleven on steroids: sympathy, sadness, anger, wanting to help—but not many feared for themselves or families or friends. When that bomb was found in Baltimore, it became like every Marine feels in his first firefight.

"Suddenly, this is about *you*. Those people down range are trying to kill *you*, and they could do it any second. A few freeze, refusing to accept that, looking for something to let them keep their sense of immortality. Most, though, react by aiming carefully and firing back rapidly. They want to kill this threat, *now*. In the moment, that's all they care about.

"When you ask yourself what the country wants you to do, Mr. President, think about that!"

Chapter 49

RICK HAD A few minutes before his meeting with the congressional leadership. He glanced at the talking points, then pushed them aside; it was gut-check time and talking points wouldn't hack it. Their half-dozen gatherings since Six-thirteen were all prelude to today's, although he would never have predicted it would come to this.

The horror of the order he might soon sign nearly overwhelmed him. He didn't want cool objectivity; he wanted resolve. What had Morales said about his choice? "Because that's better than burying people who trusted you to protect them," wasn't that it?

He realized he was attempting to armor his soul. Intellectually, he knew this armor had a chink: putting Own ahead of Other was the root of the bloody history of the human race. He had resisted that all his life. And yet . . . when faced with the choice of Own or Other on this scale, how *could* he choose Other at the cost of bloody disaster for Own?

'A man's gotta do what a man's gotta do.' That phrase had always evoked his disdain. It was a substitute for weighing the evidence, a triumph of testosterone over thought. Now he realized it was also a fundamental to the human condition, not just the evolutionary programming of the human male.

Rick smiled ruefully. *That's what Ella's been telling me. I rejected her counsel, certain I could think my way past war. War is* not *the answer! But what* is *the answer? If I kept trying, would I discover it? I'll never know, because I don't have time to keep trying.*

The knife stabbed his gut again as he permitted the thought that his next breath could be followed by news of another ruined, radioactive city.

Rick had decided, sometime over a sleepless night, to take the road that would almost certainly lead to the death of Sinpo. He hadn't told Ella because, in a way he knew but couldn't describe, he would have felt patronized by her approval; she had been certain since the beginning that he must crush Kim. He realized she knew because she hadn't asked about his meeting with Morales.

Martin hadn't made his decision in a rigorous accounting of pro and con, or in a flash of conviction. No, it had been a matter of accepting that all doors but this one had shut, one by one, and there was no time left to find others—if they existed. Realizing he had decided was frightening, but also comforting, because the strain of reexamining his options was over.

Killing Sinpo was now the default. Unless something new miraculously appeared, he would sign the order sitting within that folder on his desk like a malevolent genie in a bottle. He stared at it.

"Mr. President, the congressional leadership."

"OK."

Guarini ushered them in; Martin rose, pumping hands and mouthing greetings automatically. *God!* How he wished some atmosphere of comradeship, of uniting to do what was best for America, had developed! Instead, there had been weeks of sterile role-playing that depressed him deeply. He knew they were here to walk the tightrope again, asserting Congress' war powers authority without sharing any responsibility for presidential decisions. Do it; we'll see how it plays, and then we'll say what *we* would have done. And of course, amazingly, what *they* would have done would look just about right. He didn't resent this; it was just politics, but he wished it were otherwise.

As they were getting coffee or water and seating themselves, Easterly and MacAdoo entered. Martin felt the legislators tense.

You don't know the half of it! I used to sit where you do and believed my job was to make speeches and cast votes and let the chips fall. I didn't feel responsible for accomplishing *anything, for final results. As long as I could say I was doing my best under the circumstances, my conscience was satisfied. If my best wasn't good enough, well I'm only one among five hundred legislators.*

That's *where you are.*

Where am I? Like Truman said, I'm where the buck stops! How wrong I was to doubt Morales; it's my fellow politicians who don't understand.

When all were settled, Rick walked to a wingback chair and sat within the group, now assembled in an oval of couches and chairs. They looked at him warily.

"Gentlemen, thank you for coming over again. I think these meetings are important to allow us to informally exchange ideas, and I certainly welcome your thoughts and suggestions. I want to share my impressions of the present situation and hear yours, and then describe the courses of action we see."

He registered that their faces were carefully neutral, then continued: "I asked you over this morning to tell you that international examination of the Baltimore bomb positively identified it as North Korean. I intend to announce that tonight, and you must keep it to yourselves until then. The scientists—American, Chinese, and IAEA—are unanimous.

"So here we have it: Kim Jong-il destroyed one American city and attacked another, after being warned we were on to him and the consequences of further attack would be severe. I believe this is intolerable and Kim must now give up, or be removed from, control of the DPRK and its nuclear weapons. That's how I see it."

The Speaker, a twelve-term congressman from Minnesota, said, "I'm with you on that conclusion, Mr. President, but as they say, the devil's in the details. *How* do you propose to get Kim out?"

Well, here we go, thought Rick. "We've attempted negotiation, using all channels. Kim has turned everything down, even President Ming's offer of comfortable sanctuary in China. He has continued to deny any connection to the bombing of Las Vegas and the attempt on Baltimore. Yet, any moment, perhaps before I complete this sentence, Kim could attack us again. We have no more time." Martin felt perspiration pop on his forehead.

Looking as if he couldn't believe Martin's words, the Speaker said, "Mr. President, you're saying diplomacy is over. Many Americans, most of them in *our* party, won't accept that. You haven't made the case for war!

"When you announce, backed by international scientific investigation, that the Baltimore bomb is North Korean, Kim may become more amenable. We don't know yet. And what about continuing to work through the UN? We should give sanctions and the quarantine more time to work!"

Irritation shredded the fog of Rick's fatigue. *More* time? *Am I the only one here who hears the clocks ticking?*

"Ron, if I do that, which do you think would happen first—the sanctions bite, another city goes, or the Martin administration gets impeached?"

"Mr. President, if you think impeachment talk is because you're using diplomacy, you've been poorly advised! That talk isn't driven by your methods; it's fueled by the ineffectiveness of your administration in protecting American lives! It will really gather momentum if you turn from diplomacy to killing."

It required all of Martin's extraordinary self-control to send his rage away to its place, to listen rather than erupt at this heedless fool.

Agitated, the Speaker continued. "You've seen those videos! A lot of Americans believe war is *not* the answer; the president doesn't have to kill Korean kids to protect American kids. They want and expect your administration to protect them but don't believe for a moment that you have to start another Korean war to do it!"

"And what do *you* believe, Ron?"

"I believe it's *your* job to use all the vast powers of the presidency prudently, to protect America with a scalpel, not a meat cleaver. We don't need another ill-conceived war of choice!"

Seeing that his boss could not contain his anger, Guarini jumped in: "Mr. Speaker, you fear another bloody war in Korea. What I fear is the bloody war in *America*, begun by Kim on Six-thirteen!" Glancing at each of them, Guarini continued: "What about the rest of what the president said; what if we lose another city while we're talking? Is it *prudent* to risk that? Is it *moral* to risk it?"

The senate minority leader responded. "I'm glad that's on your mind, because it damn well should be! Listening to the Speaker, I thought maybe I'd missed the announcement of a foolproof defense against nuclear terrorists so that we could consider at our leisure how to deal with Kim.

"After Baltimore a lot of Americans are scared to death. They don't believe the Martin administration is doing what it takes to protect them from Kim's bombs. That's why they're camped out, away from cities! That's why our economy is in free fall! And that's why a lot of them are telling their senators and congressmen to give you the boot, Mr. President. They're saying 'OK, you've had your chance to do this and you didn't get 'er done.' *That's* why Bart's counting potential impeachment votes!"

The Speaker growled, jowls quivering "So, Jesse, you and your NRA crowd want to bomb them back to the Stone Age? Nuke 'em til they glow?

Will that give you more courage? Will that jump-start our economy? Are more mass graves OK with you, so long as they aren't American?"

Martin was, somehow, able to keep his voice even. "You each bring up an important point—that thousands of lives are in the balance here. We're all aware of that, and all horrified and saddened by it. I don't believe any of us want to see more mass graves of any nationality."

The president's gaze probed each congressional leader, hoping to find another soul laid bare. "However, I can't say the same about the man we have to deal with. I've stood toe to toe with Kim and I *know* he doesn't care. And, for that matter, al-Qaeda's new leader doesn't care either, so long as those graves advance the cause. Whether Kim is manufacturing and planting the bombs, or whether he manufactures them and al-Qaeda delivers them, Kim is the key. No more DPRK bombs, no more mass graves!"

He looked into their faces, each in turn, his eyes piercing the careful veils of their expressions like a bayonet. "You know what I've been trying to do, what Ming and others have been trying to do, and that it hasn't worked. So if Kim won't step down, for us, or for the UN, or for his Chinese patron, or for the good of his people, how do I get him out before he attacks us again?"

Rick wasn't surprised when nobody answered. "I can order Kim assassinated." He looked at each of the men from the Hill. *This is what they call a pregnant pause,* he thought. *And nobody's giving birth. Not one of them is willing to go anywhere near that. So, neither am I.*

"Or, perhaps we could capture Kim and put him up before the ICC. Eric, how about that?"

"Sir, the SEAL in me wants to say we can do it . . . but we can't. Kim controls the DPRK so tightly that no American special ops team could grab him and get out of the country. With a lot of luck, they might be able to kill him— but not bring him back alive."

The president resumed: "OK, Eric, we invade the DPRK and chase Kim out. Then, depending on how much help or opposition we had from China, we let Ming pick a Korean communist to succeed Kim and eliminate the nukes, *or* we assist in reunification under South Korean rule and *they* eliminate the nukes. What's the prospect of doing that?"

"Highly problematic, sir. We'd be outnumbered, since it's unlikely that South Korea would assist us or even permit us to cross their territory in invading. The Japanese might go in with us, but without ROK support we probably couldn't supply our forces in the field. Kim has said he'd attack us, the Japanese, and South Korea with nuclear weapons if we attacked him, and he's demonstrated the capacity to do it. China might well help him, either overtly or covertly. Mac and the field commanders have looked closely at this and think the odds are we'd end up in another bloody stalemate, and, unless our ABM defenses are perfect, Japan, Korea, and maybe Guam would get hit with Kim's nuclear missiles."

"And for sure Kim would be doing his best to pull off another nuclear attack in the United States!" added Guarini.

The congressional leaders said nothing. This time the president waited.

With an angry expression, the senate majority leader spoke up: "Then the Pentagon has been lying to Congress for years! You've always told us you could handle the North Koreans!"

"That's right!" said the house majority leader.

"Gentlemen," said Mac evenly, "we were always speaking about our ability to respond to the north invading the south. In that case, the ROK military would be fully with us and we'd have use of South Korea's ports and airfields. We weren't lying; we were talking a different ballgame."

The president observed the men he had summoned. *And now we all know what comes next. None of my former congressional colleagues will look me in the eye. Funny, but the Democrats seem angrier than the Republicans, as if it's unconscionable that a fellow Democrat would put them in this position.*

He spoke somberly and fatalistically, like a man who had come to terms with his advanced cancer. "In the nineteen sixties Herman Kahn wrote a book, subtitled thinking about the unthinkable. The title was *On Thermonuclear War*. That war seemed pretty close then, but we got through the next thirty years. Now we're at that precipice again; in fact we've been swept over it. We're here not by way of hostility among the five big nuclear powers, but thanks to a pissant dictator with Ray-Bans and a fondness for movies. How could we—and I include myself—have been so willfully blind?"

In a voice heavy with sadness and consequence, the president said, "Tell them, Eric."

"Yes, sir!" Secretary of Defense Easterly responded with the brisk confidence of a surgeon describing what he could do with his knife, without acknowledging that he didn't expect surgery to save the patient. A slight tremble in his hands betrayed his feelings.

"We have a full range of nuclear options, but they boil down to two.

"We can hit the DPRK with eighteen nuclear warheads simultaneously. This would ensure that Kim couldn't launch any nuclear missiles. It would destroy all cities and military bases and, ultimately, kill half to three-quarters of the population. Essentially the DPRK, including the Party, the military, and what passes for civil society, would cease to exist. Refugees, many dying from radiation, would surge into the ROK and China, maybe some into Russia. Fallout would cause some problems in South Korea and Japan but not in China or Russia. We expect no American casualties from such a strike, which could be accomplished in a few minutes using cruise and ballistic missiles."

Easterly's words left Rick faintly nauseated and a little light-headed. He reminded himself that he hadn't signed the order yet. Judging by their expressions, the five legislators were explorers scrambling away from a suddenly gaping crevasse.

With sweat beading his hairline and a slight tremor in his voice, the secretary of defense continued.

"At the other end of the spectrum, we can do a demonstration-of-resolve attack with several warheads of a type that emits lethal radiation but has relatively little explosive power—for a nuke—and leaves no fallout of consequence. This would kill most people in the target city but not obliterate it or generate cross-border fallout. We could then pause to see if Kim would give it up, or if other DPRK leaders would topple him to save themselves, or if China would intervene militarily to remove Kim and his cronies. This, too, would be done with missiles, without American casualties. Or, I should say without more American casualties, since we had about a hundred eighty thousand killed and injured on Six-thirteen."

Silence followed—the silence of the grave.

Finally, the house minority leader gave a low whistle and said, "Jesus weeping Christ!"

Martin looked at him with tired, haunted eyes. "Indeed," he said softly. His mind registered that this was their first honest comment since the "informal conversations" began.

The Speaker looked at Martin with disbelief. "You could *do* that? You could *give* that order? That's crazy!" he hissed. "You deserve to go down in history as a monster like Stalin!"

Rick felt as if his soul had been stripped bare, because the Speaker had just named one of his nightmares. But that wasn't his worst nightmare. *That* was visiting dying Americans again and knowing that he could have prevented their agony. So instead of challenging the Speaker's damning words, he said, "Then, Ron, what would you have me do instead?"

"Find another way! This is unacceptable! It cannot be beyond your wits to keep us safe without murdering tens of thousands of innocent people. I refuse to even discuss such a monstrous plan!" The Speaker waved his hands as if they could drive away the secretary of defense's words like marauding insects.

The president responded: "That's where I was until a few days ago, when we found the second bomb and then Kim refused Ming's offer. But I now believe we're beyond the point where we can decline to act decisively, where we can look for another way. You see how our country is today, even though we defeated Kim's second attack.

"Do you think I *want* to do this? Is there anything else I could do to be sure of stopping Kim before we lose another city? What else can I do to reverse the disintegration of our society?"

Rick's voice rose and cracked: "If there's something else that would do those things, for God's sake tell me what it is!"

Martin looked at five silent representatives of the coequal, legislative branch of government. The Speaker returned his gaze with contempt. Three looked at the carpet. The senate minority leader looked at Martin with an expression that said, "No, there isn't something else. And I no longer want your job someday."

Rick glanced at the folder on his desk, and Guarini knew the meeting was over.

Returning his attention to his visitors, the president said, "A few minutes ago Sam announced that I will go on the air tonight at nine. I will tell Kim, and the world, that he has a choice to make."

Martin rose and began walking the Speaker to the door. The others trailed, attended by Guarini and Easterly. When the president touched the Speaker's elbow in a friendly gesture, he pulled away. Rick banished his emotions. He didn't have time to regret this end to an important alliance and a not inconsiderable friendship. In seven hours he would give Kim an ultimatum and had a lot to do before then.

He felt as if he had been pushed into a swift river and would inevitably be swept over the falls.

Chapter 50

DOTTIE BRANSON ANNOUNCED, "President Ming is coming on now, sir." Martin punched speaker; interpreters in Washington and Beijing dialed their concentration to its highest.

"Good morning, Ming."

"Good evening, Rick.

A few minutes before seven, the president sat at his big desk. Its photos and other mementos caught Anne Battista's attention for an instant. *They're a time capsule,* she thought. *How the world has changed—and how it's changed us!* She, Dorn, and Guarini hovered; there were plenty of chairs, but nobody could relax enough to sit.

"Ming, this is a grave moment. When last we spoke, I said that consequences would surely flow from identification of the second bomb. As you know, our governments have jointly completed that identification and have agreed, along with IAEA scientists, that this bomb is also North Korean."

"Rick, what was agreed was that the fissionable material in the bomb was produced at Yongbyon, not the same thing as saying the bomb itself was produced there. And they also agreed, did they not, that the warhead was of an early Chinese design, stolen by A. Q. Khan? Will you announce that?"

"I don't intend to announce the warhead design, but if asked, the U.S. government will reply along the lines you just described.

"My purpose in calling is to give you notice of the consequences of this second North Korean act of war against the United States."

Ming frowned. "Act of war? Rick those words lead only one way and cannot be taken back!"

God, how I hate translation! Rick thought. *I can't tell if he's genuinely concerned or just tweaking me.*

"I agree, Ming. And those words fit this situation."

Martin paused. Ming waited, working a cigarette from the dented case.

"In two hours I will tell Americans who is responsible for this second bomb, and I will tell them—and Kim and his people—what may happen soon because of it. I'm telling you now out of respect for you and for China.

"Ming, Kim and his gang must go, now! My country has lost eighty thousand people and a city to Kim's attacks. And I need not tell *you* the economic damage we've suffered. Tonight I will announce that unless Kim leaves North Korea within seven days, he and his countrymen will receive a devastating attack from the United States. If he does leave, and his successor agrees to nuclear disarmament, this attack may be avoided. The United States is imposing no conditions other than these but will accept no less."

Ming nearly interrupted to say that America could not dictate to China but held his tongue, as he had many times, to his advantage, during his long career.

Rick steeled himself, praying that Ming's interpreter would convey his determination.

"Ming, I refuse another bloody ground war in Korea when I have other means to utterly defeat the DPRK! I will use our nuclear weapons. The Kim regime and North Korea's people will have one chance to recover if they make the mistake of ignoring my ultimatum. We will destroy a single city and then pause. If America's demands are not met, the pause will end with the total nuclear destruction of North Korea."

Ming remained silent, so Martin continued: "As I'm sure you've been advised, nuclear fallout would not be deposited on China. China will, however, be greatly affected. I acknowledge that and regret it. But there is, for any American president put in this situation, no other choice."

Ming's mind accelerated like a sprinter exploding from starting blocks. *So, Rick Martin, you may be the one leopard that* can *change its spots! Well, if Kim is so insane as to ignore your ultimatum, China cannot save him. And if the Korean people and the Party don't save themselves by removing Kim, China cannot save them, either. This is probably the best way, because a land war would surely force us to intervene. And the collapse of the United States, now when we hold billions in Treasuries and sell them so many products, would be catastrophic for China.*

"Rick, do you believe there is anything more for us after death?"

Martin, nonplussed as Ming intended, blurted: "Yes, Ming, I do. Do you?"

Ming ignored the question. "Do you believe in the Christian God and his son, who will sit in judgment on you in the next life?"

"I do."

"Then may they be wise and merciful to your spirit, because it will have much to answer for."

Carefully, Ming said, "China will look to its interests as this unfolds. I hope they will not conflict with America's.

"Goodbye, Rick." Ming broke the connection.

The president looked at his companions and raised his eyebrows. Battista said, "That was about the best we could have hoped for." Nodding, Martin took a deep breath and told Dottie Branson to call Premier Kato.

* * *

In Beijing, Ming arose and began a series of *tai chi* moves to calm his mind and clarify his thinking. As he continued the precise motions, satisfaction spread through him like moisture being taken up by his tomato plants:

This is surely the year of my destiny! I have ensured the peaceful return of Taiwan Province, brought China into equal partnership with America, and I'm now able to arrange that fool Kim's removal. And I have really fucked the Russians!

I'm not sure Martin will destroy a city, but if he does, even the most cautious and loyal of Kim's supporters will accept that he must go.

China's paramount objective is to prevent the second American attack, the one that will create a radioactive wasteland just south of us and send millions of Koreans to breach our border. Our second objective is to ensure Kim's successor is someone who will accept nuclear disarmament and is not such a fool.

Smiling, Ming Liu told his secretary to call the head of China's foreign intelligence service.

* * *

The Oval Office, 9:00 p.m. EDT.

"My fellow Americans, I'm speaking tonight about our analysis of the bomb intercepted in Baltimore by alert security forces and about the steps your government is taking.

"Our scientific and engineering experts have determined, and this has been confirmed by representatives of the International Atomic Energy Agency and of China, who participated in the analysis, that this bomb is North Korean."

Shifting his gaze from the text in his hand to his TelePrompTer above the camera, the president continued: "And there is more about this second bomb that establishes North Korean intent to kill still more Americans. Attached to the bomb was an asset tracking and control device that kept Kim Jong-il informed of the bomb's location. The device had a small amount of explosive and a detonator. Kim knew where the bomb was and had veto power over its use. With this device he could have, at any time, disabled the bomb's triggering mechanism. Instead, he permitted the bomb to be smuggled into Baltimore.

"It is also certain, again confirmed by the IAEA, that the bomb that destroyed Las Vegas was North Korean. Our seizure of a second North Korean nuclear weapon in another city demonstrates that the Kim Jong-il regime continues to attack us even as I speak."

Here we go, Rick thought, *I've got to keep my voice even.*

"These two attacks are acts of war.

"Your government has protected America successfully since Six-thirteen, while taking measures to end the threat from Kim Jong-il and his oppressive, murderous regime by means of diplomacy, in concert with North Korea's neighbors, whom he also threatens, and the United Nations.

"Our actions are producing results. The UN has authorized an international quarantine on all shipments departing North Korea. The Security Council has condemned Kim for breaching international peace and security and demanded that he dismantle all nuclear weapons and nuclear weapon facilities, under IAEA supervision."

Martin paused, sipped from a glass, and resumed. His voice was hard.

"It is now clear that not only is Kim a deadly threat to Americans and to our nation itself; he remains undeterred. He must not remain in control of the North Korean government and its nuclear weapons. Kim must hand over power and leave North Korea, and his successor must dismantle all nuclear weapons and the facilities that make them, under IAEA supervision."

His sweat gushed as Rick committed himself to a course of action that would change him, and the world, beyond his listener's belief: "If Kim has not complied with these terms within seven days, I will consider it my duty to respond with overwhelming force to Kim's two nuclear attacks on our country, which killed eighty thousand people on Six-thirteen, injured one hundred thousand others, and ruined a thriving city. Unavoidably, this response will be devastating to the people of North Korea as well as to Kim and his henchmen, who have enslaved them."

Rick paused, looking into the camera with eyes that seemed to see every slaughter in mankind's bloody history, yet be ready to add another. He enunciated each word: "Should Kim's regime attempt to attack us or his neighbors with a nuclear weapon, America's response will be immediate and will totally destroy North Korea. There will not be stone left on stone."

Ella was seated in a wingback chair near the Oval Office fireplace. Next to her, at Rick's invitation, was Ray Morales. Rick's eyes sought them for an instant. *See? I did it.* He saw their approval and respect, and knew he could do the rest, could bear the cost.

The president put down his text, folded his hands on the desk, and leaned forward. He was able to play the Stradivarius of his voice without connection to the pain in his heart, so he sounded supremely confident, the confidence of one with so much power he can be merciful to those he is about to defeat utterly.

"Now I want to address the people of North Korea, all of them, from farmers and ordinary soldiers to the Communist Party leadership. You have it in your power to convince Kim Jong-il that his day is over! It is my prayer and indeed the prayer of every leader I spoke with that you will do that and thus save yourselves and your descendants from unspeakable tragedy and ruin. When Kim and his cronies are gone, you will find the United States, China, and many other nations ready to help you improve your lives and realize at last the potential within you."

He picked up the text again.

"As I speak, unarmed cruise missiles are showering North Korea with leaflets relating this message in Korean.

"My fellow Americans, I have decided upon this course of action after prayer and consultation with my advisors, and with the congressional leadership. I do so with painful reluctance and, frankly, over the objections of some congressional leaders. I'm sure there will be other Americans who sincerely disagree with my decision.

"But the facts as I see them say that we cannot indefinitely defend against Kim's attacks. If we could, I would set no deadline on our diplomatic efforts. Since we cannot, I must draw the line. It is my duty as president and commander-in-chief."

Morales' blunt features split into a grin, which he immediately squelched because only the three of them would understand it.

"As I leave you tonight, hear this:

"To Kim Jong-il: For the good of those you call your dear people, relinquish power and leave North Korea, now!

"To the people of North Korea: Act now to save yourselves from the consequences of Kim Jong-il's folly. He enslaved you. Don't let him kill you.

"To the governments of North Korea's closest neighbors, China, the Republic of Korea, Japan, and Russia: Act with us, in the interests of peace and your own well-being, helping the United States remove the threat that Kim Jong-il's regime poses to all of our peoples.

"To the American people: There is a folder on this desk that contains an order I pray I will not have to sign. Please join that prayer, but pray also that God will have mercy on my soul if I must sign it. I solemnly pledge that you will not be under threat from Kim much longer. One way or the other, your government will bring that threat to an end within one week.

"Good night."

The cameras' red lights winked out.

His shirt was soaked, his head throbbed, and his heart raced. Rick didn't know if he could stand just yet. As Ella walked toward him, a proud and tender look on her face, Morales slid out the door.

*　*　*

In one of his palaces, Kim sat alone, smoking. *Events are unfolding as I foresaw: Ming's mixture of enticements and threats. Martin threatening us with nuclear bombs. But I am in control. This is going to be exciting!*

Captives of my brilliant Internet campaign, Americans will oppose Martin's desperate plan to launch a nuclear attack. Videos and blogs show it. Americans are angry and afraid and thanks to my skillful interventions have turned those feelings on their government. They will soon impeach their pathetic president for failing to protect them, even while railing against the one thing he could do that would make them safe.

Kim loved irony, so he smiled and basked in his power.

A knock signaled the arrival of Marshal Young-san.

"You summoned me, Dear Leader."

"Marshal, have your forces dealt with the American propaganda leaflets?"

"Of course, Dear Leader. Smoke from piles of burning American filth darkens our skies! Since we shot the families of a few traitorous dogs who didn't join in rooting out and destroying the lies, the dear people have themselves searched out every leaflet for destruction."

As he spoke, Young-san thought of the leaflets rather differently. They were a threat to Kim but an opportunity for him. He had received Ming's message: "You are the one. Claim your destiny." Ming had certainly told others the same thing, but Young-san knew no one but Kim had more power than he. The Chinese would anoint whoever prevailed and that would be him.

He realized Kim was speaking.

"Marshal, the American people are under my control, but Martin does not know it. Within days he will not dare to carry out his ridiculous threats against us. My next video will convince all politically active Americans that Martin is ignoring opportunities for peace, and when I ask for direct negotiations, he will be unable to refuse. We will open a dialogue with President Bill Clinton and return to the Six-Party Talks. We will talk and talk, and while we do the United States will continue to disintegrate from fear."

Kim smiled and Yong-san immediately joined him.

"Of course, Dear Leader! I will keep the people's military on high alert, because it will add to the Americans' uncertainty and ensure the southern dogs do no more than bark."

The most significant part of Marshal Young-san's response was unspoken: *High alert will enable me to shift my most reliable units to Pyongyang, where I need them.*

Chapter 51

LATE IN THE afternoon, Rick began reading the dueling op-eds in *USA Today. Two views!* he thought. *Were there only* two?

It's About Time, by Senator Rod Peters, R-Arizona

Although many believe the president's ultimatum to Kim and to the people he rules was an unnecessary turn to brute force, I disagree. Brute force, it is; unnecessary it isn't. In fact, I believe it is overdue.

All agree that Kim's rule in North Korea is a deadly abomination and must be ended. The disagreement is about how. Those who oppose the president's plan assert that diplomacy is working and, if given more time, will be successful. There is no need, they say, to resort to what all assume (although the president didn't say it) will be nuclear strikes. Others believe that an incremental use of conventional forces (code for the blood of our brave military men and women) is a better course than nuclear attack. And all Americans recoil from the prospect of devastating the captive people of North Korea in the manner that Kim brutalized the citizens of Las Vegas, who suffered and died before our eyes for weeks, with survivors still struggling to even begin recovery.

However unpleasant, however overdue their acceptance, the facts the president has now squarely faced are undeniable: Kim is well along in orchestrating the disintegration of the United States. He is not persuaded to desist by the threat of retaliation. That threat preexisted both the Las Vegas bombing and the Martin administration—

for over sixty years it has been the declared policy of the United States to respond to a nuclear attack with equally devastating weapons—and Kim, knowing it, went ahead with not one, but two nuclear attacks. Another compelling fact is that, as the president said, we can't defend ourselves indefinitely by tightening security. Conclusion: we must remove Kim, *now*. Every day Kim remains in place is another day he has to devote to his goal of destroying America.

Another reality is that if we use our nuclear power to remove Kim, we avoid a bloody, probably unwinnable, infantry fight in North Korea, a battle with truly frightening potential for pulling the Chinese in, and prevent Kim from carrying out threats to nuke South Korea and Japan.

All are saddened that, unless they assert themselves as never before, ordinary citizens of the DPRK will die by the thousands during the brief nuclear missile campaign that destroys the regime that has attacked America twice—yet remains untouched itself. But that is necessary to prevent the death and injury of hundreds of thousands more Americans and the death of America as we know it.

The president is on the right course, at last.

Why thanks, Senator, for your unqualified support! I see which way Arizona's wind is blowing. Now what does Frantic Fred have to say—although I think I know.

Martin Can't Be Allowed to Do This, by Representative Fred Stanton, D-MA

President Martin's chosen course is an immoral proposition to kill tens of thousands, perhaps millions, of Koreans in cold blood as a coercive tactic. The president is engaging in a hideous and obscene poker game with Kim Jong-il: "I'll see your Las Vegas and raise you a Pyongyang." It is comparable to the Nazi SS practice of hauling randomly selected civilians in and shooting them as a bargain offered to the resistance movements—"You stop blowing up trains and we'll stop random executions."

Not only is President Martin's decision morally repugnant; it won't make Americans safer. In fact, it will put us all in greater danger, as attacks on North Korean cities are sure to cause Kim to redouble his efforts to destroy American ones—and now with the wholehearted support of his captive people and at least the grudging approval of much of the world. And with all sympathy for America incinerated by the fireballs that claim Korean lives by the hundreds of thousands, we must consider seriously the probability of new attackers coming forward—like Iran and its Hezbollah.

Nothing can bring back Las Vegas.

I'll say it again: nothing can bring back Las Vegas. So even those who support the president's plan as retribution will find no lasting comfort in the murder of equally innocent Koreans. The dead of Las Vegas will still be dead. The city will still be in ruins. The survivors will still be living in camps and in the homes of generous strangers throughout this great nation.

So nothing about the president's plan makes sense. Except, perhaps, to a man who needs to defend himself against impeachment by the far Right. It is a grotesque irony that the impeachment the president fears would never be successful, because a great majority in the Congress, in the country, and indeed in the world, supports his diplomacy to protect America and end the crisis.

President Martin must not be allowed to carry out his murderous plan. If ever there was an issue that should bring Americans into the streets in protest, this is it!

Rick rubbed his weary eyes, feeling as if the orbs bulged from their sockets and would burst if he weren't careful. *Well, Fred has certainly gotten what he asked for! That's some crowd outside.* He couldn't see the demonstrators thronging the fence bordering the south lawn of the White House because carefully positioned trees blocked the line of sight—and any assassin's aim. But both sight and sound were only a click away.

Television showed a large crowd milling angrily; he heard their chants and taunts. Since the West Wing simply loomed indifferently about a hundred yards away, the demonstrators were more interested in each other and the reporters doing stand-ups than in the actual object of their feelings. Police, some on horseback and all in riot gear, grimly kept the groups apart and off the six-foot wrought-iron fence girdling the White House grounds.

Rick's finger twitched and the sights and sounds vanished.

He felt as if he were being circled by sharks, and criticism from both Right and Left sapped his confidence. The Right was just snarky, but the Left . . . It was much harder to be called a murderer, by standards he hadn't abandoned, when he knew he *was* one, or soon would be.

He looked at the clock, suddenly hungry, both for dinner and for conversation with Ella.

* * *

"You look a little bedraggled this evening, Mr. President," said Ella with a gentle smile. Actually, she thought he looked haunted, like the photos of FDR just before his death, bruises under eyes so distinct they looked like makeup.

"That's because people I thought were friends are calling me reckless or worse in public while telling me privately they support me. Support me . . . *when?* When they write their memoirs?"

Rick took a large bite of roast beef, acknowledging privately that he and fellow politicians accepted inconstancy and fecklessness in others so that they could forgive it in themselves.

"How about Ray Morales?"

He chewed, swallowed, then said: "The freshman congressman from Austin is in my corner!"

"Don't be snide, Rick ! How'd your meeting go?"

He cocked his head and smiled. "You were right to push it, Ella. He's a good man, and our talk helped me think this through, but I'll never be able to compartmentalize and rationalize killing the way he does."

He frowned. "And neither, apparently, can the *New York Times*. Did you read today's . . . ?"

Rick read from his Early Bird: "Listen to how it begins: 'President Martin has made a deadly misjudgment.' And their sanctimonious conclusion: 'We pray that you will not act on this misjudgment, because that act will leave you open to accusations of genocide and will leave the United States a pariah nation.'

"And what will it make me if I let Kim remain in control of half a dozen nukes and he takes out Philadelphia, or Boston, or Chicago? And what will *that* leave the nation? Answer me *that*, editors!" He flung the clip sheet to the floor.

Ella thought of commiserating but knew that would be irresponsible. Instead: "What's the hardest part of this, Rick?"

"Giving an order that will exterminate fifty thousand human beings, maybe more, like they were cockroaches! Do you know how the neutron bomb kills? Slowly. After massive radiation, thousands will crawl away and die in corners, like bugs zapped with a can of Raid."

Ella thought his eyes looked wild, as if the mind behind them was considering flight. She rose from her chair and looked down at him, arms crossed. Her eyes locked on his. "Well, Rick, Steve Nguyen and a lot of his friends and neighbors died just that way! Remember? And that's how people in Philadelphia or Boston or Chicago could die. Unless you get Kim out now or kill him. Is there some less revolting way to do that?"

Rick stood, too, his body shouting anger and fear. "Less revolting? Sure. I can order the invasion of North Korea! That would be just good, old-fashioned bombs, machine guns, and bayonets! Not like killing cockroaches at all. Bombs, machine guns, and bayonets are the proper way to kill human beings! Wouldn't bother me half as much, or the New York goddamn Times, either!"

He was shouting when his words stopped rushing.

Rick's voice returned to normal. "And best of all, it wouldn't be *me* doing the killing, would it? Soldiers pick people to kill, and, instead of piling up all the bodies in a single day, they'd pile them up a few hundred at a time. Not so dramatic. Much easier to rationalize, except on Memorial Day!"

"So, why don't you do *that*?" she said gently.

He stood silently, looking away.

"Rick . . . why not do it that way?"

He looked at her with hopeless eyes. "Because if I use neutron bombs, and Kim goes, no more Americans die. The bodies are Kim's tribe, not our tribe."

Ella stepped close and hugged him, gently pulling his head onto her shoulder. Tenderly, she stroked the back of his neck.

Then she stepped back, picked up the Early Bird, and said: "Rick, the *New York Times* is not the only editorial board that counts. What about this? 'Something horrible may happen in a week. It need not. Kim can stop it. His countrymen can stop it. We pray they will. But if they do not, it will be a necessary horror.'"

"Ah, the *Washington Post*! Always inclined to cut the home team a little slack!"

"Is it pandering to point out that either Kim or the people he rules—and who accept his rule without protest, by the way—can keep our attack from happening? They can, can't they?"

"Yes."

"And if they don't, if they choose not to act, aren't they responsible for what happens, for what you told them would happen?"

Rick raised hands in supplication, a parent frustrated by a teenager's sophistry. "Ella, that's making the victim responsible for being assaulted! A first-year law student could demolish that argument!"

"Not if I were making it!"

He's losing it! Ella thought. *He's slipping back into that parallel universe where men like Guzman and Kim don't exist, where evil is a label given by spin doctors, not a beast that comes at your throat.*

Ella grabbed his shoulders, looked explosively into his eyes, rammed her face close to his. He felt her breath. "Forget that, Rick. *Forget . . . the . . . court-room!* We're not talking about courts and laws here. Kim does not submit himself to law. As long as he controls North Korea, he remains beyond the reach of law. And as long as he controls North Korea, our country—the one *you* take for granted and the one that saved *my* life—is going to keep coming apart!

"What are *you*—not the law, *you*—willing to do to save America?"

Woodenly, a speaker with stage fright reading a speech he was too nervous to comprehend, Rick said: "During the campaign I said I'd do whatever it takes."

She gripped his shoulders with all her strength. "And *will* you?"

"Yes, God help me, but *yes!*"

Chapter 52

"AARON, ANY POSITIVE signs . . . Kim . . . coming to his senses?" said Martin, tone and expression revealing his optimism making its last stand against despair.

"Mr. President, the military appears to have completed movement into positions to attack the ROK. Overhead shows initial launch preparations at several ballistic missile sites but no sign of missiles themselves. The motorized infantry regiment we first observed near Pyongyang a week ago remains there. Imagery of sub bases shows empty, so the boats must be at sea."

"Aaron, what I asked was do you have any evidence of a move against Kim?" said Martin, loudly.

Impassive, the DNI said, "None, sir. The movement of that regiment to Pyongyang last week was probably a precaution in case of unrest, but we've seen nothing on overhead. If there were street demonstrations, we'd see 'em."

"And the U.S. Interest section of the Swedish embassy in Pyongyang tells us there's no political activity," interjected Battista.

"Yeah, but it's not mobs of peasants waving pitchforks or Pyongyang's citizens marching with placards: it's the calculation of a few powerful men in Kim's inner circle!"

"Sir, we can't see into the minds of those men. That information is simply not available to us."

Guarini's heart hurt for his friend as the DNI's reply left him twisting in the wind. Feeling like witnesses before an execution, the NSC and advisors sat fidgeting, watching the president, who would address the nation at nine that night, the zero hour. Everything was ready: if he signed the attack order, three neutron bombs would detonate above Sinpo as he spoke to the world.

Dully, Rick said, "So what can you tell us about China, Aaron?"

"Mr. President, overhead imagery and communication analyses paint a picture of Chinese preparations to move into North Korea. As we've reported, for the past week China has allotted nearly one hundred percent of all transport—road, rail, and air—to moving troops. And they've put their entire airborne force, about thirty-five thousand soldiers, on high alert, plus having their largest airborne training exercise ever. That suggests they plan on more than just putting up a human wall at the Korean border to stop refugees."

Griffith said, "Since we weren't all in on your conversation with Ming Liu, can you bring us up to speed?"

Rick suppressed his irritation at Griffith's snarky question. "Ming is tough, but he's level-headed and unemotional. I can work with him, tomorrow and down the road.

"But today . . . the bill comes due for all we've given China . . . and Ming will pay it. "

"Did he say that?"

"No, Bruce, but he has no better option if we hit Sinpo. That would force Ming's hand. He'd then believe we'd follow up with a full nuclear attack, and he can't live with that.

"Anne . . . the UN?"

"Mr. President, the Russians introduced a Security Council resolution that a nuclear attack on North Korea would be genocide. Obviously, that's not going to pass, but it will get quite a few votes. They'll also introduce it in the General Assembly, and there it *will* pass.

"The DPRK UN ambassador's invitation to President Clinton to come to Pyongyang in the interests of peace was a pretty predictable and cynical move. Clinton's turn-down is being cited by some as evidence that you don't want anything to stand in the way of nuclear war, Mr. President."

"Well, Bill might have gone if I hadn't convinced him that he was going to be held hostage." Martin paused and for an instant they saw the old insouciance. "It may also have helped that I reminded him about his decision not to reveal Chinese cooperation with Pakistan's nuclear bomb program, which probably enabled Khan to help Kim build the Las Vegas bomb. We agreed it wouldn't help if that were raked over while Las Vegas is still radioactive."

The president paused, pinching the bridge of his nose, eyes squinted. "Anything else, Anne?"

"Well, the secretary-general is as frustrated and furious as his countryman Gwon. He's trying to create a wave of condemnation that will make us extend the deadline, climb down from our ultimatum."

Well, what else did we think he'd do? He's just defending his tribe, like I am.

"I guess we have to expect that.

"Sara, what news from Homeland Security?" *That's going to make Bruce mad, asking Sara when I've put him in charge of homeland defense, but I don't care. Sara will tell the truth. Bruce won't.*

"My people are working their butts off, but the results are uneven, sir. The truth is, what triggered the first alert, which eventually led us to that bomb, was a fluke. It was the damn asset control device that led to the initial inspection, *not* radiation from the bomb.

"So, we plug away, every day, but it takes time to produce more and better radiation scanners, time to install them, time to train operators . . . and time works against us. If they get lucky once, or we screw up once . . . well, that could be another city."

"We're here to put *that* shoe on the other foot!" said the vice president, unable to contain himself any longer.

Martin sighed. "No, Bruce, we're here to *decide*. I haven't signed the order." The president's voice was tired but firm.

Guarini said, "Mr. President, Americans want Kim gone, *now*! Today most of them don't care as much about *how* that's done as they do about *getting* it done. Later, when they feel safer, they *will* care and you'll be subject to criticism, maybe a lot of criticism. But right now . . . well, we've seen people vote on this administration with their feet."

Even you, Bart? Martin seemed to shrink, to accept that his desperate hope of avoiding a slaughter was gone.

Hurriedly, Dorn said: "What about asking Congress for a declaration of war before launching the attack? I know this isn't the first time we've considered this, but I think it could be very important."

Leaning forward, Griffith pounced. "Congress will *not* take responsibility for this decision, but they may encumber it with conditions. Like no use of nuclear weapons without separate congressional approval! Like only purely military targets may be attacked! No matter what, the Martin administration owns this decision, so let's not waste time and energy—maybe even tie our hands—trying to duck it!"

In a moment of kindness to the man he had leaned on during what he now thought of as the first day of the rest of his life, Martin said, "John, you told me—when Paternity first implicated Kim—I should announce our course of action right then. You were right. That was the time to go for a declaration of war, back then, while we had diplomatic avenues to pursue as Congress debated. That wasn't the course I chose. And because of my decision then, the time is past to go for a declaration."

Dorn bobbed his head.

The president's gaze swept the room. Zimmer said, "I've said my piece, sir." MacAdoo shook his head and the two intelligence leaders returned his gaze inscrutably.

Numb, light-headed, feeling overpowered by dark, bloody forces, Rick said, "OK, now the principals." He looked at Anne Battista.

God he looks bad! she thought. *I've never seen Rick Martin with all the hope drained out of him, but that's how he is now. He looks like my uncle, at the end, when the cancer was eating his guts.*

"Mr. President, force always waits behind diplomacy, and Kim has now left us no choice but force. When Kim's gone, the new partnership we've built with Ming and his government will allow us to return to diplomacy and, with Ming, end the threat of both North Korean nuclear weapons and aggression.

"My recommendation, Mr. President, is to carry out our plan to remove Kim."

"No second thoughts, Anne, no doubts?"

"Of course I have doubts, Mr. President! But those doubts can't be resolved now. We must act in spite of doubts."

Martin nodded, whether in agreement or just in submission to the inevitable she couldn't tell.

"Eric?"

"You can't leave Kim in position to attack with nukes when and where he chooses. He's left you no means but force to stop that. And you have, correctly in the view of us all, chosen to remove him with the method that poses least risk to Americans and by far the greatest chance of success: our nuclear weapons. It's also the way that poses least risk to South Korea and Japan, because it's certain Kim would nuke them if we invaded. Not to mention that if we invade, China will come in militarily!

"So, Mr. President, I recommend you sign the attack order."

I agree with you Eric, but when your words have died away and become just part of the record of this meeting, my signature will still be on that order. I will always know I killed fifty thousand people.

Rick was sweating heavily, feeling nausea, pressure on his chest. He ignored them and turned to Griffith. "Bruce?"

Thinking of his place in history and his eventual run for the presidency, Griffith decided the dice had turned against him. Time to leave the table and cash in while he still had a stake for the next game. The trick was to be a team player, while leaving a whiff in the air that the president had only done what *he* would have done more quickly, leaving it to others, others he knew, to paint a picture of the cost of Martin's dithering since Six-thirteen.

"Mr. President, at this meeting you asked for and received the best advice of the members of the NSC, advice rendered free of coercion and not pre-cooked in any way. This is the most responsible form of presidential decision making and stands in marked contrast to the last Republican administration.

"We have not always seen eye to eye, sir—I was perhaps too early to rec-ommend what I urge again now: Sign the order. Remove Kim immediately."

Unbidden, Rick's brain recalled another Bible verse: "It is finished." He felt cold and clammy. *OK, do it now, while you can still hold a pen.*

He opened the folder, signed, handed the order to Easterly. Pain radiated down his left arm. Unsure if he could stand, he said, "Thank you all for your honesty and support. We're done now, but I'd like to have the room for a few minutes with Bart."

Chairs rustled on the carpet as the others left, with worried glances at him. Rick felt their sense of purpose—and fear. *Besides having the duty to get this right, we're all afraid of history's verdict. Are Bart and the others going to take their places with Truman's advisors, or Stalin's? And which of them will I be compared to?*

Alone with his president, Guarini heard a voice from within, speaking with the clarity and force of both mind and soul: *You've got to keep him func-tioning. He's got to make that speech.*

He saw sweat on Martin's forehead and trembling in his right hand. After a few words, Guarini called the White House physician, Captain Beck, and told him to come quickly but discreetly to the Cabinet Room.

Chapter 53

ELLA, BART, AND Captain Beck watched from a corner of the Oval Office as the president pronounced Sinpo dead. To Dr. Beck's relief it didn't take long, just over two minutes. He wanted to get his IV going again, treating the president's heart attack with a thrombolytic drug to break up any further clots and prevent a sequel.

As Rick began his final sentences with a slight quaver, Ella tensed, willing him to hold up.

"America and our allies, Japan and the Republic of Korea, will not permit an outlaw regime to attack us at the whim of its murderous leader, Kim Jong-il. That tyrant has refused repeated opportunities to turn away the horror that has engulfed Sinpo. Sadly, his countrymen have been unwilling—so far—to protect themselves from the consequences of Kim's actions by forcing him to give up power.

"If Kim still refuses to step down, and his countrymen refuse to make him do so, we will obliterate the nation that has attacked us twice, killing more Americans than any enemy since World War II. I pray that will not be necessary, but I promise *you,* and I promise all who dwell in North Korea, that I *will* give the order.

"Good night, my fellow Americans. Tonight, as on Six-thirteen, I have miles to go before I sleep. I ask for your prayers."

Dr. Beck and a navy medic moved rapidly toward the president, Ella right behind. At his side, she saw tears in his eyes and took his hand. Bart hovered silently.

Guarini and Easterly intended that after his speech the president would go to the National Military Command Center during this period of greatest danger,

260

especially to South Korea and Japan. If Kim decided to carry out his threats, artillery shells would crash onto Seoul and missiles would appear briefly on launch pads before climbing skyward with nuclear warheads.

Dr. Beck forbade that move now. He insisted that his patient sit or lie quietly. Bart didn't want outsiders to see the president hooked to an IV line, so they went to the Situation Room.

Guarini thought Rick seemed shattered by what he had ordered. Taking the Sit Room watch officer aside, the chief of staff told him not to display video of Sinpo and to give any information about the city to him alone.

Satellites gazed piercingly at North Korea, employing high-powered optics by day and infrared radar to see through night and clouds. If Kim's missiles appeared on launch pads, Martin could give an order that would turn every North Korean missile site and city into ground zero of a nuclear missile. Or, he could spare North Korea and the planet the effects of so many nuclear detonations and pray that U.S. jets swarming the launch pads, plus the Asian missile defenses so recently cobbled together, would prevent Kim's missiles from incinerating Tokyo, Seoul, Pusan, and other cities and U.S. bases.

After the initial bustle of the president's arrival, compounded by Dr. Beck's insistence that he lie down, the room was quiet. Ella sat beside her husband, gently stroking his twitching hand.

Today Rick's lived the destruction of his beliefs, not by someone else, but by his own hand, she thought. *He's not fierce. He can't wrap himself in a shield of rage. But he did it anyway, feeling all the pain. He's not a warrior like my father or Ray, but he's brave.*

She sat quietly, holding her husband's hand and savoring this new dimension of the man she'd loved for twenty-five years but never trusted, on the primal level that still lurked, as her protector. Now her doubts were gone.

* * *

Minister of Defense Chen Shaoshi looked up from the note passed by an aide.

"Aircraft with our soldiers are flying toward Pyongyang but will not cross the border until you approve. Our fighters are on the highest ground alert and will launch for Pyongyang at your command."

Ming nodded and gazed silently at images from China's satellites. Sinpo was very heavily damaged, but not obliterated. As the live feed swept the

DPRK, Ming was relieved by what he did *not* see. He didn't see any missiles in launch position. Their plan was working, at least for the moment.

* * *

It was alarming: even the heavy damage to Sinpo did not explain the thousands of bleeding, twitching people lying in the streets or staggering about. Marshal Young-san read reports impassively but worried. It was clear that that something more than blast and fire was stalking the surviving citizens of Sinpo.

He feared that perhaps the unknown killer was biological, a deadly toxin that would fell his troops and destroy his strategy for ousting Kim. Then an aide brought him information from an American press briefing. It was not a toxin, but radiation that produced the ever-growing flood of vomiting, collapsing, hemorrhaging people.

On learning that, the marshal again felt confident of success and, since he cared not a whit for Sinpo's inhabitants, became elated. Stifling that distraction, Young-san directed his rifle regiment commander to seize the national radio and television facilities. Putting on his cap bearing five red stars, he moved decisively toward his waiting limo. As he settled into the rear seat, he checked his pistol.

* * *

Kim Jong-il's fury was white hot because it was fueled by shame. Once again Martin failed to respect him and his dear people. *The American was such a fool! This attack meant Martin didn't believe he would unleash nuclear fire on the dogs to the south, on the hated Japanese, and on American bases. Such disrespect must be answered!* Hearing the guards outside his door stomp to attention, Kim spun around.

Marshal Yong-san burst into the room. "Your missiles are launching now, Dear Leader! Seoul is crumbling under the impact of your artillery and rockets. You have stood firm, faced the Americans, and sent them a fitting response for Sinpo, a response ten times Martin's minor damage to an insignificant city!

"Now, Dear Leader, we must follow our plan; we must go to your war headquarters, because the Americans will surely hit Pyongyang."

Kim longed to lead his onrushing army through the DMZ and into Seoul, killing and destroying. He wanted to bayonet enemy soldiers as his own soldiers watched, awestruck at their leader's courage and raging fury. But, he had to think of his dear people's needs. He needed to show himself and his wise leadership to the entire nation. As satisfying as it would be to slash and stab with his assault troops, he would be affecting only a tiny part of the battle. No, as he always did, Kim must push aside his own desires and steadily use his clear vision to care for his people. He could not indulge himself. He must go to Mount Jamo.

"Then let us go, Marshal."

Kim and Marshal Young-san descended to the sub-basement in the Dear Leader's private elevator. There before an unmarked door were Major Rhee Song-il, who had made a career of handling "special assignments" for Young-san, and two armed soldiers. As Kim and Young-san passed through, Rhee and the soldiers took positions guarding the door.

When the two leaders had gone, Rhee returned to the Dear Leader's office. He dialed the communications minister's direct number, which was answered not by the minister but the army colonel now controlling all national communications facilities.

Broadcasters soon announced the joyous news: the People's Republic of China Army was once again coming to stand fearlessly beside their younger cousins in defiance of the Americans.

Kim Jong-il was one of the few in the DPRK who didn't hear the joyous news. After passing through the unmarked door, he and the marshal had entered a high-speed elevator and descended one hundred fifty meters. An electric vehicle waited to carry them through a tunnel to Mount Jamo.

After standing aside to let Kim enter, Marshal Young-san shot him. Kim sprawled face down, his lower legs projecting out the door. The marshal lifted Kim's legs, bending Kim's knees until his heels nearly touched his buttocks, then pushed him in. His body slid easily, lubricated by gore from his shattered skull. From the platform, the marshal leaned in and pushed a button, setting the car in motion. Marshal Young-san walked swiftly to the elevator and returned to Kim's former office. He had much to do while Major Rhee's special security unit dealt with Kim's body.

*   *   *

"Sir! President Ming's coming up on secure one. The NMCC is also on the circuit."

The president had been in the Situation Room with Ella, Guarini, Battista, and Dorn for eighteen hours. Rick had been dozing; now he fought to clear the cobwebs.

"Good evening, Rick."

His heart pounding, the American responded. "Good morning, Ming."

"China has dealt with the terrible dangers you created by bombing Sinpo. Tell me, Rick, how did you know that Kim was going to inspect the army garrison at Sinpo yesterday?"

"Ming, I *didn't* know."

"Kim's body was found in Sinpo a few hours ago."

Martin, uncertain, said nothing.

"As you no doubt already know, China's forces are now entering the DPRK. We are responding to the invitation of Kim's successor, Marshal Young-san Ho, who asked for assistance in defending against another U.S. invasion. I told him China would stand with him if the DPRK gives up its nuclear weapons and the means of building them. He agreed."

The release of tension in the Sit Room and the national military command center was accompanied by high fives and backslapping. Amid the hubbub, Martin blurted, "Ming that is very, very good news! What are China's intentions now regarding Korea?"

"To provide the support necessary for the DPRK to remain a member of the socialist brotherhood and to ensure that neither Marshal Young-san nor his successors rebuild the nuclear weapons program. Surely this is important to American security, and America will support it politically, financially, and militarily!"

"China can count on that!"

Rick exhaled in a rush that swept his fear and weariness away. Sadness and guilt remained, and he knew he would never be as he was before the deaths of Las Vegas and Sinpo, but now there were a million hopeful things to do. He was anxious to begin.

Chapter 54

Two Weeks Later

"COME ON, JULIE, you oughta come with me!" Ray gave an encouraging grin.

"No, Ray—really! It's OK; you should go alone. You three lived this together; I wasn't part of it. That's not, oh, poor me—that's just a fact. I'd be a distraction and that would make me feel awkward. Just go! Don't keep the president and first lady waiting!"

Said with a smile, but forcefully, his wife's words propelled Ray Morales out the door. About forty-five minutes later he arrived at the main gate of Aberdeen Proving Grounds, where his four-star identification card produced the snappiest salute the Federal Protective Service policeman could muster and drew a smile from a waiting Secret Service agent. It was the agent who had escorted Ray into the White House on his secret visit, and this time he was much friendlier. They chatted about the Marines and outfits they had served with, while the agent drove to dockside.

The Martins welcomed him aboard a Hunter Thirty-six and got it under-way expertly. Aware of the president's preference for quiet, Ray munched a sandwich, nursed a beer, and didn't say much. After maneuvering the boat into the broad mouth of the Gunpowder River, Rick laid her on a starboard tack and smiled at Ray and Ella.

"Ray, I don't know exactly where to begin. Certainly I should start by thanking you for your wisdom and discretion. You helped me steady myself when I needed it a lot.

You've never revealed our meeting . . . never asked for anything. The country owes you and I owe you."

"This is where the cowboy hero would say, 'Aw shucks—t'warn't nothin'—and really, it wasn't—but if I may, I'd like to ask some questions, Mr. President."

"Go ahead, Ray—anything!"

"Do you think al-Qaeda did it, or Kim's people?

"I don't know. My best guess is al-Qaeda."

"So you went ahead with the nuclear attack on Sinpo without knowing if Kim was directly involved in the attacks on us?"

"Yes. Because our attack wasn't about punishing the guilty. I wouldn't have done it for punishment or revenge. It was to get Kim out, quickly, after all else had failed to do it. I believed regardless of who was setting the bombs off, getting Kim out of power would stop the bombing by cutting off the bomb supply."

Feeling a wind shift, the president adjusted the boat's course.

"I had to convince Ming that if he didn't remove Kim, I would. Ming knew that invasion of the DPRK would fail and he knew that I knew it. He also knew that if I had the stomach for it the United States could end Kim's regime using nuclear missiles and leave the mess on China's doorstep. The nuclear destruction of their neighbor and 'younger cousin' would be a disaster for China, sucking them into the chaos no matter how they tried to avoid it. I had to convince Ming I *did* have the stomach for that and it took the destruction of Sinpo to do it."

Morales thought for a moment. "Do you believe it was Ming who took Kim down? The DPRK announced he was killed at Sinpo."

"Well, I don't believe he was killed at Sinpo. That's just too much of a coincidence, unless I were to believe that China has an agent in here so deep that he could tell Ming Sinpo was the target *and* Ming could somehow maneuver Kim to Sinpo at the right time. I don't buy that!

"Ming took Kim down indirectly, by cutting a deal with Marshal Young-san: get rid of Kim, give up the nukes, and you'll have Chinese resources and a free hand to rule. That's a pretty sweet package for a thug like Young-san and I'm not surprised he took it. I think Young-san killed Kim, or ordered it, and had his body deposited in the wreckage of Sinpo to tie up the loose end."

As the wind increased, Ella moved across the slanting cockpit to the high side. *I wonder if Rick is going to get to what's really on his mind and soul,* she thought.

"Now I have some questions for *you*, Ray," said the president.

"Fire away, sir."

"What about me, Ray? Did I do my duty? Did I save hundreds of thousands of Americans by killing fifty thousand Koreans? Did I do the right thing? Or was the bombing already over because Kim got cautious after we intercepted the second bomb? You've read the *New York Times*. Am I the bloodiest ruler since Stalin?"

Morales saw a pinched, fearful squint on the president's face that reminded him of an iconic newspaper photo of a Viet Cong guerrilla, his captor's pistol inches from his temple, moments before being executed.

Poor guy! thought Morales. *He's really at the center of a firestorm, some of it fed by people who don't consider that they might be dead now if he hadn't acted. But some also from folks who would have been willing to bet their own lives that we could get through this without using our nukes; that somehow, given more time, diplomacy would have worked.*

"All I can tell you, sir, is that I would have done the same. I can say you did your duty. But were you right? Was it the best outcome? Would somebody else, like Vice President Griffith, have done better?

"Well, sir, as that Marine instructor I told you about said, 'This is about *you*, Lieutenant. You're the platoon commander. What are *you* going to do, *now?*'

"You were the one who had the responsibility and the duty to decide. *You* know if you made the best decision you could. That's all you get to know in this life, except that there'll be other tough decisions coming along, because that's what leaders get. You make 'em and go on.

"You carry the decisions you've made in your rucksack. Some of them are really heavy. For the rest of your life, early some days and late some nights, you'll wonder if you could have made better choices, better decisions. You'll open that ruck and lay them out. You'll revisit them. But you don't get any do-overs. That's just the way it is."

Rick gazed back at him for long seconds, face still pinched. Then he relaxed, nodded, squeezed Ella's hand, and eased the boat onto a broad reach. It left a wake straight as an arrow as it rollicked through the green-brown waters of the Chesapeake.

* * *

After dinner, the president and first lady sat on the porch of the guest house, enjoying the spectacular play of sunset reflected in clouds over the bay.

"How do you feel, Rick? What do you think about the things Ray said?"

"About what he said: obviously, that works for him, as he lives the rest of his life with the decisions he's made. It doesn't for me; it's too pat."

"Does it have to be complicated to work for you?"

"Maybe . . . I don't know; I'm just saying how I feel."

"No, you're saying how you *think*!" Ella smiled, then grew solemn.

"Rick, how *are* you going to live with the order you gave to destroy Sinpo?"

He leaned forward, elbows planted on thighs, hands clasped. "I'm going to focus on the good that could come out of it and work as hard as I can, for the rest of my life, to squeeze every bit of progress from it. A better life for Koreans. Tighter international control of nukes. The end, I pray, of nuclear terrorism."

"What about the country's reaction?"

"I don't know . . . Ella, should we run again? Or am I such a symbol of anger and bloodshed that we couldn't win a second term and shouldn't even try?"

"Rick, it's too soon to tell! But do you *want* to be president for eight years?"

"I don't know. Nine months ago, I was so sure of everything. Sure that I could thread the needle and solve any dispute. A few days after Las Vegas I was sure I could lead a transformation, truly change the course of history for the better."

He twisted and looked intently into her eyes. "And it *was* the right policy—but I couldn't get it done because of one man, Kim Jong-il, and one philosophy, bin Laden's version of Islam. Evil plus unreasoning, undying hatred stopped me and nearly destroyed America.

"So I'm no longer sure of much. Now, all I'm *sure* of is that someone—maybe Kim, maybe Kim and al-Qaeda—destroyed Las Vegas, and *I* destroyed Sinpo, and because of us about a hundred and thirty thousand people are dead."

Ella put her hand on his forearm and squeezed it hard. "Rick, you can be sure of more than that! You can be sure that a really dangerous man, Kim

Jong-il, no longer rules a country with nuclear weapons. And you can be sure that never again will a country with nukes give or sell one to the crazies, because that had consequences as terrible as the terrorists' act. And that every country will keep much tighter control over all nuclear materials. And that the UN will not just debate and watch again if someone like Kim starts building nukes and missiles."

Rick shook his head. "No, Ella, other than the Kim part, I can't be sure of any of that! I thought the bombing of Las Vegas changed the world, changed the ways that Ming and other leaders thought about security. I was wrong—it only changed *my* way of thinking!"

"So you can't believe in something unless it's certain? And nothing is resolved unless it's resolved forever? Come on, Rick!" Ella smiled, taking the sting out of her words.

She's right. I'm afraid of getting comfortable with what I did, afraid of letting myself off the hook. But I accomplished a lot and I can acknowledge that without forgetting what it cost.

"You're right . . . I didn't let Steve Nguyen down. I suppose I let that woman down, but I *did* try to find a way without more killing, and maybe another time I'll succeed.

"But how do *you* feel, Ella? You wanted to kill the bombers, very slowly and painfully, as I recall."

Ella threw back her shoulders. Her dark eyes flashed. "Kim's dead. I hope he died in pain and knowing it was payback for Las Vegas! But probably he didn't; probably he got a quick bullet in the head. Still, I feel good knowing he was killed for what he did. Same for bin Laden—and I'm glad he had time to know what was coming!

"But we didn't get the others. Whoever planted the Las Vegas bomb, whoever was waiting for that second bomb—they're still out there, somewhere. I want them dead, too!"

Taking a deep breath, Rick plunged, driven to ask but fearing her answer: "But, Ella, I was also asking how you feel about *me*. I know there was a time you thought I wasn't up to this job, to being president in these circumstances."

"Rick, I've always thought you were a good man! I've never wavered from that. But you're a good man born and bred in a place of law and safety and abundance. You had never in your life been at physical risk. You had never faced an opponent who didn't accept the rules and conventions that you had come to believe governed human life. In all of this you were like so many Americans. So I *did* fear that you wouldn't be able to understand that this was kill or be killed, or, perhaps, would understand but be unable, or unwilling, to kill. Thank God, I was wrong!"

Rick preened a little. Ella knew the signs: her husband was about to launch into one of his lectures. *He's going to be OK!* As her heart jumped, she suppressed a smile.

"Ella, you *were* wrong! But I understand why. Like I was, presidents are constrained by their own beliefs, which typically lean toward pragmatism and compromise, and the beliefs of a small but politically potent group of Americans who believe that both safety and morality dictate always acting in concert with others, always following the rules. So presidents are reluctant to use our enormous military power—and they should be!

"But as a nation we are a fierce, passionate people, capable of determined action and ruthless—sometimes mindless and unnecessary—violence. So if you threaten and frighten and kill Americans, they demand, and will have, your blood.

"Our political conversation can hide that reality and convince really dangerous people and groups that America won't destroy them if they attack. Maybe it goes in cycles, because that's what led to Pearl Harbor and to Hitler's declaration of war on us a week later. Kim was probably crazy, so it's hard to be sure, but I think that's also what led to Six-thirteen.

"Pakistan's leaders understood us and cut a deal that saved them and their country. Kim Jong-il didn't, and he and fifty thousand of those he ruled are dead, lives thrown away by their ruler's miscalculation like the millions of German and Japanese lives. I killed them and I'll be sick over that forever, but now I'm sure I had to . . . I guess I'm closer to thinking like Ray than I realized."

"Rick, do you think this is *over* now, with Kim and bin Laden dead?"

* * *

Fahim kept his nimble fingers and restless mind occupied repairing the old cabin in the Idaho mountains. Most evenings he took a cup of hot sweet tea to the porch and watched the sun go down. And waited for The Base to give him another mission.

Afterword and Acknowledgments

"THE COMMISSION BELIEVES that unless the world community acts decisively and with great urgency, it is more likely than not that a weapon of mass destruction will be used in a terrorist attack somewhere in the world by the end of 2013." So states the opening paragraph of the Executive Summary to the report of the Congressional Commission on the Prevention of Weapons of Mass Destruction Proliferation and Terrorism, December 12, 2008.

Code Word: Paternity is a novel, not a prophecy. But much of it is, unfortunately, fact. The spread of nuclear weapons, dubbed "nuclear proliferation" by scholars and governments, is real. A. Q. Khan's nuclear smuggling ring significantly increased the risk of a nuclear weapon getting into the hands of terrorists. The late Kim Jong-il and his father did, indeed, buy and sell and barter nuclear weapon and missile technology with regimes controlled by other dangerous, unpredictable—perhaps unhinged—dictators. They did, indeed, engage in the astonishing assassinations, kidnappings, and warlike acts recounted by President Martin's secretary of state and his CIA director. All of the technologies described in *Code Word: Paternity* exist: in fact analyzing the debris of a nuclear explosion is old hat, having been mastered some fifty years ago during the days of nuclear weapon testing in the atmosphere.

The Paternity Project is my invention, in the sense that the name is my creation and to my knowledge there has been no government announcement of such a capability. I had no access to classified information. But one can find press reports from the late 1940s through the early 1960s describing the use of techniques like those of my fictional Paternity Project to analyze nuclear detonations. My surmise—indeed my expectation—is that the U.S. government has such a program, perhaps resident in the Department of Homeland Security's National Technical Nuclear Forensics Center.

Although nuclear terrorism hasn't happened, America's shield against it may be wearing thin. That shield, called nuclear deterrence, is the belief of all rulers possessing or developing nuclear weapons that should the United States be attacked anonymously with a nuclear weapon, the U.S. government has the scientific capacity to rapidly identify the nation that manufactured the weapon's nuclear core and would retaliate against that country in kind, regardless of the affiliation of the operatives who emplaced and detonated the bomb.

But our deterrence shield is constructed largely of two materials: the assumption that all who control nukes regard U.S. nuclear retaliation as their own ultimate catastrophe, and their belief that the president of the United States possesses both the resolve and the political capital to order nuclear retaliation in circumstances when the identity of the enabler nation is not established beyond all doubt. Unfortunately we live in a period when the first of these factors can no longer be taken for granted and the second depends on the ability of every ruler controlling nukes to accurately perceive the qualities of both America's president and its politics.

America's political discourse now features frequent attacks on the character of our president, regardless of party. And the proliferation of cable television and Internet outlets catering to micro-audiences offers great temptation for someone—be he or she a "shock jock" or a head of state—to substitute googling for thought and simply reinforce beliefs already held.

Kim Jong-il, "the Dear Leader," died in 2011. I don't think it's too much of a stretch to imagine that he, given his life journey and probably psychotic personality, was at risk of making the colossal misjudgments portrayed in *Code Word: Paternity*. Perhaps his successor, son Kim Jong-un, is unlike him and will take North Korea in a different direction. But, then again, perhaps not. And there are other autocrats who, should they possess nukes, could have the same combination of absolute authority and delusional thinking as Kim Jong-il and make the same catastrophic error that "my" Kim made.

I wish to acknowledge a number of works that were essential to my research for *Code Word: Paternity*. I benefited enormously from them; any errors in the novel are my own. Professor Graham Allison has written widely and authoritatively about nuclear weapon issues, especially the dangers of nuclear proliferation. The title of his 2004 book, *Nuclear Terrorism, The Ultimate Preventable*

Catastrophe, cannot be surpassed as a summation of the situation in which we now live. Professor Allison describes the risks and proposes solutions much less sanguinary than the one that Rick Martin ultimately employed. May they come to pass!

Besides Allison's book, I relied on Gordon Corera's *Shopping for Bombs*, also on *Nuclear Jihadist* and on *Fallout*, both by Catherine Collins and Douglas Frantz. Michael Levi's *On Nuclear Terrorism* was important for its discussion of nuclear forensics, the techniques behind my fictive Paternity Project. Though first published over sixty years ago, *The Effects of Nuclear Weapons*, edited by Samuel Glasstone, remains an essential resource on the topic and implies how much may be deduced from analysis of a nuclear detonation. I depended on Bradley K. Martin's *Under the Loving Care of the Fatherly Leader* for information about North Korea's ruling dynasty of Kims. My copy of Don Oberdorfer's *The Two Koreas* became well thumbed. I got a key story idea from Senator Jim Webb's *A Time to Fight*: the kernel of Ray Morales' conversation with President Martin—Martin's epiphany.

With great pleasure I express appreciation for the support of family and friends—and writing instructor Steve Alcorn—during my journey to the completion of *Code Word: Paternity*. Besides her steady encouragement, my wife, Janie, gamely read the entire manuscript and made comments that improved it. So did Robert Bishop, Sandra Bovee, John Dill, John Fredland, Dan Hahne, Bill Mason, Bob (the WO) Miller, Ted Mussenden, Barbara Sheffer, Chip Sterling, Kathy Sterling, and Bob Williams. P.T. (Pete) Deutermann gave me pithy comments on the writer's craft and life that helped me find perspective. My thanks also to Robert Brown, Jr. whose contribution went beyond his eagle-eyed copy editing. Paul Chamberlain of Cerebral Itch and Megan Hahne gave me my first inkling about cover creation. Connie Reider, friend and wonderful portrait photographer, created my author photo. And my appreciation to the staff of Nimitz Library at the U.S. Naval Academy where I did most of my research.

GLOSSARY OF ABBREVIATIONS AND TERMS

ACLU. Abbreviation for *American Civil Liberties Union*. The ACLU is a membership organization that advocates in courts, legislatures, and communities to defend and preserve the individual rights and liberties that the Constitution and laws of the United States guarantee.

Andrews. *Andrews Air Force Base*, near Washington DC, houses the squadrons that provide transportation to the president and other senior government officials. It is the airport normally used by the president.

BMEWS. Abbreviation for the cold war-era *Ballistic Missile Early Warning System*, which could provide long-range warning of a ballistic missile attack over the polar region of the northern hemisphere.

CBP. Abbreviation for the U.S. *Customs and Border Protection Agency*. It is one of the Department of Homeland Security's largest components, with a priority mission of keeping terrorists and their weapons out of the United States. It also has a responsibility for securing and facilitating trade and travel while enforcing hundreds of U.S. regulations, including immigration and drug laws.

CIA. Abbreviation for the U.S. *Central Intelligence Agency*. The director of the Central Intelligence Agency leads the organization and reports to the director of National Intelligence (DNI).

Dear Leader. Term used by North Koreans to address or refer to Kim Jong-il.

DHS. Abbreviation for the U.S. *Department of Homeland Security*. The secretary of homeland security is an officer of the cabinet, responsible to the president.

DMZ. Abbreviation for the *Demilitarized Zone*, a buffer free of soldiers established along the border between North Korea and South Korea.

DNI. Abbreviation denoting the U.S. *Director of National Intelligence*, who serves as the head of the intelligence community, overseeing and directing the implementation of the National Intelligence Program and acting as the principal advisor to the president, the National Security Council, and the Homeland Security Council for intelligence matters related to national security.

DOE. Abbreviation for the U.S. *Department of Energy*, responsible for insuring the integrity and safety of the country's nuclear weapons, promoting international nuclear safety, advancing nuclear nonproliferation, and continuing to provide safe, efficient, and effective nuclear power plants for the U.S. Navy. The secretary of energy is an officer of the cabinet responsible to the president.

DPRK. Abbreviation for the *Democratic People's Republic of North Korea*, commonly referred to as North Korea.

DSP. Abbreviation for the *Defense Support Program*. DSP satellites are a key part of North America's early warning system. They help protect the United States and its allies by detecting missile launches, space launches, and nuclear detonations.

FAA. Abbreviation for *Federal Aviation Agency*, which is among other things responsible for U.S. air traffic control.

FEMA. Abbreviation for the *Federal Emergency Management Agency*, a unit of the DHS. FEMA is tasked with handling all possible disasters in the United States. This includes both natural disasters, such as hurricanes and earthquakes, and manmade ones, such as hazardous substance spills, bombings, and war.

GOC. Abbreviation for *Government of China*. This formulation is sometimes used in American diplo-speak to refer to other governments, e.g., GOJ for the Japanese government.

Gulf One. A term referring to the UN-authorized international military operation that drove invading Iraqi forces out of Kuwait in 1990.

Great Leader. Term used by North Koreans to address or refer to Kim Il-sung, father of Kim Jong-il and his predecessor as dictator of North Korea.

HEU. Abbreviation for *Highly Enriched Uranium*. The fissionable material of particular interest in natural uranium ore, U-235, occurs naturally in low concentration, too low for powering a nuclear reactor or serving as the fissionable core of a bomb. For those purposes it must be concentrated, or enriched. When enriched to a concentration of twenty percent U-235 or greater, uranium is said to be highly enriched. The degree of enrichment wanted for a bomb is much higher than twenty percent.

IAEA. Abbreviation for the *International Atomic Energy Agency.* The IAEA is an independent, intergovernmental science-and-technology-based organization in the United Nations family that serves as the global focal point for nuclear cooperation. Among other functions, it verifies through its inspection system that nations comply with their commitments, under the Non-Proliferation Treaty and other nonproliferation agreements, to use nuclear material and facilities only for peaceful purposes.

ICC. Abbreviation for the *International Criminal Court.* The ICC is the first permanent, treaty-based, international criminal court established to help end impunity for the perpetrators of the most serious crimes of concern to the international community. It came into operation in 2002. Unlike the International Court of Justice (ICJ), the ICC tries individuals and is not part of the UN system.

JCS. Abbreviation for the U.S. *Joint Chiefs of Staff.* They are the chairman, the vice chairman, the chief of staff of the army, the chief of naval operations, the chief of staff of the air force, the commandant of the marine corps and the chief of the national guard bureau. The collective body of the JCS is headed by the chairman, who is the principal military advisor to the president, secretary of defense, and the National Security Council (NSC). However, all JCS members are by law military advisors, and they may respond to a request or voluntarily submit, through the chairman, their advice or opinions to the president, the secretary of defense, and the NSC.

Juche. An ancient Korean philosophy adapted and perverted by both Kims to sustain their absolute rule. North Koreans are immersed in its teachings and shielded as much as possible from contrary views. Among its tenets are the absolute subordination of the people to their wise rulers and the idea that Koreans are a chosen people who can be completely self-sufficient and who have no need of contact with the inferior, outside world.

NATO. Abbreviation for the *North Atlantic Treaty Organization.* The signatories, including all major European powers, Canada, and the United States, are pledged by Article Five of the treaty to treat an armed attack on one member as an attack on all members. Formed to resist the Soviet Union's westward push after World War II, the institution diminished greatly in the twenty-first century.

NEST. Abbreviation for *Nuclear Emergency Support Team.* Its mission is to provide specialized technical expertise to the federal response in resolving nuclear or radiological terrorist incidents. NEST capabilities include nuclear materials search and identification, diagnostics and assessment of suspected nuclear devices, technical operations in support of render safe procedures, and packaging for transport to final disposition.

NORAD. Abbreviation for the *North American Aerospace Defense Command,* a bi-national United States and Canadian organization charged with the missions of aerospace warning and aerospace control for North America. Aerospace warning includes the monitoring of manmade objects in space and the detection, validation, and warning of attack against North America whether by aircraft, missiles, or space vehicles. Aerospace control includes ensuring air sovereignty and air defense of the airspace of Canada and the United States. These missions are managed from a command center at Peterson Air Force Base in Colorado.

NSA. Abbreviation for the *National Security Agency,* the U.S. government organization that makes and breaks codes that protect information. One very important task of the NSA is to intercept, decode, and analyze all forms of communication. NSA's listening mission is specifically limited to gathering information about international terrorists as well as foreign powers, organizations, or persons.

NSC. Abbreviation for the U.S. *National Security Council,* the president's principal forum for considering national security and foreign policy matters with his senior national security advisors and cabinet officials. The NSC is chaired by the president. Its other statutory members are the vice president, the secretary of state, the secretary of defense, and the assistant to the president for national security affairs. The chairman of the JCS is the statutory military advisor to the NSC, and the director of national intelligence is the intelligence advisor. Other officials, such as the director of the CIA, the secretary of homeland security, and the secretary of the treasury, attend as appropriate.

Pak. English slang term for Pakistan and its peoples.

Pantex. Pantex Plant, located near Amarillo, Texas, maintains the safety, security, and reliability of America's nuclear weapons stockpile. The facility is managed and operated by B&W Pantex for the U.S. Department of Energy/National Nuclear Security Administration. Among its functions is the dismantling of nuclear weapons that are surplus to the strategic stockpile.

Predator. The MQ-1 Predator is a medium-altitude, long-endurance, remotely piloted aircraft. The MQ-1's primary mission is interdiction and conducting armed reconnaissance against critical, perishable targets. It is used extensively against insurgents in Pakistan and Afghanistan. Although the pilots and their remote control gear can go anywhere, the major drone control site is Creech Air Force Base, thirty-five miles from Las Vegas.

ROK. Abbreviation, usually pronounced "rock," for the *Republic of Korea*, frequently called South Korea. Its derivative, ROKs (pronounced "rocks") is sometimes used in reference to ROK officials or military forces.

RFID. Abbreviation for *Radio Frequency Identification*. A technology similar in application to bar code identification, RFID can be used just about anywhere, from clothing, to missiles, to food. Attached RFID tags use transponders to transmit significant amounts of data to a receiver; often such tags are used as part of a real-time locator system.

Sandia Labs. *Sandia National Laboratories*, near Albuquerque, New Mexico. Sandia's primary mission is ensuring the U.S. nuclear arsenal is safe, secure, reliable, and can fully support U.S. deterrence policy.

SECDEF. Abbreviation for the *Secretary of Defense*. The secretary is an officer of the cabinet, responsible to the president.

SCIF. Abbreviation for *Sensitive Compartmented Information Facility*. The most sensitive of classified information is allowed to flow only to particular individuals—each specifically cleared for access to that source of information—and is called "Sensitive Compartmented Information," or "SCI." SCI may only be discussed in an SCIF, an ultra-secure facility colloquially known as a "skif."

SEAL. Acronym for *Sea, Air, and Land* used in reference to the navy's Special Operations Forces. Navy SEALs operate in all of those environments.

Situation Room/Sit Room. The *Situation Room* is actually a five- thousand-square-foot complex of rooms on the ground floor of the West Wing. The staff of the Situation Room helps the president connect with intelligence agencies and important people overseas. The Sit Room watch provides continuous monitoring of world events and briefs the president. Because of its location, security, and high-tech bells and whistles, the Sit Room complex is often used for national security meetings and for monitoring crisis events.

Tenet, George. CIA Director at the time of Nine-eleven. He served from 1997 through 2004.

WMD. Abbreviation for *Weapons of Mass Destruction*. Nuclear, biological, and chemical weapons are considered WMDs.

Yongbyon. North Korea has several known facilities that produce nuclear material for bombs. Most are located at Yongbyon, sixty miles north of Pyongyang, which has a staff of about two thousand. The major installations include a five-megawatt electric research reactor, a fifty-megawatt reactor under construction, and a plutonium reprocessing facility. Yongbyon is also the site of the Radiochemical Laboratory of the Institute of Radiochemistry, the Nuclear Fuel Rod Fabrication Plant, and a storage facility for fuel rods.

CPSIA information can be obtained at www.ICGtesting.com
Printed in the USA
LVOW041842220113

316772LV00010B/1538/P